JoeE

SECRETS, SECRETS, SECRETS

BOOK ONE

A Novel By

Gordon J. Goss & Teresa J. Richardson

© Copyright 2014 Gordon J. Goss & Teresa J. Richardson
All Rights Reserved

ISBN: 1500966460
ISBN 13: 9781500966461
Library of Congress Control Number: 2014915412
CreateSpace Independent Publishing Platform
North Charleston, South Carolina

Published by N.S.D. Books
Website: www.secrets3.com
Email: books@secrets3.com

DEDICATION

The main character of this novel is based upon the loving and caring personality of Joe Edward Rogers Jr., a dedicated athlete and diehard sports fan. His life was cut tragically short, but he still lives in the memories of those whose lives he touched.

PROLOGUE

Driving the five words into my heart like daggers, she lets the silence that follows twist them at their hilts. Five little words, as sharp and deadly as knives, plunged straight into my heart. That's all it takes to tear my world apart.

Trying to speak, all I can do is sit there, stunned and mute. I struggle to form words, but the questions die in my throat. It's as though the ground has shifted out from under me. The world wobbles, the planets scatter out of alignment, and the stars fall from the heavens.

And in the end, all I can manage to mumble is, "What did you say?"

But already the truth is settling in. The five little daggers are doing their work. The damage is done, the curse cast, the façade shattered forever. Like a house of cards teetering on the edge of collapse, my new life suddenly comes tumbling down.

Maybe that's where we could start this story: those five terrible words. But if you want to understand them, first you have to understand what they're killing. Even when the first big secret surfaced and the grinning skeletons ambled out of their closet, I told myself that this too shall pass.

Unfortunately, secrets inevitably lead to lies, and lying always leads to further deceit. But now, it's clear that this chronicle of deception and betrayal runs deeper than I ever could have imagined. Secrets have been stacking up since well before I was born. I'm starting to think they'll eat away at my life like caustic poison until the day I die. You can't outrun the truth any more than you can turn back time.

Part 1

TOO MANY SECRETS

Chapter 1

UP AND AWAY

People are quick to point out, "JoeE, you're so grown-up and act so mature for sixteen."

Accepting their praise graciously, I recognize that my maturity has been forged by years of training to be a leader, on and off the football field. Even if I'd ever wanted to act like a child, my father made sure that it wasn't an option. However, without this rigid foundation and extensive preparation, I could now easily be suffocated by the tangled web of deceit hanging all around me. Instead, along with the love and support of family and friends, I'm capable of meeting these challenges head on.

With knots forming in my stomach as I wait in line, I nervously check my cell phone for the time. Pushing everything out of my mind, I simply focus upon a few basic facts. It's a trick that Dad taught me to calm my jangled nerves prior to football games. He preached that it's better to plant your feet in what you know than drown in what you can't control.

Closing my eyes, I calmly think: My name is Joseph Edward Collins the Fourth, but JoeE to friends and family. Today is Wednesday, December 26. I'm about to fly from Syracuse to Atlanta, where I'll switch planes to Jackson, Mississippi. From there, I'll start my new life in the nearby suburb of Brandon. This major upheaval has been well thought out and chosen of my own free will. I'm ready to face the consequences of my decisions like the man I've become.

Now feeling somewhat reassured, I take a deep breath and open my eyes, ready to face my destiny. Thanks, Dad. Your trick works, not just in football, but in life as well.

Walking down the passageway, I step aboard this Delta Airlines flight, leaving the only place that I've ever called home. After negotiating the narrow aisle, I place my backpack and heavy coat into the overhead compartment and squeeze into my assigned seat.

For months, I've struggled to gather the courage to make this drastic life change, knowing that my entire future hung in the balance. It's a decision based upon forgiving both the living and the dead who've kept me shrouded in a veil of secrets and lies my entire life. I take comfort in the thought that if I'm wrong about the path I've chosen, my grandparents will welcome me back into their home with open arms.

Peering out the tiny portal that the airline calls a window, I watch the concrete slowly slip past as we begin to taxi to the head of the runway. Feeling a kinship with this plane, I too am eager to soar into the heavens but forced to wait until the tower clears us.

I'm reminded of a jockey trying to guide his chomping-at-the-bit thoroughbred into the starting gate of the Kentucky Derby. After finally cajoling the prancing animal into the gate, both horse and rider are required to await the signal to charge ahead.

Suddenly, I sense the urgency of the vibrating engines that are ready to power us into the foreboding gray sky. The brakes are finally released and the throttle eased forward. My mount charges forth as the engines sigh in relief like an antsy horse might snort to ease its nerves.

At first, I'm able to count the lines painted along the edge of the runway as my modern Pegasus slowly canters forward. Then the runway becomes a blur as my winged stallion of Greek mythology gathers speed, galloping for the horizon. As the wheels leave the tarmac, this metallic steed gives a mighty leap, bounding effortlessly skyward, finally free from earthly constraints.

After briefly losing itself in the misty clouds, my chariot of fire breaks into the bright blue, sun-lit sky. New York will rapidly vanish as we head south. The last glimpses of my home state remind me of the soft white comforter on my grandparents' bed. With snow clinging to almost everything, I can distinguish only a few oddly shaped patches outlined by the browns and grays of barren trees.

Although I try to relax, my brain is bombarded with questions. Am I ready for this new life? Will I leave turmoil behind, or will it follow me? Could I feel like a stranger in this new land? Will this move alter anything or everything? I know that I'm not the only one with questions about what the future holds. Realistically, is anyone ever fully prepared for what's to come?

Even though I'm only a high school sophomore, I really have nothing to fear. This flight just might be the gateway to the most exciting and happiest times of my life. Thinking philosophically, I recall the veil of clouds we've passed through and marvel at how much my life mirrors a flight pattern. Sometimes a plane is forced to barrel through stormy weather searching for clear skies. After my recent troubles, I too am seeking the most direct path to a golden patch of sunshine.

Exhausted at trying to guess what the future holds, I pretend that the nightmare of the last few months never occurred. My mind drifts back to the end of last summer, before I began to dread what the future held in store. At that time, I assumed that my trek through life would follow my dad's beat for beat, footprint for footprint.

One second, my future was crystal clear; the next, an unseen hand yanked the rug from underneath me, turning my whole world upside down. In vivid detail, memories of one particular night flood my mind. It was a warm evening in late August, only four short months ago, perfect for opening our high school football season. Recalling the sweet smell of the field's freshly cut, emerald-green grass, I still remember the nervous sweat glistening in the palms of my hands. The slight taste of an orange-flavored Gatorade still lingered in the back of my mouth as we charged out of the locker room and onto the field.

The temperature was in the high sixties, without a whisper of wind. Even though I'd celebrated my birthday just days before, that milestone paled in comparison to being named starting quarterback for the opening game. It seemed as if our entire student body, as well as everyone else associated with G. Ray Bodley High School, shared my exhilaration. Fans of all ages—most clad in bright red, some with red face paint—filled the bleachers at our home field. They were there to cheer on the Red Raiders in the initial contest of what promised to be an exciting season.

As we went through our pregame drills, I took in the thrilling scene unfolding all around me. At a distance, I admired our cheerleaders, who were warming up on the sidelines. The girls' nervous energy was evident as they practiced flips and cartwheels, chattering and giggling. Members of our award-winning band were taking their seats in the stands while the drum line played a heart-pounding cadence. The band would soon be accompanying the crowd in an awe-inspiring rendition of the national anthem. I was anxious for the drummers to begin the rhythmic beat of our fight song, signaling that the game was about to get underway.

Some enthusiastic students began to chant, "We're number one!" This, of course, was premature, but a tangible hope of the entire community. Repeating as state Class A champions depended upon many factors. I was also acutely aware that how well I executed my duties at quarterback was a key to our success. A swarm of butterflies fluttered through my stomach, making sure I didn't forget the enormity of my responsibilities.

Our opponents that evening, the Fowler High Falcons, were wearing their coal-black uniforms with bright-white numbers. Fowler's team had taken a forty-minute bus ride from nearby Syracuse, which the residents of my hometown of Fulton consider to be the "big city." About thirty miles away from my hometown, the fifth most-populous city in the state is the home of Syracuse University, where my father attended college.

Fowler's black uniforms reminded me of Atlanta's team in the National Football League. Fantasizing that the NFL Falcons had come to test me in my first varsity game as quarterback, I felt empowered and more anxious than ever to get on with the game. My entire life up until then had been preparation for that moment. Hardly able to wait for the starting whistle to blow, I was ready to unveil JoeE Collins, future Heisman Trophy winner. Well, that was my dream—and for that matter, it still is.

"Bring it on, Falcons!" I wanted to shout arrogantly. "Play your cover-two or blitz me if you dare. Try single coverage, and I'll burn you!" I actually said nothing, keeping my eyes open and my mouth shut, just like my dad taught me.

"Let your play on the field do the talking," my father had drilled into me. "Winners walk the walk, letting the losers talk the talk."

My dad, Joseph Edward Collins the third, either called Joseph or Coach Collins, was the head football coach at my high school. My hometown is a small community straddling the rather swift-flowing Oswego River, about halfway between Syracuse and Lake Ontario. As in most of this country, high school football is an integral and cherished part of our heritage. The sport has provided entertainment, developed athletes, and been a time-honored fixture in Fulton for over a century.

Ever since I was old enough to hold a football, my father has spent countless hours teaching me the fundamentals of the game. The sport was his passion, the focal point of his entire life. He was a star athlete in several sports during his four years at G. Ray Bodley High, impressive enough at quarterback to earn a football scholarship to Syracuse. He majored in history, now my favorite school subject. I desperately wanted to make him proud by following in his footsteps.

My father's considerable success playing in college for the Orange led to him being drafted by the NFL Oakland Raiders. A first-round draft pick, Dad impressed the team's coaching staff with his leadership ability and an outstanding preseason performance. That fall, they named the rookie as their starting quarterback in the first regular-season game. Unfortunately, fate stepped in, making that opener the last football game that he'd ever play. Nearly seventeen years later, I was poised to take the reins of a high-powered offense. What a proud legacy to live up to.

After that one injury-shortened season with the Raiders, as well as the tragic death of my mother in a car accident, Dad returned to New York with me, his infant son. He never spoke about either of those heartbreaking events. Obviously, they weighed heavily upon his mind and were why he chose to retreat to the familiarity of his hometown.

Soon after his return, the ex-star athlete became a history teacher and football coach at his former high school.

Although Bodley doesn't have enough students to be classified with the larger Class AA schools, our team is highly ranked among the somewhat smaller Class A. Following the grandeur of playing for Syracuse and in the NFL, my father eventually adjusted to this much smaller stage. I can only imagine how he regretted not being able to live his lifelong dream of starring in the National Football League. That dream was now squarely upon my shoulders.

Even though my life with Dad wasn't a normal one, it was fairly routine. Little did I know back then that just below the surface there were incredible secrets. Whether recent events were directed by fate or the hand of God, they triggered a chain of almost inevitable actions and reactions. A door has now been opened that can never be closed.

Chapter 2

MY DAD

Often on quiet nights in our small, thin-walled apartment, I was awakened by the sound of my father mumbling or even ranting in his sleep. Sometimes, it sounded as if he were calling the next play in a football game. Other times he would scream out in agony, "My knee, oh, my knee!" Occasionally, Dad would seem to be arguing vehemently with someone, then shout cruel accusations and threats. I'd hear words like betrayal, lies, and secrets as well as assorted four-letter words that I'm forbidden to use.

Of course, none of this made any sense to me at the time, but I suspected that the relationship between my parents had been stormy at times. On those unsettling nights, I just rolled over and attempted to go back to sleep. Losing your wife and dream career at the same time would be enough to give anyone nightmares, especially if you were left to raise a child alone.

Even though I'd known from a young age that my mother died soon after I was born, the topic was taboo. I had no recollection of the woman, and no one ever mentioned her. Never having been shown a picture of my mother or even been told her name, it was as if she'd been systematically erased from my life.

When I asked Dad once about my mother's family, he told me that she'd been an only child and that her parents were deceased. Then he said, "The subject is too sad to discuss," but what I heard was, "Don't ask any more questions about your mother." My dad didn't like to repeat himself, so I never questioned him about her again.

Yet, sometimes late at night, I'd try to imagine what she looked like. I didn't resemble either my dad or my grandparents, so I suspected that I must favor my mother. I often wondered what kind of person she had been and if she'd loved me. The woman was a dark, faceless mystery.

Until a few months ago, my life was highly structured and reasonably simple with everything in black and white. My father established my priorities as football, school, eating, and sleeping, in that order. During the summer, school was replaced by various activities, all of which kept me physically active. My family's prestigious football legacy inspired me to stay in top shape year-round. Staying fit has always been a key component for aspiring football players.

"Keep it simple" was one of Dad's favorite mottoes. My life was simple, and I expected it to stay that way, at least through high school.

Football and family have been the center of my world since I was a youngster. I had few playmates; my closest was Jonathan Grabowski. Like me, he's an only child, tall for his age, extremely shy, and likes to read. Sometimes, we played at my grandparents' house with Josh Moretti and his twin sister, Cassandra, who lived nearby.

While I lacked the abundance of toys and electronic gadgets that most of my classmates enjoyed, I never felt deprived. It was only last year that my dad permitted me to have a cell phone. We had a television, and Dad had a computer. Frankly, I'm not attracted to sitting in front of either one for hours on end, except to watch football.

My father brought me up the way the male children of ancient Sparta were raised, which most people these days would consider quite abnormal. I've learned a lot about the Spartans, first from books on ancient Greece, and then from the movie *300*, which dramatizes the Spartans' heroic last stand at Thermopylae. Like the son of a Spartan, I was raised to be physically strong, mentally alert, and in strict control of my emotions.

I've trained at every position in football, both offense and defense. Dad believed that this cross-training would help me better understand my essential role in the game. For as long as I can remember, I've been raised with one goal in mind: to be an elite quarterback.

Spartan boys were focused singularly on becoming fierce warriors who could defend their homeland. A Spartan test of manhood meant facing a hungry wolf while attempting to survive in the wild. My test of manhood is confronting a pack of eleven angry defensive players as I try to survive on a football field. Sometimes, I believe that I'd rather face the lone, hungry wolf.

On the plane, I try to settle back into my seat, letting my thoughts drift back to September 1, the day after the opening game against Fowler. The Syracuse *Post Standard* printed a brief article about our victory. In the lower left-hand corner of the sports page were three short paragraphs entitled "Fulton Smashes Fowler." After reading the article, I could hardly wait for Dad to see it. The newspaper referred to our high school as Fulton, although the official name is G. Ray Bodley. It goes by both names, since it's the only high school in the city.

Reading the article, I was pleasantly surprised to find that my name was in the very first line. It read, *"Led by sophomore quarterback Joey Collins, who threw four touchdown passes and ran for another, Fulton High dominated Fowler 40 to 12. Last night's contest was the season opener for both squads."*

Preferring my name to be spelled "J-o-e-E," I'm disappointed that it's misspelled in the article. Adding my middle initial is my attempt to distinguish myself from those who go by Joey, Joseph, or Joe. At least they got the facts about the five touchdowns correct.

It went on to say, *"Collins is the son of former Syracuse University and Oakland Raider quarterback, Joseph Collins, who also happens to be the current head football coach at his alma mater. It looks like the Red Raiders might just have a dynasty in the making."*

Awesome! Both of our names right there in the same article. I've often perused my grandparents' scrapbooks filled with newspaper clippings, programs, photographs, and other memorabilia from my father's illustrious gridiron career. Now they can start a scrapbook on me too.

I could hardly wait for Dad to come to the kitchen and read the article so he could share my enthusiasm. Deciding to make lunch, I couldn't fix anything fancy, knowing only some fundamentals that my grandmother taught me. After a quick inventory of our rather poorly stocked cupboards, I heated a can of tomato soup and made grilled cheese sandwiches, hoping the savory aromas might entice my father to the kitchen.

"Dad, lunch is ready! Come and get it while it's hot," I shouted, knowing the offer of food usually got his attention.

Waiting impatiently for him to appear, I thought about how surprised he'd be at this delicious meal. Dad wasn't much of a chef; ordering pizza was his specialty. Most of our nutrition came from school lunches and eating often at my grandparents' home.

My father finally came into the kitchen, wearing his normal gray warm-ups. His probing brown eyes automatically surveyed the room like a quarterback checking out the defensive alignment prior to the snap of the ball. Knowing that he couldn't help but notice the neatly folded newspaper on the table, I'd opened it to the sports page. Next to the paper were a steaming bowl of soup and a grilled cheese masterpiece. My heart rate increased, and my mouth felt as dry as when I took the field at the previous night's game. Nearly choking on my sandwich, I stuffed it into my mouth to keep from shouting, "Come on, Dad, read the paper!"

Despite being forty years old, at six foot one with a very muscular physique, my father appeared as if he could still play professional football. Every once in a while at practice, Dad would show off his incredibly accurate passing arm, spiraling a pass fifty or sixty yards down the field. He always claimed that he was "just demonstrating how it was done," but his look of joy revealed the truth. He loved throwing a football and obviously longed for the days when those passes meant the difference between victory and defeat.

Before sitting down at the table, he made himself a cup of black coffee. Finishing my lunch, I sat nervously. It dawned on me that he was intentionally dragging this out, teaching me one more lesson about patience. Finally sitting down, he picked up the newspaper.

After reading the three concise paragraphs, Dad lowered the paper so I could see the muscles around his mouth form a smile. As I waited with bated breath for him to speak, I'm sure he saw the eagerness in my eyes.

He merely asked, "JoeE, have you read the article on our game?" He knew darn well that I had read it, so I just nodded. His smile faded quickly, and his expression turned serious. "I don't think that they gave our defense enough credit. Reporters tend to praise quarterbacks far too much." As my heart began to sink, his face suddenly brightened again as he added, "But this time, the quarterback deserved the praise."

My heart skipped a beat, and for some reason, the biblical words, *"This is my beloved son in whom I am well pleased,"* flashed through my mind. Apparently I had read those words somewhere besides the Bible, which isn't a text that I've studied. At that moment, I could relate to how that son must have felt hearing those words. A joyful heart certainly made this simple meal before us seem like a fabulous awards banquet. The grilled cheese sandwiches might as well have been lobster.

I recalled the years of training, thinking about the countless exercises, sweating in the weight room, endless wind sprints, and never-ending constructive criticism. The bone-weary fatigue of my bruised and battered body came vividly to my mind. Suddenly, these sacrifices, as well as the absence of a normal childhood, were a small price to pay for my father's words of praise. Now, I was the one with the enormous smile.

Of course, Dad never let an opportunity for a teaching moment slip through his fingers. Sounding more like my coach than my father, he warned, "Remember, all games won't end in victory, no matter how well you may play. Passes will be dropped, balls will be fumbled, and blocks will be missed. Whether it's you or a teammate who makes the mistake, as quarterback, it's your responsibility.

Hanging on his every word, I commit everything Dad says to memory.

"You need to do whatever it takes to elevate the team's performance. As the leader, it's your team, on and off the football field. JoeE, enjoy the victories, but no matter how much you prepare, how hard you try, how strong you believe, events will happen that are totally out of your control. You must learn to deal with failure as well as success."

I've heard that Knute Rockne, the immortal football coach of Notre Dame, was amazing at delivering inspiring speeches. My dad may have had him beat.

Allowing his words to sink in before continuing, my father then said, "It's easy to move ahead when your life goes well. The sign of a real quarterback, as well as a real man, is one who can pick up the pieces and move on proudly after failure or tragedy. I failed that test, but you don't have to make the same mistake. I've already made it for the both of us."

My dad knew that, as always, I was listening to every word. He was my idol and my superhero, on and off the football field.

When I was young, I tried my hand at a variety of sports, including basketball, baseball, lacrosse, wrestling, and hockey. But as I grew older, Dad discouraged me from those sports, explaining that they increased my chance of serious injury, especially to my knees. Outside of football, I now play only tennis, and I excel at it to some degree. My six-foot-five height, along with my strength, enables me to be a formidable server. Dad approved because the activity is relatively safe and improves my hand-eye coordination.

"Football is dangerous enough," he told me repeatedly. "We don't need to take any unnecessary chances." His use of the word "we" was interesting—he made it sound as if he was also at risk.

My father suffered a serious knee injury while playing baseball in the spring of his sophomore year in high school. Luckily, he recovered in time for football the following fall. However, Dad believed that the blow to his knee permanently weakened his joint and contributed to his career-ending knee injury years later. My father didn't want me suffering a similar fate. However, not all dangers are of a physical nature.

Chapter 3

JUST A PLAY

On September 21, three weeks after our game against Fowler, the leaves on the maple trees were beginning to abandon their bright greens for hues of orange and red. A slight breeze whispered through the air. It was not strong enough to affect the flight of a football significantly; it was more like a cool, refreshing aftershave. The temperature was still in the sixties at game time, another perfect night for a gridiron clash. All day, it had been bright and sunny, one of those exceptional days for central New York.

We were prepping for our fourth game of the season that fateful night. Over the previous two weeks, we had chalked up victories over a very talented Watertown team and a gritty Mexico High squad. Our newest opponent was Jamesville-Dewitt, which we simply called J-D. The contest was an early season clash between two highly rated Class A schools. Jamesville and Dewitt are eastern suburbs of Syracuse, about forty-five minutes from Fulton.

In extremely high spirits, our team left our high school to head to the game. During the ride, my dad was extremely quiet, which was more than a little unusual for him. He had a drawn, almost tired look, and he kept clutching the seat, as if in pain. However, Dad was never one to complain, and I expected that by game time he would be back to his normal, boisterous self.

Our offensive coach, Gerald Maribito, delivered a short pregame pep talk. My dad, who usually gave all of these speeches himself, was nowhere in sight. The assistant coaches took us onto the field and through warm-up drills. We went through the first few plays that the coaches wanted us to run, designed to slow down J-D's aggressive defense. As the game was about to start, my dad came out of the locker room and took his usual place along the sidelines, while I focused my attention on the battle before us.

As one of our team's captains, I joined Jordan Maxwell, a senior linebacker, at the center of the field for the coin toss. Maxwell's nickname is Mad Max, owing to the fact that he was always chasing down runners at full speed like a maniac. A real leader on defense who seemed to be in on almost every tackle, Jordan's place on a college football team was all but guaranteed. As we waited for the toss to commence, butterflies fluttered around in my stomach even as my heart hammered against my chest.

As the coin spun in the air, Mad Max shouted, "Tails!"

"Tails it is!" confirmed the ref.

After I told him that we wanted to receive the ball to start the game, the referee asked the other team's captains which goal they wished to defend. They chose the goal to our right. Even though the team's nickname is the Red Rams, they were wearing their white home uniforms with red numbering. With the preliminaries out of the way, we shook hands with the other captains and trotted back to our sideline.

As I stood by Coach Maribito, he reminded me about the first few scripted plays. The reminder was unnecessary. I knew our game plan as well as our entire playbook, forward, backward, and upside down. Also aware that my teammates would precisely execute whatever play I called without question, I was confident that we'd be triumphant. We were a well-drilled, well-conditioned, and well-disciplined machine. My dad had seen to that.

Our kickoff return team took the field, a whistle blew, and the J-D kicker slammed his foot into the pigskin with a familiar thud. We returned the kick to around the thirty-yard line. I trotted onto the field as my teammates huddled up. It was time for me to report to work. The butterflies were now in high gear, and every muscle in my body felt like a rubber band stretched to the breaking point.

As ten helmeted faces stared at me, I barked out, "Trips right, fake zero blast, bootleg left, on two."

Like all football plays, it only sounds complicated to those who don't speak the language. If we were on the playground, I'd just say, "You three go out to the right; we'll pretend that we're going to run up the middle, and when I say 'hut two,' I'll take the ball and run to the left." I guess we make it sound complicated so that girls will think we're smart.

After pausing for a moment so my teammates could visualize their assignments, I shouted, "Break!"

Leaving the huddle in unison, we approached the line of scrimmage. The linemen crouched into their stances as I quickly surveyed the field. As expected, the J-D defense shifted to our right, where we had three wide receivers (*trips right*). As our coaches predicted, J-D was already overplaying the strong side of our formation. We would make them pay dearly for their error in judgment. The play was designed to go to our left, away from our strong side. We were about to teach the Rams a little lesson about over shifting.

I took my place behind the center, remembering that Dad had taught me to identify which player is the key defender on each play.

"Keep the game simple in your mind, JoeE," he would say. "If everyone does their job, the play is designed to be a success."

I took a quick glance to the left and saw J-D's outside linebacker, number 51. He would be the key defender on this play. If we were able to get past him, we could make some good yardage and put the Rams back on their heels.

Placing my hands under the center, I barked out loudly, "Hut one." No one on either side moved. It was as if they were frozen in place. In that same tone, I shouted, "Hut two."

I felt the slight sting of leather as the center snapped the ball into my waiting hands. The lineman in front of me erupted into action. I whirled to my right, pivoting with footwork that I had been taught when I was just seven years old.

Our running back was barreling toward the line of scrimmage with his arms open, one above the other, ready to take the hand-off that he knew would not be made. As he came forward, my arms jutted out as if I were handing him the ball. Then, just as quickly, I pulled my arms back as if I had given the pigskin to him (*fake zero blast*). The running back rushed past me as I drifted, almost leisurely, away from the line of scrimmage, acting as if my part in this play was over. It was not.

Although I couldn't see any of the action, I knew that chaos was erupting just a few feet away. I could hear the slamming of pads and helmets, the grunts of exertion verifying that teenage warriors were putting exclamation points on their physical effort. Our linemen, including my best friend, Jonathan, at left tackle, were making sure that no J-D defenders penetrated into the backfield. At over three hundred pounds of almost pure muscle, Jonathan regarded himself as my personal protector.

The ball was in my left hand, held along my thigh, shielded from the view of the linebacker (*bootleg left*). Luckily, I'm not only tall at six foot five, but my hands are large enough to hold the ball easily and securely with one hand.

Rolling out to the left and picking up speed, I saw out of the corner of my eye that the linebacker had been fooled by our well-executed fake. He had moved to help tackle our running back, who he mistakenly thought was carrying the ball.

Meanwhile, I accelerated toward the sideline before the linebacker realized his mistake. Stopping in his tracks as if he'd hit an invisible wall, number 51 whirled around, but he was too late! I was headed up the field, and now all he could do was pursue me.

Sprinting up the field, I automatically shifted the ball into an even more secure position. My left hand was now firmly around one end of the football with the other end tucked securely into the crook of my elbow. Countless times in practice, holding the ball in that manner, I'd run down a line of players while each of them tried to punch it loose. The bruises on my arms from their misses never had time to fade before we were running that drill again. Dad emphasized that fumbling the football was unacceptable.

As I reached full speed, I checked out the field ahead. No safety was in sight. There was just one defender to beat now, the cornerback on this side of the field. He was in what my dad called a chicken fight with our wide receiver, Josh, another one of my good friends. As they pawed at each other, I instinctively angled slightly toward the sideline. The cornerback reacted, moving to cut me off. At the last second, I made a quick cut toward the middle of the field. This move gave Josh just enough of an angle to make his block.

Slipping past them, I saw nothing but green grass between the goal line and me. However, as I went by, the cornerback made a desperate lunge. He caught the back of my foot, throwing me slightly off balance. As I began to stumble, I wished that I had better balance.

When I was ten, Dad read that football players could benefit from dance lessons. When he started talking about enrolling me in a beginner ballet class to improve my balance, my grandfather talked him out of the idea. He pointed out that such a class might destroy my self-confidence, as I was likely to be shown up by five-year-old girls in little pink tutus. However, at that moment as I clumsily lurched forward, I wished that Dad had persisted. Besides, it certainly would give me something to talk to girls about other than pass patterns, zone coverage, and blitz packages.

The more I stumbled, the more I slowed down, trying to regain my balance. Then, *wham*! Something that felt like a small truck slammed into my back. Muscular arms wrapped around my midsection, and I was driven face-first into the grassy field.

Momentarily dazed, I shook off the hard hit and pulled a clump of grass from my facemask. One of my teammates helped me to my feet. As I rose, I saw that number 51, the linebacker we'd originally fooled on the play, had applied the bruising hit.

"Nice tackle," I said, turning toward him.

He mumbled something back that sounded like a surprised thanks. Dad taught me to recognize a good play, no matter the color of the player's jersey. Even though we fooled him, this linebacker had hustled and made a perfect tackle.

Our team gained two benefits from the play: we were nineteen yards closer to the goal line, and my butterflies were completely gone.

Everything had happened in a matter of seconds. That play now runs through my mind in slow motion as if it were a video recording.

Obviously, I don't remember every football play in such vivid detail. It was what happened next that seared it into my memory forever. Now, less than four months after that game, I'm on this plane, facing major uncertainty for the first time in my life. It's hard for me to believe that I'm the same JoeE Collins who faced the Red Rams that tragic night.

In so many ways, I'm not.

Chapter 4

LOVING GRANDPARENTS

Still gazing out the plane's window, I think about the simple life in Fulton to which I'd become accustomed. Encouraging me to stay as active as possible, my athletic father was always suggesting activities that would help develop or enhance my football skills. I took gymnastics to improve my agility, volleyball to sharpen my reflexes, and swimming to build strength and stamina. Running (weather permitting), weight training, and sit-ups and push-ups were simply normal parts of my daily routine.

My friends play the popular video games like *Halo* and *Call of Duty*, but Dad thought they were a waste of my time. One of my friends, Paul Murphy, who doesn't play sports, is absolutely hooked on *Grand Theft Auto*. At Jonathan's house, I've played *Madden Football* a few times and really enjoyed it. Fearing that I might lose my focus on physical activities, Dad never allowed me to play such games at our apartment. Thankfully, he didn't try to control my actions when I occasionally stayed with my best friend. Possibly, those rare weekend nights were time off for good behavior.

As the still-accelerating aircraft continues to press me back into my seat, I settle in for the two-hour flight. On the way to the airport this morning, my grandfather said, "JoeE, plunging into unknown territory and unfamiliar surroundings would be a daunting prospect for anyone. However, you're an exceedingly level-headed, intelligent, and mature young man, wise beyond your years. The changes in your life during these past few months have helped prepare you to face your future. You'll be fine. Our door and our hearts will always be open to you. Remember, we're just a phone call away."

For as long as I can remember, my paternal grandparents have been a significant part of my life. While I have almost no knowledge of my mother's family, I've learned a considerable amount about my father's. When I was young, Dad and I lived with my grandparents. Now in their midsixties, they live in Fulton on West First Street in the house where my grandfather grew up. Since I didn't have a mother or siblings, Dad and my grandparents comprised my immediate family.

Soon after I turned eleven, my father and I moved into our own small apartment and an even more structured life. It was as if I'd been sent off to military school or, in my case, football school. Although my father never said so, I believe that we moved so he could more easily control my life with as little outside interference as possible. Daily routines were established and bedtimes rigidly adhered to, even on weekends and holidays.

However, even after moving to the apartment, both Dad and I spent some time at my grandparents' house. At their home, I was taught many important life lessons in a softer, gentler fashion. Besides teaching me the basics of cooking, my grandmother gave me some necessary chores to perform and made sure that I followed good hygiene habits. My grandfather would sometimes regale us with tales from his youth or talk about any subject under the sun. Those hours spent with my loving grandparents are the fondest of all my childhood memories.

My grandfather's name is Joseph Edward Collins Jr., but everyone knows him simply as Eddie. Standing just under six feet with intense blue eyes and a full head of curly, white hair, my grandfather also sports a rather pronounced belly. It most likely results from his disdain for exercise and propensity for snacking. For as long as I can remember, I've called him Papa. My grandmother told me that when I was learning to talk, I couldn't say "grandpa" and that "Papa" was the best I could do.

With soft hazel eyes peeking from behind trifocal glasses, hair that is rapidly turning to wisps of gray, and a short, chubby frame, my grandma is the dictionary image of the typical American grandmother.

Born Margaret Flynn in eastern North Carolina, she moved with her family to the Boston area when she was ten. Her unique manner of speech combines a New England accent with a slight Southern drawl. Growing up, I loved to hear stories of her childhood, especially about her working on her cousins' farm when the extended family helped with the tobacco harvest. I can't imagine what kind of person I would be without her.

Yesterday morning, on what may have been the last Christmas I'd spend with my grandparents, I asked my grandmother what she really thought of my decision to move so far away.

"JoeE," she said, putting her arm around me, "you're sixteen going on sixty, and you know how to think through a situation. We don't have a crystal ball, so only time will tell if you've made the right decision." As I sat at the kitchen table that snowy morning, she planted a kiss on the top of my head, adding, "If you use your God-given brain, follow your heart, and remember what you've been taught, you'll be just fine. Call us as soon as you get there, or I'll get sick with worry. Remember, we're your backup team, right here on the bench. We love you and always will."

I couldn't help but notice that Grandma wiped her eyes with her apron as she hurried over to the stove to start a pot of tea.

My grandparents have passed on much to me about our family history. Both of my great-grandfathers served honorably in World War II. Grandma's father was a tail gunner and bombardier in the skies over Europe, flying missions on a B-17. One of my fondest memories is of my grandmother and me eating popcorn and watching *Memphis Belle*, a World War II drama that gave me a glimpse of what my great-grandfather had endured during wartime. The survival rate of B-17 aircrews was incredibly low; over half of them were killed, wounded, or captured. When my grandmother was young, she was often awakened at night by her father screaming, "Bombs away! Bombs away!" He and his wife passed away long before I was born.

Papa's father, Lieutenant Joseph Edward Collins, called Joe, served in the South Pacific during that same war as a member of the Army Signal Corp. The most unusual story that Papa tells about his father's wartime experience concerns "weekend warriors." During his time in the Philippines, Joe's unit was given the weekends off to rest after grueling, sixteen-hour days restoring communications. Some soldiers in his outfit from Southern states joined infantry units fighting remnants of the Japanese army. The soldiers from states outside the South, relaxing at their relatively safe quarters, thought that the boys from Dixie were not quite right in the head.

I was fortunate enough to meet my Great-grandfather Joe before he died. We have an old photo of all four generations of the Collins men who shared the same name, taken on my fifth birthday. I'm extremely proud to be a part of that particular photograph. I've heard the old saying that's based upon a quote from the Bible. It warns, "Pride goeth before a fall."

Chapter 5

ME TOO

Bringing me back to the present from my little daydream, the smiling flight attendant with a hint of a Southern accent asks, "What would you like to drink, sir?"

Out of habit, I mumble, "Just water, please."

The flight attendant is a nice-looking woman, probably in her forties. She's wearing a navy-blue dress that comes down to just below her knees. Slightly beneath her left collar is a small set of silver wings with her name, Joyce Bailey. As she hands me a small package of peanuts across the elderly woman seated to my left, I tell her, "Thank you, Joyce."

"You're very welcome, sir," she tells me sweetly. I like the sound of "sir," mostly because it makes me feel important.

A plump woman with salt-and-pepper hair nudges me and offers her peanuts with a sweet smile. "These are a bit rough on my stomach. Would you like them?"

After thanking her, I gobble down her peanuts before opening my own. The salty taste reminds me of watching football games at my grandparents' home in Fulton. There were always some peanuts, chips, or other snacks for Dad and me to munch as we analyzed every televised football game possible. My father and I, as well as my grandfather, were the ultimate football fans.

The woman beside me interrupts my thoughts about my family. "So are you going to be staying in Atlanta?" she asks.

"No, I'm going on to Mississippi."

"Oh. Well, I'm going to Florida to visit my grandchildren." She pauses a moment as if waiting for a response. "I've never been to Mississippi. How do you like it there?"

"I don't really know since I've never been there myself. I understand that it should be warmer than New York and they talk much differently than us."

Those two facts are pretty much all I really know for sure about the state. I know almost nothing about Mississippi, having much more knowledge of ancient Greece, many European countries, and several other parts of the world. My knowledge of that state, and the whole South, for that matter, pretty much begins and ends with the Civil War.

The elderly woman then asks the obvious question. "So, you're just visiting Mississippi?"

"No, I'm moving there." My words hang in the air for a moment like laundry on a clothesline.

"Oh," she says, reacting with surprise. "Well, I hope that you enjoy it."

I simply reply, "Me too."

After the flight attendant brings bottled water, I check the time, noting that we'll be in Atlanta shortly. Sipping my drink, I turn toward the window again, losing myself in thoughts of my hometown. A Brad Pitt movie, *A River Runs Through It*, perfectly describes Fulton, a working-class community of about twelve thousand.

Several of Dad's friends have commented that I look like a young Brad Pitt or even Leonardo DiCaprio, possibly a result of my sandy-brown hair and chiseled body. I consider the "movie star" comments simply nice exaggerations. Good looks or not, I'm painfully shy, unlike everyone else in my gregarious family. Especially after a couple of drinks, my father and Papa are extremely outgoing, almost brash at times. Even my grandmother can strike up a conversation with anyone as if she and that stranger were lifelong friends.

Off the gridiron, I'm shyer than Bashful in *Snow White and the Seven Dwarfs*. But when I step onto a football field, everything changes: the reserved, quiet JoeE is gone, replaced by a take-charge guy, a leader brimming with self-confidence. And as soon as the clock hits zero, the spell is broken. I've always wondered where this shyness comes from.

Chapter 6

TWO-WORD MESSAGE

As our plane descends for its landing in Atlanta, I try to remember what my grandfather told me about this airport. Papa said something about how it was gigantic and has some kind of subway connecting the concourses. Although I usually pay close attention to him, it just so happened that two cute girls walked by as he was explaining what to do. I didn't catch most of it. I'll just follow the signs to gate B-7, which is stamped on my ticket.

Although I've never flown to or through Atlanta before, it isn't as though I'm new to flying. When I was only five, my dad took me to Arizona to watch Syracuse play Kansas State in a bowl game. Since then, I've been in many airports, all of which seem to be pretty much alike, with some bigger and others smaller.

Each year, after the high school football season ended, Dad and I traveled to college or NFL games almost every weekend. We primarily attended Syracuse University and New York Giants games. Once, we flew to California to watch the Oakland Raiders play when the team offered my dad a front office position. Although he turned the job down, I could tell that he was tempted by the offer.

I've even been to a couple of Super Bowls, both times watching my beloved Giants beat the New England Patriots. Although my father and I lived rather simply, like a couple of Spartans, Dad never hesitated to fly or drive to football games and stay at awesome hotels. My father's top priority was the game he loved, and he made sure that we shared that passion.

Dad knew coaches and players on many college and professional teams and could usually arrange great seats. Some he played with, or for, while at Syracuse or during his brief NFL career. Others he had coached when they were at Bodley. Sometimes college coaches would visit Fulton on recruiting trips. Dad said that someday soon those same coaches would be recruiting me.

Exiting the plane, I say good-bye to the nice woman who sat beside me and thank her again for the peanuts. Following the crowd, I walk a long distance, more than the entire length of the Syracuse airport. This concourse continues for as far as the eye can see. Papa was right; this airport is humongous. The signs lead me to the longest escalators I've ever seen. A pair of them plunges down to an outlet far below. As I descend, I feel like we are plummeting into the depths of the earth.

As we reach the bottom, I find myself in an area that opens into a long, wide tunnel. Along the wall, across from the escalator, there is a series of sliding doors with large windows. This must be where I catch that subway Papa told me about. I hope that I don't have long to wait. Not wanting to relive the past anymore, I'm not too keen to consider the future either. Even as I attempt to clear my mind, the nagging memories tug at me.

Finally, I simply give in, and the events of September 21 roll over me like a freight train.

After our successful opening play against J-D that night, I'd started walking back to our huddle. Glancing toward the sidelines to make sure that Coach Maribito wanted me to continue our preplanned series, I noticed that our coaches were gathered around someone lying on the ground.

At first, I thought that one of our players had been injured on the play. A whistle blew, and the head referee waved his hands above his head and tapped his shoulders, signaling an official's timeout.

As I jogged to the sideline, a nervous chill crept up my spine. Just like that, alarm quickly turned to panic. That's when I saw that it wasn't a player lying facedown on the sidelines. Time froze as I realized that it was my dad.

By the time I reached the spot where he had collapsed, I could see our team doctor kneeling over him. The doc yelled, "Get an ambulance, *now!*"

"Back off, boys!" yelled one of the coaches as the players pressed in closer for a better look. "Give the doc some room."

We moved back as requested. I began to shake ever so slightly as the whole scene turned surreal. Time slowed. Breaths shortened. The whole world seemed to stop. As clear as everything that day had been up until that moment, the rest of that night was a bit of a blur. Only a few minutes here and there jump out in my memory.

Standing on the sidelines with Jonathan beside me, I felt his gigantic arm around my shoulders as if he were trying to shield me from danger. Even off the field, the big guy was still my personal protector. In any other situation, I would have felt awkward and pushed his arm away in embarrassment, but right then and there, I was too numb, too stricken, to feel anything at all.

A rescue squad must have had an ambulance parked by the field. Almost immediately, they drove it over to our sideline. My grandparents stumbled out of the stands and came down to where I was standing. Papa went over and asked the doctor some questions as my dad, now wearing an oxygen mask, was lifted onto a stretcher.

I was unable to hear what they were saying, but their dire expressions didn't make me feel any better. As the paramedics put the stretcher into the ambulance, Papa came back to where my grandmother had replaced Jonathan, wrapping her arm around me.

"The doctor says it's a heart attack," Papa told us. "They have to get him to the hospital before we'll know more. JoeE, are you OK?"

"I'm fine," I replied, not knowing until later that I'd turned as white as a sheet. My grandmother was trying not to cry as she hugged me tighter. I was too numb even to try to hug her back.

Coach Maribito came over to me. "Go along with your grandparents, JoeE. We'll take care of things here."

I turned to Jonathan and Josh. "I'll be back as soon as I can. Play hard."

They looked at me as if I were insane. "JoeE, it's your dad. This is just a game," Josh said.

I didn't understand what my friend meant. Football wasn't a game to me; it was my life.

Following Coach Maribito's instructions, I tailed my grandparents to the parking lot, feeling guilty about leaving.

"Do I need to take my cleats off?" I blurted out before getting into the car. My dad had warned me not to wear them in the car several times before. Those were the last words that I uttered for the next hour.

"No, it's OK, JoeE," said Papa as my grandmother shot me a nervous glance.

Papa told her that he'd obtained directions to a nearby hospital. We drove away from the field in a tense silence, each of us lost in our own thoughts. Sitting in a small waiting area outside the emergency room, I looked around. The three of us were the only people waiting at the small facility. Papa went up to a counter to talk to a woman who gave him some forms on a clipboard to fill out.

When he returned, he told us, "No word yet."

After what seemed like hours but was probably only twenty minutes, a nurse came out to tell us that they were attempting to stabilize Dad. After he was stable, she said that he'd be moved to one of the large Syracuse medical centers.

"How is he?" Papa's voice was strained.

The nurse didn't answer, at least not at first. My grandfather closed the distance between them, and they spoke in low, hushed whispers. I couldn't hear what they were saying, but when my grandfather returned, his face was somber. As the nurse walked back through a set of swinging double doors, Papa put a hand on my grandmother's shoulder.

"All we can do now is pray," he said, his voice cracking under the weight of the words.

My grandmother began reciting the Lord's Prayer under her breath. She and Papa are devout Catholics. They've taken me to their church a number of times and probably had me baptized there as a baby. Having not received First Communion or Confirmation like many of my friends, I don't consider myself Catholic.

Dad didn't want anything to do with Catholicism—or any other religion, for that matter. He claimed that he'd "paid his dues" when he was young. Papa told me that my father had been very involved with the church as a youth and even served as an altar boy. Dad once told me that God didn't listen to prayers.

"We have football instead of church, JoeE," he explained when I was about nine years old. After my father made that statement, I never thought of football as just a game again.

With no other option available, I decided that I should at least try to pray.

My silent prayer was, "God, please let Dad get better so he can be back on the sidelines for my next game." It wasn't much of a prayer, but it seemed appropriate.

About fifteen minutes later, a doctor stepped out of the swinging doors of the emergency room. In a cold, clear voice, he delivered a brutal two-word message: "He's gone."

God didn't listen to my prayer either.

Chapter 7

THE STRANGER

My grandparents went off to sign some papers and arrange for Dad's body to be transported to Fulton, leaving me in the small waiting room. Although I probably appeared calm on the outside, the turmoil inside my head was nearly unbearable. Unable to fathom what my life would be like without my father, I was lost in my own desperate thoughts, failing to notice that I was not alone.

"JoeE," the stranger standing beside me said in a soft, peaceful voice. Snapping my head around, I was startled that someone knew my name. He had an average height and build, with an ordinary face. The only distinctive thing about him was his collar. I assumed he was a Catholic priest.

"You're stronger than you think." His voice filled me with a peaceful feeling, washing over me like warm water from a steaming shower after a strenuous workout. "Believe it or not, this too shall pass."

I nodded, but only in politeness. To tell the truth, I didn't exactly agree with his statement.

"You now have your own special path to follow, JoeE," he went on, not bothering to introduce himself. "Others will help you along the way as you help them on their difficult journeys through life. You have been given many gifts and much talent. Remember, however, the greatest gifts are those that you bestow upon others, like love, compassion, acceptance, and understanding. Most importantly is forgiveness, which, although given to others, also releases you from your burdens."

So caught up in what the stranger was saying, I didn't hear my grandparents return.

"Excuse me, please," I told him politely. "This'll just take a moment."

I walked over to the counter where Papa was handing the woman some papers. "The priest that you sent to see me is here."

"We didn't send anyone to see you, JoeE. Where is he?"

Turning around to point out the stranger, I was surprised to find that he was no longer in the waiting area.

"Maybe he was just a priest here at the hospital," I said. "This isn't a Catholic hospital," Papa said.

My grandfather asked the woman behind the counter about the priest. "As far as I know," she told him, "there's been no one out there except for the young man in the football uniform."

Apparently, I'd just imagined the entire conversation, but it seemed so real.

When we got to my grandparents' car, I asked, "Are we going back to the game now?"

"No, JoeE," Papa responded. "We're going home."

"OK." I didn't see why we weren't going back. Dad was dead, and there was nothing anyone could do about it. The logical course of action would've been to return to the game. My teammates needed me, and I didn't want to let them down.

Chapter 8

DREAM GIRL

I hear the *whoosh* of a silver subway streaking past behind the closed doors. When it comes to an abrupt stop, the doors slide open quickly, letting out several passengers. Those of us waiting waste no time boarding. A female computerized voice informs everyone that the doors are closing and the next stop will be Concourse B, like bravo. I feel like I'm in *Star Wars*. Was that Princess Leia's voice telling us the doors were closing?

The subway rapidly gains speed, requiring me to grab a metal pole to maintain my balance. Thinking about how sweet it'll be telling the kids at school about this airport, it suddenly dawns on me that the next time I step into a classroom, I won't know a soul.

As the computer voice announces our arrival at Concourse B, the subway again stops abruptly. I hop on another long escalator, and it takes me up to another concourse. Following the signs to gate B-7, I see, displayed behind the counter, "Flight 2478, Jackson, 2:55 p.m." As each minute passes, Mississippi becomes more real to me. There it is on a sign, not just a shape on a map, a name in a book, or a word in a conversation.

I check my cell phone and see that it's already 2:05, meaning I don't have long to wait. Glancing at my ticket, I see that my flight arrives in Jackson at 3:20. Only twenty-five minutes? No way!

Stepping to the counter, I decide to verify the flight times. Before me is a nice-looking woman with rich, coffee-colored skin entering information into a computer terminal. I'm not used to talking to black people, or people of any other minority for that matter. Fulton is almost 100 percent white, as is much of central New York.

Grinning brightly at me as if I was a friend, she asks, "May I help you, sir?"

There's that "sir" again. It makes me feel older. Showing her my ticket, I ask about the flight time. She explains that Atlanta is on Eastern Time and Jackson, Mississippi, is on Central Time. The flight is actually an hour and twenty-five minutes.

I thank her for the information, feeling embarrassed that I failed to figure out something so simple. Apparently, my mind is too preoccupied with other thoughts. Now I know three things about Mississippi: It's warmer than New York, they talk with a strangely fascinating accent, and it's on Central Time.

During the last few months, I considered researching Mississippi on the Internet. Papa warned me that facts and figures alone wouldn't tell me very much about what the state is actually like. He said that I needed to experience being there awhile, meeting the people, and living from day to day.

I've seen several movies that generally portray Southerners as poor, uneducated, and racist. I've also noticed that movies tend to make it seem as if all New Yorkers live in New York City. I figure that if films are so wrong about my state, they're probably wrong about Southerners as well. Actually, I have no idea what it'll be like living in Mississippi. With only thirty bucks in my pocket, if they're all poor, I'll fit right in.

Locating a seat nearby, I remove the latest issue of *Sports Illustrated* from my backpack and begin reading an article about Vikings running back Adrian Peterson. Immediately noticing a small patch of reflected light darting around the waiting area, I try to determine its source. Standing near the large plate-glass windows is a girl about my age wearing Wonder Woman bracelets. Both of her two-inch-wide, cuff-style bracelets are magically catching rays of sunlight, generating small reflections that dance around the area like Tinker Bell.

Even facing away from me, she looks amazing. Anxiously, I wait for her to turn around.

The young lady accompanied by what appear to be her parents and younger brother. Although she's several inches taller than her mother is, she isn't nearly as tall as her father, who's close to my height. Her gorgeous, long, blond hair is neatly pulled back into a ponytail. The girl's comfortable-looking attire isn't overtly designed to attract attention. She's wearing a feminine, yet demure, short-sleeved pink blouse with a short blue-jean miniskirt over capri-length, pink leggings. Her eye-catching figure has my head practically spinning.

My new "dream girl" and her family are silently observing the planes as they roll into and out of the gates. Her much younger brother is wearing Mickey Mouse ears. It's not hard to figure out that they're probably returning from Disney World.

As she turns toward me, I retreat into my magazine. Out of the corner of my vision, I see the face of an angel, accented by amazing dark-brown eyes. I observe her bronzed skin. It's obvious that she didn't get her awesome tan simply from a few days in Florida. Maybe she's from the Jackson area. It certainly appears that her family is flying home.

Of course, I know some strikingly beautiful girls back at my high school in Fulton. However, Dad strictly forbade me from going on dates, visiting a girl's home, or bringing one to our apartment. He warned that they can be a serious distraction from football. He also told me that there'd be plenty of time for girls and dates later. However, he never actually specified when "later" might be, and I was afraid to ask. Being so shy, the best I could manage was an occasional "hi" or "'bye" when face-to-face with a girl near my own age.

I've never engaged in a real discussion with a girl, with one exception: my friend Josh's twin sister, Cassandra. But she's more like one of the guys than an actual girl. We've never talked about anything but sports. I'm able to handle an all-out blitz, repeat our playbook word for word, and spit out the next play in the huddle without any problem, but talking to girls isn't one of my skills.

My tongue refuses to work properly, and my feet want to run away when some smiling teenage female tries to lock eyes with me or engage in conversation. And from what I've heard girls at my high school discussing, we have little to talk about anyway. Hair, cosmetics, fashion, reality shows, romance, and the latest gossip aren't topics that I care anything about, much less want to discuss. Wouldn't it be nice to find a female who knows as much about football as she does about putting makeup on her face?

Until our flight is called for boarding, I continue to steal glimpses of my dream girl. As I squeeze into another window seat on the plane, obviously designed for someone much smaller than I am, As passenfers continue to board, I pray that the girl in the pink shirt has been assigned the empty seat next to me. I wait in hopeful anticipation, but, instead, a heavy-set man sits next to me.

Possibly, when we land in Jackson, there will be an opportunity to speak to my dream girl. Maybe I could introduce myself and ask for her phone number. How would I even start such a conversation? Maybe by asking her about football in Mississippi? Seriously, whom am I kidding? Probably all I could get out is "What's up?" if that much. Besides, she's unlikely to know anything about my favorite sport anyway.

Trying to distract myself, I focus on the bustling activity on the airport tarmac as our plane is prepared for departure. Realizing that in a little over an hour, I'll be starting my new life in Mississippi, I take a deep breath, letting it out slowly. As children say when playing hide and seek, "Here I come, ready or not."

Chapter 9

UNUSUAL EVENTS

As our plane pulls away from the gate, my mind drifts back to last September once more. The first few days after my father's death were strange, to say the least. Staying at my grandparents' home rather than the apartment, I felt like a ship without a rudder, sailing aimlessly through uncharted waters. I never shed a tear or even felt the need to do so.

"Crying is for girls and babies," Dad always cautioned, assuring that I grew up to be as manly as possible. It actually helped that I didn't feel emotional about him dying. Numbness can be a blessing at times.

The evening after my father died, an unusual event took place. I'd left my backpack on the backseat of Dad's car before we took the bus to the game. My grandfather told me that the car was parked out back on Austin Avenue, a little-used road at the back of their property.

When I went out to grab the backpack, Paula Worminski was leaning against the rear fender of Dad's car. She was a fifteen-year-old freshman with pretty brown eyes and long brunette hair. I didn't know her well, even though she lived nearby and had been going to our school for several years. She was wearing a red sweater with a revealing deep V-neck and skin-tight jeans while drinking a beer and smoking a cigarette.

"Want a smoke?" Paula asked in a slurred voice as she reached for the pack.

"Sure," I said impulsively, although I'd never smoked before that night. It was the first time I'd deliberately done anything that I knew was wrong. For some reason, no longer being required to answer to my father made me feel a strong urge to rebel.

Paula smiled and handed me one from her pack. As I clumsily tried to light it, she tilted her head at me. "You don't talk much."

Sweat beaded on my forehead. I was embarrassed by my ineptness. Once the cigarette was lit, I immediately took a huge drag. As my lungs filled with smoke, I began coughing my head off. Laughing, she popped open a beer and handed it to me. Upset with what seemed like her ridicule, I dropped the cigarette to the ground, stomping it out with my foot. Without thinking, I chugged half the beer down, coughed some more, and drank the rest as my eyes watered. I didn't care for the taste, but it was a heck of a lot better than the medicinal flavor of the menthol cigarette.

Before she could offer me another beer, I opened the car door to retrieve my backpack. The sweet smell of Paula's perfume hung in the air inside the vehicle. I realized that Paula had been inside Dad's car doing Lord only knows what, and I momentarily felt outrage.

Seeing that my backpack had been moved from the backseat to the floorboard, I had a good guess at what had recently transpired but no idea who had been with Paula. As anger mixed with jealousy, suddenly I wanted her in that backseat with me.

Before I returned to the house, we promised each other to keep secret what had happened. With the lingering scent of her perfume clinging to my clothing, all I could think about that night was Paula. Her enticing body and the thought of her in the backseat was burned into my memory.

Needing another escape from the real world full of pain and sadness surrounding me, I turned to my oldest friend, my closest ally: my imagination. Papa taught me to read even before I started school. With all the characters from books running around inside my head, I was never lonely. The amazing words and unique phrases of many authors kept me both intrigued and fascinated. Books became an escape from the straightjacket of my highly regimented life.

Countless mourners poured into my grandparents' house, day in and day out. Dad's two younger sisters, Sandra and Kelly, came to stay with us. Aunt Sandy flew in from Chicago the day after Dad died; Aunt Kelly and her husband Steve arrived from Southern California on Sunday.

Friends and relatives alike tried to offer words of comfort, but it would've been nice if someone could've explained why Dad was taken from me. Doubting that any kind of God would be so cruel, the only logical explanation seemed to be a random act of chance.

One of the last people to stop by was Scott Brown, Syracuse University's offensive coordinator and a longtime friend of my dad's. He stayed only a few minutes, but it was obvious that Coach Brown was having a hard time controlling his emotions. He and Dad remained close friends even after playing football together at college. Having never seen a grown man, much less a macho football player, so emotional, it surprised me. I wondered why I hadn't cried or, at least, felt like doing so. Was it because I'd been trained so well to control my emotions?

On Tuesday, there was a huge funeral at the nearby Catholic church. Wading past a sea of mourners, I was directed to sit in the front row with my grandparents. It seemed as if there were a million flowers of every variety and color, their fragrance making it seem like springtime. The young priest, who'd probably never even met my dad, spoke some kind words. After the funeral, there was a graveside service that, thankfully, was brief. Following the service, my grandparents and I went back to their home.

Afterward, Dad's sisters said their good-byes, since they had to catch an early flight the next morning. Soon after they left, Jonathan and Josh stopped by to talk with me. I learned that Coach Maribito had been promoted to head coach. He'd assured them that whenever I returned to the team, I'd start at quarterback. When I told them that I'd play in our next game that Friday night, my friends seemed a little surprised, but relieved.

That evening, a strikingly beautiful woman with long, golden hair came to my grandparents' house. Her sad, robin's-egg blue eyes were cozily nestled between soft brown eyebrows and long lashes. A flawless complexion emphasized the perfection of her facial features. Her black dress was the ideal backdrop for her translucent, alabaster skin. Even as a teenager, I could appreciate her unique beauty.

I'd seen the tall, stately woman talking to Coach Brown at the graveside service earlier, but I didn't recall seeing her before that afternoon. It was quickly obvious from their friendly greeting that she knew my grandparents rather well. My grandfather introduced her as Sarah Lindley, a friend of my father who had traveled a long distance to be with us.

It was difficult to tell how old Sarah might be, but I would have guessed at least thirty. With her red eyes, her face matched the many tearful faces I'd seen around the house over the previous days. While Sarah may have come to comfort us, she appeared to need solace herself. However, there was something in her dazzling blue eyes other than sadness.

When I reached out to shake her hand, she hesitated briefly as if she didn't know what to do. Then, she grabbed my hand with both of hers and squeezed it quite hard. Her trembling fingers were noticeably cold despite our unseasonably warm September weather.

"JoeE, it's so nice to see you," Sarah said, a tiny smile tugging at the corners of her mouth and lighting up her eyes.

Her strong Southern accent reminded me of magnolias, mint juleps, and antebellum mansions. Her smooth, liquid drawl and rich accent suggested that she was definitely from somewhere sunny.

Besides her accent, I heard a faint choking sound when she spoke, as if she were about to cry at any moment. Obviously, she must have been a good friend of my father's. Thinking that she was about to say something else, I waited, but there was only silence. Leading her into the kitchen, Papa closed the door behind them. Never having seen that door closed before, I assumed that whatever they were discussing was extremely private.

I asked my grandmother how Dad knew this woman. She hesitated, thought for a moment, and then replied, "They met when your dad was at Syracuse University."

If Sarah had been in college with my father, she was obviously about forty. Either my grandmother was mistaken, or women must age a lot slower in the South.

"Papa said she came a long way to attend the funeral. Where is she from?"

"Somewhere in Mississippi, dear. Why do you ask?"

I just shrugged my shoulders. To be honest, I didn't know why I cared.

After about an hour, Sarah and Papa returned from the kitchen. He asked her when she was flying home.

"Not until Saturday," she replied, glancing over at me.

Seeming pleased, Papa told her eagerly, "Great, that gives us plenty of time to talk." Perplexed, I thought, *How much more time could they possibly need after already talking for an hour?*

As she reached the door, Sarah turned to me and said sweetly, "JoeE, it was so nice to see you. Hopefully, we'll see each other again soon."

"It was nice to meet you, Sarah," I replied, curious about this beautiful woman's relationship to my father.

Was she a friend of both my parents? Possibly this woman could shed some light on my mother, who remained a total mystery to me. Just like Papa, I found myself eager to see her again and planning what questions I wanted to ask. It's likely that my mother attended Syracuse University, although I'd never been told that for a fact. Some of the people who Dad knew from school would ask him about his wife. He always said that she was no longer with us.

Without talking to me, my grandparents went directly into the kitchen, and Papa closed the door again. Obviously, those conversations weren't for my ears.

Tired after the long day, I slipped off to bed. As I lay back on my pillow, Sarah's face and voice kept popping into my head. It seemed as though she had wanted to say more but had been restrained by an invisible force. The squeeze of her hand had seemed more like a hug or a subtle embrace. Where had I seen Sarah before? As far as I knew, I'd never been in Mississippi. I was unable to shrug off the feeling that there was something extremely important that she needed to tell me. Her voice continued to haunt my thoughts until I drifted off to sleep.

Waking up at about six o'clock the next morning, I followed my normal exercise regimen and decided to return to school. Without Dad around, I'd either have to walk or ask Papa for a ride, which meant hearing how he'd walked to the old Fulton High School.

According to Papa, he braved the winter cold, crossed an icy bridge, and plowed through drifting snow. He'd told me this story for years. Each time, the weather got a little colder and the snow was a little deeper. Listening to his story again wouldn't kill me. Then again, with almost three more years of high school, I might have to hear that story a hundred more times. Chuckling to myself, I projected that by the time I graduated, it would be minus one hundred degrees with snow over his head. It was a nice day, so I decided to walk.

I knew that I could get through the school day with little problem, but after school was football practice. That was a different story. Football and my dad were irreversibly linked. Of course, over the years, I'd played for different coaches, but Dad was always a part of those experiences.

As I prepared to leave, I wished that I could attend a school where nobody knew my dad or me. That way, I could walk down the hall without his ghost lurking behind me every step of the way.

At that moment, the idea of a new school seemed like such a simple escape. It's hard to believe that I was so naive.

Chapter 10

CONFUSION

The thud of the plane landing at the Jackson airport jars me from my daydream. My next thought is, *Watch what you wish for—it might just come true.* In a few days, I'll be attending a new high school where nobody knows me or knew my dad. My best friend, Jonathan, won't be there to have my back. With new classmates, teachers, and friends, it will seem like a different world. I've been granted my wish of anonymity but at a very steep price.

Although I'm anxious about these changes, I try to organize my thoughts. Thinking of my life simply in football terms, moving to Mississippi is like playing a team for the first time. At first, you're unfamiliar with the players, not sure about their strengths and weaknesses. After a few plays, you begin learning about your opponents. They don't know much about you either. You hide your weaknesses and take advantage of your strengths.

Inside the confines of my mind, all this logic sounds reasonable. However, even at sixteen, I realize that life doesn't work that simply. In football, there's one set of rules for everyone and a level playing field. In life, neither is the case.

Passengers begin exiting very soon after we arrive at the gate. The girl with the reflective bracelets disembarks ahead of me. I grab my backpack and coat from the overhead bin and head down the aisle, following the crowd. I notice my dream girl and her mother go off to the restroom. I hope to see her again at baggage claim.

Glancing outside through plate-glass windows along the hallway, I'm welcomed by bright blue skies without a hint of snow. Sunlight is streaming through the glass, making me wish I were wearing sunglasses. Approaching a security area, I see several people beyond it, obviously waiting for arriving passengers. At the rear of the crowd, I see a familiar face with a broad smile.

Immediately I think back to my first day at school after Dad's funeral. It went pretty much as I expected, with everyone offering sincere condolences. I called my grandparents to let them know that I'd catch a ride to their house after school. I felt that I required another day before stepping onto a football field, but I gave myself *only* one more. I swore that I'd drive out the nagging emotions that were bugging me. Grief had no place in this Spartan warrior.

People kept telling me that I needed some time to deal with Dad's death. All I really needed was to play football. Upon hearing that we'd lost the game to Jamesville-Dewitt after my premature and unnecessary departure, I knew that my team needed me. Our next game would be a clash with a powerful East Syracuse team. I couldn't let my teammates down again. Dead father or not, I would play.

Arriving at my grandparents' house after catching a ride with Paul, one of my few friends who didn't play football, I saw an unfamiliar car in the driveway. Thanking Paul for the lift, I entered the house to find Papa sitting in his favorite chair. On the couch across from him were my grandmother and the mysterious Sarah. Their apprehensive expressions gave me the distinct impression that they had been anxiously awaiting my arrival.

"What's up?" I asked, trying to break the foreboding silence.

The three adults exchanged ominous glances. Sarah's eyes flicked from me to my grandparents and then back.

"JoeE, you remember Sarah, don't you?" my grandfather asked. His voice was strained, his usual confident tone gone.

"Of course, Papa," I replied. "How are you, Sarah?" I tried to hide my eagerness to find out what was going on.

"I'm fine, JoeE," Sarah said, but it was obvious from her eyes that again she was holding something back.

"Bring a chair over here, JoeE. We want to talk to you," Papa instructed, motioning to where he wanted me to sit.

While I pulled a chair toward the three of them, my grandmother started the conversation. "Do you remember me telling you that your father met Sarah when they were in college?"

I nodded affirmatively, so my grandmother continued, "That is true, but I didn't tell you everything about their relationship."

"Oh?" I responded, shifting anxiously in my chair.

"You see, JoeE, while they were in college, they got married."

"Oh my God!" I blurted out. I was shocked as questions flooded my mind. It was like opening a door to a hallway lined with more doors. My father was married to Sarah before he married my mother? Why did Dad keep this secret from me? How long were Sarah and my dad married before they got a divorce?

Apparently seeing the puzzled expression on my face, Sarah jumped in quickly. "JoeE, your father and I had been goin' out for over a year before we got married."

My shock started giving way to disbelief. So, that's what Dad had meant when he told me, "There'll be plenty of time for girls later." Later meant college.

"Joseph wanted to start a family right away," Sarah went on. "When I failed to get pregnant after several months, I checked with a doctor. He told me that I might never be able to have children of my own. Joseph was devastated, as he wanted a son. We talked about adopting a boy after we graduated."

My mind quickly began filling in what I assumed to be the rest of Sarah and my dad's story. Obviously, they divorced, Dad remarried, and I was born. The end. At least, that should've been the end.

However, my mother died in a car accident, and my father was now gone. Apparently his first wife, who couldn't have children, had come to offer this poor little orphan…what? Pity? Maybe some help with college tuition? Or possibly she wanted to be a surrogate parent? Did she really expect me to move to Mississippi to regroup and find myself a new life?

My ego was a little resentful at Sarah's presence, insulted that she felt sorry for me. Another part of me was grateful for her thoughtfulness.

Mostly, I was curious as to exactly what she was going to say and if she would be willing to answer questions about my mother. All I knew was that I'd never leave my grandparents, much less to move to somewhere I had never been before. Of course, she hadn't offered me any such option. I was quiet. I was going to let her tell me the whole story.

Glancing at Papa, Sarah asked in a soft voice, "Should I go on, sir?"

"Certainly, Sarah," my grandfather replied emphatically. "JoeE deserves to know the truth. We owe him that."

"After Joseph and I graduated, we moved to California so he could be near the NFL team that drafted him. My husband was so excited to be livin' his lifelong dream. When he was named the startin' quarterback for the openin' game of the season, both of us were on cloud nine." Hearing Dad being referred to as "my husband" seemed very strange to me. I couldn't picture him with a woman, much less a wife.

The delightful expression on Sarah's face indicated that sharing this particular memory was exciting. She went on enthusiastically. "I recall Scott Brown, Joseph's best friend and teammate at Syracuse, bringin' us back to earth. My husband called his friend to tell him the news about startin' at quarterback. Scott warned him kiddingly that when a NFL team starts a rookie quarterback, it may not be that the rookie's that good. He said that it usually means the team is desperate. Only Scott could insult Joseph and still make him laugh."

My grandparents and I chuckled at that comment. It helped break the growing tension in the room. As Sarah's expression turned to a somber one, she reminded us, "Then, as you know, Joseph had that horrible knee injury in his first regular-season game."

Sarah stopped, as if she was at the end of the story, so I blurted out, "So when did you get divorced from my dad?"

Sarah glanced at my grandparents. Immediately trying to clarify my question, I added, "I mean, when did you two get divorced so my father could marry my mother?" There was utter silence for several seconds as if no one wanted to answer.

My grandfather finally put an end to the awkward silence by calmly stating, "JoeE, Sarah and Joseph never got a divorce."

"Never? I don't understand, Papa," I stammered, my heart beginning to pound in my chest. "Then what about my mother? You mean that she wasn't even married to my father?"

All at once, the nice, clean package that I believed about my parents' lives was thrown out the window. The pieced-together image that I'd created of their lives turned to sand. It was gone in a heartbeat, like breath on a mirror. A thousand different possibilities fluttered through my mind—my mother could be this, mother could be that.

But I've had logic drilled into me. Everything has an explanation. Dad taught me the Occam's razor theory, which states that the simplest assumption is the most likely. I suddenly knew what Papa was going to say before he even opened his mouth.

Looking me straight in the eyes, my grandfather confirmed that simple explanation when he slowly said, "JoeE, Sarah *is* your mother."

Chapter 11

ECHOES FROM THE PAST

When Sarah and I approach each other at the Jackson airport, she throws her arms wide open. We hug as she says softly, "I'm so happy that you're finally here, JoeE."

Having not seen her since those life-changing days just after Dad's funeral, my heart fills with joy to be with her.

Easing apart after the long embrace, my mother asks predictably, "How was your flight, dear?"

"It was a totally awesome flight, Mom. Thank you for the ticket. It was a nice Christmas present."

This was the first time that I've called Sarah "Mom" in person. In one of our phone conversations over the last three months, she and I had discussed what I should call her. Calling her Sarah had begun feeling awkward. I knew that in the future, it would be weird to introduce her as, "This is my Sarah."

When I asked her what she'd like me to call her, she simply left it up to me. Considering my choices, I felt that "Mommy" was too childish while "Mother" was too formal. When I told Sarah that I'd decided to call her "Mom," she seemed extremely pleased.

"I really like that, JoeE," she'd said with a smile in her voice. However, for a while I still referred to her as "Sarah," as it was difficult for me to believe I actually had a mother.

As we walk toward baggage claim, my thoughts once again drift back to that night at my grandparents' home when I first learned that Sarah was my mother. I was certainly happy to know that she was alive, but there was still one big question: Why had I been lied to all these years?

When my initial shock wore off, she tried to explain. "A couple days after Joseph's knee injury, my husband underwent surgery. We all hoped that Joseph would recover quickly and be able to play football again."

The grim looks on my grandparents' faces indicated that they too were reliving those horrible days as Sarah continued. "Joseph began rehab, but his knee didn't respond as everyone had hoped. The doctors told him that he might be able to walk again but that returnin' to football was completely out of the question."

Knowing my father, I'm sure that he didn't take that news easily. I remembered my dad's nightmares and mumbled cries about his knee drifting through the thin walls of our apartment. There's no doubt that those memories haunted him the rest of his life.

After taking several moments and a number of deep breaths, Sarah went on. "Bein' a football player's wife can be tough; bein' an injured player's wife is next to impossible. Joseph became more and more despondent. He often released his frustration by yellin' at me as if somehow everything were my fault. Bein' the target of so much undeserved venom was too much for me. Finally I couldn't take the vicious accusations anymore and returned to Mississippi."

It was clear that Sarah was having trouble holding it together. She took a minute to compose herself, taking more deep breaths. "When I returned home, I began usin' my maiden name of Lindley. As far as I was concerned, my marriage was over. I thought that Joseph would file for divorce since I'd left him."

While Sarah was speaking, my grandparents remained quiet. Their silence and failure to defend their son's behavior confirmed that my mother was telling the truth. I knew that Dad was prone to occasional fits of anger, so I was not that surprised that he had lashed out at his wife. Although my father never physically abused me, his verbal assaults could hurt just as much, if not more.

After what seemed like an eternity of icy silence, Sarah finally went on. "I'd been back in Mississippi for a month or so when Joseph began callin' and beggin' me to come back to him. He said that he was sorry that he treated me so badly. My husband informed me that he was checkin' into coachin' positions and promised that things would be different if I returned. Believin' that our marriage deserved a second chance, I made plans to fly to California."

She paused to ask my grandmother if she could have something to drink. I noticed tears forming in Sarah's eyes. While she waited, she hesitantly went on. "When I returned, I quickly found a position workin' at an investment firm while Joseph searched for a coachin' position. I started to feel poorly, so I saw a doctor and was shocked to learn that I was pregnant."

My grandmother brought Sarah a glass of water. She took several swallows and wiped her eyes with her sleeve before picking up where she left off.

"When I told Joseph that I was pregnant, he was so happy. I talked to some people back home and learned that there were a couple of football coachin' jobs openin' up in the Jackson area. I suggested to my husband that he apply. With his experience and knowledge of the game, I knew that he'd have an excellent chance of being hired."

A combination of disappointment, bitterness, and sorrow racked her voice as she candidly told me about life with Dad. A small tear glistened on her cheek as she continued.

"Joseph said that he wasn't goin' to the South. He wanted to return to central New York to coach, even if it meant waitin' for a position to open up. I told him that I didn't want to go back to the North and couldn't see why he refused to give the South a chance. I gave him all my reasons for wantin' to return to Mississippi, but it didn't seem to matter. Joseph began to yell at me again, and nothin' was resolved."

Taking another short break, Sarah sipped some water and shot a glance at my grandparents, as if silently asking for permission to continue. My grandfather gave her a kind, knowing nod. Apparently, that was enough. "I was scheduled for a sonogram that would let us know whether the baby was a boy or a girl. The day before the procedure, Joseph made a shockin' proposal that he said would resolve our stalemate over where to live once and for all."

Although it was clearly becoming more and more difficult for my mother, I was actually fascinated to hear about these events that occurred before I was born. A kind of nervous excitement had taken hold of me; my heart was practically in my stomach.

"I eagerly asked my husband what he had in mind," she went on. "He said that if the baby was a girl, I should take her to Mississippi without him, raising her as I saw fit. Joseph seemed to have no interest in raising a daughter. But if the baby was a boy, he wanted take him to New York to raise him without any interference or assistance. At first, I didn't believe that he was serious!"

Of course, having been brought up by my father in New York, I knew the rest of the story. Normally, it requires death to sever the strong ties between parent and child. My father had come up with a new way, the chaotic randomness of chromosomes that determine one's gender—basically, a glorified coin flip.

It sounded exactly like Dad to use cool, crisp logic in a totally emotional situation. When I hit a home run to win a Little League game, instead of a hug, he asked if the pitch was a fastball. When I ran seventy-five yards for a touchdown in an important game, instead of a pat on the back, I received a lecture on handing the ball to the referee in the end zone.

Regret tinged every word as my mother went on. "You need to understand, JoeE, we were young, just in our early twenties. We were desperately tryin' to solve what seemed like an impossible situation. Joseph gave me all kinds of reasons why his proposal was our only practical option. We couldn't continue to live like we had been, in constant, bitter turmoil. We needed to part before we destroyed each other. I was heartbroken and confused. He simply wore me down, so I agreed to his proposal, terrified to do otherwise."

Her gaze falling to the floor, Sarah looked exhausted. I shook my head, trying to comprehend how my parents could have come to such an insensitive bargain. I felt as if I should say something, but I was simply speechless. It was like the biblical story of King Solomon threatening to split the baby in half. However, in my case, the decision was based on my potential to play football.

Understanding that I was the baby to which Sarah was referring made the whole story seem totally surreal. I begin feeling sorry, not for myself, but for my mother. Knowing Dad, I could suspect that she actually had little choice once his mind was made up. At times, he could be a bit of a bully until he got his way. As a coach, this technique may have had its place. Off the field, however, such behavior was uncalled for and at times downright mean.

"JoeE, I know that it was wrong of me to agree to Joseph's plan. I really messed up and just hope that someday you'll be able to find it in your heart to forgive me."

I knew that I should be angry with my parents for their selfish agreement, but I just couldn't feel that emotion. Instead, I simply forgave them. Maybe it was because I missed my father or because I'd always wanted a mother. Possibly, it was because of the words that I'd heard, or thought I'd heard, from the stranger in the hospital waiting room. It may have been that I felt sorry for Sarah, knowing how persuasive and demanding my father could be at times. My mother had already suffered enough, and I had no desire to add to her pain.

Without a word, I threw my arms around her. For a brief moment, I thought I would never let go.

"It's OK," I said, my heart suddenly overflowing with love that seemed to appear out of thin air. "You did what you thought you had to do."

If forgiveness was all that it took to ease my mother's suffering, then I was ready, willing, and able to forgive both her and even my father. I realized that my grandparents had known about my mother all this while. Even though their silence for sixteen years hurt worse than I cared to admit, I couldn't blame them for it. They'd been caught in the middle, and they done the best they could in a delicate situation.

I hoped to learn much more about what forces influenced my parents to part ways in such a strange manner. That afternoon in Fulton, I was simply happy not to be going down the crooked path of anger, resentment, and revenge. I forgave them even though I did not know all of the circumstances.

Immediate, unconditional forgiveness allowed me to get on with my life. With no residual bitterness or regret, the specters of the past couldn't cast their gloomy shadows on me. Keeping my focus on the future, my heart was open to the joy of my mother's love.

Chapter 12

BYE-BYE DREAM GIRL

Walking silently through the Jackson airport, I note the ticket counters of several airlines and another security checkpoint beyond. Maybe the Jackson airport isn't quite as small as I first imagined, and possibly, I shouldn't jump to conclusions about my new home.

We take an escalator down a level to baggage claim. Along with the other passengers, I patiently wait by a long conveyor belt, chatting with my mother about nothing in particular. When my dream girl's family arrives, she isn't with them. Keeping an eye out, I hope to see her once more. If I do, I swear that I'll talk to her.

Interrupting my little daydream, Mom asks, "How many suitcases do you have, dear?"

"Just one," I reply. "Papa said that he'd ship anything else I might need." Suddenly a loud buzzer sounds, and the conveyor begins to move. Spotting the new blue suitcase that my grandparents gave me for Christmas, I snatch it off the conveyor and head for the door.

"You were able to get everything into that one suitcase and your backpack, JoeE?" my mother asks, sounding as if I'd performed an amazing feat of magic. As we walk outside, she adds, "I needed two suitcases for my short trip to Fulton."

Chuckling, I reply, "You have a son, not a daughter, Mom."

I'd made the comment jokingly, but I catch a strange, more serious expression on Mom's face as she says, "Oh, yeah."

As we exit the terminal and cross to the parking garage, I learn what "Mississippi is warmer than New York" feels like. Early this morning, I

left a cloudy central New York with a bone-chilling mist and a temperature of around thirty. I'm now enjoying sunny skies with humid, sixty-
degree air. I hope that I'll have little need for my heavy winter coat.
My dad often remarked that in the winter, the national weather maps
always had a snowflake directly over Fulton.

"Mom, does it snow here?" I ask, hoping for a negative response.

"We've had snow a few times in the last five years, but it's usually
gone within a day or so. It does get cold, but never like central New
York. Once in a while, it gets below freezin'. The last week or so, it has
been unusually warm, and it's predicted to get even warmer over the
next couple of weeks."

"Wow!" I smile. "Warm days in December and January. No more
shoveling snow!" Many of my friends in Fulton are into winter sports,
such as snow skiing, hockey, and snowmobiling. However, I prefer
swimming, water skiing, and tennis, none of which mixes well with
snow.

As we near the parking garage, I glance over my shoulder and
finally spot my dream girl standing alone at the other end of the
arrival area. Just then, a bright-red car pulls up in front of her, and
she gets in. Assuming that the driver is some lucky guy whom she's
dating, I quickly turn away with a little twinge of jealousy, wishing I
were he.

In the parking garage, we place my belongings into my mother's
light-tan Cadillac Escalade. Her vehicle is a newer model with a dash-
board that resembles the cockpit of an airplane. Why would Mom own
a luxury utility vehicle rather than just a car? Of course, this roomy
SUV is ideal for traveling. Hopefully, we will be going to places like the
Superdome in New Orleans. Maybe I should mention to her that the
Super Bowl is there this year.

Leaving the airport, I notice a sign that reads, "Jackson Medgar
Willey Evers International Airport." I ask, "Who's this guy that the airport is named after?"

"Medgar Evers was a civil rights advocate," Mom tells me. "He was
killed in the sixties. Not long ago, they finally arrested his killer and
convicted him of murder."

"Was Evers black?" I ask, curious to see her reaction to a question regarding race.

"Yes, he was a black man," my mother said simply.

"I suppose there have been a bunch of incidents like that here," I say, pursuing the inquiry.

"Like everywhere else, there are murders in Mississippi, but they are rarely racially motivated. Now it's mostly drug-related," Mom says. Approaching a small traffic circle, she drives three-quarters of the way around it. "This area is part of the city of Pearl, JoeE," she informs me. "Brandon is just a little piece up the road."

"Is my new school in Brandon or Pearl?" I ask, trying to familiarize myself with the area.

"You'll be attendin' Brandon High School."

Mom has told me very little about the city during our phone conversations. She didn't wish to influence or "sell" me on moving here. Rather, she wanted me to decide based upon my own criteria. Making that choice was the most grown-up thing that I've ever been allowed to do, and I really appreciate her letting me make the decision for myself.

As she drives, Mom tells me about my new hometown. Like a tour guide, she informs me, "Brandon is a small but growing city. It has about twice the population of Fulton. The high school is a mile or so from our house in the southern part of the city."

I'm relieved when she says that Brandon has essential restaurants like McDonald's, Wendy's, Burger King, and, even more importantly, a variety of pizza places. Mom also informs me that there aren't any movie theaters or large malls in Brandon but there are several of both in other nearby suburbs of Jackson. When she mentions that it has a Super Wal-Mart, I know that I'm still in the civilized world.

The day after I learned that Sarah was my mother, she asked me if I'd like to live with her in Mississippi. Before that time, I'd just assumed that I'd be living with my grandparents until I finished high school. Of course, moving to Mississippi meant that I'd be leaving my grandparents as well as my friends and teammates. After talking it over with everyone, I finally decided to make the big move. By waiting until after Christmas to leave Fulton, I was able to finish the school semester and the football season. Dad always said, "If you start something, son, you need to finish it."

My mother reassured me that if I ever wanted to return to Fulton—for a visit, or to live—I was free to do so. Since my parents never filed for divorce, there was no question about Mom's custody rights. By not divorcing, they'd provided a type of insurance policy that I just cashed in.

Of course, I never realized that Dad was still married all of those years; that explained why he never went out on dates. Although it seems unlikely, the possibility remains that my mother has seen other men. She seems to be quite secretive, so anything is possible. So many of the so-called facts about my parents have proved to be false that it would be foolish of me to make any more assumptions.

I'll start living life like I play football, simply one play at a time. No more will I make big plans for the future. Today is all the future I need.

Chapter 13

WELL-OFF WORKS

While still in Fulton, I learned from my mother that the sizable bonus that Dad had received for signing his NFL contract was later used to set up a trust fund for me. He had never mentioned such a trust. Mom said the funds were designated for the costs of college and I'd receive the remainder when I turned twenty-one.

I've never worried about having money for college, always assuming that I'd be offered an athletic scholarship, as my dad was. Informing me that the money had been invested in various assets over the years, Mom stated that it was now a "very substantial" amount. According to her, it could be used sooner, at the discretion of the trustee. She said that Papa would need to be consulted before any of the money could be withdrawn early.

Of course, my first question to Papa after hearing about the trust fund was predictable. Like a child itching for a new toy, I asked, "Can I have Dad's old car or use money from the trust fund to buy one?"

His answer was just as predictable: "We'll see, JoeE." I intend to keep reminding Papa how much I need my own wheels.

My friend Paul, who's six months older than me, was given a car by his parents when he got his license. He said that it gave him freedom and that girls really like guys who have their own cars. I need all the help I can get when it comes to the opposite sex. Of course, I never said anything to Dad, believing that we couldn't afford a second car.

Taking a left, Mom tells me, "This is Highway 80, also called Government Street. It's the main street through Brandon and where many of the businesses are located. I'm goin' to a bank to open a checkin' account for you."

With only thirty bucks to deposit, it wouldn't be much of an account. "That's nice, Mom. Thank you."

I've never had a bank account of my own or a job, either. My ten-dollar-a-week allowance was always gone quickly, usually blown on fast food. In the next half mile or so, I note that we pass at least five banks. "What's with all the banks?"

"There are a bunch. I believe ten different ones in the city, some with branch offices. I've got accounts in all of them." So much for the movies portraying Mississippi as poor. I guess I won't fit in as well as I thought.

"Why not just have all your money in one bank, Mom? Wouldn't that be easier?"

"Yes, it would, honey," my mother agrees, "but the government only insures your money in a bank up to a certain amount. By havin' accounts in several different banks, our money is much safer. It also helps me keep my various accounts straight."

We pull into the parking lot of Community Bank. Entering through two sets of heavy double doors, we walk into a large, open area with a high ceiling. The counter, like the floor, appears to be made of marble. The wooden desks, as well as the furniture in a small sitting area, have a polished antique look.

"How old is this bank?" I ask, glancing at the fine furnishings.

"It was built about a dozen years ago," Mom informs me to my surprise. "Why do you ask?"

"Just wondering. It's pretty impressive." I look around, admiring the place. "It definitely looks a lot older, kinda like Papa's bank in Fulton. That one is real old."

The woman at the first desk on our left greets us. "Good afternoon, may I help y'all?" she asks politely.

My mother turns toward her. "Yes, Jane. Is Jennifer here?"

With her sweet smile, Jane informs us that Jennifer is in her office. Approaching the open door of the corner office, I see an attractive woman with dark hair sitting behind her desk.

The woman looks up from her computer. "Hey Sarah, please come on in." With her eyes fixed on me and a grin playing at the corner of her lips, she asks, "So is this JoeE?" How many other people in Brandon has Mom told about me moving here?

"Yes, this is my son," Mom answers with a hint of pride in her voice.

Practically jumping out of her chair, Jennifer reaches out to shake my hand. Like my mother's, this woman's hand is like ice. Don't these people have any circulation, or could Brandon actually be Vampire South? My mother informs me that Jennifer and she are old friends who went to high school together.

I say somewhat jokingly, "She doesn't look all that old to me, Mom." Of course, my mother doesn't look her age either. Maybe Brandon's real secret is a fountain of youth.

Jennifer laughs. "I like him already!"

Maybe I've actually made my first friend in Brandon. Why can't I talk to girls my own age? It isn't as if they bite. At least, I don't think so.

My mother tells Jennifer that she wants to set up a checking account for me. After we sign some papers, I offer my paltry thirty dollars. But my mother tells me to keep my money and hands Jennifer a check instead. Asked if she wants a debit card on my account, Mom says, "Definitely." I can't believe that I'm getting my own plastic. Jennifer leaves for a couple of minutes, apparently to finalize the paperwork.

I thank Mom politely for the checking account and debit card.

"Honey," she tells me, "just use good judgment. I'll set up something so that money is deposited into your account each week."

"That'd be awesome," I tell her, wondering if it will be ten dollars a week like Dad gave me.

Jennifer returns, handing me a small set of checks and telling me that my printed checks would arrive in about two weeks. Mom and her friend start talking about something going on after church on Sunday as I thumb through my new checkbook proudly. Noticing the account balance written into it, I'm concerned.

Interrupting their conversation, I ask, "There's something wrong here—is this the right amount?"

When I hold up my checkbook so Mom can see the balance, Jennifer has a worried look on her face. She's obviously hoping that there's no error on her part.

"That's right, dear," my mother says casually.

I look at the balance again. "Twenty-five hundred dollars? Isn't the decimal point in the wrong place?"

"Just use it wisely," my mother tells me as Jennifer sighs in relief.

I look at Jennifer and ask quite seriously, "Is this above what the government insures for one bank?"

"No, JoeE," Jennifer responds. "The FDIC insures up to $250,000 for your accounts in this bank."

Does that mean Mom has more than a quarter million dollars? Before I can ask anything more, my mother is leading me to one of the tellers to obtain my debit card.

"Hi, Maria," my mother greets the woman at one of the spaces.

"May I help you, Mrs. Lindley?" Maria asks. The teller, who appears to be around thirty years old, has shiny black hair and beautiful bronze skin.

As Mom hands her one of the papers, she says, "My son needs a debit card on his new account."

"We'll fix him right up," Maria tells her. Glancing at the paper, she enters some information into her computer, and then locates a small electronic box with a numbered keypad. She asks me to punch in any four digits for my access code. "Make it a number that you can remember."

I punch in my favorite quarterback's jersey number twice—now all I have to do is think of Eli Manning to remember my password. After walking over to a machine a short distance away, Maria soon returns with my card in hand.

I must have a gigantic smile, as Maria observes, "You look so happy, JoeE."

"I am really happy." Of course, like most teenagers, I'm never satisfied. Now if I were the starting quarterback for Brandon High, had my own car, and had a girlfriend, my life would be perfect. Right now, I'm not sure about my chances for any of them.

Leaving the bank, I ask my mother, "So, do you know everyone in Brandon?"

"Not everybody, dear," Mom replies. With a little smile, she adds, "But it never hurts to be friendly. I'm actually pretty shy. I was never much of a talker, so my trick is to get people talking about themselves. For example, just by askin', I've learned that Maria is from Hawaii and is actually married to a guy who was stationed at Pearl Harbor. Can you believe she has grandkids?"

In addition to finally confirming the source of my shyness, Mom has even provided a suggestion for combating it.

"Are you sure she's a grandmother?" I exclaim, shaking my head. Now I'm sure that somewhere in Brandon there's a fountain of youth.

Heading back the way that we came on Highway 80, I think about what my mother said earlier. She told me that she has accounts in all of the Brandon banks. If the federally insured amount is $250,000, then obviously Mom has well over that total in her accounts or she wouldn't need so many.

Taking my math a step further, I realize my mother could have several times that sum. In phone conversations, Sarah mentioned owning several houses and other property. Considering that she just deposited $2,500 into my account, I think that my next question is appropriate.

"Mom," I blurt out, "are we rich?"

"Rich is a relative term," my mother answers carefully. "I'd just say that we're well-off. Just because we're wealthier than most people makes us no better than anyone else."

Feeling myself grin, I think about our apparent lack of financial worries. Well-off works for me, especially if it means that I'll get a car soon.

Retracing our route to the corner where an expansive Ford dealership is located, we turn south. Crossing over Interstate 20, we pass Home Depot, the Honda dealership, and various smaller businesses. I've not seen any older-looking buildings since we entered Brandon. Unlike Fulton, it appears as if everything has been built in the relatively recent past.

We drive over railroad tracks, passing a Pepsi plant with a large pond beside it. The pond, which is about forty yards in diameter, has a small fountain at the center that's spraying water about a dozen feet into the air. I think I've found the fountain of youth. After all, that Pepsi slogan a few years ago said, "Taste the one that's forever young."

If I suddenly begin feeling younger, at least I'll know why.

Chapter 14

MISSISSIPPI ROOTS

During our phone conversations over the last few months, Sarah gave me a broad overview of our family history. It was extremely fascinating, information that I've hungered for my entire life. My new roots run deep, interweaving with Mississippi's rich history, giving me a sense of belonging.

Forming a mental picture of my maternal family, I try to imagine the young girl who eventually became my mother. Despite our many phone conversations, I still feel as if I barely know Sarah. Although she's opened up to me about our heritage, her own life is still somewhat shrouded in mystery. She often sounds guarded, as though she's choosing her words carefully. Then again, maybe it's just her shyness.

I found some interesting similarities between the generations. One little tidbit that really made me feel linked to her is the fact that she, along with her parents, Dean and Kimberly, was also an only child. I guess that "one and done" runs in my family. Meeting at college also seems to be a familiar theme, since Sarah's parents became acquainted while at Delta State University in northwest Mississippi just like she and my dad did at Syracuse.

"JoeE, you get your height from my daddy," Sarah told me in one of our early phone conversations. "I saw a picture of him when he was in eighth grade, and he was already over six-feet tall."

It's another link to her family and explains why I got so big so fast. Her statement suddenly made me feel connected to Grandpa Dean who, like me, endured the awkwardness of being so much taller than those around him in school.

Sarah seemed to bubble up whenever she mentioned her father. "Your grandfather Dean's ancestors were among this state's original plantation owners. They owned thousands of acres of prime land near the Natchez Trace north of Tupelo."

"Is their plantation still there?"

"Their plantation home was burned by the Yankees during the Civil War," Sarah told me, sounding bitter despite the fact that the event occurred a century and a half ago. "His family held on to most of the land after the war. Since then, it has mostly been rented out."

"It's nice that the land could stay in our family," I told her in that conversation last fall.

"It gives us a real connection to our ancestors," my mother said. "My daddy's family became involved in banking. They became major stockholders in a number of banks in north Mississippi. Your great-grandfather was a banker, and his son ended up following in his footsteps."

In another of our little talks last fall, Sarah told me about her mother, Kimberly Lee Bowen, and that side of our family. There wasn't the same excitement in her voice as when she told me about her father. The main insights she shared about her mother were that she majored in music in college and played in the Jackson Symphony. My grandmother Kimberly was from Brandon, where her parents owned an insurance agency along with several rental properties.

"There was a General John Bowen in the Civil War," I mentioned to her. "I wonder if we're related."

"I don't know, JoeE, but maybe," my mother told me. "Your great-grandmother, Paralee Sarah McRaven, was from Vicksburg. Her family has lived in that city since before the Civil War. Her parents were well-to-do and doted on their only child. Her father was a successful attorney, involved in state and local politics."

"How did your parents end up living in Brandon, Mom?" I asked in yet another one of our conversations.

"They got married just after graduating from Delta State," Sarah informed me, "and moved into a home given to them as a wedding present by my mother's parents. I grew up there and still own that house. It's really big, so I've rented it out for over twenty years. Daddy Dean went to work for a local branch of a bank headquartered in Atlanta, while Mama became a middle-school band director."

In subsequent talks, my mother presented me with a broad overview of her life. However, she was very sketchy when it came to details, pretty much giving me only the facts. I hope that over time, she will open up. Unfortunately, tragedy and loss seemed to be the overriding theme of Sarah's stories.

A few years after marrying Dean, his wife gave birth to a daughter: Sarah Louise Lindley. She was named after her grandmothers, both of whom had died by the time she started school. In fact, all four of her grandparents passed away before Sarah reached her eighth birthday. Her early life was marred by funerals and, all too often, grief-stricken parents.

During her early years, Sarah spent a considerable amount of time developing her musical talent. My grandmother devoted many hours to teaching her daughter how to play the piano. Expanding her musical ability, Sarah played clarinet in the school band.

When Sarah was ten, death visited her again. On a stormy night, her father was driving home from the airport when his pickup skidded off the highway. According to the police, Sarah's father was killed instantly. Having a hard time accepting his death, Sarah spent months believing that he was still coming home.

Not only was Grandpa Dean heavily insured, he also left behind the bank stocks along with the extensive property that he'd inherited. Although his devastated family lost a husband and father, at least financial worries weren't added to their already heavy burden.

Growing up, my mother had two close friends: Marty Booth and Jules Barbour. Since grade school, they'd spent much of their spare time together. The three girls often gathered at Sarah's large home, since Marty lived in a small trailer and Jules had younger brothers. Sarah's mother loved the sound of their laughter, especially after losing her fun-loving and gregarious husband. Kimberly called them the Three Musketeers.

By the time the teenage girls reached high school, boys were their main topic of discussion. Sarah confessed that she had a particular fascination with Brandon's star linebacker, whose nickname was "Rhino." The name fit him perfectly, since he played football like a charging rhinoceros. As outgoing as she was shy, he was her only romance during high school. When Rhino went off to Mississippi State on a football scholarship, they drifted apart.

"How did you end up going to Syracuse, Mom?" I had asked her, curious as to why she chose a college so far away from home.

"I loved writing poetry and short stories," Sarah responded. "I researched schools of journalism, thinking that I could develop my writing talent and have a career. Syracuse University had one of the top-rated journalism schools, so I applied and was accepted. My mother wanted me to attend a college closer to home, so I also checked out schools in Mississippi, but I ended up going to New York."

In the spring of her senior year in high school, tragedy again struck Sarah's life. Her mother was diagnosed with brain cancer. A delay in diagnosis, coupled with the aggressive nature of the cancer, severely reduced her chance of survival. Early that summer, Kimberly Lindley died. Later I would learn that at eighteen, Sarah found herself financially set for life but all alone in the world. It wasn't anywhere near an even trade.

"How did you meet Dad?" was another of my questions.

"As a freshman, I was a journalism major, but I changed to finance the next year," Sarah told me without explaining why. "In one of my business classes, I met Scott Brown, who was at Syracuse on a football scholarship. We became friends, and he introduced me to his roommate, Joseph Collins."

"What was Dad like back then?" I asked, hoping she might open up a bit.

"Oh, Joseph had a really dominant personality. It was like a magnet," Sarah admitted, finally giving me a little glimpse into her feelings. "He reminded me of my daddy with his zest for life. If I hadn't met Joseph, I might have just dropped out of school and returned to Mississippi. After adjustin' to the loss of my mother, I began to miss my hometown. Although I tried, I could never convince Joseph to travel here, not even for a visit."

Apparently, Sarah felt that if I knew more about her trials and tribulations, I would forgive her for letting Dad take me away. Even though I've told her repeatedly that she's already forgiven, my mother seems to find it difficult to accept that fact.

Maybe my mother had been using her stories to point out how difficult life can be. Was she trying to warn me about emotional pitfalls, especially with regard to the opposite sex? My current problem is much simpler. To have a relationship with a girl, I believe it's helpful, if not mandatory, to actually have a conversation with one first.

In one of our last phone conversations, I asked Sarah, "Why didn't you and Dad ever get a divorce?"

Seeming uncomfortable, she simply replied, "I guess that we just never got around to it." It wasn't much of an answer, but I felt that I shouldn't pursue what appeared to be a touchy subject.

Admitting that even now she finds it difficult to be close to people, Sarah attributed it to the many tragedies she'd endured. "Reuniting with you has given me a whole new outlook on life, JoeE," she confessed.

Perhaps my mother will trust me enough one day to fill in all those years of her life that she just skimmed over. Until then, I'll be thankful for what she has shared and patiently wait for the rest.

For some reason, I have the uneasy feeling that Mom really wants—no, desperately *needs* to—share something extremely important with me. However, I haven't the slightest idea what it could be. I hope it doesn't take another sixteen years to find out.

Chapter 15

LOOKING FOR TRUTH

Thinking back upon my years in Fulton, I wonder why I was so incredibly shy around girls. Often they tried to engage me in conversation, but I certainly did nothing to encourage them. I would listen politely but never volunteered anything. Some girls probably believed that I was a deaf-mute. Although I attended school dances, I never intended to dance. Several girls even asked me, but all I could get out was a polite, "No, thanks." Pretty pathetic for the star quarterback.

Even my equally shy friend Jonathan occasionally danced with Josh's twin sister, Cassandra. It was always weird seeing her in a skirt or a dress, since I've always considered her to be just one of the guys. When she talked to me, I'd listen but do nothing else except give one- or two-word answers to her questions.

Before moving to Mississippi, I promised myself that things would be different when it came to girls. "No balls, no glory" is the locker-room way to say courage. Tired of being like the cowardly lion in *The Wizard of Oz*, I was going to find some courage. I planned to come out of my shell. Well, at least I hoped I would.

At the first traffic light, Mom turns right onto Highway 468, which I recognize from when she gave me her home address.

"If we'd continued straight, JoeE," my mother says, "we would've been at Brandon High School in less than a mile."

"Are we almost to your house, Sarah?" I'm curious about how far I'll be living from my new school.

"Yes, it's just a little piece down this road, dear."

"Mom, it's nice that I won't have to go too far to get to school."

The transition from referring to her as Sarah to calling her Mom has been more difficult than I expected. I've caught myself going back and forth between the two names. Being here, even for this short time today, has made me feel much closer to her. From now on, I'm going to redouble my efforts to call her Mom.

While back in New York, I'd found some information about Brandon High's football season. Only able to find scores, it was obvious that the team had done well, losing only two games all year. "Do you know anything about Brandon's football team, Mom?" I ask, not expecting her to be very knowledgeable about the sport.

"We played for the state championship last season."

I ask, "Do they have a good quarterback?"

"Yes, honey, he's excellent and only a junior."

"Did Brandon win the championship?"

"No, but it was a close game right until the end."

I want to say that with me at quarterback, Brandon would've won that championship, but that would sound arrogant. Although Dad cautioned me not to brag, he always stressed that if I'm not confident in my abilities, no one will believe in me. He simply urged me to show my talent on the field.

"Mom, how did you hear about the game?"

"I was there. I go to all of Brandon's games," she answers, shocking me. "Brandon did win the state championship in girls' soccer. We also have other excellent sports teams, a terrific band, fantastic cheerleaders, and a great dance team."

"Well, Mom, if I don't make the football team, maybe you can teach me some cool dance moves."

She laughs.

Looking around, I think about how different this area feels compared with anywhere in Fulton. Much of the history that I know about my ancestors comes from Papa's entertaining family legends. Although he has a tendency to exaggerate, I believe that most of his stories are based upon fact. The furthest that he's traced back his ancestry is to his grandmother's grandfather, John Conley.

Born of Irish parents, as a young teenager John ran away from his home in Canada in the early 1800s. Finding work on the cargo boats on Lake Ontario, one day he got off on the American side of the lake. From that point on, he was an American, but he was what we now refer to as an "illegal immigrant." I wonder if I could be deported back to Canada.

Half a century later, one of his granddaughters married Thomas Collins, also the son of Irish immigrants. He and his young wife moved to Fulton and raised four children, including a son named Joseph Edward. Called Joe, he was the first of four generations of Collins boys to play football for what was then called Fulton High School.

His mother didn't want him to play such a rough sport, so for three years, he played without her knowledge. His father kept his son's secret, telling his wife that Joe was working in the family's hauling business. This deception ended in the fall of 1929 when Joe scored four touchdowns against archrival Oswego in the final game in his senior year. Word travels fast in a small town, and that night there was hell to pay in the Collins household. The crash of the stock market that year may have been mild in comparison to his Irish mother's wrath.

For a long time, I believed that my great-grandfather secretly playing football was my family's biggest secret. Of course, it paled in comparison to those of my parents.

I can't help but excitedly anticipate what wondrous adventures await me here in Brandon.

Chapter 16

HOME SWEET HOME

We turn into the driveway of a medium-size, one-story brick home that appears comfortable but certainly nothing spectacular. However, after living in a small apartment with Dad, this place looks like a mansion to me. Pressing an automatic door opener, my mother reveals a two-car garage. It will be the perfect place to park my car as soon as I get one.

In an extraordinarily motherly tone, my mother says, "Well, honey, welcome home."

"I'm happy to be here, Mom."

Exiting the Escalade, I retrieve my suitcase, backpack, and the heavy coat that's destined for the back of a closet. Entering the house, I see a glass door that leads to a patio. Straight ahead of me is an open doorway leading to a large bedroom. On the other side of that room is an adjoining bathroom.

"That's my bedroom, JoeE," Mom says, indicating the room straight ahead. Pointing to the left at a louvered folding door, Mom informs me, "Behind there is the laundry room. Let me show you to your bedroom."

Walking through the kitchen into a nicely decorated dining room, I gaze out a picture window to a panoramic view of the expansive back-yard. Beyond the lawn is a heavily wooded area.

The yard is well over half the length of a football field. A chain-link fence encloses an area near the house. There's a small fountain, a grill, and some lawn furniture. Pots and planters of various sizes line the inside of the fence. On the right is a long, double row of extremely tall pine trees. They separate the property from the expansive front lawn of the house next door which is set back from the highway.

There's plenty of room to pass around a football. Of course, I need to meet someone who would be interested in catching those passes. I doubt that my mother enjoys playing catch, but she does continue to surprise me. I figure she'd probably worry more about breaking a nail than holding onto the ball.

Against the far wall of the dining room is an exquisite upright piano constructed from either rich mahogany or maybe dark cherry wood. It's obviously very old. "Do you still play the piano, Mom?" I ask curiously.

"I stopped playing for a long time after my Mama, your grand-mother Kimberly, died. She and Daddy were both wonderful pianists," Mom says nostalgically. "But I've begun playing again recently."

"I can't wait to hear you play," I tell her as she smiles wistfully, obvi-ously still lost for a moment in the memories of bygone days.

Smiling, she goes on. "My grandfather bought this piano for my mother when she was a young girl. It was nearly seventy-five years old when he bought it. That was over sixty years ago, so it's quite an antique."

In the middle of the dining room, there's an elegant wooden table with eight matching chairs. The impressive set was constructed from a light-colored wood, probably oak. On both sides of the piano are tall cabinets that match the wood of the table.

From the dining room, we go into a comfortable-looking living room. There's a gigantic big-screen television, an ivory sectional couch, and a very cozy-looking armchair. There are also several shelves with many books and assorted collectibles. However, there are few pictures on the walls, and some of shelves have open spaces as if something is missing.

That television and couch would be perfect for watching football games, especially cuddled up with a hot girl. However, I dismiss the fantasy quickly. I suspect that few girls, hot or not, are interested in spending their time watching football on television. Maybe none.

Hanging a left down a short hallway, we pass a closed door and a bathroom. The door probably leads to a spare bedroom, since Mom doesn't mention it. I follow her into another bedroom at the far end of the hallway. Except for the kitchen, which is tiled, the remainder of the house has immaculate white pile carpeting. Muddy shoes and spilled drinks will definitely not be welcome here. Cleanliness may need to rise on my list of priorities.

My mother turns to me. "This is your room, darlin'. I hope you like it."

The walls of my new room are painted a shade of light brown. It's one of those colors with a name that only a female would know. On the far wall, there's a window, and I can see the backyard through the venetian blinds. The furnishings include a single bed, a four-drawer dresser, a wooden desk, and a nicely padded recliner. There's also a large flat-screen television mounted on one of the walls.

Attached to the television is a DVD player, which is sitting on top of a bookcase with various types of storage units. On the desk is a black laptop computer, an iPad, a printer, and what appears to be a combination CD player and radio.

"What's not to like?" I ask, giving her a bear hug. "This is totally awesome and then some." This bedroom is at least twice as big as my room at the apartment in Fulton.

Across the room from the window is a large closet with ample space for far more clothes than I own. It's the kind of room that I've only dreamed about. Now I'm living that dream.

"Merry Christmas, sweetie," my mother says cheerfully.

"Thanks. I may forget about school and just stay in here for the rest of my life. Maybe I could just have pizza delivered. You would be welcome to visit me, of course," I joke. She's obviously trying to make up for her absence at my last sixteen Christmases and birthday celebrations. Maybe she can't make up for those lost years, but Mom sure is making a valiant effort.

After I swing my suitcase and my backpack onto the bed, I find a hanger for my coat. Mom asks tentatively, "After you get unpacked, dear, could you please come out to the dinin' room? I need to talk to you about something important."

"Sure, Mom," I answer, wondering why she waited until we got to the house if it was something important. "May I call my grandparents first? They asked me to call as soon as I got here."

"Of course, JoeE, take as much time as you need," Mom says as she leaves my room, sounding a little nervous. She's probably about to set down the house rules. Dad had his for the apartment: no eating in your room, put your dirty dishes in the sink, keep your room picked up, etc., etc., etc. As nice as Mom is being to me, she still has to try to be a real mother despite her inexperience. In my humble opinion, she's doing just fine so far.

All my friends back in New York said I should feel bitterness toward my mother for giving me to my father to raise. However, after the loss of Dad, I'm just happy to have even one parent. Mom is making every effort also. I just can't be upset at her, considering that she lost both of her parents. It would be like someone who's lost one leg being bitter toward someone with no legs. Forgiving her was the best thing that I could've done for both of us.

Taking out my cell, I call my grandparents. "I made it," I inform Papa when he answers.

When he hears my voice, my grandfather asks, "How's Mississippi, JoeE?"

"Awesome so far, Papa. My room is incredible, and I've got my own laptop!"

"Did you have any problems in Atlanta?"

"No," I answer truthfully. "Man, you were right. It's humongous! My mother has something that she needs to tell me, so I've got to go, but I wanted to make sure I checked in with you."

"Sure, JoeE," Papa tells me, seeming very understanding. "We're glad that you have arrived safely. We love you."

"I love you guys. I'll call you tomorrow. 'Bye," I tell him as we hang up.

As I approach the table in the dining room, Mom has a strange look on her face, making me doubt that house rules are what she wants to discuss. "JoeE, do you remember the story I told you about your father and me when we lived in California?"

"Of course, Mom. I'll never forget it!" I reply, recalling my shock and surprise at learning her secrets.

"Well, I didn't finish the story that day at your grandparents' house," she explains.

My heart skips a beat. What important details might she have omitted?

Pausing as if she's trying to summon the courage to continue, Mom finally says, "You may remember that I was goin' for a sonogram that would let us know whether the baby was a boy or a girl. When the doctor showed us the pictures from the ultrasound, we saw you and…"

Part 2

LIES, LIES, LIES

Chapter 17

AND WHAT?

The word *and* has defined me for my entire life. It's a word used to connect one person, place, or thing to another. Football *and* I have been connected for as long as I can remember. We're made for each other, or, at least, I'm made for football. I've been raised with a single goal in mind, being a football player. Not just any football player, but a star quarterback. Reaching that goal, I led my high school team to an exceptional season. Yes, football and I are definitely connected.

Fulton, New York, *and* I are also connected. I'm the fourth Joseph Edward Collins from Fulton. For the past hundred years, our family has weathered economic ups and downs in this small city in central New York. We shared in Fulton's growing industrial prosperity, and we suffered through its economic decline. Fulton is the only place that I've ever lived. Its history and culture are a part of me. Fulton and I are definitely "joined at the hip."

My father *and* I were more than joined together. Dad tried to create in me a younger version of himself, a clone to accomplish what he couldn't. He failed to recognize that I could never be exactly like him, no matter how hard either of us tried.

Dad's untimely death led me to a new connection with a mother who I believed to be long dead. After my father's funeral, she suddenly appeared with a fantastic story. After much soul searching, I finally decided to leave my grandparents, my friends, my school, and my roots in Fulton to join her in Mississippi. Now she *and* I are most definitely connected.

After today's long flight to Mississippi, I have begun solidifying this connection with my mother. Now, she enlightens me that the amazing story begun in New York has another chapter. Mom said, "When the doctor showed your father and me the pictures from the ultrasound, we saw you *and...*" Who or what in the world am I going to be linked to this time?

Chapter 18

YOU'RE KIDDING

Pausing again, my mother takes a deep breath before finishing her sentence. "And your twin sister, dear," she finally reveals with a sigh of relief. It's as if an unbearable burden has just been lifted from her shoulders.

"You're kidding, right? A twin sister?" I blurt out, more incredulous than someone who has just been told that he's won the lottery.

"It's yrue, JoeE."

Then, like a machine gun, I rapidly shoot out questions. "Did she live? Where is she now? What's her name?"

My mother answers calmly. "She has lived with me for the past sixteen years. Her name is Mary Anabella. I've always combined the two names and called her MaryAna."

So Dad had *his son*, and Mom had *her daughter*. How convenient! A line comes to mind from the movie *The Parent Trap*, in which twin sisters were torn apart by their parents in a similar manner. One of the twins complains, "His and hers. It makes us feel like a set of bathroom towels!"

Nervously, I ask my next question. "Does MaryAna know about me?"

"Yes, dear, she knows all about you. When I returned from New York, I told her. MaryAna is anxious to meet you. She's waitin' at a friend's house for me to call."

"Call her, please. Call her now," I plead, still trying to grasp the concept of having a sister.

Picking up her cell, she makes the call. A few seconds later, she says, "JoeE's here. You can come home now, honey." After a short delay, she follows with, "Yes, I've told him about you. He's anxious to meet you." Mom pauses for a few more seconds as then finishes by saying, "Sure, sweetie, you can bring Coree with you. I'm sure JoeE would like to meet her."

Getting off the phone, she tells me, "Your sister will be here in a few minutes. She's bringin' her friend, Coree."

Another girl? Oh, great! I'll be so tongue-tied that they'll think that I'm a mute.

My mother explains, "The girls have been friends since first grade. Coree spells her name in a peculiar manner, with a double *E*."

Although I've never met anyone named Coree, one of my favorite songs is "Corey's Coming" by Harry Chapin. When Dad listened to his music, it could be heard throughout our small apartment. Eventually, I began not only to appreciate the music of older artists but also to prefer many of their tunes to more modern ones.

"What's Coree's last name?"

"It's Calhoun. Why do you ask, dear?"

"Oh, just curious," I answer. "Is my sister's last name Collins or Lindley?"

"Your sister's legal name is Mary Anabella Lindley-Collins, but she goes by MaryAna Lindley." Seeing my puzzled expression, Mom explains, "People just assumed that I never married her father, since we both go by Lindley. It certainly was easier lettin' them think that was the case than explainin' the truth."

"I can understand why that would be much easier," I agree. "People probably wouldn't have believed the truth anyway. It's hard for me to grasp it."

"Just like Joseph told you that I died in a car accident, I told MaryAna the same about him. I also told her that he was an orphan so I wouldn't have to explain about grandparents." I can hear both regret and sorrow in my mother's voice as she adds, "Sayin' it out loud makes me realize just how cruel we were to you children. I'm so sorry. We just didn't think it through and were too prideful to admit it." Crocodile-size tears well up in my mother's blue eyes.

"It's all right," I say, trying to make her feel better. "You know that I've already forgiven you. Everybody makes mistakes. You guys just made a whopper!"

"You sure are much more understandin' than your sister was when I told her about Joseph and you," Mom informs me, shaking her head slightly.

"Did MaryAna ever ask about her father before you told her?"

"When MaryAna was about four, she asked me about her daddy and if I could show her a picture of him. Explaining that his name was Joseph Edward Collins, I showed her an old photograph of him in his college football uniform. Even at that early age, MaryAna quickly realized that her last name was actually Collins. But she preferred Lindley to using the name of a father she never knew and thought was dead."

"What is my sister like?"

My mother smiles. "She's kind, compassionate, athletic, smart, fun-loving, and artistic. MaryAna's always plannin' something with her friends—trips, activities, and so forth. She's popular, very outgoin', and no one's ever a stranger to her. Your twin is fairly—no, extremely—outspoken, letting you know in a heartbeat exactly what she's thinkin', good or bad. Such bluntness isn't a typical Southern trait, especially for females. If she's spoiled, it's my fault. I've tried to give her everything she wants."

Hearing my mother talk about my twin seems weird. Let's see—I lose a father, gain a mother, and now add a sister. At this rate, I'll need a scorecard to keep up with my growing family. Thinking about how to tell people back in Fulton that I have a twin sister, I ask Mom, "Do my, I mean our, grandparents know about MaryAna?"

"Yes," Mom says. "Your father never told them about havin' a daughter, but I told your grandfather about your sister when I came to the house the night of your father's funeral. I always thought that they had a right to know about MaryAna, although my husband insisted otherwise. Your grandparents kept me secretly informed about you all these years. I'll always be in their debt for that kindness. I've kept everything that they sent me in a scrapbook."

"I bet they were totally shocked to learn they had another grandchild," I say, trying to imagine the look on Papa's face. My grandmother would've taken it all in stride. Papa might not have said too much, but he was probably upset that my father never told him about MaryAna.

"They were surprised and pleased," my mother continues. "Your grandparents and I decided that you had been through enough in September. We also felt you should meet MaryAna face-to-face the first time, not just over the phone. I knew it would take your sister some time to get adjusted to the idea of havin' a brother."

Now I'm about to meet MaryAna in a manner of minutes. I wonder if she's going to like me.

Mom goes on, "MaryAna talked to your grandparents on the phone a few times when you weren't there. They plan to come down here for a visit sometime in the next few months. Hopefully, the three of us will be able to take a family trip to Fulton next summer."

"That sounds terrific," I exclaim. "It certainly would be better than introducing MaryAna to Fulton this time of year."

About then, there's the sound of a car pulling into the driveway. The garage door opens. There goes my parking space, I think. I already have sister problems and haven't even met her.

As my heart pounds and my muscles tense, suddenly the door to the garage swings open. The two girls bound through the kitchen and into the dining room. They stop abruptly and stand side by side, as if they're challenging me to guess which one is my sister. The smirks on their faces indicate that they've been plotting this little charade for some time.

Carefully surveying the two lovely teenagers before me, I note that both girls are tall, about five foot eight. They're dressed alike, wearing white tennis shorts, pink V-neck T-shirts, and matching tennis shoes. My sister and her friend are both wearing pink headbands, but only one of the girls has matching wristbands. Could pink possibly be their favorite color?

In most aspects, the two amazing young ladies standing before me are close to identical, maybe not enough to be twins, but certainly enough to be sisters. Both have super tans and the same golden-blond hair pulled back into ponytails. The only major physical difference between the two is the color of their eyes.

However, I know immediately that for certain, the blue-eyed young woman without the wristbands is my sister. It isn't the fact that I have blue eyes that leads me to this conclusion. Although my mother has blue ones, our father had brown eyes. Therefore, genetically speaking, it's fifty-fifty whether my sister's eyes would be blue or brown.

Stepping in front of the one that I know is MaryAna, I put my arms out tentatively for a hug. As I smile at her friend, I can't help but get lost in Coree's hypnotic dark-brown eyes. My sister jumps forward and throws her arms around my neck, squeezes hard, and impulsively kisses me on the cheek.

She whispers in my ear, "JoeE, how in the world did you guess so quickly?"

Her friend's brown eyes silently ask the same question.

The answer is simple—it wasn't a guess. Ignoring the question for the moment, I thrust out my right hand to her beautiful friend, asking, "What's up?" The girl with the hypnotic eyes smiles, and before she can speak, I summon all of my courage to add, "How did you like Disney World, Miss Calhoun?"

Chapter 19
WHO'S CRAZY?

"JoeE, how do you know that I went to Disney World?" Coree asks in her delightful Southern accent. With a wide-eyed expression of amazement, she gazes at me as if I've just performed a mystifying feat of mind reading. For a moment, I fail to respond, enjoying her admiring yet bewildered look. Having thought that I'd never again lay eyes upon my dream girl, I can't believe that she's right in front of me.

Before everyone gives me credit for sorcery, I tell them about seeing Coree and her family in Atlanta. Explaining how her brother's Mickey Mouse ears had given me the Disney World connection, we all have a good laugh, relieving my terror. However, I quickly learn that around my sister, talking is optional.

"So you were checkin' out my best friend?" MaryAna asks. I sheepishly nod.

Thinking for a moment, Coree says, "Oh yeah, I remember you now. You were the guy pretendin' to read *Sports Illustrated* while you were lookin' at me. Did you like the article on Adrian Peterson?"

With redness flooding my cheeks, I admit, "Y-yeah, that was me. It was an interesting article." Apparently, girls are more observant than I've given them credit for in the past. I want to ask her how she knows about the Adrian Peterson article, but I'm too embarrassed to open my mouth again.

MaryAna promptly jumps in. "Yep, guys are always checkin' us out, pretendin' that they don't even notice us. So, JoeE, you think my best friend is hot?" Without giving me a chance to reply, she adds, "At least you're willin' to admit you checked her out. Most guys wouldn't even own up to it."

Standing up for both myself and my fellow males, I bravely answer, "You can't blame us for looking." It's pretty lame, but I'm proud that I'm able to respond without stammering.

I immediately learn that debating my twin sister is a losing proposition when MaryAna counters, "It's not the lookin'. It's what y'all are thinkin'."

Both girls giggle, sounding just like my female classmates back in Fulton. I'm always amazed that a giggle can be so charming yet sometimes downright annoying. Apparently expecting me to respond, my sister gives me a moment.

While I sit there silently, Coree comes to my defense. "I'll betcha he was just thinkin' about askin' me about football. Weren't you, JoeE?"

With my face now as red as a ripe tomato, I stammer honestly, "Ye-yes."

"See there, y'all," Coree says jubilantly, "JoeE has total respect for us girls. He just wanted my little ole opinion on the football article."

That may have been the moment that I started falling in love with Miss Coree Calhoun. Suddenly, I saw much more than her amazing beauty and her dark-chocolate eyes, and I heard more than her charming accent. I sensed her caring and compassionate personality. Unable to take my eyes off my dream girl, I catch a glimpse of the inner beauty that's masked by the eye-catching package in which it's wrapped.

As if she's reading my mind, MaryAna quickly adds, "I'll bet you football isn't all that JoeE wants to be talkin' to you about, Coree!" The girls giggle again as I just smile. Apparently, my mother was right—my sister says exactly what's on her mind.

Mom explains that the two girls have been best friends since grade school and in the last couple of years, they've become almost inseparable. "Mama," MaryAna asks, "has JoeE seen his bedroom yet?"

Mama is one name that I never considered calling my mother. I remember Mom used it earlier to refer to my grandmother Kimberly. Apparently, it's another signature of the South.

When my mother tells MaryAna that I've already started unpacking, my twin proudly announces that she personally picked out everything in my room. Obviously feeling overlooked, Coree interjects, "I helped too, didn't I, Mrs. Lindley?"

Mom referees. "MaryAna picked out everything with Coree's help. It was a team effort."

I say appreciatively, "You guys did a great job. It's awesome." They appear pleased by my praise.

"Wait till you get our bill," MaryAna says jokingly. At least I think that she's joking. Realizing that I'm going to enjoy being around my sister and her friend, my initial fears begin to melt. First of all, they seem to do most of the talking, which is fine by me. Secondly, their exuberant attitudes and sweet Southern drawls make everything they say sound so delightful.

MaryAna informs me, "I told Coree that you played football for your high school. Her father is the head football coach at Brandon High."

Coree's the coach's daughter? Oh my God! This is one girl I definitely don't want mad at me. One word from her, and I might find myself with a permanent seat on the bench.

Turning to me, Coree says, "I hear that you're a quarterback."

Suddenly extremely nervous again, I answer, "I've played several positions, but mostly quarterback."

"Are we all havin' a *Friday Night Lights* moment?" Knowing that MaryAna's comment refers to a television series by that name, I feel my face turning beet-red again. In the show, the high school football coach's daughter falls in love with a young quarterback. Mom has a puzzled expression; apparently, she's unfamiliar with the show.

Turning to my sister, Coree giggles. "Y'all know how much we love our quarterback." Then, she looks back at me with a devilish grin.

For the next couple of hours, I listen to MaryAna's nearly non-stop description of her adventures. Almost all include Coree, who fills in like a tag-team wrestler when my sister needs a break to catch her breath. My twin's vivid storytelling makes it seem as if I was there with them.

The stories range from tornadoes and hurricanes to dirt biking and four wheeling. Two of the girls' favorite summer activities are "goin' to the sandbars upriver" and "tubin' down the Bogue Chitto." They've been to a number of Civil War battle reenactments in and around Mississippi as well as other battlegrounds and museums. I also hear stories about trips to Panama City, Gulf Shores, Ship Island, and other places along the Gulf Coast.

When my sister tells me that Nawlins is awesome, I'm confused. Finally, when they mention "watchin' the Saints play football in the Superdome," I realize that they're talking about New Orleans.

It's fascinating to listen to the girls telling me about their lives. Their Southern accents and colorful sayings magically transform every story into an amazing experience. Their Mississippi accents are nothing like those of hillbillies, which are so often derided. Neither is their drawl the one of Georgia and South Carolina so often imitated in movies and on television. It's certainly not akin to the Texas twang of so many popular country songs.

There seem to be three features that make the way they talk distinctive. First of all, the "g" is almost always dropped in words ending in "ing." Therefore, *going* is pronounced *goin'* and *talking* becomes *talkin'*. Although I've heard this elsewhere, it's far more noticeable and consistent here. The dropping of the "g" softens these words, making the girls sound gentler than their Northern counterparts.

Secondly, the girls pronounce the "er" at the end of words as if it were an "ah." This changes words like *ever* to *evah* and *over* to *ovah*. Sometimes, *you* is pronounced *yah*. For example, "Do yah evah go ovah tah the rivah?" These changes smooth sentences and give their Mississippi accents a flowing nature. It reminds me of pancakes with syrup slowly dripping down the sides.

While they often combine words, like *alotta* for *a lot of,* they're equally likely to make a normally one-syllable word into two or even three syllables. They don't think twice about saying *gonna* rather than *going to* in the same sentence that *oil* is pronounced *oy-i-ull.* The cadence is almost musical and rhythmic.

The most adorable aspect of the girls' accents is their Southern drawl, where they extend the duration of some words. Often, they pronounce the vowels "a" and "e" as if they're two syllables. Thus, *bed* is pronounced as if it's *bay-id* and *sad* like it's *sa-id*. The drawl tends to slow their delivery, making the conversation more relaxing.

Both MaryAna's and Coree's speech patterns remind me of waves rippling onto a seashore. Sometimes the water eases a little farther inland than it does at other times. Just like the waves, the languid ebb and flow of their gently spoken words is hypnotizing.

With my fresh arsenal of linguistic knowledge, the girls' exciting adventures become much more understandable. Their smooth-flowing, singsong manner of speaking is a far cry from the rapid-fire, clipped dialogue that's characteristic of upstate New York. However, some of the more unusual terms like *itty-bitty, hissy,* and *ornery* will require advanced study on my part.

The two girls continue to relate story after story about their friends, teachers, and activities in and out of school. It's so enjoyable that I could literally listen to their enchanting tales all day. During a rare respite in their nearly nonstop chatter, I ask my sister, "Are all of the girls in Mississippi like you two?"

"You mean crazy like Coree and me?" MaryAna answers blithely.

Where I grew up, the word "crazy" means "insane." It's certainly not a compliment and often used as an insult. In Fulton, crazy people are sent to mental institutions and often reside there indefinitely.

"No, I don't think you're crazy," I reply, not yet aware of the Southern meaning of the word.

"Well, we all are sure enough crazy and proud of it, aren't we, Coree?" MaryAna responds as she giggles. Her friend just nods in agreement. It's confirmed. I've got a twin sister, and she's insane! I'm not so sure about her friend.

After mostly sitting back and listening to the girls' entertaining narrative, our mother interrupts to ask, "Are you hungry, JoeE?"

Having not eaten anything except peanuts since leaving home this morning, I reply, "I'd love something."

She and MaryAna go to the kitchen to fix sandwiches, leaving Coree and me sitting across the table from each other. If I'm going to have a one-on-one conversation with a girl, this seems as good an opportunity as I'll ever get.

Taking a deep breath, I lean forward and ask softly so that my sister won't hear, "MaryAna doesn't really think that you two are mentally ill, does she?"

Tilting her head to one side slightly, Coree looks at me strangely. After thinking for a moment, suddenly the look in her big brown eyes becomes one of understanding. Moving around the table, she sits beside me so we can talk quietly.

"No," Coree whispers. "Here, 'crazy' is more commonly used to describe someone silly or fun-lovin' but generally in a nice way."

Realizing the differences in meaning, I nod and smile, saying, "MaryAna is definitely your Mississippi version of crazy."

Still in a whisper, Coree asks, "Do you know anyone who's actually mentally ill?"

"One of my good friend's father," I answer, also keeping my voice hushed. "He's in the Hutchings Psychiatric Center in Syracuse. I've gone with Jonathan and his mother several times to visit him."

"Didn't it bother you to be there?" Coree asks, leaning even closer to me and seeming intently interested in my response. Getting a whiff of her sweet perfume, it's difficult to concentrate on her question.

"Honestly, the first time was kinda weird, not knowing what to expect. After that, it seemed pretty normal. Jonathan and his mother really appreciated me being with them, and his father enjoyed our visits."

"What did you think of Jonathan's daddy?" Her gaze becomes even more intense, as if my answers are critical.

"His father was very nice to me," I reply, suddenly wanting to talk to her. Feeling my fear of teenage girls magically melting away, I continue. "One time, he was a little disoriented, probably from medications. He always asked us about football. We would tell him all about our most recent games. It was like visiting someone who had suffered a heart attack or had some other serious illness. His father's mental problems are a sickness and not his fault."

Coree smiles. "JoeE, that's a nice way to look at it."

Wanting to continue my first real conversation with a girl, I recall what Mom said about asking people about themselves. Taking a deep breath, I ask, "Coree, do you know anyone in a mental institution?"

"Yes, I do," she answers but stops abruptly as my sister brings chips and dip to the table.

Wiping my sweaty palms on my jeans, I'm proud of myself for having a conversation with a girl my age for the first time. Not just any girl, but someone who seems to value my opinion on something other than football. Of course, I recognize that most boys accomplish this incredible feat by the third grade.

My mother serves us delicious roast beef sandwiches. The girls alternate between talking and eating, while I finish my sandwich quickly. When I begin hungrily munching down the chips, Coree offers me half of her sandwich, explaining that she grabbed something to eat when she got home from the airport.

As I reach for the sandwich, Coree's fingers brush against my hand, possibly unintentionally, but almost like a tender caress. A spark of electricity pierces my hand and sends cold shivers tingling through my body. I've never experienced a burning-hot, icy-cold chill quite like that before. It dissipates quickly, practically taking my breath away. Did Coree and I just make some kind of supernatural connection?

Looking around to see if sparks are flying, I finally assume it was just static electricity. Gazing into Coree's eyes again, I wonder if she felt the same cold chill. As she smiles at me, I note that her expression has changed from her earlier smile. My sister's friend now appears to have a more relaxed expression that lights up her entire face. It's the warm smile that you might give to an old friend whom you're happy to see again.

After another thirty minutes of listening to the girls talk, MaryAna says, "I need to carry Coree home. JoeE, do you wanna ride along with us?"

It's obvious that "carry," in this context, is their term for take or drive. Having always needed my father's permission before going to a friend's home, I glance toward my mother. "Mom, I'd like to ride along with them, if it's OK with you?"

Apparently surprised that I asked for permission, my mother hesitates for a moment before answering. "Of course, dear, if you wanna go."

Entering the garage, I see MaryAna's fire-engine-red Chevy Malibu, the same vehicle that I saw my dream girl get into at the airport. The flashy car looks as if it were just driven off a showroom floor. "Sweet ride," I tell my sister, probably with a slight twinge of envy in my voice.

"Thanks," she responds. "It was a Christmas present from Mama."

I know that our mother already spent a small fortune on my bedroom, but maybe if Mom thinks that she still needs forgiveness, she can buy me a car too! I need to keep up with my sister.

MaryAna commands her best friend, "Let my brother sit up front."

Climbing into the backseat, Coree mutters, "Great, there goes my front-seat status."

Starting to get in, I say, "I'll get in the back instead."

Giggling, Coree replies, "Not necessary, but if you want, you can ride back here with me." That sounds like a wonderful offer to me.

MaryAna orders sharply, "Coree, stop hittin' on my brother. Now, JoeE, just get in the front seat."

I obey meekly. I've learned who is in charge.

Buckling my seat belt, I note that there are a couple of open beer cans in the cup holder. Since I can't smell beer over the fragrance of the girls' perfumes, I'm not sure whether the cans are empty or not.

As we turn out of the driveway, I notice Coree raising her cell phone and pointing it at me. MaryAna snaps at her, "Did you just take a photo of my brother?"

"Maybe," her friend responds, smiling at me.

"Well, maybe JoeE wants to take a picture of us, too."

"I wish I could," I respond, "but I can't take photos with my phone. It's kinda lame."

MaryAna glances at me in disbelief.

As we wait at a traffic light, my sister asks curiously, "What was your—I mean, our—father like?" Obviously, even after several months, she is finding it difficult to believe that Dad was her father.

Trying to be as concise as possible, I tell her, "He was very strict with me and didn't have much tolerance for mistakes. We lived a simple, disciplined life centered on football."

"So, was he kinda ornery?" MaryAna asks.

Seeing me hesitate, Coree clarifies, "She means, was he irritable?"

I recall the Winston Churchill quote about Great Britain and the United States being two countries divided by a common language. It seems that the North and the South share that same challenge.

"Oh," I respond, adding the word *ornery* to my mental dictionary. "Sometimes he got pretty upset, especially when our team was not playing well. Dad taught me a lot of things besides football. However, that game was his whole life."

Her next question is considerably tougher. "Do you think he ever thought about me?"

I really have no idea but say reassuringly, "He probably did, just like Mom says that she constantly thought about me."

With bitterness in her voice, MaryAna asks, "Can you believe their crappy agreement? Splittin' us up like that? When Mama first told me, I couldn't believe it. I just wanted to scream!" Obviously, my sister has given considerable thought to our parents' questionable child-rearing arrangement.

Coree asks me, "What did you think when you learned that you had a twin sister?"

Apparently, MaryAna has told her friend all about our family situation. Thinking about Coree's question for a moment, I decide that we all need a little comic relief. "To tell the truth, I was hoping for a brother or at least a dog."

"JoeEeee!" MaryAna yells, instantly reaching over and punching me in the arm.

"Ouch!" I cry out, actually feeling some pain.

They both laugh, and Coree says teasingly, "Maybe he thinks you are a dog."

My twin sister then barks, "Ruff, ruff," and begins panting as she adds, "If my brother wants a dog, when we get to your house, I'll just roll over for belly rubs."

My sister is definitely crazy.

Chapter 20

THE CALHOUN FAMILY

We drive only about a mile before arriving at Coree's home, a large two-story brick mansion surrounded by beautifully landscaped grounds. Pulling into the circular drive in front of the house, I glance up at four giant white columns, providing the elegance of an antebellum plantation home. An equivalent house in Fulton would cost a fortune. I doubt that this place is affordable on the salary of a high school football coach. Of course, Coree's mother may have a high-paying job, or they could've inherited a great deal of money.

"Welcome to Calhoun Castle," says Coree graciously. "Your sister gave it that name."

"Nice house," I tell her politely as she exits the car.

"Thanks. My father sure thinks so," Coree replies. "We just moved in last summer. According to Daddy, our old house was too small, so now we have this gigantic place."

Noting the slight disdain in Coree's voice, I just nod. It doesn't sound as if she's overjoyed to be living in such a large house. Apparently, her father believes that a family of four needs an enormous amount of space. I don't know the size of their previous home, but a small army could be comfortable here.

MaryAna is preoccupied, typing away at a furious pace. Texting is quickly becoming an art form and, judging by the way my sister's thumbs fly across the keys, apparently she's a modern artist.

We enter through the big double doors and walk across a *Home Is Where the Heart Is* welcome mat. As soon as I step inside, I'm sure that there's been a mistake. I'm pretty sure that ceilings can't be that high. There are laws, right?

Coree's father is in the den with his feet propped up lazily on the recliner and a beer in his hand. Most of the downstairs appears to be one gigantic room: you could pass a ball from the living room into the den and watch the receiver carry it into the kitchen without a single wall to stop you. The room is arranged in sections, with one for watching television, one for formal dining, and another for quiet conversation.

Even though the kitchen is separate, it's visible through a large, open archway at the rear of this room. The furniture includes a comfortable-looking couch, a loveseat, several curio cabinets, various bookshelves (mostly full of trophies), and a variety of chairs, lamps, and small tables. Everything appears to be arranged for comfort and utility rather than stylish design.

On the right wall is mounted a gigantic flat screen above a brick fireplace. The room's inlaid wooden floors and long wooden beams give it a rustic appearance rather than the formal colonial style that the exterior suggests. If you moved the furniture to the walls, you could hold a magnificent ballroom dance or a small battle reenactment in the open space.

Before I can take it all in, Coree is already making enough noise to raise the dead, shouting, "Julie, MaryAna's twin is here."

Her father rises from his recliner and walks toward me with a slight limp. With the beer still clutched in his left hand, he extends his right for me to shake.

Coach Calhoun is dressed in the same maroon golf shirt and tan slacks that he was wearing on the plane. The five o'clock shadow on his chin adds a rugged appearance to his otherwise handsome face. About an inch shorter than me, the coach is a burly, barrel-chested man with a thick neck and wide shoulders. He looks like a football player. He has sandy-brown hair and bright-blue eyes. I grab his large hand, and we exchange a firm, manly handshake. As he surveys me, a jovial smile suddenly stretches across his unshaven face.

In a deep, almost gruff voice, he says, "I'm Rhyan Calhoun, one of Coree's slaves here at the castle."

I grin at his little joke.

Hearing her father, Coree responds quickly, "Daddy, please behave yourself. Besides, you know I'm the slave here at your castle."

At this point, her mother enters the room. She's changed out of the clothes she was wearing in Atlanta and is now wearing white shorts and a light-blue sleeveless blouse.

At the airport, I was so captivated by my dream girl that I hardly noticed her mother, so it's almost as if I'm seeing her for the first time. She's petite, maybe five feet tall, with short brunette hair, and coffee-colored eyes. She looks to be the same age as Coach Calhoun, and he towers over her as they stand next to each other. Although not particularly attractive, she seems to have a sense of self-confidence about her.

Apparently hearing a noise, she glances at the stairs. Coree's little brother is joining us, still wearing his Mickey Mouse ears. With sandy-brown hair like Coach Calhoun's but eyes like his mother's, the youngest Calhoun mostly resembles his father.

After Coach Calhoun introduces his wife, Julie, and son, Logan, he turns to me, saying, "We were shocked when MaryAna told us that she had a brother." I smile as he adds jokingly, "Thankfully, it wasn't a sister. One more teenage girl prancing around this place, and I would've blown my brains out."

His wife interrupts him. "Rhyan, stop it! JoeE doesn't know that you're kiddin'."

"Who says I'm kiddin'?" the coach roars as a great smile again breaks across his face. However, there's a slight hint of anger in his tone.

Coach Calhoun is somewhat like my father. However, Dad would never joke with someone he'd just met. He often kidded around with those he knew, and he was usually the life of the party. I often wished I were more like him off the football field and not just on it.

"JoeE actually saw us on the way home from Disney," Coree says timidly, cutting through the silence.

Examining me carefully as if I were a patient, Julie asks curiously, "So you saw us at the airport?"

"Yes, Mrs. Calhoun," I respond.

"Please, call me Julie," Coree's mother requests cordially.

"I hear that you play football," Coach Calhoun says, obviously seeking a response from me.

"Yes, Coach," I tell him, adding proudly, "I started for my high school team this season." I suppose that I'm trying to impress him, but from the look in his eyes, I failed.

"What position?" he asks like a game-show host questioning a new contestant.

"I'm a quarterback," I reply in a self-assured manner, watching intently for his reaction.

Speaking as if faced with a dilemma, he says hesitantly, "Oh? Well, you have good size. How fast are you?"

"I can run the forty-yard dash in under four-point-six seconds in pads," I tell him proudly, "and bench press well over four hundred pounds."

"Impressive," Coach Calhoun replies. "Have you ever played any defense?"

"Some," I reply honestly, "mostly in the secondary, but I've played some at linebacker and on the defensive line also."

The coach explains that one of his safeties, who was also the defensive captain, graduates this year. He informs me, "If you're a player, we'll find a place for you."

Less than enthusiastically, I respond, "That sounds good, Coach." What I really want to say is that starting quarterback would be the perfect spot, but I realize that he already has someone in that position.

Motioning toward Coree and MaryAna, he quips, "These are my Brandon Bulldog cheerleaders."

His young son, Logan, who hasn't made a sound since coming downstairs, springs into action. "They're not *your* cheerleaders, Daddy," he corrects his father. "They're the team's cheerleaders."

"Thank you for pointing that out, Logan," Coree tells her little brother, giving her father a disdainful look.

Just then, the front door flies open, and a young man bursts in carrying a backpack. I note that the newcomer is in his late teens and well over six feet tall with sandy-brown hair, blue eyes, and an athletic build. Is this Coree's boyfriend? Why the backpack and no knock on the door? Then, I notice that both MaryAna and Coree are excited to see the latest arrival.

Solving the mystery, Coach Calhoun greets him, saying, "How was Nawlins, son?" Apparently, Coree has two brothers, but she didn't mention that fact. Does she have more siblings?

The young man replies, smiling, "I bet it was better than Disney World, sir. We saw plenty of pretty girls."

"There were plenty of cute girls at Disney World," Coree says. "You should've come with us."

"I mean girls over ten," he replies sarcastically.

"I wish I'd been with you, Son," Coach Calhoun jokes, a little twinge of jealousy in his voice. Gesturing at me, he says, "Mason, this is MaryAna's brother, JoeE."

Striding toward me, Mason thrusts out his right hand. As we shake, I notice his extremely firm grip and broad smile.

"So, you're the famous JoeE. It's great to meet you. On Bourbon Street this week, I met some college girls from New York. You sure have some fine ladies up there."

"It's nice to meet you, Mason," I reply, returning his friendly smile. Glancing toward the two girls with a little nod of my head, I add, "And don't give us all the credit. Mississippi has its fair share also."

Coree grins, but MaryAna continues to stare at the newest arrival as though she is a deer caught in headlights.

"I lovingly call these girls the Airhead Twins," Mason points out, putting his arm around his sister in a little half hug. "Then I found out that your sister actually was a twin." Mason laughs loudly as Coree puts her hands on her hips, looking a little cross with him. The "airhead" insult finally brings MaryAna out of her trance. She purses her lips in disapproval at his comment.

Coree complains, "Julie, do something. Mason is bein' ugly to us." Apparently, "ugly" doesn't mean the same thing here either.

"Mason, please stop teasin' the girls," Julie asks tentatively, as if she feels awkward correcting him.

"Yes, ma'am," Mason replies with a scowl.

Coach Calhoun takes up the verbal assault. "But these girls are *my* little airheads!"

Coree gives her father a "ha-ha," and then she sticks her tongue out at Mason. MaryAna returns to her hypnotic trance, quiet for the first time since I met her. It's fairly obvious that Mason's presence has created a dramatic transformation in my twin sister.

Logan, not to be left out of the conversation, adds, "No, Daddy, they're the *team's* little airheads." Everyone, including Coree and MaryAna, have to laugh at that remark, breaking the almost visible tension.

When Mason excuses himself politely and goes upstairs, MaryAna comes out of her trance and reverts to her vivacious self. The next few hours are packed with nonstop joking and storytelling as well as questions about growing up in New York.

I learn that besides coaching football, Coree's father is a physical education teacher at the high school, and her mother works at a hospital. We finally take a break, and Julie serves sandwiches and iced tea in the living room. Every once in a while, MaryAna glances at the stairs as if she were hoping that Mason would come join us, but he doesn't.

At one point, Logan asks Coree if I'm her boyfriend. "No," she responds, "I just met JoeE today."

"I just wondered," says Logan, shrugging innocently. "Y'all been staring at each other."

"Logan, hush," says Julie.

As the others attempt not to laugh, Coree and I turn as red as my sister's Malibu. It must be obvious that I'm smitten if a seven-year-old picks up on it. After we eat, my twin tells me it's time to go. Although the stress of the long day is beginning to catch up with me, I hate to leave. After I thank Coree's parents for their hospitality and say that I hope to see everyone again soon, we head to the door.

Tugging on my arm, Logan pulls me aside where no one can hear. As I lean down, he whispers in my ear, "JoeE, I know when it's OK to kiss a girl. Want me to tell you?"

"Sure," I say, needing all the help I can get, even from someone his age.

Whispering again, the little guy says with a huge grin, "When she's rich!"

"Thanks, buddy." I grin back. "I'm glad you're looking out for me." Tousling his straw-colored hair, I once again head for the front door, wondering who drilled that nonsense into his head.

Saying good-bye, Coree gives me an unexpected but most welcome hug. I want to say something nice to her, however, the "shy JoeE" returns. Instead, I just walk out to the car. Turning to take one last look at my dream girl, I see her silhouetted in the doorway. As I wave to her, she puts her hand to her mouth and throws me a kiss.

Suddenly, there's a tightness, almost a knot, in my stomach. I have the sense that a magical spell has just been cast over me. Is this what love at first sight feels like? Then I realize that my stomach is probably just reacting to all the peanuts that I ate on the flights today.

As I join MaryAna in her car, she offers me a Tic Tac. Taking a couple from her, I notice that she has replaced the opened beer cans in the cup holders with two unopened ones. Apparently, MaryAna enjoys an occasional brewski. Maybe the drinking age is lower in Mississippi, but I doubt that it's legal at sixteen.

As soon as we're on the road, I ask her, "Why didn't one of you mention that Coree has two brothers?"

"We didn't want to disappoint you on your first day here. Mason will be a senior next year, and he's also a football player just like you."

"And so?" I ask, still not understanding the need for secrecy.

"Mason is the coach's son."

"I know that now. Why would that disappoint me?" I ask, beginning to get frustrated at what I perceive asevasiveness.

MaryAna glances at me, "Mason isn't only the coach's son, JoeE. He's Brandon's quarterback."

"Oh, I see. So you don't think I have any chance of being Brandon's quarterback next fall?" I ask, probably with a bit of sarcasm in my voice. At least now I understand what Coach Calhoun meant when he said, "Maybe we can find a place for you."

"Coree and I just think that it would be difficult for Coach to change quarterbacks, even if Mason wasn't his son."

"So Coree and you are experts on football?"

"JoeE, I may not know that much about the sport, but I'll bet Coree knows as much about football as you. Maybe more."

I don't challenge her ridiculous statement, trying to avoid a needless quarrel. Seeing that I'm holding back and probably guessing what I'm thinking, my twin concludes, with anger in her voice, "And Coree sure as heck knows a ton more about Brandon Bulldog football than you!"

I have to admit that my sister has a good point. "That's true," I tell her, hoping it'll end our first sibling argument.

When we get back home, my mother is hanging pictures on the walls. Most of the photos are of MaryAna at various ages. There are photographs of my sister as a baby and as a small child at the beach, in a karate outfit, wearing gymnastic tights, and a recent photo in her cheerleading uniform. On the shelves, there are now smaller pictures in frames as well as several trophies and plaques. Mom must have taken everything down before I arrived. Obviously, she didn't want me asking her, "Who's the girl?"

"I guess you'll have to take some photos of me too, Mom," I say, smiling.

"Your grandparents already sent me photos of you for Christmas. Tomorrow, I'll buy some nice frames and figure out where to hang them."

MaryAna butts in, "I vote for hangin' them in the bathroom or maybe just usin' them as dart boards." Apparently, she's still fuming about our exchange in the car.

Attempting to curtail our verbal jousting, Mom tells her, "Stop bein' ugly to your brother, Pumpkin."

"Bein' ugly" must be a Southern term for being mean.

I can't let this opportunity to tease my sister slip away. "A nickname like Pumpkin? That must be really handy on Halloween." That smart remark costs me another punch in my upper arm. This time it really hurts. "Hey," I say, rubbing my shoulder, "where did you learn to hit like that?"

"Eight years of karate," she responds. "You wanna call me anything else?"

I put up my hands in surrender. "No way! I should've known you were dangerous when I saw your *Karate Kid* photo."

MaryAna warns, "And Coree has a black belt too. So you better behave yourself."

The three of us stay up awhile, just talking and getting to know one another. MaryAna, seemingly no longer upset with me, says that she can't wait to introduce me to all of her friends. If her other friends are anything like Coree, I can't wait either. Totally exhausted, I finally say good night. We have a long group hug, and I head off to try out my new bed.

As I lay my head upon the pillow, my rambling thoughts are about my new friends and family. I begin to feel like Dorothy in *The Wizard of Oz*. Falling asleep, my last thought is, *Toto, I've got a feeling we're not in New York anymore.*

Chapter 21

BATHROOM PROTEST

Thursday morning, I awaken for the first time in my new home. Although it's still dark outside, six o'clock is my usual time to rise. No one else is stirring in the darkened house. Turning on my bedroom light, I automatically do a couple hundred push-ups and sit-ups. These exercises have been a part my morning routine for as long as I can remember. They seem as normal as brushing my teeth and as necessary as breathing.

Back in Fulton, I enjoyed year-round access to the weight room at the high school. In recent years, I would run, weather permitting, the mile or so to the school, having my own key for access. I've used the high school facility since junior high. No one ever questioned that because my father was a coach. A few years ago, the workout room was expanded and updated. I hope my new school has an equally nice facility.

Preferring to run at least a couple of miles every day, I usually go in the early morning when the air is the freshest. Unfamiliar with this area, I decide to wait until the sun is up. In Fulton, the weather often failed to cooperate with my training regimen. A sense of anticipation has me eager for the sun to rise. Like a racehorse's, my legs are clamoring to stretch out and gallop. Papa used to say that I liked to run almost as much as I liked to eat. Thinking about my grandfather, I wonder what the weather is like in Fulton today. Most likely, it's cold and cloudy with a chance of snow.

After a hot shower, I sit down in the dining room to enjoy breakfast. When I finish, I return to my new room, noting that MaryAna's bedroom door remains closed. Since my bathroom is between our two bedrooms, I suspect that it was previously my sister's. Realizing that she has made sacrifices to accommodate me being added to her little family, I hope that my twin isn't upset that I'm here. Since she states her opinions rather bluntly, she probably won't keep it a secret if I fail to live up to her expectations.

Back in my room, I examine the contents of my desk, finding several pushpins. They're perfect for mounting my bright-orange Syracuse University pennant from the first college football game I attended. Attaching it to the wall above the end of the bed, I recall Dad buying it for me when I was only five.

On the wall next to the bed, I put up my huge, life-size poster of the New York Giants quarterback, number 10, Eli Manning. The Giants are by far my favorite NFL team, and their quarterback is my favorite player. I'm extremely disappointed that they're struggling to make the playoffs after such a promising start to the season. I'm probably the only Syracuse University and Giants fan in this area.

Continuing to unpack, I place a stand-up silver frame on my desk. It's a photograph of Dad and me taken just prior to last football season. Next to it, I set a gold frame containing a photo of me with my grandparents. It might be too early to say, but my new room is starting to feel like home.

Also on the desk, I place a football that the guys on my high school team presented to me as a going-away present. The ball, which they all signed, means a lot to me. I'll miss all those guys, but mostly Jonathan and Josh. We've been friends and teammates so long that it's hard to imagine not seeing them nearly every day.

The few CDs I brought with me are actually from my dad's collection. Although I appreciate a wide variety of music, these are my favorites. The music varies from sixties and seventies rock 'n' roll to eighties heavy metal and power ballads. My father had little use for the music produced after the 1980s. We'd have lengthy discussions where I would defend the more contemporary artists, but in the end, I would have to admit that some of the most incredible music was produced long before I was born.

The first rays of sunlight peek through my window, reminding me that it's time to run. Hearing my mother rattling around in the kitchen, I return to the dining room.

"Good morning," I greet her cheerfully.

"How did you sleep, dear?" she asks in her motherly tone.

"Like a baby," I reply, giving her the standard answer to her standard question.

"I'm just fixin' to get some breakfast. Want something?" Mom asks as she prepares bacon and eggs.

"Yes, please," I answer politely, never passing up a chance to eat. Some people say that you shouldn't eat before you run. They don't have my appetite.

As Mom takes out another plate, I tell her, "I put a poster of Eli Manning up on my wall. I hope that's all right."

"Honey, anything you want to do in your bedroom is OK with me," she responds. "It's *your* space, so whatever makes you feel at home is fine."

This is a huge difference from Dad with his strict rules. My father wanted to dictate everything that went on in my room and, for that matter, in my life. He controlled me as he did our football team. I never felt the need to rebel against his authority. I'm beginning to enjoy my newfound freedom, but I know that it comes at a price. Now, I'm responsible for my decisions.

Mom pulls some bread out of the cupboard. "So, Eli Manning is your favorite player?"

"He sure is. I know a lot about him."

"Did you know he played for Ole Miss?" she asks hopefully.

"Of course!" I reply. "But he was actually born in Louisiana."

"You did your homework," my mother says, sliding two slices of bread into the toaster. "His father, Archie, was born in Mississippi. He's among many great football players from this state—like Walter Payton, Jerry Rice, take your pick. We can claim Brett Favre, who I believe is the best quarterback of all time. He's a Mississippi boy, and he played at Southern Miss."

"Wow!" I stammer, surprised at all the great players from Mississippi and that Mom knows so much about football.

"Do you know, JoeE," she says, astounding me further, "that Brett is one of the coaches at Oak Grove High, near Hattiesburg? Brandon beat them last fall. Next season, they'll come here to play."

Driving home last night, MaryAna had told me that Coree knew all about football. Now, I learn that even my mother knows about Brett Favre and Brandon's opponents. Have I moved to football heaven?

"I'm surprised at how much you know about the sport, Mom."

"In Mississippi, honey, football is more than a sport. High school and college teams are a cherished part of our Southern culture. Most of us identify closely with our favorite teams. If you have any questions about football, just ask Coree."

"Does she really know that much about football?" I ask, still not convinced.

"More than I do, that's for sure," Mom responds.

"For Dad and me, football was like our religion."

"Oh, we have plenty of religion in the South. You're in the Bible Belt. If you like football or religion, you've moved to the right place."

While she takes our dirty dishes to the kitchen, I tell her, "I'll take the football and pass on that Bible stuff, if you don't mind."

I hear the sound of a door opening behind me, and MaryAna comes prancing out of her room. My sister is wearing a nearly see-through pink teddy and matching panties. At first, I don't believe she sees me sitting at the table and think she'll be totally embarrassed when she does. Walking into the dining room, my twin gives me a little smile. Recalling that my mother omitted "modest" when describing her, I now see why.

"Mary Anabella!" my mother cries out, seeing her daughter's attire, or more accurately, lack of it. "For heaven's sake, young lady. Go back to your room and put some clothes on!"

Flagrantly disregarding our mother's command, my sister proceeds to the kitchen, opens the refrigerator, and replies casually, "Mama, it's only my brother, for heaven's sake. How I'm dressed doesn't bother you, does it, JoeE?"

I take a deep breath, let it out slowly, and consider her question. If it were Coree looking like a *Playboy* centerfold, it certainly would "bother" me. The two girls look so much alike that I can't help but imagine my dream girl dressed in a similar manner. However, since it's my sister, it certainly does make a huge difference.

"It doesn't bother me if it doesn't bother you, Sis."

"See, Mama," my sister says, pouring herself some orange juice, "it doesn't bother JoeE, and it sure enough doesn't make any sense for me to get dressed just before I take a shower, does it? If my bathroom wasn't so far away now, I could've already showered and been dressed."

"Young lady, do as you're told," Mom insists, not swayed by my sister's bathroom-location logic. It appears that my twin isn't overjoyed at the new arrangement, and this apparently is her not-so-subtle protest.

"Yes, ma'am. Don't have a hissy fit," MaryAna grudgingly concedes, trudging off to her bedroom, texting with her left hand while drinking her juice with the right. Almost immediately, she returns, having thrown on a short silk dressing gown. My frustrated mother just sighs. "MaryAna, you're incorrigible."

My twin turns to me and teases, "So, Mr. JoeE, you think that you can handle a bunch of girls runnin' around the house in the mornin'?"

I just shake my head in surrender, trying to ignore her. She's far better at these little verbal duels than I'll ever be.

"Maybe I'll just have a slumber party this weekend," MaryAna threatens, pouring herself another orange juice. "We'll see if Coree and some of my other friends dressed like this bothers you."

"Aren't you a little old for slumber parties, Sis?" I say, secretly intrigued by what she's describing.

"Aren't you a little young to be so judgmental?" she counters, getting in a parting jab.

Mom ends our teasing. "You two, play nice. Do you want some breakfast, MaryAna?"

"Yes, ma'am," she replies politely, grinning at me as if she's won some little victory. Apparently, MaryAna wants to make it quite clear that it's still her home and I'm here on probation as far as she's concerned.

Returning to my bedroom, I call my grandparents, telling them about my sister and the Calhoun family. I explain that Coree's father is Brandon's head football coach and her brother, Mason, is the starting quarterback. I complain, "It appears that no one here believes that I can compete for the job next fall except me."

My grandfather tells me, "Don't worry. They'll change their minds when they see you play."

"I sure hope so," I respond, currently believing that being the starting quarterback is my highest priority in life. We discuss when my grandparents might be able to come for a visit. I tell Papa all about MaryAna's car, hoping that it'll help my case for one of my own. I'm amazed at how much I have to tell him since we talked less than twenty-four hours ago.

Out in the hallway, I hear MaryAna shout, "Has anybody seen my phone?" This is surprising, since I thought it was permanently attached to her hand.

"No!" Mom and I yell simultaneously.

"Hey JoeE, call me, please," my sister requests. She gives me her number, and I call. When her Taylor Swift ringtone echoes down the hallway, I can't believe that she actually lost her phone in her own room. Apparently, unlike me, she hasn't had it drilled into her head that there's "a place for everything and everything in its place."

"Found it! Thanks," MaryAna yells. She then announces, "I'm gonna get a shower." I hear her leaving her room, heading to the bathroom off my mother's bedroom.

"You can use my bathroom if you want," I shout, hoping to appease her.

"Yuck!" she yells back in disgust. "After you were in there? No way, but thanks."

I'm surprised that MaryAna hasn't complained directly to me about having to give up her bathroom. Of course, the day isn't over yet.

Chapter 22

RACHEL TAYLOR

"Mom, I'd like to go for a run. Is that OK?" I ask, still feeling as if I need permission. It's a hard habit to break.

"Certainly, dear," she informs me. "Across the street there's a subdivision that would be much safer than runnin' along the highway."

"Great, I'll go there," I readily agree as Mom gives me a sweet motherly smile.

Racing past the homes in the nearby subdivision, I soon find the fresh morning air filling my lungs. Unlike Fulton, these homes are primarily one-story structures. There are a few people moving about and only an occasional vehicle. Those I do see give me a friendly wave. In Fulton, it would be unusual for complete strangers to acknowledge my presence. Although it feels awkward at first, I return their greetings, realizing that this friendliness must be normal behavior in Mississippi.

Along the way, I notice a strange little bird that seems to be following me. The lone blue jay finally alights upon the branch of a small tree near the road.

"Hi, bird," I call to him, slowing to a jog when I pass his tree. "My name is JoeE. I'm new around here." Suddenly the blue jay bursts into song. It seems that even the birds in Mississippi are friendly.

Returning home, I notice a girl about my age raking pine needles in the yard next door, on the other side of the double row of tall pine trees. Her front yard is spacious, nearly as large as a football field. She isn't tall, less than five feet, with bright-red hair cut short. Our neighbor has a very slender build with a rather pale complexion. She's wearing a drab tan jacket and black jeans.

As I begin to cross our yard, she yells to me, "You must be JoeE."

Surprised that she knows my name, I change direction and jog toward her. My sister and Coree are both tall, tanned, and athletic. This girl appears extremely fragile in comparison. Although certainly no beauty queen, she has a pretty face and a pleasant smile.

"Hey, JoeE. I'm Rachel Taylor," she announces. "Welcome to Brandon."

"How do you know my name, Rachel?" I ask as she stops raking.

"A good friend of mine told me," she answers. "You met him yesterday—Mason Calhoun."

"Oh, Coree's brother," I reply, acknowledging the connection.

"Yes, her older brother," she confirms with a smile.

"Do you go to Brandon High?" I ask, forcing myself to follow Mom's advice about asking people about themselves.

"I sure do. I'm supposed to be a sophomore, but I missed a year," she says. "I guess I'll see you around school or maybe at Mason's house. Your sister is over there quite often."

"Hopefully I'll see you a bunch, then. It's nice to meet you, Rachel." I add, "Have fun raking."

"Oh, I just love the smell of pine needles in the mornin'," she says sarcastically with a little grin.

"I guarantee that raking pine needles is better than shoveling snow," I tell her.

"I suppose," Rachel says, returning to her work. "It's nice to meet you."

"Later," I say cheerfully.

Returning home, I'm extremely proud of myself for carrying on a normal conversation with another teenage girl. Possibly, I left the tongue-tied schoolboy in Fulton.

Walking toward my bedroom brimming with confidence, I pass my sister, who's still wearing her immodest outfit, apparently continuing her bathroom protest. She's sitting at the dining room table with her feet propped on a chair, performing some kind of toenail-painting ritual.

I notice that she's using her left hand. "Are you left-handed, Sis?"

"Yeah, aren't you?"

"No, I'm right-handed, but I do a lot of things with my left. Painting my nails isn't one of them, though."

"I sure hope taking a shower is one, bro." MaryAna pretends to hold her nose. Considering the pungent smell of her blue nail polish, I doubt that she can smell anything else. Apparently, my twin is simply trying to catch up after being denied sixteen years of teasing me.

"On my way," I promise, wiping my hand across my face, still flushed and sweating from my little jaunt. Leaving the dining room, I add, "While I was out, I met Rachel Taylor. Mason told her about me."

Immediately, I get a reaction from MaryAna that I'm not expecting. She says angrily, "We need to talk right now, Brother!"

Setting her polish on the table, my sister leads me to my room. Following like an obedient puppy, I find that I'm intimidated by her hostile demeanor.

Closing the door behind us, apparently so our mother can't hear, she demands, "Sit down."

I sit on the edge of my bed, totally unsure of what's going on and afraid to ask. Pulling her flimsy dressing gown tightly around her, MaryAna plops down on the recliner and swings her legs over one arm of the chair.

Gritting her teeth, she pounds the chair with her fist. "Oh, that Rachel! I don't understand what Mason sees in that girl. She makes me madder than a wet hen!"

My sister's bright-blue eyes have a tinge of green from the jealous rage that has suddenly erupted like a volcano at the mere mention of Rachel's name. I've never seen a wet hen. If they get as mad as my twin is at the moment, I certainly plan to avoid henhouses during rainstorms.

She rants on. "Mason probably just feels sorry for her with all that cancer stuff."

When Mom was describing my twin sister, she included the words *kind* and *compassionate*. It appears that jealousy trumps both kindness and compassion. Also, I believe that I just received my answer to the question about the "missing year" that Rachel mentioned. Apparently, she suffered from cancer sometime in the past. That may also explain her slender, almost frail body.

I dive headfirst into unknown waters. "So, you like Mason?"

"I don't just like Mason. I've loved him for a long time." My twin sniffs back a tear, obviously emotional and completely serious.

Oh, great! I kick myself for being so curious. Note to self: don't ask your sister about boys. Unfortunately, I've already let the toothpaste out of the tube, and there's no putting it back now.

I can tell from her expression that MaryAna is deciding how much she wants to tell me. "When Coree and I were eight, I talked her into takin' karate lessons 'cause Mason was in karate. When we were nine, I convinced her to take gymnastics with me 'cause Mason was into gymnastics. In junior high, I begged Coree to try out for cheerleadin' so we could be on the sidelines to cheer for her brother. Mason is nice to me but treats me like another little sister. We were meant to be together, and I really want to go out with him."

Seeming even more agitated, MaryAna renews her attack on our neighbor. "Mason has been friends with Rachel for a long time. Now, he has started goin' out with that she-devil. They're out on dates all the time. I'm more popular than Rachel, I'm prettier than her, I wear nicer clothes, and I've got a much nicer car! Mason should be goin' out with me, not her!"

Witnessing much more than just a glimpse of MaryAna's fiery temper, I ask, "Why do you think Mason likes Rachel so much?"

With her imagination in high gear, my sister speculates, "Maybe she's some kind of red-haired witch who cast a spell on him. Did you ever notice that a bunch of witches in movies have red hair?"

Waiting a few seconds to make sure that my sister is back on earth, I tell her, "MaryAna, you have to be realistic. Rachel seems pretty normal to me, red hair and all. It's doubtful that she's a witch."

"Maybe," MaryAna concedes reluctantly. "You're probably right. Possibly she just found an old book at the library that contains secret love spells."

I try to be logical again. "As for charms and magic spells, I suspect that Mason may think she has a charming personality. He doesn't seem to be someone under a love spell. If anyone was under a spell last night when Mason came into the house, it was you."

Pursing her lips, MaryAna just nods sadly, actually conceding the point. Apparently, Mason hasn't gotten the memo that says that the quarterback is supposed to date the hot cheerleader. Isn't that what all the movies tell us? At least Mason is dating someone, while I'm sitting on the sidelines.

"Have you ever told Mason how you feel about him?"

"No!" she says emphatically. "I'm afraid that he might really hate me. Maybe you can talk to him."

Shocked at her suggestion, I tell her, "I barely know the guy."

"Come on, JoeE." She bats her sad eyes at me. "You're both football players. Y'all can start talkin' about football, and then ask him why he likes Rachel so much."

"No way." But somehow, I know that my sister isn't about to take no for an answer.

"*Pleeease*. I'll help you get to know Coree better," MaryAna adds with a devilish grin. The bribe does the trick, since I need all the help I can get when it comes to girls.

Finally agreeing, I promise, "OK. I'll talk to Mason. Maybe he doesn't even know that you like him that way. Last night when you saw him, you turned into a zombie."

"Really?" she asks. "You think that deep down he loves me too but doesn't know how I feel about him?"

"I have *no* idea," I answer. "The first chance I get, I'll try to find out at least why he likes Rachel so much. No promises on the result."

Stepping into the middle of this teenage drama is easily the most idiotic thing that I've ever done. Maybe I *shouldn't* be allowed to make my own decisions.

MaryAna throws me a little kiss. "Thank you, Brother. It's nice to have someone who will listen to me about this stuff."

"What about Coree? Haven't you talked to her about your feelings toward her brother?"

"Well." My sister hesitates. "Of course, Coree knows that I love Mason. She just tells me he really likes Rachel and that I should start goin' out with other guys. She just likes whatever boy she's with at the time. Believe me, she's been with plenty of them."

Was Coree's attentiveness to me yesterday simply how she treats guys in general? It seemed as if we connected in a very personal way. I suddenly realize that it was probably just wishful thinking on my part. Having no experience with girls, I suppose that I just jumped to conclusions.

MaryAna goes on, "When we were thirteen, Coree sneaked off to her bedroom with a guy at a party. Later, she began goin' off with guys all the time. Luckily, her real mama in Atlanta got her on the pill."

"Isn't Julie her mother?" I ask, somewhat confused.

"No, Julie's her stepmom," my sister says. Taking a couple of breaths before continuing, MaryAna updates me on the current Calhoun family. "Coach Calhoun married her about ten years ago, after he divorced his first wife, Martha, who remarried and moved to Atlanta. Then they had little Logan seven years ago. Have I confused you enough?"

"Just another messed-up American family," I say, smiling. "Compared to our family, they almost seem normal."

"Totally," MaryAna agrees with a laugh. "After Coree started takin' the pill, she would never tell me who she was seein' or where they went. Guys like her, and she sure enough likes them back."

Listening to my sister talk about her friend, I'm amazed. Coree doesn't seem to be the wild temptress that MaryAna is describing. However, she's so beautiful that I've no doubt that any guy would be attracted to her. After her antics this morning, I'd be more willing to believe that MaryAna is the "wild child."

"What about Mom? Can't you talk to her about your feelings for Mason?"

"I can talk to Mama about most things. However, when I mention Mason, it's almost like she can't wait to change the subject. Once, I told her that I loved him, and she acted as if I had just said I had an upset stomach. Mama's clichés—like, *you'll get over it* and *everybody has puppy loves*—show that she just doesn't get it."

"Does Mom have some problem with the Calhoun family?" I ask, surprised at our mother's dismissal of my sister's feelings.

After considering my question for a moment, MaryAna answers, "She never lets me spend the night at their house, but it's not like she cares if I visit. Mama encourages me to spend time with Coree, but she stays over here a lot. Mama would probably freak out if I went out on a date with Mason."

"Mom may just think that you're too young to have a serious relationship," I tell my sister, trying to explain our mother's behavior logically.

"Maybe." MaryAna considers the possibility. "Do you think it's because of you, JoeE? Maybe she sees Mason as just some kind of substitute brother for me."

"Could be," I say. "Mom has carried some pretty painful secrets around for a long time. By now, she probably has a few warped ideas about families and relationships. I bet Mom will act just as weird if I start going with someone."

"Well, I know one girl who already wants to go with you for sure."

"You're kidding, right?" I say, my ears perking up.

Confirming my hope, MaryAna informs me, "Apparently, you made quite an impression on my best friend last night. She's already texted me a dozen times and called me three times this mornin' just to talk about you. Coree says something about you gives her goose bumps! Isn't that nuts?"

"Wow!" I exclaim, thinking about the exciting shiver that I'd felt when Coree touched my hand the night before. "Could it be my awesome good looks, Sis?"

"No way!" MaryAna cries out, adding teasingly, "I sure enough got all the good looks in this set of twins!"

"Yeah, right," I come back at her, "and I see that you got all the humility, too!"

With a little twist of her head, my sister proceeds to stick her tongue out at me. Then she tells me much more seriously, "Coree is really sweet. We really have been best friends, like, forever."

"So she really is your BFF?" I ask.

"For sure. There's nobody nicer than her," my sister says. "I just thought that you should know about the other guys. That doesn't make her a bad person. She's just adventurous and wants to please everyone. I think boys just take advantage of her."

"I don't really have a problem with all that stuff. That's her business, not mine," I say, trying to hide my growing jealousy.

"I bet you can't wait to hook up with her."

"MaryAna! I can't believe you said that." I'm shocked and embarrassed by her suggestive remark. "Mom was right when she said that you say whatever's on your mind. You know that's not always a good thing, don't you?"

"Oh, JoeE, don't get upset," my sister says, realizing that I may not be used to such plain talk from a girl. "Coree said that she's really lookin' forward to totally gettin' to know you, talkin' to you about football, and learnin' about livin' in New York. She didn't mention anything about doin' that other stuff."

"I really want to get to know her, too," I respond, hoping that I'll get that chance soon.

"I've never heard Coree talk about a guy like she's talkin' about you. Of course, she did say that she thinks you're really hot and totally buff."

I turn crimson with embarrassment.

"Well, I think Coree is the most beautiful girl that I've ever seen," I tell my sister, hoping that MaryAna will relay the message.

"I'm sure Coree will be glad to know that you like the way she looks. I think she gets with so many guys 'cause she craves the attention. Julie and her daddy hardly ever do anything with her. The trip to Disney World was a Christmas present for Logan. Coree's parents insisted that she go along to babysit."

"Oh," I say, trying to understand Coree's family.

MaryAna speculates, "It probably goes back to her mama movin' away when she was so little. She never hears much from her. Mamas movin' away is something Coree and you have in common, JoeE. She may open up to you about it."

As I think about Coree's friendly, caring personality, unique sense of humor, and cute Southern accent, I simply can't wait to see her again. Nothing that my sister has told me about her friend's past or the relationships that she may have had deters me in the least. She's still my dream girl. The past is the past, and it shouldn't influence the present.

. Maybe my thinking is naïve. Do things that happened long ago shape our futures? Are we products of what has gone before?

Chapter 23

A KEN DOLL?

MaryAna says that neither Coree nor she could find me on Facebook. To her amazement, I inform her that Dad didn't allow me to have a Facebook page.

"Seriously?" my sister asks, obviously upset. "Was he tryin' to keep you in the Stone Age? I'm glad he left Mama, but I wish that she'd taken you with us!" My sister's bitter resentment toward our father is quite evident. Forgiving him for abandoning her as a baby doesn't appear to be on her to-do list.

Pausing to take a deep breath, MaryAna continues, "Oh, yeah, I gave your cell number to Coree. She wants to text you."

I shock my sister once again. "My cell doesn't accept text messages. Dad had them blocked. He thought that texting would be too much of a distraction for me."

About to explode, my sister's so irate that she practically screams, "No Facebook! No textin'! Who was this guy? Hitler? I know he was my father and that he's dead and I should go easy on him, but get real!"

This time, I just laugh at her obvious frustration.

In a few seconds, she bursts out laughing too. "Please tell me that you at least have e-mail."

"Nope," I tell her, shaking my head. MaryAna just drops her head, speechless at the thought that I'm so technology deprived.

"I'm not even gonna ask about Twitter," MaryAna says, totally defeated. "I'm textin' Coree to tell her to get her butt over here and help me drag you into the twenty-first century."

Drying my hair after my second shower, I hear Coree and her brother, Mason, pulling into the driveway. MaryAna rushes out the front door to meet them. Apparently, Mason has a car and Coree doesn't. When I get outside, he's telling the girls that he's going next door to see Rachel. Noticing the look of bitter disappointment on my sister's face as he heads toward his girlfriend's house, I actually feel sorry for her. The advice that Coree gave my twin to start dating other guys seems reasonable, under the circumstances. However, it appears that MaryAna may have a fixation on what she can't have—in this case, Mason.

I call to him, "I met Rachel earlier. She was out raking pine needles."

"What did you think of her, JoeE?" Mason asks looking back at me.

"She seems very nice."

"She is very nice." Coree's brother smiles and disappears around the corner of our house.

MaryAna glares at me, pursing her lips as she stomps back toward the front door.

"Well, she did seem nice," I say in my defense, shrugging my shoulders.

"Get into the house now, Brother!" MaryAna commands. Her blue eyes narrow as if they are about to shoot poison darts. My sister saunters back inside, adding threateningly, "We're fixin' to straighten you out, boy!"

With sunrays streaming through her blond curls, giving them a soft golden glow, Coree smiles and says mockingly, "I reckon' it's best not to upset Miss Scarlett here at Tara." Her *Gone with the Wind* reference is made more effective by her sweet, Southern drawl.

Then, in almost a whisper, she adds, "I hear you and MaryAna had quite a little heart-to-heart this morning."

So does Coree know about my entire conversation with my twin? Apparently, they have no secrets between them. Then I remember my pitiful batting average on assumptions lately.

The next hour is the MaryAna-Coree show. The girls set up a Facebook page for me. My sister uses her phone to take my photo, and she uploads it. When I answer the relationship question as "single," I hear some giggles.

"If you need to change your relationship status, it's easy," Coree says as both girls giggle again. My cheeks are turning a rosy red.

MaryAna sets up an e-mail account for me, demonstrating how to access and send messages. I send an e-mail to Coree. Reading it, she giggles and shows it to my sister. It simply reads: "How do you change that relationship status again?"

"Well, at least he's trainable," MaryAna tells her friend, making me sound like a circus animal.

I ask Coree, "Do all sisters treat their brothers like this?"

MaryAna answers for her. "Well, guys are such simple creatures; it's easier if we take care of y'all."

Still unaware that I'll never win any kind of verbal battle with my sister, I make the fatal mistake of challenging her statement. "We aren't that simple. We're highly evolved."

MaryAna flies into combat mode. "Life has been made so simple for y'all because guys can't handle very much." Before I'm able to respond, she adds, "Guys don't require makeup and can't have babies. Your underwear is cheap, and the world is your urinal. Girls don't stare at your chest while you're talkin' to them. You can belch and just laugh about it."

When my sister stops for a breath, Coree takes the baton. "Males can vacation with just one suitcase and walk by a mirror without makin' sure everything is in place. You only need a couple of pairs of shoes, and apparently, wrinkles are invisible to you. Chocolate is just another snack, not an essential food group. Boys can't seem to remember birthdays, anniversaries, or to put the toilet seat back down. And you get to play football. It's just not fair!"

Listening to what my dream girl is saying, I feel the sting of her words. Heaven help me if she learns that I *moved* here using just one suitcase. But then, what's wrong with being a guy? We do enjoy many advantages. Thinking about the bowl games this week, I miss a word or two as they continue their little tirade. However, I've got enough sense to look their way and pretend to be listening.

As I start to say something, my relentless sister gets in a few parting zingers. "Guys can have just one hairstyle, like, forever. You only have to shave your face, and then only if you want to. New shoes don't hurt your feet, and paintin' your nails isn't even a thought. Pick up your wallet, and you're good to go. Are you listenin', JoeE?"

"Oh yeah, every word," I swear, but my mind had again drifted off topic.

Probably not believing me, MaryAna finishes her point. "Girls are the ones who evolved. Males are still stuck in caveman mode." The girls snicker at each other.

I have to admit that some of those points are probably valid. Refusing to give up completely, I simply say, "Well, I guess I'll just have to muddle through, along with my fellow cavemen."

Ignoring my sarcastic comment, the girls begin taking inventory of my clothes. Shaking her head, MaryAna says, as if she's a member of the fashion gestapo, "No way is he wearing any of this to school! I'd never hear the end of it!"

As they check out my shirts, MaryAna often points her finger at her open mouth and makes gagging sounds.

When Coree comes to one of my rugby shirts, she says, "MaryAna, do you believe this! JoeE has a shirt like the one Michael Oher wore in *The Blind Side*."

I love that movie and think about how lucky Michael was in real life to be accepted into the Tuohy family. While watching that film, I had wished for a mother like Sandra Bullock's character. Now that I've got the mother and the sister, all I need is a new father and a pain-in-the-butt little brother.

Being brutally honest as usual, MaryAna says about my favorite shirt, "Where did you get that one, JoeE? The Big, Tall, and Ugly store?" When she sees my heavy coat hanging in the closet, she adds, "That coat would only be useful if you were on a dogsled."

Coree comments a little more sympathetically, "You really don't spend much time thinking about clothes, do you?"

My sister doesn't wait for me to answer. "Face it, Coree, his clothes are hopeless, but we can fix the problem." She grins at her friend. "Makeover?"

"Yes, makeover," Coree confirms. Apparently, the girls are slaves to fashion, and they intend to put me into chains right along with them. "We need Mama's credit card and a trip to the mall," MaryAna announces gleefully.

I tell the girls proudly, "Mom got me a debit card and put money in a checking account. We can use that."

"Are you kiddin'?" MaryAna asks, raising her eyebrows in disbelief. "We'll use Mama's money. She feels so guilty about you, there's no way she's gonna refuse to buy you anything, much less clothes. Let me talk to her."

My sister leaves my bedroom, and for the first time, I'm completely alone with Coree. Sitting next to me on the bed, she smiles, causing my heart to beat faster. A lump appears in my throat, and I can't think of anything to say.

Luckily, Coree doesn't seem to be at a loss for words. "I sure hope that we didn't hurt your feelings about the clothes."

"No problem," I answer truthfully, adding with a smile, "They were all gifts."

"Have you ever been shoppin' for clothes?"

"Nope," I reply honestly, having hoped that I never would.

With a giggle, Coree changes the subject unexpectedly. "I know that MaryAna told you that I've been with a bunch of guys." She then asks bluntly, "Does that bother you?"

Answering quickly, I blurt out, "Not really."

She fidgets with one of her bracelets. "Do you have a special girl back in New York?"

"Nope, no one,"

Her eyes widen. "Really?"

"I'm kinda shy," I tell her, making the biggest understatement of the century.

Sliding closer, she says hesitantly, "Well, you shouldn't believe everything that your sister—"

Coree stops abruptly when MaryAna bursts back into my bedroom. She's holding up our mother's credit card.

"Road trip!" my sister announces excitedly.

On the way to the mall, Coree says, "Julie wants me to invite y'all to our house to watch Ole Miss play Pittsburgh in the bowl game tomorrow. She's plannin' a big spread with fried chicken, catfish, hush puppies, cornbread, fried okra, and all the fixin's. Y'all are gonna come, aren't you?"

"I'd love to come," I say enthusiastically, looking forward to spending more time with Coree and her family. I want to ask what the heck okra is, but I'll just find out tomorrow.

"Is Mason bringin' Rachel?" MaryAna asks in a tone of voice indicating that she already knows the answer.

"Most likely," her friend replies. "That's why he went over to Rachel's house today to ask her."

My sister accepts the invitation. "OK. I'll bring JoeE over before the game, eat something, and maybe stay a little while."

"If you're busy, MaryAna," I offer, "I could walk. It's only a mile or so."

"JoeE! Are you serious?" my sister shoots back at me. "Nobody in Brandon walks anywhere! We have walkin' tracks for that!"

I just shake my head and laugh.

Coree explains, "MaryAna thinks that if God wanted us to walk, we'd be born with walkin' shoes on our feet."

For some reason, Mason's nickname of the Airhead Twins suddenly comes to my mind.

The trip to the mall with my sister and her friend is intense, to say the least. They say that they're just going to start with the "essentials" and fill in the rest of my wardrobe later.

At the first store, the girls have me try on a couple of items to establish sizes. From there on, I have one purpose and one purpose only: to carry packages.

They are like two whirling dervishes, going from store to store and searching rack after rack. I'm hardly able to keep up with them; the girls even find time to pick out a few items for themselves. They inform me that they share clothes, giving them a much wider selection.

When I state that one of the shirts looks really expensive, MaryAna says, "We aren't goin' to pay for it. We're just goin' to charge it!" Somehow, my sister's logic eludes me. "Besides," she continues, "I'm already plannin' a shoppin' trip with Mama to spend the *big* money."

I wonder if I'll have to carry packages on that trip too.

We drop Coree off at her house, and on the way home, MaryAna explains that on Thursday afternoons, her friend works a couple hours for a psychiatrist friend of Julie's. When I ask, she says she's unsure of exactly the type of work her friend does for the doctor.

I spend the next few hours practicing to be a male model. I'm required to try on each of my new outfits and prance into the living room like a show pony. My mother and MaryAna relax on the couch as they evaluate how well the new clothes fit. They also decide which outfits are appropriate for what occasions and what additional clothing and accessories are necessary. Now I know why girls must have Ken dolls to play with when they're young. Apparently, the male dolls are practice dummies.

The two of them spend more time discussing each of my outfits than I've spent thinking about clothes in my entire lifetime. Apparently, how I dress for school will reflect directly upon my sister. I doubt that the Spartans took this much time worrying about their attire.

Chapter 24

FASHION CENTRAL

On Friday, I again rise before daybreak. After completing my exercises, I begin a several-mile run through the nearby subdivisions. The air is cool and crisp against my face. Amazingly, I'm already beginning to feel at home in my new surroundings.

My lone blue jay sings to me as I approach his small tree, which the little guy has apparently staked out. I officially name him JoeE's Bird. Hopping from branch to branch, my new acquaintance continues to sing his little heart out simply for the pure joy of it.

As the sun peeks over the horizon, I behold a landscape dominated by the deep, rich green of tall Southern pines. They seem to reach to the sky while their pungent scent reminds me of a car air freshener. Although there are brown pine needles and prickly pinecones strewn everywhere, the trees themselves maintain their majestic, emerald beauty. Mixed with the various shades of brown of the leafless hardwoods, the panoramic scenery is a delightful way to begin the day.

For school, I had to memorize the Joyce Kilmer poem, "Trees." Back then, it had simply been words upon a page, another assignment completed. Recalling that poem today, I begin to understand that it isn't just about a clever rhyming scheme. The author brilliantly explains the joy and awe I'm feeling when nature unexpectedly amazes me.

With my pace now set to the beat of the poem, I pick up speed, and time flies as fast as my feet do. Feeling isolated from the cares of the world, I'm comforted and protected by these regal sentinels standing guard above as my feet pound silently across their domain.

Returning home, I take a hot shower, and Mom fixes me a hearty breakfast. Water has never felt more refreshing, and food has never tasted more delicious. After I eat, I pick up my cell to call my grandmother, who is also an early riser.

Hearing her cheerful hello reminds me how much I miss her and Papa. It now seems like I have two homes, and I hate the distance between them. I begin to empathize with my parents and their dilemma of where to live.

Following my phone conversation, I sit at the dining room table, trying out my new iPad. After checking out some of the apps, I play a few games that I've never tried before. It's really fun, and I feel a twinge of resentment that Dad denied me so many childhood pleasures.

Obviously not an early riser, MaryAna finally wanders out of her room a couple of hours later. She's dressed more modestly today. Apparently, she's made her point and abandoned her bathroom protest. Going to the kitchen, she pours herself some orange juice, texting as usual.

"I'm plannin' your day, JoeE," my sister says with a grin, intently working her iPhone. "Before I give you your itinerary, I need to ask a serious question. Just how much do you like Coree?"

"A bunch," I blurt out without hesitating, knowing my answer will be forwarded to my dream girl. "I think she's great."

"OK, I kinda thought so," MaryAna says. "In that case, I've got your day set. After you watch the bowl game, Coree will give you a ride back here in her brother's car. That way, you two can have some quality time together."

A short ride in a car is quality time? Of course, it's better than nothing. Now I have to think of what to say to Coree. Obviously, I have an anxious expression on my face, because MaryAna adds, "Don't fret; you're in my expert hands."

After that, my sister returns to her room. Mom joins me in the dining room, and I spend the next few hours playing around with my iPad while I talk to her. When I mention that the Super Bowl is in New Orleans this year, to my surprise, she says she already has tickets.

"How do you like the Calhoun family?" Mom asks, as if she were reading my mind.

"They're great," I answer. "In fact, MaryAna and I are going there this afternoon to watch a bowl game, if that's OK with you. Are you going?"

"It's fine with me, dear. I've got a bunch of work to catch up on, so I won't be goin'," she replies.

"I'm really looking forward to playing football with Mason and for his father," I say enthusiastically.

"Rhyan and his assistant, Coach Butler, have developed an excellent football program," my mother informs me. "JJ Butler was a classmate of mine in high school. He was also one of my mother's piano students. I know that you'll like him."

"It's too bad Dad didn't take the coaching job here,"

"I wish that he had come here with us," Mom says, sighing as if fantasizing about how different our lives might have been.

While we talk, MaryAna spends her time preparing to go to the party, hustling back and forth between bedroom and bathroom. How can it possibly take her so long to get ready? Of course, I have no idea what is involved in the process and probably don't want to find out. Doing everything while texting must increase the time requirement significantly. Returning to my bedroom, I see that my sister has taken the time to lay out some of my new clothes.

MaryAna keeps her door closed, as if her room is a secret laboratory where she brews up new perfumes and cosmetics. She does take a break from her preparations to instruct me on how I should start combing my hair, adding that it would look better if I let it grow out some. She also tells me that I need to shave before we leave.

"I shaved early this morning," I tell her. "I don't need to shave again."

"OK," MaryAna tells me. "But I know some girls don't like that stumble rubbin' against their soft skin when kissin'." Getting her drift, I quickly go shave again.

Earlier, I was worried that we might show up far too early at Calhoun Castle. Now, I worry that the game will be over by the time we arrive. Knocking on my sister's bedroom door, I ask if she's about ready to go. She tells me to come in and that she just needs to finish putting on her makeup.

Prior to this moment, I'd only seen quick glimpses into Fashion Central. Her bedroom is the same size as mine, but where my room is neat with the bed made and everything put away, MaryAna's is just the opposite. She has a room full of furniture with almost nowhere to sit. Clothes and undergarments are strewn everywhere. Calling this room messy would be an insult to a mess.

Hanging over her windows are sheer curtain panels in the colors of the rainbow. The brilliant hues are mirrored in her lampshades, a lava lamp, electronic gadgets of all sorts, and small boxes overflowing with trinkets, souvenirs, and things for her hair. The walls of her room are covered with amazing abstract paintings, blazing in vivid colors. I notice the signature, *M. A. Lindley*, indicating that she's the artist.

There are piles of women's magazines on the floor, including *Vogue,* and *Cosmopolitan.* Her unmade double bed has clothes strewn all over it. The dresser, with its large mirror, is covered with everything from makeup supplies to empty juice glasses and a half-eaten bag of potato chips. My sister's open closet reveals that her fancier dresses are hung neatly. However, her shoe rack is overflowing with every type and shade of footwear imaginable.

Looking very attractive, my sister is wearing a black-and-gold University of Southern Mississippi football jersey with matching black pants and gold shoes. Her jewelry complements her outfit.

"Are you a Southern Mississippi fan?" I ask.

"Oh, not especially," she answers, "but Tyler will be at the party, and he loves Southern. Since Rachel will be with Mason, I need someone to talk to. Maybe Mason will get jealous."

"Who's Tyler?"

My sister continues to put on her makeup. "Tyler Richardson is Mason's best friend. They're both seventeen and juniors. Tyler is on the football team. He's real fast and catches the ball for touchdowns."

"A wide receiver?" I ask, wrongly assuming that my sister is familiar with basic football terminology.

"I suppose," MaryAna answers, seeming annoyed at my interruption. "He also plays baseball with Mason. They both are pitchers and do something else."

"Bat?" I ask condescendingly.

"Whatever!" she says sharply, again perturbed by my interruption. "Coree had a thing for Tyler when we were in seventh grade. I didn't blame her; he was buff even back then. But he did something at a party once that really ticked her off. She was like really mad at him, like forever. Now they're friends again, but I don't think she's ever totally forgiven."

"What did he do?"

Shaking her head, she answers, "I've asked them what happened, but neither of them will discuss it. It's some kind of big secret."

Pausing briefly, she adds, "Tyler's sister, Lainey, will be there and maybe her friend, Noe. They're both fifteen and play softball. Tyler tells me his sister is really good."

Finishing her makeup, MaryAna says, "Tyler is funny and always sweet to me. I didn't used to like him 'cause he was really immature. Now we talk a lot and kinda hang out. If I didn't love Mason, I..." Not finishing her sentence, she says, "OK, time to leave."

Chapter 25

PARTY TIME

When MaryAna and I exit the car at Calhoun Castle, Coree grabs my hand, giving me an unexpected hug and a peck on the cheek. Entering the house, I note that the bowl game is already underway. Coree introduces me to a couple of young women waiting for us just inside the door. If I looked up "adorable" in the dictionary, their photo would be there.

Coree says, "JoeE, I want you to meet Ilaina Richardson, who we call Lainey, and her friend, Noe Howard."

"Nice to meet you," I say, pleased by their friendly smiles.

"Hi, I'm Lainey," the first girl says. Tyler's sister has long, straight, dark hair and matching eyes. She's maybe five foot four and wearing a bright-red, short-sleeved baseball shirt with black shorts. On the front of the shirt in small letters it reads, "Lady Bulldogs."

Brushing her hair back behind her right ear, Lainey continues, "I'm glad to finally meet you, JoeE. Your sister and Coree have been talkin' about you for a couple of months. Hopefully, your football season went well."

"It ended on a good note," I reply. "Thanks for asking. MaryAna tells me you're an exceptional softball player."

Blushing slightly, Tyler's sister smiles and then nods toward the beautiful young woman who's dressed similarly. "Noe plays softball, too."

"Hi, Noe," I say, trying to keep my nerves in check with all these girls surrounding me. With her reddish-blond hair and almost ridiculously blue eyes, Lainey's friend has the kind of striking beauty usually reserved for the movie screen.

"Hey, JoeE," Noe responds, seeming a little shy herself. Quickly looking away when we make eye contact, she takes a half step back as if she's trying to hide behind Lainey. Barely speaking above a whisper, she stammers out the rest of her greeting. "I'm glad to meet you."

Breaking the short, awkward silence that follows, Coree informs me, "I'll introduce you to Tyler, if he ever leaves the kitchen. That boy has a healthy appetite!"

Hearing Tyler's name, MaryAna excuses herself and hustles off to the kitchen. She doesn't acknowledge either Mason or Rachel, who are sitting by themselves in one corner of the huge living room.

Laughing, Lainey says, "We can't keep food at our house. Between my brother and Mason, they eat everything in sight. I worry they might eat our dog if we run out of food."

Laughing at Lainey's comment, I turn to wave to Mason and Rachel. Smiling at me, Coree's brother asks, "Have y'all come to watch Ole Miss kick some butt?"

"They may have a little problem today with Pittsburgh," I tell him. He just flashes his awesome smile back at me and goes back to talking with Rachel.

Relaxing in his recliner with Logan on his lap, Coach Calhoun is intently watching the game. This is the first time that I've seen his younger son without the Mickey Mouse ears. He's a cute kid and pretty tall for a seven-year-old.

"I saved a place for you next to Daddy," Coree informs me, pointing to the end of the couch by her father's recliner.

Before we sit down, Rhyan puts out his hand without getting up. As we shake, he says, "We're glad you could make it, JoeE. Maybe Coree will finally stop talkin' about you."

"Hush, Daddy!" Coree complains, looking a little embarrassed.

"Sorry we're late, Coach."

Laughing boisterously, Coach Calhoun says, "If MaryAna was on time, it'd be a first."

I take my place on the couch, and Coree sits beside me. Lainey and Noe squeeze onto the other end, and my dream girl scoots up against me to give them more room. As she takes my hand, I've no idea how to respond in a room full of people, including her father. Apparently, MaryAna relayed my message to Coree about how I feel about her.

Coach Calhoun can't help but notice his daughter's flirtatious behavior. Finally, he commands, "Coree, give the poor boy some room. You're practically pushin' him off the sofa."

As Coree slides slightly away from me, she says to her father flippantly, "Oh, Daddy! We're just fine. Watch the game." Although her attitude is similar to MaryAna's rebellious antics yesterday morning, there's a sharper, more defiant tone to her voice.

Looking at Coree, I smile, letting her know that I don't mind the closeness. She slides right back up against me. Coach Calhoun simply ignores her, concentrating on the game. Trying to distract myself from the father-daughter tension, I note that there's no score. I ask the coach if he's an Ole Miss fan.

"My loyalty lies with Mississippi State," Rhyan explains. "I played there in college."

"Where did you play in high school?"

"Right here in Brandon," the coach answers proudly. "Once a Bulldog, always a Bulldog." Since the nicknames of both Mississippi State and Brandon are the same, Coach Calhoun's statement is literally true.

Pausing to take a big gulp of beer, he continues. "I have to root for several colleges now. Some of the boys who played for me are now on various college teams. There are two players from Brandon in this game."

I tell the coach, "MaryAna mentioned that there would be a Southern Miss fan here today. After they lost all their games this past season, it's a wonder they have any fans left. Apparently they're looking for a new head coach."

Coach Calhoun nods. "Both Tyler and Lainey are big Southern Miss fans. Their daddy graduated college there. In my opinion, they need a topflight head coach to turn that mess around."

Realizing that Lainey just heard everything I said, I'm mortified that I've just insulted her favorite team. I turn to her, saying, "I'm so sorry, Lainey. I shouldn't have brought up Southern's season."

Despite my unthoughtful comment about what undoubtedly is a sore subject, Lainey says, "That's OK. Southern Miss will rise again." Then she yells, "Southern Miss to the top!" Lainey is obviously a true fan of the team. I hope that they'll fulfill her dream someday.

From the kitchen, I hear a male voice yell, "To the top, Golden Eagles!" I suspect that might be Tyler.

Coach Calhoun adds, "Go Eagles!" He then gives a chuckle, as if his comment was a joke.

Coree further enlightens me. "Logan, Noe, and I are State fans, just like Daddy. Julie likes Ole Miss 'cause that's where she went to college. Mason roots for whatever team State is playin' so he can argue with Daddy. Rachel likes LSU 'cause both of her parents are from Louisiana."

At the mention of LSU, a chorus of boos fills the room. Rachel, who I didn't think was even listening, says rather softly, "Go Tigers." Mom was right. Everybody seems to have a favorite.

"What about MaryAna? Does she have a favorite team?"

Coree replies with a grin, "Your sister is a diehard fan of any team whose jersey she thinks looks good on her. What's your favorite college team?"

"Syracuse University," I reply proudly.

There's total silence for a moment. Then little Logan breaks the hush with, "Is that a high school, Daddy?"

His father answers him with a big grin. "No, Logan. But I think they only play high schools."

Coming to my defense, Coree admonishes them. "Stop pickin' on my JoeE! Syracuse used to have really great teams, especially when his father was quarterback there. They've even won a national championship."

I've got to admit, I like the sound of "my JoeE." However, I'm more impressed by the fact that Coree knows about Syracuse football.

"Syracuse won a bowl game this year," I say.

Impressing me even further, Coree adds, "A couple years ago, they beat Kansas State in a bowl, too."

She's absolutely correct. Could MaryAna and my mother be right? Does Coree know as much about football as I do? Of course, that's impossible! If she really understands the sport, she's beyond a dream girl. Coree is all my fantasies come true.

Entering the living room from the kitchen, Julie greets me. Thanking her for inviting me to their home, I tell her that I'm looking forward to tasting the food that she has prepared. She tells me that I'm most welcome anytime and that the food will be ready at half time. Rhyan informs her that the small cooler beside his chair is out of beer. He hands it to her, and she dutifully returns to the kitchen to refill it.

Next, it's MaryAna who comes from the kitchen, followed closely by a teenage guy munching on a piece of fried chicken. "Guess who couldn't wait till half time," MaryAna announces as she sits down on a nearby loveseat.

"Surprise, surprise," Coach Calhoun responds.

"Tyler, that's my brother, JoeE," MaryAna informs him. Tyler Richardson is about six feet tall with short, dark-brown hair and brown eyes that remind me of his sister's. He has a very muscular build and a dimple in his chin. Like MaryAna, he's wearing a Southern Miss jersey. Standing up, I extend my hand toward him.

Wiping his greasy hand on his jeans, Tyler shakes my hand firmly. "Hey, dude. 'Sup?"

"They're dumping on the Syracuse Orange," I complain with a little smile.

"The Calhoun clan is always dumpin' on Southern Miss too," Tyler sympathizes, adding, "I call them SEC elitists."

Tyler is referring to the Southeastern Conference to which LSU, Ole Miss, and Mississippi State all belong. The conference is considered the strongest in the nation.

With a devilish little grin, Coree asks, "Hey Tyler, do you know how the state of Mississippi could win a national championship in football?"

"How?" Tyler asks reluctantly, probably knowing that he's about to get dumped on again.

"By combinin' Ole Miss's defense, State's offense, Brandon High's coachin' staff, and the Southern Miss bus!" she teases with a giggle.

As we all laugh, Tyler retorts, "Coree, do you know what they call a pretty girl at Mississippi State?"

"What?" she says, knowing that it's her turn to have her favorite college insulted.

"A visitor from Southern Miss!" he exclaims. I can't help but laugh. Pursing her lips, Coree shoots me a disapproving look. Obviously, laughing at jokes aimed at her favorite team is dangerous territory.

We all settle in and watch the Pitt Panthers mount a nice drive down the field against Ole Miss, which is already leading in the game. Coach Calhoun makes brief comments on several plays. Surprisingly, everyone else just watches the action in silence. Pittsburgh attempts a screen pass. The ball is tipped and then intercepted, ending the promising drive.

When the game goes to a commercial break, Coach Calhoun asks, "What did you think about that play call, JoeE?"

Looking directly at him, I reply truthfully, "I didn't like it—or the execution, for that matter."

"Why?" the coach asks.

I take a deep breath. "Well, first of all, the running back they were throwing to on the screen is fairly short. It was hard for the quarterback even to spot him in all that traffic. Secondly, the quarterback never set his feet, causing his errant throw. He should've just stood in there and made a decent pass. I actually prefer screen plays to the H-back or a wide receiver myself. Motion can give the quarterback a clue about the defense. If they're in man-to-man coverage, you have a better feel for which defender will be covering your intended receiver. I wouldn't have called a screen play in that area of the field, anyway, since the defense is likely to be in some kind of zone."

Suddenly I realize that Coach Calhoun has muted the television. When I stop talking, there's total silence. Glancing quickly around the room, I see that all eyes are glued on me. With a gulp, I sheepishly conclude, "I would've called a swing pass or a quick out."

The coach takes a swig of his beer before addressing me. "That was an interestin' analysis. Maybe they do know something about football up North, after all."

"Thanks, Coach," I respond, now totally embarrassed and planning to keep my answers much shorter in the future.

Squeezing my hand, Coree whispers in my ear, "That was awesome."

Whispering back, I simply say, "Thanks." I doubt that she understood much of what I said. She was probably just being nice.

The highlight of the bowl game is half time, when we invade Julie's kitchen for a veritable feast. The fried catfish is amazing—pure white meat and absolutely no fishy taste. The hush puppies are so awesome that they should be the next fast-food sensation. There are vegetables, including black-eyed peas, which I believe should be called "black-eyed beans." It turns out that okra is a vegetable. After taking a bite of the fried okra to please Coree, I don't ask for seconds. It must be an acquired taste.

After eating, Mason and Rachel leave. When we return to watch the game, Coree stays in the kitchen to help her stepmother clean up. Grabbing the opportunity, Logan quickly takes my dream girl's place next to me on the couch.

Seeming very curious, Logan begins to pepper me with questions. Understandably, the youngster is confused as to why I grew up so far away from my twin sister. "What's New York like? Have you seen the Statue of Liberty? Your face is so smooth, are you old enough to shave?" He barely takes a mental breath between his inquiries. He seems extremely bright and, like my sister, says what's on his mind. In some strange way, he reminds me of myself at that age.

Lainey and Noe, who have been as quiet as church mice most of the afternoon, also begin asking me questions. Over the years, I've had almost no opportunity to talk with anyone younger than myself. I find that I'm enjoying our little conversation immensely.

Sitting on a nearby loveseat, MaryAna ignores the game in favor of chatting with Tyler after commenting that she thinks the Pittsburgh uniforms are ugly. When Coree returns to the living room, she evicts her little brother from his seat. He asks if he can sit on my lap. When

I agree, he eagerly scampers up as his father continues watching the game, ignoring the five of us on the couch.

Whispering in my ear, Coree says with that devilish grin, "When will it be my turn to sit on your lap?"

I just smile at my dream girl.

Near the end of the third quarter, my sister tells me that she'll see me at home later. Before leaving, she whispers something in Coree's ear. They giggle, and Coree thanks my twin. For what, I have no idea.

Just after MaryAna's exit, I notice Tyler going out the door. He reappears near the end of the game, which Ole Miss wins rather easily thirty-eight to seventeen. We join Tyler, who's already back in the kitchen devouring additional quantities of the fine Southern cuisine. After we eat, Tyler takes his sister and Noe home.

Logan goes to his room, returning with a board game that he wants me to play with him. While my new buddy and I play, I notice that he's left-handed like my twin. Coree again helps Julie in the kitchen. Soon, they both join us while Coach Calhoun watches television and drinks more beer from the little cooler by his recliner.

After I play several games with Logan, Coree receives a text and tells me that it's time for us to leave. Promising Logan that I'll come back to play with him again, I tell Julie and her husband that I had a wonderful time.

As we're about to leave, Coach Calhoun makes my day when he says, "Come over tomorrow and watch the game." I accept his invitation gratefully.

Although I've enjoyed the afternoon immensely, I'm anxious about the ride home with Coree. This will be the "quality time" that my sister promised me this morning. It'll be nice to have an opportunity to speak privately, although I still have no idea what I'll say. I'm extremely curious about what Coree was about to tell me yesterday morning before my sister came back into the room.

Mason had taken Rachel home in her car, leaving his white Toyota Corolla in the driveway for us. Coree tells her parents that she's driving me home, and she'll ride with Mason when he's ready to come home later. All this shuffling of vehicles must be part of my sister's master plan. I wonder if I have severely underestimated my twin's matchmaking ability.

Getting into Mason's car, Coree looks over at me, smiling. "I loved havin' you here today, JoeE."

I return her smile, unsure how to respond.

Her next statement takes me completely by surprise, especially considering what MaryAna has told me about my dream girl and the opposite sex. "You're the first boy that I've ever invited to watch a game with us. Football is too important to share with just anyone."

At first, I think that Coree might be kidding. However, she seems to be completely sincere. "I really enjoyed everything today," I say. I want to say much more but only add, "Especially being with you and your family."

Looking directly into my eyes, Coree says, "MaryAna told me that you like me. Although I haven't known you very long, I really like you too."

"That's great," I manage to utter, despite feeling completely awkward. I want to express my intense personal emotions, but I still lack the courage. Blushing again, I attempt to change the subject. "Your father was still limping today. Did he injure his leg recently?"

From her confused expression, I'm pretty sure that Coree wasn't anticipating such a drastic change in topic. "It's from an old football injury. Daddy was a linebacker at Mississippi State. Before he injured his knees, he was an All-American candidate. He injured one knee and then tore the ACL in the other. That ended all hope of ever playin' in the NFL. It makes Daddy bitter. He really loves the game more than anything else in the world," she says with a sad tone in her voice.

"Gee, that's too bad." I understand her feelings because of my father's shortened NFL career. "I bet your father was a heck of a football player."

"I suppose, but I never saw him play," Coree says rather matter-of-factly, adding, "Those injuries got him into coachin'."

"I hope that I get a chance to play for him," I say, no longer so sure what the future might hold.

Smiling again, Coree says, "If you're good enough, you'll play." The confident way in which she says it makes me believe her.

It's threatening rain as we arrive at my house. I suddenly realize that I've just used up my quality time with Coree. I still don't know what she was about to tell me yesterday. I'm about to ask her, but we reach the front door.

Figuring that I can delay going inside for a couple of minutes, I say, "My mother gave me a key; I've got it here somewhere."

"Oh, I've got one," Coree informs me as she unlocks the door and steps inside. There goes my chance to learn her secret.

My dream girl then takes me completely by surprise when she announces, "Nobody else is here. We've got the whole house to ourselves."

She sits down on the couch and pats the cushion, and I meekly sit beside her. I wonder if I'm ready for this. Of course, I'm not sure what "this" is.

Chapter 26

A CHOICE

Sitting next to Coree on the couch, I feel my stomach muscles tighten. It's as if I'm about to plunge into the deep end of the pool and don't know how to swim. Although I want to talk to my dream girl privately, I'm not sure that a conversation is exactly what she has in mind.

"How do you know that nobody is home?"

Coree smiles. "MaryAna and your mama have gone to the mall, and they won't be back for a couple of hours. Your sister will text me when they're on the way home."

Obviously, MaryAna worked all of this out with her best friend earlier in the day. My sister is proving to be quite the matchmaker, and apparently Coree's in on it too. Maybe this is MaryAna's way of rewarding me for agreeing to talk to Mason.

With her sweet smile fading away, Coree adopts a steady stare that seems to penetrate right through me. It's as if she's using an MRI to bypass my outward appearance and investigate my inner being, all the way down to my soul. My dream girl is lightly biting her lower lip and twisting one of her bracelets nervously.

In a slow, deliberate monotone, Coree begins to speak. "JoeE, I'm gonna offer you a choice." She pauses, takes a deep breath, and continues. "Do you want to just make out, or do you want a glimpse into my soul?"

"Is this a trick question?"

"If you just want to make out, I understand," she says, not amused. "If you choose the second option, I'll share some of my deepest secrets. The choice is yours."

Swallowing hard, I ponder my choices. All my training on making tough decisions on the football field is useless at this moment. Starting a physical relationship with her is appealing; my raging teenage hormones cast all of their votes for that option. But I'm curious as to what dark mysteries lurk in the soul of my dream girl. Secrets are the last thing I want between us.

Looking deeply into her big brown eyes, I say, "Let's explore door number two."

Her eyes light up, and she places the softest of kisses on my cheek. There's a lone tear that she wipes away quickly with the back of her hand.

In almost a whisper, as if she's afraid someone else might hear, Coree begins, "Like I told you earlier, I really like you. It might sound silly after only knowin' you for a couple of days, but MaryAna told me that you feel the same way about me. She also said that you were a great listener. I want you to know the truth about me, not just falsehoods and rumors."

Pushing her hair out of her face, Coree tucks it behind her ear, locking her eyes with mine. "Your sister thought she was tellin' you the truth, but I haven't always been completely honest with her. There are secrets that even my best friend has no idea about."

I squeeze Coree's hand to let her know that I appreciate her trust in me. Now I'm more than just curious; I'm intrigued. Why is Coree willing to share so much with me but not with my sister?

Taking a deep breath, Coree continues. "I've been MaryAna's best friend since we were in first grade. We've done almost everything together. Her body matured early, and she was one of the most popular girls in our class. Some of my brother's macho football buddies wanted to date her."

"I can see why guys might like my sister," I concede.

"Your sister is beautiful and friendly, JoeE. Guys just naturally love her bubbly personality," Coree says. "On the other hand, I was kinda pretty back then, but I sure wasn't MaryAna. She always seems so happy and carefree and ready to have fun, but I was never that person. I wanted so much to be like her. Some boys must have thought that a good way to get to know your sister was to hang out with me. I craved their attention, never questionin' what they saw in me."

Now really animated, Coree continues to share her memories. "At Mason's fifteenth birthday party, Tyler Richardson and I sneaked away to my bedroom. I really liked him and honestly thought he liked me too. I wanted to show him some of my football stuff. We were sittin' on my bed, lookin' at a sports magazine, when he kissed me right on the lips. Being my first real kiss, I was embarrassed but excited at the same time. Before I got a second one, he asked me if I'd give him MaryAna's cell number."

"That wasn't very cool," I say.

Obviously retaining considerable bitterness toward Tyler, my dream girl says, "I was totally mad and wouldn't talk to him for, like, over a year."

This certainly explains their little verbal jabs at each other at the party.

With a guilty expression spreading across her face, Coree goes on. "Although I never did too much more than kissin' with guys after that, I kinda led MaryAna to believe that a lot more went on. I just wanted her to think that they desired to be with me as much as her. She enjoyed hearing my little fantasies, believin' every word was true."

"Yeah, that's what she told me—that you'd been with a lot of guys."

"The truth is," Coree says as she begins to tear up, "I made most of it up. Sure, I've made out with boys, but I've never slept with any of them. I'm not a slut."

"I believe you," I respond truthfully, giving her a little hug.

When Coree asks if I could get her a glass of water, I recall that my mother asked for the same thing when she was sharing her amazing story back in Fulton. Coree's expression has turned fearful, and she now seems extremely nervous. I begin to get the distinct impression that her secrets go a lot deeper than a few white lies to my sister.

When I return from the kitchen, Coree takes a couple of big gulps. Grabbing a tissue, I wipe away some of her tears. This simple gesture brings a little smile back to her beautiful face.

Hesitantly, she asks, "If I tell you the next part of my story, will you promise not to tell anyone? Not even MaryAna?"

I say, "All right, but under one condition."

"What's the condition?" she asks with a quizzical look.

"Since I'm shy around girls, I'm in desperate need of some kissing lessons," I reply, trying to amuse her a little.

It works. She smiles, asking, "Seriously?"

I nod. "It's the only way that you can buy my silence."

"It's a deal!" Coree agrees with her devilish little grin. My dream girl goes on with her narrative. "About a month before my fourteenth birthday, I had some really rough times."

Taking another swig of water, Coree draws several deep breaths before continuing. "My real mama never called me. Daddy refused to give me her phone number, which pretty much confirmed my fear that she was dead. At one point, I was cryin' for almost two days when Julie came to my bedroom to console me."

A picture of her stepmother trying to comfort a distraught thirteen-year-old flashes through my mind. She is unable to control her tears, and they stream down her face as she continues. "I was only five when Mama left, but I still remembered how she used to hold me when I was sad. Nobody but Mason would talk to me about her. Actually, I could bear the thought of her dying a whole lot easier than thinking she deserted us. What mama would leave her children unless the children deserved it? I was so mixed up."

"I kinda know how you felt," I say, thinking about how I used to desperately long for a mother.

Wiping her eyes once more, Coree goes on. "That's part of the reason why I wanted to talk to you about all this. Maybe you can understand how utterly desperate I felt."

Incredible pain racks Coree's eyes, and it's obvious that her memory of these events is crystal clear. My memories of the night Dad died

147

are just as vivid. The day that she's describing is obviously one of those traumatic times that you just never forget, no matter how hard you try.

I say, "Actually, it was much rougher on you. Your mother left when you were old enough to have memories of her. With me, there was nothing to miss, but I still wanted the love that only a mother can give."

Holding back her tears for a moment, Coree resumes. "I was horrible to my stepmother that day. At one point, I yelled to her on the other side of my locked bedroom door, 'I want my real mama, not *you*! Get away from my room!' I felt more and more abandoned by everyone except Mason and MaryAna. It seemed my whole world was crashing in on me, and I just wanted to die so I could be with Mama."

"That was a long time ago. I'm sure Julie's forgiven you by now," I respond.

Now crying uncontrollably, Coree can't speak. She buries her tear-dampened face into my shoulder. I softly caress her long blond curls, wondering what bad experiences could've driven her into such a depression. What secret is so terrible that even the thought of it can make my dream girl break down like this?

Finally, in a shaky voice, she mutters, "I'm so sorry, JoeE. I shouldn't bother you with all this stuff. Do you understand how messed up I was back then? How I could be so desperate?"

"It isn't that bad, Coree," I tell her reassuringly. "We all go through rough times. Yours was just a bit extreme."

"So you're OK with it?" she asks timidly, like a child who has just broken her mother's favorite vase. "You don't hate me?"

"Of course not," I reassure her again, thinking about the pain and shock of my father's death. "I could never hate you."

"You're so understandin'," Coree says. Seeming relieved, she adds, "Somehow I knew I could tell you."

"Nothing that you have ever done would make me think less of you," I tell her. She's my dream girl, after all.

With my arm wrapped around her shoulder, I squeeze her to emphasize the point. She gazes up into my eyes, smiling as if a heavy burden has just been lifted from her shoulders.

Pressing her lips together and swallowing hard, Coree continues revealing her closely held secrets. "A couple weeks after that horrible day, Julie came along with Mason to talk to me.

"My stepmother told us, 'I don't care what your daddy says, y'all are old enough to know the truth about your mama.' What Julie told us is another secret that you must promise to keep. OK?"

"Your secret is safe with me."

Taking another sip of water, Coree continues, "Julie asked us if we remembered the house fire. We told her that we definitely remembered it."

What in the world is this all about? A house fire? I'm now totally taken aback by Coree's story, yet captivated at the same time.

She finally seems completely over her crying jag, and she enlightens me further. "You see, when I was five and Mason was nearly seven, our parents were separated and we lived with our mama. One night, our house caught fire. Mama and my brother were badly burned, but got out alive."

After a gulp of water, Coree makes eye contact with me again. "Mason was in the hospital for several months and then had to go through a bunch of surgeries."

As if her head is too heavy for her to hold upright, Coree rests it against my shoulder again. "Normally, I remember everything clearly. However, what happened that night is all jumbled up in my head. I'm not sure what's real and what I imagined. Daddy took me to live at his house and later told us about Mama remarrying and moving to Atlanta."

With a little cough to clear her throat, Coree continues, "Julie told us that Daddy was lyin'. My brother asked if Mama died from her burns. Our stepmother told him that she was still alive but never moved to Atlanta and wasn't remarried."

All I can do is sit motionless, completely spellbound as if I were watching a movie or a TV drama. After taking another deep breath as if to build up her courage, Coree reveals, "Julie cautioned us not to let Daddy know that she was tellin' the family secrets. She totally stunned us when she said that Mama was at the Mississippi State Hospital Also know as Whitfield."

"The state hospital?" I ask, not familiar with Mississippi's medical facilities.

Coree sighs. "You see, it's the state mental institution."

Chapter 27

CHERRY CHAP-STICK

Less than an hour ago, I saw Coree Calhoun as a lovely, carefree creature, the object of my hormone-driven desires. Unaware of her troubled past, I failed to recognize a fellow traveler, also lost in a labyrinth of deceit. Although I'm having an onslaught of new feelings that are difficult to explain, there's no longer any doubt that I've fallen in love with the girl of my dreams.

Coree trusting me with such deep, personal secrets draws me even closer to her. Clearly, she's a kindred spirit. We are both haunted by ghosts from the past. Buried under the debris of multiple lies and endless secrets, our lives have become intertwined like grapevines on an arbor.

Fortunately, we bring to the table complementary strengths. Our diverse personalities will help us survive as our uncertain, but parallel, paths merge into one. My dream girl will provide wisdom gained from dealing with intense emotional traumas. Her fire is defrosting my icy demeanor and frozen heart. Meanwhile, I offer calmness in times of stress, crisp logic to assuage her fears, and a deep reservoir of love to comfort her troubled soul.

.To my dream girl, I'm apparently more than an attentive ear or a shoulder to cry on—I may represent salvation from the loneliness of her agonizing secrets. As for me, in the last hour, she's replaced football as my reason for living.

Cheeks flushing, Coree explains, "Julie said that Mama suffered a complete break with reality while she was hospitalized with her burns.

My stepmother said Mama's condition was diagnosed as severe bipolar disorder based upon a long history of manic-depressive behavior."

If Coree's mother suffers with depression, genetics may explain why her daughter was so depressed and crying for days. At the least, it's a viable possibility.

After taking a momentary break, Coree continues her now epic tale: "Julie said that Daddy thinks Mama started the fire. He feels strongly that she was tryin' to kill herself and take us children with her. He convinced a judge to commit her to Whitfield under her maiden name, Martha Jo Booth. He didn't believe that she deserved the Calhoun name any longer. Daddy was granted a divorce and full custody of Mason and me."

Rubbing her eyes, Coree pauses before saying dejectedly, "I'm so ashamed to have a mama who's not only insane, but also may have tried to kill my brother and me." After another long pause and a tissue break, she says, "Over the last couple of years, Mason and I have visited Mama at Whitfield quite a few times. Usually she seems perfectly normal, but she doesn't remember much about the fire. Julie has helped us sneak away to visit her without Daddy findin' out."

Taking another swallow of water, Coree says, "When MaryAna found out that I was sneakin' out, she just assumed that I was with boys. Your sister was worried that I might get pregnant, so I made up the story about Mama gettin' me on the pill. MaryAna already thought that I was sleepin' around, so I just let her keep thinkin' that way. She kept askin' me about what it was like bein' with guys, and I kept makin' up romantic fantasies for her. The truth is that I was ashamed to let your sister know about Mama."

"Coree, it's not your fault that your mother has mental problems," I say.

"It may be that way in New York," she replies, "but I live in Mississippi where *everything* your family does reflects directly on you. Maybe that's why we have so many secrets."

"So, do you have any other ones?" I ask innocently.

Giving me a surprised look and pursing her lips, Coree pauses a moment as if she's evaluating my question, and then she snaps, "You mean other than that I'm really messed up and did a really dumb thing? That my mama is off her rocker and may have tried to kill me? That I sneak off to a mental hospital and make up lies to tell my best friend? That your sister mistakenly believes that I'm on the pill and sleep around? Is that your question?"

Before I can respond, Coree stares at me with those big brown eyes flashing. She counts off on her fingers. "I'm not a movie character, JoeE. I'm not a vampire. I don't know any werewolves. I don't go to a school for magic. I'm not carrying a magic ring. I'm not an expert with a bow and arrow. I don't have a light saber. I can't use the force. I don't possess any superpowers. I don't even dye my hair!"

Recognizing that Coree has cleverly avoided my question about having other secrets, I figure that she has revealed enough for one evening. With a smile, I say, "Well, I believe that about covers it."

Turning the tables on me, she asks, "So, Mr. JoeE, do you have any secrets that you want to share?"

Thinking for a moment, I admit, "Well, I tried to smoke a cigarette and once chugged a whole beer."

Coree waits patiently for me to go on, finally asking, "Is that it?"

"Pretty much. But I didn't like the cigarette. It made me cough a lot," I reply sheepishly. Maybe I should admit the whole story surrounding Paula Worminski, but I don't want to mention her—at least not yet.

"I guess I'll have to start callin' you Mr. Perfect," Coree says, shaking her head slightly. "By the way, I really hate cigarettes. So in the future if you take up smokin', please don't smoke or even light one up around me, OK?"

"I'll never smoke," I tell her honestly. "However, if you being a virgin is a secret, then I do have something to admit."

"Oh, JoeE," Coree says tenderly. "I already figured that out. But you have kissed girls, haven't you?"

"Well, not exactly," I respond sheepishly.

With a genuine smile where the corners of her eyes crinkle slightly, she says sweetly, "You're like a big cuddly teddy bear." Getting up from the couch, she says, "Come on. Let's get something else to drink besides water. There's another bowl game on TV. We can watch it till Mason comes to get his car." She leads the way to the kitchen with me close behind.

"Speaking of kissing," I say, "I've got one more question for you."

She looks at me curiously. This time, I have the devilish grin. "What if I'd taken the first choice? Would you really have made out with me?"

"I guess you'll just have to wonder," my dream girl replies. "Do you think I would've?"

"Maybe," I answer, grinning at her again. "We *do* have some time to kill before Mason gets here."

Looking directly into my eyes, Coree slowly says, "So, Mr. JoeE, you want both choices? That's kinda greedy."

We grab a couple of Dr Peppers from the refrigerator and return to the couch. She reaches into her little purse, removes some lip balm, and tantalizingly applies it.

"Well, sir," she says with a little giggle, "if it wasn't getting so dark outside, we could throw a football around. Of course, I did promise you some kissing lessons, and I always try to keep my promises, no matter how difficult the task. Hopefully, you'll be a good student and behave yourself."

Far too soon for me, Mason arrives to retrieve his car and take Coree home. Before she leaves, my dream girl promises to continue my educational course at another time. For the next half hour, I sit on the couch with the television still tuned to the football game. If anyone had told me a week ago that I wouldn't be interested in a bowl game, I would've thought he was insane. However, back then I didn't know how much I'd like the taste of cherry ChapStick.

When MaryAna and my mother return home, I'm still relaxing on the couch, evaluating the intense events of the last couple of hours. My sister can't wait to show me her purchases. Of course, she bought some items for herself, including a beautiful new dress and a cute little bracelet.

Handing me a small bag, she says excitedly, "Merry Christmas a few days late."

"Does this mean I have to give you a present, Sis?" I say kiddingly.

Giggling, my twin commands, "Just open it, silly." Inside is the latest iPhone. I give my sister and my mother big hugs. "Mama added you to her callin' plan. Now you can text me, JoeE," my sister says, almost giddy with excitement. She must be on a "shopping high."

"And I can now text the girl I'm going with," I quickly add.

My mother jumps in with a tinge of panic in her voice. "You aren't goin' with Coree, are you? You just met her."

Again, I feel that my mother is about to say more. Instead, she rushes off to her bedroom without another word. MaryAna glances at me with that "I told you so" look as we walk back to my room.

I say to my sister, "Thanks for giving Coree and me some time alone. She's really an awesome girl."

"No problemo," MaryAna responds. "Coree told me that y'all needed some private time."

"We needed to talk," I tell MaryAna. "I really don't understand why Mom is so upset. Sure, I just met Coree, but you've known her forever. From what I've seen, you have super-good taste in friends."

"And in everything else," my sister informs me with her haughty little grin and a twist of her shoulders.

"Mom sure seemed extremely upset, almost in panic mode, didn't she?"

"Coree is a Calhoun," MaryAna reminds me. "You know how Mama feels about them."

"Speaking of romantic involvements," I observe, "I noticed that you and Tyler spent some quality time together over at the Calhoun house this afternoon."

"Tyler's sweet," MaryAna admits. "He keeps askin' me to go out. But he usually double dates with Mason and Rachel, so I turn him down." Then she adds, "Maybe I should go out with Tyler. It might make Mason jealous."

"You know, that isn't a good reason to go out with someone, Sis. Maybe you can set up a double date with Tyler, Coree, and me."

Immediately lighting up like a Christmas tree, my twin says, "Brilliant! I can wear the dress that I just bought. How about dinner and a movie? I need to make plans!"

Someday, my sister is likely to be some kind of social director. For now, I don't know whether she's more excited about going on a date with Tyler or showing off her new clothes, but I suspect the latter.

Chapter 28
A HISTORY LESSON

On Saturday morning, I wake up at my usual time, eager to face my exciting new world. Finishing my exercises quickly, I decide to take a day off from running, since it's raining quite heavily. Instead, I'll do some research about the history of my new hometown. Using the Internet, I find plenty of information.

Prior to the arrival of white settlers, the area around the present-day city was very active with more than fifty American Indian villages. The current city was founded in 1829 and named after Gerard C. Brandon, the first native-born governor of the territory. About thirty years later during the long Civil War, Vicksburg was a major target of the Union army. Before attacking the stronghold on the river, General Ulysses S. Grant needed to capture the city of Jackson. After several battles around central Mississippi, Grant burned the capital city before laying siege to Vicksburg. With only chimneys remaining of many buildings in Jackson, it earned the unenviable nickname of Chimneyville.

Brandon was also looted and burned at the same time by one of Grant's top commanders, General Sherman. Later, Sherman's infamous "March to the Sea" would make his name synonymous with terror in the South. A statue at the center of Brandon's town square was erected to mark the spot where the despised Yankee soldiers stacked their rifles when they occupied the town. Like much of the South, Mississippi has many reminders of those terrible years.

Over the last century and a half, Brandon has earned a proud reputation as the "city of red hills laden with golden opportunities."

The "red hills" refer to the rust-colored clay soil that dominates the landscape. Supposedly, Brandon has produced more governors, senators, congressmen, judges, district attorneys, physicians, and teachers than any other town in the state.

The phenomenal success of my new hometown is normally attributed to its excellent public school system. If this information is correct, I'll be attending a school that offers a quality education for all the students in the city. So much for the movies portraying Mississippi as uneducated.

Since the year 2000, Brandon has grown by about 30 percent to a population of over twenty-two thousand, which is 86 percent white, 12 percent black, and 2 percent indicated as "other." It has a much more positive economic outlook and certainly more racial diversity than Fulton does.

Glad to know a little bit more about my new hometown, I close the laptop and pick up my new phone to text Coree. Less than a minute after hitting SEND, my phone rings.

Answering, I hear the sweet voice on the other end say, "Hey, JoeE."

"Coree? Why are you up so early?" I blurt, wondering if she's a morning person like me.

"I usually get up early. This mornin' I've been talkin' to your sister," Coree enlightens me. "We're tryin' to decide on everything we're goin' to wear tonight on the double date with Tyler."

I can't believe that my sister is awake too. Apparently, this date is like a quest for her. MaryAna must be in the back bathroom, as I've not heard a sound from her room.

"Has she talked to Tyler yet?" I ask, wondering if he has been made aware of the big plans.

"No, not yet."

"What if he already has plans?" I ask with concern.

"Are you kiddin'?" Coree laughs. "Tyler will drop anything for a date with MaryAna. That boy's been tryin' to get with her forever."

"Well," I say, pretending to be hurt, "so I guess my sister got to ask you out on our first date."

"Oh, JoeE, I'm sorry," Coree says. "You can ask me now if you wish. I'll pretend that I know absolutely nothin' about it. There, I've deleted it from my memory." I can hear a little smile in her voice.

In the most Southern accent that I'm able to muster, I ask, "Miss Coree Calhoun, will you give me the great honor of accompanyin' me to the movie theater this evenin'?"

I hear her giggle.

Sounding as if she were on the porch of her daddy's plantation sipping a mint julep, Coree replies, "Why, yes sir, Mr. Collins. I'd be most honored and so delighted to accompany y'all to the movie theater this evenin'."

We laugh as if someone just told us the most hilarious joke. Love must make laughter bubble up, like pouring a warm Coke over ice.

After an hour-long conversation about nothing, really, in which Coree does most of the talking, I reluctantly get off the phone. After showering, I sit down at the dining room table to eat my usual breakfast of orange juice and cereal. In a few minutes, MaryAna comes flying by, heading back toward her bedroom. She has upgraded her morning wardrobe to pajamas with fairy tale characters on them and slippers that resemble bunnies. Now she looks like a six-year-old.

My sister stops long enough to say, "Good mornin', Brother," as she gives me a sisterly peck on the cheek.

"I hear that you've been busy."

"Busy, busy. Gotta hurry. Workin' on jewelry now. Only ten hours to get ready."

"I'm going over to the Calhoun Castle this afternoon to watch a football game with Coree and her father," I say. "What time do I need to be home?"

"About five," MaryAna says. "I'll carry you over there. Just let me know when you're fixin' to leave."

"Thanks, Sis. Are you sure you have time to work me in? Remember, you *only* have ten hours left," I say, having now resigned myself to the fact that "nobody walks in Brandon."

Ignoring my sarcasm again, my twin rubs in the fact that she's six minutes older than I am. "Of course I'll make time for my precious little brother. Coree will figure out a ride back here for both of you. When you get home, I'll have some clothes laid out for you. I'll make sure that you have everything your little pea-pickin' heart desires."

"I'm not a Ken doll, you know," I say. "I can pick out my own clothes."

"Yeah, right!" is all I get out of my sister as she disappears into the inner sanctum of her bedroom.

She shuts her door before I'm able to object further, so I just shake my head in frustration, as usual. My sister seems to live in her own fantasy world where everything is either perfect or she'll endeavor to make it that way. MaryAna obviously tries to achieve perfection in herself, her clothing, her friends, her life, and now, her brother. Heaven help her when her little fantasy world inevitably comes tumbling down.

My mother is now awake and joins me at the dining room table. "Did I hear that you're goin' to watch a game at the Calhoun Castle this afternoon?" Mom asks.

After her negative comments last night, I expect her next question to be, "Aren't you spendin' too much time at her house, JoeE?"

Instead, Mom surprises me by saying, "I'm glad that you are gettin' along so well with the Calhoun crew. MaryAna tells me that y'all are goin' to the movies tonight."

"Yes," I tell her cautiously, "we're going with Tyler Richardson and Coree." I intentionally don't use the word "date."

"That sounds wonderful, dear," Mom says cheerfully. "I think that your sister should see more of Tyler, don't you? He seems like such a nice young man."

Is she kidding? Last night, my mother asked me, "You aren't goin' with Coree, are you?" Yet today, she wants my sister to "see more of Tyler." Is Mom implying that I'm less mature than the leader of the Airhead Twins is?

Chapter 29

LITTLE BLACK DRESS

By the time MaryAna drives me to the Calhoun Castle, the heavy rain has stopped. The iron-gray skies indicate that the showers could resume at any moment. I notice that the beer cans are gone from my sister's cup holder. Since my mother rode to the mall with my sister yesterday, I suspect that MaryAna cleaned out her car.

Getting out of the car, I thank her for the ride. My sister tells me to have fun and that she'll see me later. I let her know that Coach Calhoun has offered to give Coree and me a ride back after the game on his way to restock his beer supply. She has a guilty little grin as she drives off to her tanning bed appointment.

Turning toward the large house, I see Coree at the front door with an inviting smile. She's wearing a maroon-and-white Mississippi State football jersey. Goose bumps cover my body as my excitement meter goes off the scale. Is she a modern-day Helen of Troy, the face that launched a thousand passes?

Walking to the door, I see that my dream girl is also wearing white tennis shorts and socks that reach the middle of her calves. She has on the same pink tennis shoes, headband, and wristbands that she wore the day I met her. Making a mental note, I decide that future presents should be pink.

Entering the house, I hardly manage to get out, "Hi, Coree," before she greets me with a tight embrace, locks her lips onto mine, and practically jumps into my arms. The feel of her moist lips is a greeting that certainly requires no words.

However, I'm totally embarrassed once again when I notice that Coach Calhoun is watching us from his recliner with a rather dour expression. It appears that his daughter's exuberant greeting doesn't meet with his approval. Fearing that we may be in store for an understandable rebuke, I at least expect a cautionary warning of some sort.

Surprisingly, Coach Calhoun's expression quickly shifts to a friendly smile as if he isn't upset by his daughter's behavior. Coree extends the long kiss, acting as if we were totally alone, not in plain view of her father. The whole scene confuses me, but I'm certainly not going to complain about such an awesome greeting.

As he stands up to shake hands, Coach Calhoun says almost gratefully, "It's nice that you could come over and give an old coach some company, JoeE." Settling back into his recliner, he motions for me to sit down on the couch beside him, commanding his daughter, "Get your men something to drink, darlin'."

Replying obediently like a well-coached player, Coree says "Yes, sir." She turns to me. "Do you want tea, JoeE? I just brewed some up fresh."

Recalling the tasty, sweetened iced tea that I drank the last time that I was at their home, I reply with a smile, "Iced tea, please."

"Be right back," Coree says, bouncing off to the kitchen in a seemingly carefree mood. To see her today, you'd never know that she was the same girl who wept on my shoulder last night.

Coach Calhoun tells me, "Well, it's just the three of us today. Everybody else has abandoned us, off doin' their own thing."

In a couple of minutes, Coree returns with giant glasses of tea for us and a small cooler filled with beers for her father.

"Let me help you," I offer when I see her loaded down with the drinks.

"Thanks," she replies, giving me a little peck on my cheek. We settle in to watch another bowl game.

My grandfather told me that when he was my age, there were only about a half dozen bowls each year, almost all on New Year's Day. Now there are a gazillion of them, starting in the middle of December. It seems that every time they added a bowl game, Papa added an inch of snow to his story about walking to school in Fulton.

Unlike my last visit to the Calhoun Castle, Coach starts talking and making comments about plays in the game right from the start. He asks me several probing questions while I keep my answers as short as possible. I'm in my element when talking football, but after a while, I realize that I'm practically ignoring Coree.

Although her father doesn't direct any of his questions to her, my dream girl is intently watching the game as well as following our discussion. For someone who has never played the sport, she appears to be extremely interested in what we're saying but offers no comment.

Trying to work Coree into the conversation, I turn to her when one of the teams takes a sack on a third down. "What do you think about that play?"

Scrunching her cute little nose, my girlfriend thinks for only a second. "The right defensive end has been givin' them trouble all game. If they would've had the motion man chip on him, the quarterback would've had plenty of time to hit the slot receiver as he dragged across beneath the linebackers. They dropped far too deep on a third and five."

"Wow, impressive," I blurt out. Most people would've called what she said gibberish. I heard a sweet symphony. It's obvious that she knows her football.

Looking at me seriously, Coree asks, "You know I'm right, don't you?"

Just nodding with a big smile, I acknowledge that she's absolutely correct. I could've driven a bus in front of those linebackers. Coach Calhoun takes another swig of his beer and again completely ignores her. Maybe this is his unspoken punishment for her passionate little greeting at the front door.

At halftime, her father and I raid the fridge. After joining us for a quick bite, Coree says that she'll be upstairs during the second half of the game.

"I want to make myself beautiful for tonight," Coree proclaims. "Your sister is doin' the same for Tyler."

As she's leaving the kitchen, Coach Calhoun says, "I heard Tyler and Mason talkin' earlier about goin' to a monster truck show at the Coliseum. Sounds like they've been looking forward to it for a while."

"No, Daddy," Coree tells her father. "Tyler cancelled those plans and is goin' to the movies with MaryAna and us." Apparently, Coree is right. Tyler will drop anything for a date with MaryAna.

Coach Calhoun and I watch the second half of the bowl game by ourselves. It seems like Coach is enjoying himself more without his daughter's presence. Between plays, he tells me some rather wild stories from his days playing football.

After the game ends, Coach gets up from his recliner and turns to me. "Next time I'm in my office at school, I'll get you a copy of our playbook."

"Thanks, Coach," I say enthusiastically, getting off the couch.

Coach Calhoun continues, "I'm now more of an administrator myself. I've got two darn good assistant coaches: JJ Butler and Sammy Brantley. After you have a chance to look over our plays, I'll set up a little sit-down so you can meet them. JJ can answer any of your questions. We're always open to fresh ideas for our team."

I'm pleased that Coach Calhoun is that impressed with my football knowledge.

Having no idea how long she's been there listening to us, I notice Coree just standing on the stairs. I've always wondered why an already-beautiful girl thinks that some makeup, clothes, hair styling, and jewelry will make her more beautiful. Seeing my dream girl, I wonder no more. Now she not only gives me goose bumps, but the vision before me completely takes my breath away.

Having gone upstairs as a cute teenager, Coree reappears as a radiant super model, confidence now oozing from every pore. Apparently, her knowing smile indicates she received the acknowledgment of her beauty that she desired from my open-mouth stare.

She descends the staircase wearing a sleeveless black dress. The dress comes down to a couple of inches above her knees, leaving visible an ample stretch of shapely, tanned legs. Wearing black, high-heeled, strappy sandals, Coree is carrying a black velvet jacket with a matching black purse. Wide gold bracelets adorn her wrists, and dainty dangle earrings and an exquisite black-pearl necklace complete her transformation.

In a masterpiece of understated elegance, my dream girl's hair is nothing like her normal ponytail. Blond curls sweep across the top of her forehead and disappear behind her head, emerging as cascading golden locks that softly brush against her almost-bare shoulders. Her sparkling dark-brown eyes seem even larger and brighter than usual.

As Coree descends the stairs, I'm afraid they might just melt beneath her feet.

Chapter 30

SPEAKING FRENCH

Coach Calhoun barely spares a glance at his stunning daughter. He asks, "Coree, are you goin' to the movies or an opera?"

"Daddy!" she answers coyly. "I'm just tryin' to look pretty for JoeE on our first date. Don't you think I look nice?"

"Well, it's definitely an improvement over those outfits you used to wear," her father says gruffly, grabbing a beer for the road.

Apparently taking his comment as a backhanded compliment, she says, "Thanks. You know this was Mama's black-pearl necklace. Julie gave it to me. Isn't it surprising that Mama left it behind when she moved to Atlanta?"

Coach Calhoun ignores her question, grimacing as he heads to the door. As my date descends the last few stairs, I put out my arm just as Jack did for Rose in *Titanic*. Smiling, Coree takes my arm, and we stroll out of Cinderella's castle.

We drive to my house in Coach Calhoun's red Ford pickup truck, which has various Bulldog decals plastered all over it. The radio is blaring some country music, but I'm unfamiliar with the song. He proudly informs me that this truck is his "Country Cadillac."

Getting out, I thank him for the lift. He waves and says, "It's nice to have someone to watch the games with besides Coree. Come over anytime."

"I will, Coach," I mumble as he shifts his truck into reverse. My head is now filled only with thoughts of Coree. She's so close I can see the pulse flutter in her throat and feel the heat radiate from her bare arm, which is almost touching mine. She's lit up like a black-clad angel in the truck's headlights as her father backs the truck out of our driveway. My pulse matches hers as we walk toward the front door of my home, hand in hand.

Drawing in deep breaths of the crisp night air, I embed the scene next to my fondest memories. A slight breeze delicately scents the air with the heady aroma of her honeysuckle perfume, making me wish this moment could last forever.

As her father disappears down the highway, I break the silence. "It was nice of you to keep us company during the first half of the game today."

"Nice?" she says rather sharply. "I love watchin' football as much as Daddy. I wish that girls could be on the football team."

"Maybe you'll get a chance to play sometime," I say, trying to take the edge off her obvious resentment.

My patronizing comment only infuriates her as she adds bitterly, "I can run a pass pattern just as good as Tyler, maybe better. I can catch a football and take pain as well as any player on Daddy's team!"

Gulping hard, I attempt to change the subject. "By the way, you look awesome tonight."

"Thank you, sir." She adds jokingly, "I wore black to match my evil reputation."

Smiling, I nod. "I guess that your reputation is no better than the poor girl's in *The Scarlet Letter*."

Mischievously, Coree replies, "Maybe I'll just sew a giant *A* onto the front of my dress like that girl in *Easy A*." Laughing, I visualize her stunning dress with an enormous red letter on the front.

Entering the house, I walk back to my bedroom to change clothes while Coree disappears into MaryAna's room to check on her progress. Catching a quick shower, I shave again, and put on the outfit set out for me, actually liking the choice. When I finish getting ready, I duck into the kitchen to get something to drink, and then sit down at the dining room table. My mother is there, busily punching keys on her laptop.

"What are you doing, Mom?" I ask.

"I'm just sendin' your grandparents an e-mail, honey," she replies, looking up from her keyboard.

"Could you please ask Papa about getting me a car sometime soon?"

"Actually, dear," Mom informs me, "that's one of the topics that I've been discussin' with him. Maybe tomorrow we can sit down and talk about it if you have a few minutes."

I smile. "I believe that I might be able to fit you in on my busy social calendar. Let me check with my sister, who schedules my appointments."

My mother grins at me as the door to MaryAna's room swings open. Emerging from my sister's room, Coree clears her throat loudly.

She sweeps her hand in an upward arc, announcing, "May I present Miss Mary Anabella Lindley-Collins." Apparently, my twin has updated her friend on her legal name.

As my sister struts out of her room, I have my second vision of stunning beauty for the day. MaryAna's hair is parted in the middle, curves around her face, and then comes to rest on her bare shoulders. This elegant hairstyle seems to accent her sparkling blue eyes.

The way MaryAna enters the living room reminds me of a scene from the Harry Potter movie, *Goblet of Fire*, when Hermione makes a spectacular entrance at the Yule Ball. Hermione has transformed herself into such an amazing beauty that one of her best friends, Ron, initially fails to recognize her. My twin has undergone a similar transformation.

Like Coree, MaryAna is wearing high-heeled sandals, but they are silver to match her necklace, earrings, and a thin bracelet on her left wrist. She's holding a small purse and a little jacket, both of which match her cranberry-red sleeveless dress, which has a rather revealing neckline. Suddenly, an extremely weird thought shoots through my brain. If we were identical twins, would I look like that? Thankfully, the doorbell rings, shaking the thought away.

Peeking out the window, my sister says, "It's Tyler." When she opens the door, her date's jaw drops slightly. From the expression on his face, I know that he's having the same reaction to my sister that I had to

Coree. As he steps backward to let her out the door, he almost falls into the bushes. The poor boy is suffering from beauty shock.

Coree and I say good-bye to Mom and leisurely walk outside. Tyler's older-model, dark-gray Ford is parked next to MaryAna's shiny new Malibu. Later, I learn that he's worked a part-time job for a couple years just to afford any vehicle at all. He's very proud to have a car of his own and tries to keep it immaculate, despite its age.

Tyler says, "MaryAna, I suppose you wanna take your car?"

My sister pleasantly surprises me when she answers, "No, Tyler, let's take yours. I've always liked ridin' in it."

His face lights up like a kid opening a Christmas present. Beaming, he tells her, "Sure, we can take mine if you want."

When I glance at Coree, she gives me a little wink of acknowledgment. We both know that MaryAna parked her car outside the garage with the full intention of taking it tonight. Why, then, did my sister change her mind? Possibly, she wanted to reward Tyler for his shocked, slack-jawed response to her considerable efforts to enhance her natural beauty. Whatever the reason, by asking to ride in his car, my sister just made Tyler's day—or maybe even his week, month, and year.

We talk and joke during the ten-mile-or-so drive to the movie theater. It seems like I've known them forever. Tyler is really funny, and the girls are their usual "crazy" selves. The theater is a vast multiplex with about twenty movie choices. Apparently, MaryAna has decided that Coree and I will see a different flick than she and Tyler will see. Going along with the plan, I buy some popcorn and drinks before we head to our theater.

"Is the back OK?" Coree asks, leading us to a couple of seats in the last row, far from the few others in the theater.

"Sure," I whisper back, realizing that perhaps she wants a place where we can be alone.

When the movie starts, I put my arm around her shoulder, and she snuggles up against me. The beginning of the action/adventure film is decent, but it quickly deteriorates into too much action and not enough adventure. Reaching for some popcorn, I notice that Coree is staring at me rather than at the screen.

I whisper, "What's wrong?"

She whispers back, "Nothin'. I just wanna look at you."

Smiling, I ask softly, "Don't you like the movie?"

"Nope," she says, not really surprising me. "It's kinda stupid. They lost me when the aliens blew up the Eiffel Tower."

"Oh," I say. "It is pretty lame."

Responding by snuggling up even closer, Coree whispers in my ear, "Since they're in France, maybe I should give you French lessons."

"I didn't know you spoke French."

As she looks at me with that devilish smile, I suddenly get her drift. Needless to say, I don't see much more of the film. Although still unable to speak French, by the time we leave, I have a new appreciation for their customs.

Leaving the theater, Coree and I talk about movies we've seen as well as books we've read recently. When I mention *The Hunger Games*, I'm surprised that she knows it's based upon the Greek myth about Theseus and the Minotaur. However, when I learn that she's familiar not only with Greek mythology but with the Peloponnesian War, I'm flabbergasted. There's no doubt that we'll never lack for things to discuss.

On the ride back, the four of us stop at a restaurant called Fernando's. As we munch on homemade chips and salsa, I look over the extensive menu of nachos, tacos, burritos, enchiladas, and other enticing cuisine from south of the border. Tapping me on the arm, Coree informs me that Fernando's makes the best fajitas in the world. We order the mixed fajitas for two.

After placing our order with the friendly server, I ask my date curiously, "By the way, what's a fajita?"

The three of them look at me as if I have two heads. "You've never eaten fajitas?" my twin sister asks incredulously.

"No. In fact, I've never been to a Mexican restaurant before tonight. We don't have one in Fulton. I've heard that there is one in Oswego. It's about a dozen miles away from where I lived, but I've never been there."

Coree asks, "Don't you even have a Taco Bell? What about Chinese restaurants, or Mongolian or Greek?"

"No Taco Bell, but we have a new Chinese takeout and an Italian restaurant," I inform her.

Tyler, who has not said much since he started devouring the chips and salsa, joins the interrogation. "Does Fulton have McDonald's, Wendy's, Burger King, and pizza places?"

Before I can answer, MaryAna jumps in. "Tyler, don't be silly. You can't be a city in America if you don't have those places."

I'm not sure where my sister learned that "fact." However, envisioning the multitude of fast-food restaurants across our nation, she might actually be right.

Coree asks, "So all Fulton has is fast food, pizza, an Italian restaurant, and Chinese takeout?"

"No," I say, coming to Fulton's defense. "There are diners, other restaurants, and three Dunkin' Donuts. Also, some of the bars serve food."

The other three teenagers have looks of curiosity. Tyler asks, "What's a diner?"

When our meal is served, it interrupts our interesting comparison of the cuisines available in Fulton and Brandon. The fajitas are served on a red-hot, cast-iron skillet placed upon a wooden holder. Billows of smoke rise from the fiery-hot metal as it sears the meat and veggies.

"Be careful. That's *really* hot," the server warns, placing the sizzling fajitas on the table between Coree and me.

"They smell incredible," I tell them enthusiastically as my mouth begins to water in anticipation of my first bite. "If they taste half as good as they smell, I'm in for a real treat." It turns out that I'm wrong—they taste twice as good as they smell. "Fulton definitely needs a Mexican restaurant!" I exclaim.

As we eat, Coree finally answers Tyler's question. "Diners are like those places where they eat in old movies. Remember Xan's restaurant on Lakeland Drive?"

"Yep," Tyler answers in between bites of his tacos. "I went to a birthday party there. We blew toothpicks through straws and stuck 'em into the ceilin' tiles."

"Well," Coree explains, "they were tryin' to make it look like an old diner. Obviously, it was new. JoeE's Fulton has the real thing, just like in the movies."

Trying to grasp the concept, Tyler says, "I got it. We have new things of their old things." Then he asks, "Do you think they'll ever build any bars in Brandon?"

It's now my turn to look incredulous. "You mean that you don't have bars here?"

Seeming annoyed, MaryAna says, "Nope, and we'll never have bars if the churches have anything to do with it. Legalizing liquor sales comes up for a vote again next year."

As the other two eat, Coree explains that it's been only recently that restaurants in Brandon were allowed to serve beer and wine. She also says that a few years ago, this county was completely "dry." No alcoholic beverages were sold. At one time, it was necessary for her father to drive into Jackson even to buy beer.

"What's the drinking age in Mississippi?" I ask, catching my sister's eyes. MaryAna looks away quickly, avoiding my stare.

"It's twenty-one," Coree informs me, "like every place else, I suppose."

My date says that she doesn't drink but has some friends who do.

Although I don't know about Tyler, I suspect that my sister is one of those friends. My twin and her date now seem far more interested in their meals than in the conversation about drinking. Explaining to Coree that there were always plenty of alcoholic beverages at our apartment and at my grandparents' home, I admit that I've tried beer, wine, and whiskey. However, I believe that all of them taste so bad that I definitely have no desire to be much of a drinker. Apparently, I'm not much of an Irishman.

My dream girl says that her favorite eating place in Brandon is a Greek restaurant called Kismets. Hearing the restaurant mentioned, MaryAna reminds Coree of a night when they attended a dinner theater there. Apparently, the girls had a fabulous time and even won T-shirts for solving the "whodunit" mystery that was presented that night.

Tyler asks, "Are those the T-shirts that say 'The Detectives' on the back?"

MaryAna answers, "Those are the ones. They were out of all the adult sizes, so we have to squeeze into them."

"Those shirts are amazin'," Tyler says between bites. "JoeE, you need to see them. They make the girls look like they belong in *Playboy*!"

"Tyler Richardson!" MaryAna scolds him as if he were her child. "What are you doin' readin' that magazine?"

Before Tyler can answer, Coree says, "Tyler doesn't read; he just looks at the pictures!"

Not fazed by either the scolding or the sarcasm, Tyler goes back to his meal. On the other hand, I'm now visualizing my dream girl in an undersized green T-shirt. I agree with Tyler; she looks amazing!

Chapter 31

TICKETS FOR SERVICES

After finishing dinner, we take Coree home. On the way, she and I make plans for her to come to my house on Sunday afternoon to watch the NFL games. Arriving at Calhoun Castle, I walk her to the door and kiss her good night. What starts out as a simple kiss quickly develops into a very passionate embrace. We finally break apart, and I return to Tyler's car.

As I get into his vehicle, my sister can't resist making a snide comment. "You two need to get a room."

I ignore her, but Tyler says, "*We* could get a room, MaryAna."

"In your wildest dreams," my fiery sister says emphatically.

"Have you been eavesdropping on my dreams, MaryAna?" he asks, causing me to let out a little laugh.

"You can both just go to Hades as far as I'm concerned," my flustered sister blurts out as we continue to chuckle. Quickly recovering, MaryAna changes the subject. "JoeE," she asks, "are you goin' to church with Mama and me tomorrow?"

Since moving here, I haven't thought about attending church. While living in Fulton, I occasionally accompanied my grandparents to the nearby Catholic Church, but it was just a polite gesture to please them. My mother told me that she and my sister were Baptists. Attending a service to please my new family seems reasonable.

"Sure," I agree, but I can't help my lack of enthusiasm.

"Awesome," MaryAna says cheerfully, seeming extremely pleased that I'm willing to make the effort.

Of course, my sister seems to do everything in an extreme manner. It's another example of how different we are. I'm much more calm and cautious. My bold move to Mississippi was completely out of character.

I ask hopefully, "Will Coree be at the Baptist church?"

"No," MaryAna answers matter-of-factly. "She's a Methodist. For a while she went with me. Now she usually goes with her brother to their church."

"Oh," I respond, actually having no idea what the difference is between a Baptist and a Methodist. In Fulton, Catholicism is the predominant religion, and they normally refer to all other Christian denominations simply as Protestant. Papa says that he was taught that Roman Catholicism is the "one true religion." I suppose that all the other religions believe that theirs is the true one. I don't see how they all can be right.

"JoeE, I'll lay out some of your new clothes for you in the morning," MaryAna tells me.

Tyler teases, "Aw, does little JoeE need his sister to pick out his clothes for him?"

"Hush!" MaryAna snaps. "I just want JoeE to look nice for Mama. By the way, Tyler, you could use someone pickin' out your clothes too. Maybe Lainey could help."

"Do you want the job?"

"Sure," my sister says. "If you burn all your clothes and let me pick out the new ones."

Tyler comes right back with, "As soon as I sign a major-league baseball contract, we'll do just that."

"OK," MaryAna agrees. "You sign a contract, and I'll go shoppin' for the clothes. When you play in the World Series, you need to have tickets for Mama, JoeE, Coree, Mason, and me waitin' at the box office."

Thinking for a moment, Tyler responds, "No problem. But don't you think that five tickets is a little expensive for your services? Maybe you could throw in some little extra personal perks."

"And just what do you suggest?" MaryAna asks as we pull into our driveway.

Seeing that this matter will require some serious negotiations, I thank Tyler for driving and leave him and my sister to work out the details of their contract. Negotiating unpurchased clothes, imaginary World Series tickets, and heaven only knows what else may take them some time.

Reaching the front door, I hear music. Mom is sitting at her piano in the dining room, and melodic tones emanate as her fingers caress the keys. This is the first time I've heard her play, and I'm extremely impressed.

"Did you have fun?" Mom asks, looking up when she notices me but continuing to play.

"I had an awesome time," I answer. "I had fajitas for the first time. They were amazing, almost as wonderful as your music."

Mom stops playing, turns toward me, and smiles at the compliment. She says, "You must have eaten at Fernando's."

A moment later, MaryAna comes storming through the door, fuming. "Oh! That Tyler Richardson is sooo darn frustratin'."

I tease her, saying, "Yeah, I like him too."

My sister glares at me, throws her little jacket over her shoulder, and struts off to her bedroom without saying another word to either of us.

"What was that about?" my mother asks, looking perplexed.

"I don't think that Tyler was offering enough World Series tickets for MaryAna's wardrobe services," I offer as an explanation.

"Huh?" Mom is still confused.

"I believe that MaryAna likes Tyler but just won't admit it, even to herself," I explain more adequately.

Mom exclaims, "Thank God!"

This strikes me as a very strange response, especially from someone who thinks that I shouldn't be going out with Coree.

"Speaking of God," I say, "MaryAna wants me to accompany you guys to church tomorrow. What time do we leave?"

"Are you only goin' to the worship service or to Sunday school also?"

I've heard of Sunday school, but I've never attended one. "MaryAna didn't say, but I suppose both," I tell her.

"Then we'll leave around 9:30." She pauses for a moment and then asks, "Do you really want to attend church with us, sweetie?"

"Not really," I admit, "but MaryAna seems to be excited that I'm going. Don't you want me to go?"

"Whatever you want is fine, honey," she says, avoiding the question. "I know MaryAna is lookin' forward to showin' you off to her friends."

I begin to wonder if I've agreed to participate in a religious ceremony or a social event.

Changing the subject again, I ask Mom tentatively, "Is it OK if Coree comes over tomorrow afternoon and watches the football games with me?"

"Of course, dear. Coree will always be welcome here." My mother pats the piano bench beside her. "Come sit by me, baby."

I sit down on the bench, expecting to listen to my mother play. Instead, Mom asks, "Would you like to learn a duet?"

"Sure," I tell her, "but I don't know the first thing about playing a piano."

"I'll teach you," she says sweetly. "Have you ever heard the song, 'Heart and Soul'? It's great for two people to play."

"Wasn't that the song the Tom Hanks character and his boss played on that giant piano in the movie *Big*? They were in the toy store and played it by dancing on it."

"That's the song," Mom confirms. As she teaches me some basic piano terminology, I feel that I'm not only adjusting well to my new life here in Brandon, but that it's far exceeding my expectations.

Chapter 32

A BIBLE LESSON

Sunday morning, I awaken early but don't get up right away. I lie there wishing that I could relive yesterday over and over again. On my run this morning, my friendly blue jay is waiting in his favorite tree. I apologize for not coming by yesterday, but my "it was raining" excuse seems weak. He seems to accept my apology like a true friend, as evidenced by another wonderful little concert.

After a leisurely breakfast, I call my grandparents. I know that whether in Brandon, Fulton, or any other place in America, Sunday is church day. Following an enjoyable conversation about bowl games, beautiful girls, and fajitas, I text some of my friends in Fulton. Next, I check e-mails, Facebook, and exchange several texts with Coree. I'm amazed at how this new world of communication keeps me busy.

Like a stealthy fashion coordinator, my sister has laid out my clothes without me even noticing her. A stylish yet conservative light-brown jacket with pants to match, a cream-colored shirt, and a striped tie appear on the back of the recliner. Brown leather shoes with matching socks are next to the chair. At least for now, she's allowing me select my own underwear.

Promptly at 9:30, Mom says it's time to leave. Of course, MaryAna is not quite ready, and it's another fifteen minutes before she's good to go. Both my sister and my mother are wearing modest yet attractive dresses. The weather is sunny but a bit chilly, so they both have light jackets that coordinate with their outfits.

I shiver recalling the bone-chilling cold I endured accompanying my grandparents to church just a few days ago. Everyone at church that day was bundled up in a heavy overcoat. People could've been wearing their Sunday best or just pajamas under their coats for all I could tell.

When we arrive at the Baptist church, I notice that nearly everyone is dressed up, at least by Fulton standards. MaryAna begins introducing me to people around our age so fast that I'm forgetting their names as quickly as I'm hearing them. Several of the girls have double names like Krista Marie, Avery Amber, and Bonnie Lee.

After the many hurried introductions, we proceed to a small classroom, where more than two dozen teenagers are milling around talking. My sister explains that there are Sunday school classes for each grade through high school, and normally one for boys and another for girls. She informs me that the woman who usually teaches the sophomore girls just had a baby, so for a few weeks, the classes for our age group have been combined.

I recognize several teenagers that I met only minutes before. However, matching names to faces is difficult. Several of the guys look like athletes, as their well-defined neck muscles indicate considerable time spent in a weight room. Several girls flash smiles in my direction, which I return. I'm probably lucky that Coree is a Methodist and not here to monitor me.

While MaryAna talks to an extremely attractive girl with brown hair, who I believe is named Bonnie Lee Wilson, I notice a man almost my height entering the room. Leading me over to him, my sister introduces me to Brother James, the Sunday school teacher.

Everyone finds a seat, and Brother James instructs us to open our Bibles to Leviticus, chapter 18, verse 6.

With a rustling of pages, everyone complies. Looking on with MaryAna, I listen as Brother James explains that the day's Bible lesson is about incest and how it's crystal clear that incestuous relationships are strictly forbidden.

Oh, great. Just what I've always wanted to learn about on a Sunday morning—or any morning, for that matter.

After pausing to make sure that the entire class has located the passage, Brother James continues. "In this verse, the term *uncover nakedness* means havin' sexual relations. As you've learned in other lessons, holy Scripture often uses phrases that are no longer in common use today."

My sister holds her small King James Bible where I can see the passage. Brother James begins slowly reading the text in a manner that allows everyone to follow along easily:

6: None of you shall approach anyone who is near kin to him, to uncover his nakedness: I am the LORD.

7: The nakedness of your father, or the nakedness of your mother, shalt thou not uncover: you shall not uncover, she is your mother; you shalt not uncover her nakedness.

8: The nakedness of your father's wife you shall not uncover: it is your father's nakedness.

9: The nakedness of your sister, the daughter of your father, or daughter of your mother, whether born at home, or elsewhere their nakedness you shall not uncover.

After reading the passage, Brother James explains that the following few verses expand on the prohibition of sex with other close relatives, such as aunts and uncles. He then opens the class up to questions, and that leads to a frank and lively discussion. The questions center primarily on cousins.

I'm expecting to hear some Jeff Foxworthy "you know you're a redneck" jokes about family trees with no branches or picking up girls at family reunions, but apparently the church setting encourages even teenagers to act somewhat restrained. Explaining that most states, including Mississippi, ban marriage between first cousins, Brother James surprises me with his next statement: New York and California allow such a practice. Needless to say, I don't contribute anything to the discussion.

Posing a hypothetical question, Bonnie Lee asks, "If you don't know that someone is a close relative, is it a sin to get with them?" Before Brother James is able to answer, she adds, "Like MaryAna didn't know that she had a brother until just recently. If she had, say, met

JoeE in college and they, well, you know…" She didn't finish, but we all knew what she meant.

Considering the possibility of the situation she just described, I find her question both interesting and embarrassing. What if Dad hadn't died? I might have met MaryAna somewhere. I doubt that I'd have been attracted to her. Of course, there I go assuming again.

I realize that over the last few months, my sister has told her friends all about the unusual circumstances surrounding our upbringing. Beginning to feel extremely self-conscious, I slouch down in my chair, wishing that I could melt away. If MaryAna hadn't told anyone about having a twin brother, my sudden appearance would now need explanation. That might be even more embarrassing. I suppose that I've been the topic of gossip in Brandon for months.

Brother James ponders Bonnie Lee's question. Finally, he says in a scholarly tone, "Although ordinarily ignorance doesn't excuse breaking the law, I feel sure that God is merciful in extraordinary circumstances."

Of course, his answer makes no sense whatsoever. God is supposed to be merciful in all circumstances, not just extraordinary ones. As I've noticed with difficult religious questions, the answer usually involves reliance upon God to sort out the messes that mankind creates. Maybe that's the way it should be. Let the Almighty handle the tough stuff, as he's much better equipped than we mere mortals are.

After Sunday school, MaryAna and I walk to the main sanctuary for Sunday worship. It's a beautiful church with stained-glass windows, polished wooden pews, and a marble floor. The church is almost full, but we find seats. Why are the empty seats always near the front in church? At sporting events, the same people are willing to pay extra for front-row seating.

The service includes plenty of singing, both by the choir and the congregation. A gigantic organ accompanies us, lending a sense of grandeur. My sister sings like an angel. However, I refrain, not wanting to offend the ears of those nearby. If God wanted me to sing, he would've given me a better voice.

The minister gives a powerful sermon on "Love Thy Neighbor." He points out that treating people as Christ would treat them should not be just a "Sunday thing." Such behavior is how we should strive to act seven days a week. Finding myself almost hypnotized by his deep, baritone voice, I admire his skillful delivery. All in all, my first exposure to the Baptist religion is quite pleasant. Compared to a Catholic service, it seems more dynamic.

As we leave the church, MaryAna and I find our mother. She introduces me to several more people, including the minister, Reverend Thomas, and his extremely friendly wife, Dacia. He seems very mild-mannered out of the pulpit, nothing like the impressive orator with the booming voice. He says he hopes that I will join their church. I tell them that I'll consider the invitation.

Although I may feel differently when I'm older, I don't see myself becoming tied to any one religion. MaryAna is a Baptist because Mom is a Baptist. Papa is a Catholic because his parents were Catholics. Coree is probably Methodist because of her family. If any of them were born to Lutheran, Jewish, Muslim, or Hindu parents, in all likelihood, he or she would belong to that religion instead.

Probably less than 1 percent of the world's population is a different religion than their parents. For now, my religion is football, the religion of my father. I'm sure that most of the world doesn't perceive the sport in any religious capacity; however, my religion serves many of the purposes of the other denominations.

Football teaches me that I should play by the rules and that there are penalties if I violate them. That's like the Ten Commandments, sin, heaven, and hell. To be successful and reach the "promised land" of the end zone, football players need to believe in their coaches and each other. At some schools, it's customary to pray before games. Many football players thank God for victories, although they don't seem to blame him for their defeats. Maybe football is the one true religion. I'm open minded and willing to listen to everyone, but I'll judge for myself.

MaryAna tells me that she and Mom will drop me off at our house, since they're going out with several of their girlfriends to eat. I suspect that I'll be a major topic of discussion at that luncheon. After being dropped off at home, all I want to do is catch up on the sports news, watch some football with Coree this afternoon, and relax for the rest of the day.

It's been an eventful week and, after all, Sunday is supposed to be a day of rest.

Chapter 33
AN UNEXPECTED VISIT

Arriving home, I'm on a natural high, feeling like I don't have a care in the world. Somehow, knowing that Coree will be here soon makes everything else trivial. Making myself a sandwich, I locate the sports page of the newspaper and flip the TV to ESPN Sports Center.

One short segment on the show catches my attention. It's devoted to the offensive coordinator at Syracuse University, Scott Brown. Apparently, my dad's old friend and teammate is a leading candidate for open head-coaching positions at several universities. Before coaching in college, Scott played and coached in the NFL. I'd love to play for him someday.

Finishing my lunch, I hear the doorbell ring. Opening the door, I'm surprised to see Coree's brother, especially since she isn't with him. He's holding a rather thick black notebook with a red-and-white bulldog decal on the cover.

"What's up?" Mason asks, giving me a dynamic smile that lights up his whole face as he enters the house.

"Just chilling," I answer, leading him into the dining room and gesturing for him to sit down at the table.

Handing me the notebook, Mason explains, "Coree said Coach wanted you to have our playbook. I told her that you could borrow mine until you get your own. I hear that you're a quarterback."

"Yeah, I started at that position last season. Thanks a lot," I tell him, adding, "There was no need for you to make a special trip."

"No problem," he responds. "I just dropped Rachel off after church. Coree needed to help Julie with a couple things before she comes over to watch the game. I'll give her a lift when she's ready."

"Thanks. Hopefully, I'll have my own wheels soon," I reply, adding, "I can't wait to start learning these plays."

Mason enlightens me on Brandon's offensive scheme. "We run a no-huddle with plays signaled in from the sideline. The coaches like to keep our offense up-tempo, so the defense has less time to react. I've had years to learn the system, so you've got some catchin' up to do."

I'm surprised at how Mason is encouraging me to prepare myself to challenge him for the starting quarterback role. Why isn't he more defensive? Maybe he doesn't see me as much of a threat. Possibly, he's doing it as a favor to Coree. Either way, far be it from me to look a gift horse in the mouth.

"I've jotted down a bunch of notes in the margins," Mason explains. "If you have any questions, just send a text or give me a call. Here's my number." Grabbing a pen lying nearby, he writes it on the first page of the book.

"So you're a lefty?" I ask, noticing that he wrote the number with his left hand.

"Yeah, I do everything with the wrong hand, just like my daddy," Mason jokes as we both chuckle.

"MaryAna's left-handed too," I point out. "Of course, she's ambidextrous when it comes to texting."

He gives a little grin but says nothing.

Remembering my promise to my sister, I ask timidly, "I know that it's totally none of my business, but would you mind telling me what you like about Rachel?" I feel really stupid asking such a personal question. A promise is a promise, though.

Mason studies me for a moment, shakes his head, and grins again. With surprising candor, he responds, "You mean, why do I like Rachel rather than your sister?"

I nod, realizing that he's aware of the source of my question.

"Before I answer," Mason goes on, "let me say that MaryAna's a lovely girl. However, I feel toward her just like I do about Coree. Your twin is like another sister to me."

His statement isn't surprising, since I've seen the interaction between them in the last few days.

Mason pauses for a moment before continuing. "It's a different feeling with Rachel. We share certain life experiences that enable us to talk about things on a much deeper level. It's difficult to explain. Both of us faced the real possibility of dyin' when we were quite young. We both spent a considerable amount of time in hospitals. It's easier to talk with her, especially about serious topics. Maybe our misfortunes make us both realize that tomorrow isn't guaranteed."

Before my father's death, I wouldn't have understood so clearly what Mason meant. "Thanks," I tell him. "I really appreciate you sharing that with me. Do you mind if I talk to MaryAna about it?"

"Not at all," Mason replies, again flashing his amazing smile. "I certainly don't want to hurt your sister's feelings, JoeE. Maybe you'll be able to explain how I feel in a way where she realizes that I want to remain her friend."

"I'll try," I tell him, realizing that I have no idea how to accomplish that feat.

"By the way," Mason says, "in case you haven't noticed, Tyler worships the ground that MaryAna walks on. He wants her to like him about as much as he wants to play in the World Series. I see that your sister is finally payin' him some attention."

I tell Mason candidly, "I think she likes Tyler but isn't ready to admit it."

Sounding serious, Mason says, "Tyler's a great guy. It's about time she recognized that fact. I'll admit that he has some rough edges, but he'd give anyone the shirt off his back."

Changing the subject, Mason says, "Well, there's no doubt about Coree likin' you, JoeE. You're all she talks about now. If she says you're a great guy, I believe her. She's far from the airhead that I make her out to be."

"I like her too," I admit, beginning to blush.

Still serious, Mason tells me, "Coree has been through a lot. Things have really been rough for her. Our daddy is not the easiest man to live with."

"I'll try to be there for her," I reassure him.

Sounding more upbeat, Mason asks, "Do you play baseball, JoeE?"

"I've played a little baseball but mostly softball," I answer.

"Well, if you want to try out, we can always use another strong arm," he offers. "We start practice next month."

"Next month is January," I interject, knowing that back in Fulton, winter and baseball aren't synonymous.

"Yeah," Mason continues. "Our season opens in February. Maybe Tyler and I can help you since we both have played forever. Just let us know if you're interested."

I've heard of Southern hospitality and I guess that I'm witnessing it firsthand. "Thanks," I respond sincerely. "It's nice of you to offer."

After Mason leaves, a million thoughts swirl through my head. My former simple life is no more. Unfortunately, the faster my new life goes, the more likely it is to spin out of control. There are no road signs warning me of what lies ahead.

Chapter 34

TIME TO REFLECT

Walking back to my bedroom in a terrifically good frame of mind, I peruse my CDs, finding some music to match my upbeat mood. I lie back on the bed, thinking about my new family and friends.

First, I consider my mother. The more I get to know her, the more unlikely it seems that she could have allowed Dad to take me away. There must be more to their story. I sense that she's holding something back. But what? Like a giant puzzle, there are important pieces missing.

Next, I consider my twin sister. Unlike many single-parent households, money is not in short supply here. MaryAna has all the advantages that come with affluence. Beautiful, athletic, talented, and popular, my sister seems to have it all. Yet she obsesses over a guy who treats her like his kid sister. MaryAna is a delightful mix of contradictions. She never ceases to amaze and confound me. Now I need to explain to her why Mason prefers Rachel. I have no idea if she'll be devastated or simply feel free of the totally one-sided romance.

Then there's my dream girl, who's even more complicated than my sister is. Despite lying to her best friend for years, she opens up to me soon after we meet. Coree is so beautiful that she could stop traffic, but to me her attraction has little to do with physical beauty. Maybe I'm the one who's complicated.

There's a movie called *Weird Science* in which two teenage boys create a "perfect" woman. For me, Coree is my perfect woman—well, maybe not a woman yet but certainly my perfect dream girl. I realize that I'm naive when it comes to girls, but I can't imagine finding anyone more ideal for me. I already know that I want to spend my life with her.

Of course, there's also Mason, an enigma wrapped in a riddle. After our conversation today, I'm in total confusion. Is he just a nice guy who wants to help a fellow football player? Does he believe that I'm not a threat to his starting status? Did Coree put him up to helping me? Is there something between him and his father that's prompting his actions? I have plenty of questions but no answers. My mind whirls like a runaway clock.

"Son," my dad would say, "be the best that you can be at whatever you do." I fully intend to follow that advice. However, would it hurt Coree if I knock her brother out of his starting quarterback role in his senior year? Maybe this is what Dad meant when he preached, "Girls are a distraction from football."

My reflections are interrupted when I hear my mother's and MaryAna's voices in the kitchen. Turning off my music, I yell, "How was lunch?"

"Dinner was nice," my sister yells back, correcting me on their term for a noontime meal. Entering my open bedroom door, she informs me, "We talked a lot about you."

"Surprise, surprise," I say, sitting up on the bed. In Brandon, I'm probably a bigger subject of gossip than Kim Kardashian, Lindsay Lohan, and the Real Housewives of wherever put together. Plopping down on the recliner, my sister slips out of her shoes. She makes herself comfortable by hanging her legs over one arm of the chair. Apparently, she enjoys the well-padded recliner but has invented her own peculiar way to utilize it.

"All the girls were askin' questions about you," MaryAna begins, assuming that I want to hear the latest gossip. "I said you were still in the social dark ages, that we even had to create an e-mail for you. They were shocked that you couldn't text on your old cell. I also told them that we had to buy you new clothes 'cause yours were so nerdy."

"That's very flattering," I respond. I've become used to her forthright manner, which often borders on ridicule.

Ignoring my sarcasm as usual, MaryAna goes on. "I also told them that you were so sweet, a great listener, and that I'm happy that you're my brother."

At first, I don't believe my sister, but she seems sincere. She continues to surprise me. "I informed the girls that you were already goin' with Coree. There were some jealous faces at that announcement. A couple told me that you were smilin' at them during Sunday school. I won't tell Coree this time, but you better behave yourself from now on."

Beginning to blush, I realize that the whole world now probably knows about Coree and me. Apparently, I'll never have a secret around my sister.

MaryAna continues, "I also mentioned that next year, you may replace Mason at quarterback."

"What changed your mind from the other night?" I ask, actually astonished.

"Something Coree said," MaryAna answers without explanation.

"I just hope to be *one* of Brandon's quarterbacks," I say. "It's all speculation now anyway."

Since my sister brought up the subject of Mason, I figure it's as good a time as any to reveal what I've learned. "Mason stopped by," I inform her. "He dropped off his playbook."

"Did you talk to him 'bout me?"

"You were one of the subjects we discussed, and we talked about Rachel as well."

Looking at me nervously, she acts as if I'm about to announce an Academy Award and she's a nominee. I hate to crush my sister's dreams, but I don't wish to give her false hope, either.

I collect my thoughts and then I tell her frankly, "If you want to compete with Rachel for Mason's affection, I suggest you have a near-death experience and spend some serious time in a hospital."

"The cancer thing, huh?" MaryAna asks despondently.

"Did you know that Mason almost died once and spent a long time hospitalized?"

My sister answers, "Kinda. Coree told me once that he was badly burned. Is that it?"

"Yes, he was seriously burned when he was about seven," I reply. "It gives Rachel and him a common experience that shapes the way they relate to each other and see life in general."

The expression on MaryAna's face indicates that she isn't getting my drift. Deciding upon another approach, I ask, "Do you remember when you said that Coree might open up to me because our mothers left us when we were young?"

Contemplating my question for more than a few moments, MaryAna finally says, "Ah, I see." The look in her eyes verifies that, indeed, she understands my point.

I go on. "Papa once told me that you can communicate on three different levels—things, people, and ideas. Usually we simply talk about things, like 'the weather is nice' or 'that was a great game.' When we know people better, we often talk about other people. This can lead to gossip, like what you were doing today at lunch—I mean dinner."

My sister smiles. I can see that she's listening closely.

Pausing long enough to allow her thoughts to catch up to me, I continue my impromptu lecture. "When we really get to know some-one, we can talk to them about ideas, opinions, and other more seri-ous subjects. Sharing uncommon life experiences, especially traumatic ones, helps us connect much quicker."

"Wow, JoeE! You're like a philosopher or something."

"Not really, Sis," I say. "I just try to listen to people who know a bunch more than me."

"So I guess Mason will never like me," my sister says in a rather pathetic tone.

"He likes you," I inform her, "but like another sister."

MaryAna seems to accept my assessment and says in a more upbeat fashion, "Well, I better call Tyler before he goes fallin' for some base-ball babe 'cause they both struck out once."

We both laugh as I sigh with relief.

My sister adds, "Thanks, Bro. We've talked about ideas, haven't we?"

"Yes," I answer. "We broke through that barrier pretty quickly, espe-cially concerning the concept that I have no idea how to dress."

MaryAna smiles, gets up, grabs her shoes, and glides off to her bedroom. She already seems resigned to her fate. I really didn't tell her anything new. All I did was confirm her beliefs.

After she leaves, I feel extremely proud at how I handled the situation. My pride extends to my newfound ability to speak with girls, my amazing toys of technology, and my undoubtedly correct decision to move to Mississippi. Most of all, I'm proud that I'm going with a girl as exceptional and caring as Coree is.

Chapter 35

LOVE INTERRUPTED

Around two o'clock, Coree arrives to watch the NFL games. A beautiful white-shell necklace looks amazing against her tanned skin, and wide coral bracelets adorn her wrists. Apologizing for being late, she explains that she was helping Julie get caught up on the laundry. Apparently, she tries to help around the house as much as possible, since both of her parents work.

Mom tells us that she has soft drinks and tea in the refrigerator and the cabinets are stocked with snack food. "That's great," I tell her thankfully, as we raid the kitchen. "You really know the way to a teenager's heart."

Carrying our haul to the living room, we spread our minipicnic out on the coffee table. Turning on the TV, I find the first of two NFL games is already into the second half. In the central time zone, these games start at noon instead of one o'clock, as they do in New York. Sitting down on the couch, Coree and I make ourselves comfortable. She kicks off her shoes, apparently a Southern custom, and rearranges the pillows for maximum comfort.

"Football, junk food, and a beautiful girl," I say to her. "Life can't get any better than this!"

Smiling at the compliment, Coree reminds me, "JoeE, tomorrow is New Year's Eve."

Having lost track of time the last few days, I respond apologetically, "I forgot all about it. Have you already made plans?"

"Actually, I was hopin' that y'all would come over to our house. Mason and Tyler have bought a bunch of fireworks, and they plan on settin' them off startin' around eleven o'clock."

"That sounds awesome. So you can buy fireworks here? Are they legal?"

"Of course, they're legal. Can't y'all buy them in New York?"

"No way!" I inform her. "You aren't even supposed to bring them into the state. One of my friends brought some back from a trip, and he got into trouble when the police caught him setting them off."

"Well, that's a bummer. What do y'all do on New Year's Eve?" she asks.

"Parties mostly, but definitely not much outside unless you love the cold," I say, recalling many frigid nights in Fulton.

After looking around to make sure that neither MaryAna nor Mom is close enough to hear her, Coree whispers, "I need to ask you a favor."

I look at her in anticipation. "Sure, what is it?"

"On Tuesday morning," she continues to whisper, "I'm goin' to visit Mama at the state hospital. I'm wonderin' if you might go with me." My dream girl takes my hand. "I'd really like it if you would. It would mean a lot."

I whisper back, "Of course I want to go. It would be nice to meet your mother."

Giving me a grateful hug, she looks as if I've just given her an expensive present.

A few minutes later, Mom walks into the living room. "Is MaryAna in her room? I haven't heard a peep from her since we got back."

I say, "Earlier I asked MaryAna if she wanted to watch football with us. She said that she'd rather let spiders crawl over her. I think that she's in her room painting her nails again."

Mom says she needs to go to the grocery store and run a couple of other errands. Coree asks her if she'd like to come over to Calhoun Castle on New Year's Eve. Mom thanks her but says that she already has plans to attend a little get-together at the governor's mansion.

"Mom, you know the governor?" I ask.

"I know people close to him," Mom says without further explanation. "Do y'all need anything from the grocery store?"

I reply kiddingly, "Just a case or two of beer."

For a moment, she looks as though she thinks I'm serious. Then, realizing that I'm teasing her, Mom shoots back, "It better be light beer. You don't want a beer belly at sixteen." She leaves, grinning, while we settle in to watch the game.

"Does my mother ever go over to your house, Coree?" I ask.

"No," she replies. "Before MaryAna got a car, your mother would drop her off sometimes, but she never came inside. I always invite her to parties and cookouts, but she's never accepted."

Soon after Mom leaves, MaryAna comes through the living room wearing a coral romper outfit. She informs us that she's going over to Tyler's house. My sister seems very upbeat, almost joyous. Maybe her teenage drama with Mason is finally over.

"Coree," she asks, "would you mind letting me borrow that shell necklace? You know how good it goes with this outfit."

"Sure," my dream girl responds, removing the necklace and handing it to my twin. Apparently, the girls weren't kidding about sharing their attire. Coree tells her about the New Year's Eve fireworks. MaryAna says that Tyler has already texted her about it and that they both plan to be there.

MaryAna tells us that she'll be back later to carry Coree home. This again reminds me of how much I need a car.

As my sister puts on the necklace and a black leather jacket, I ask, "How are the negotiations going on the World Series tickets?"

"In the bag, Brother," she answers. "Tyler is cavin'. I'm takin' him to the nursing home with me. See y'all later." MaryAna is gone before I can ask her why she's going to a nursing home.

Seeming perplexed, Coree asks, "What's that ticket thing all about?" Amazed that my sister hasn't shared the story with her friend, I explain the clothes-for-tickets negotiation from last night.

"I thought you were serious," Coree says. "Major league baseball scouts have already been to Brandon to check out Tyler. He's really good."

I ask her curiously, "So both Mason and Tyler are pitchers?"

"Yes," she answers. "Mason might actually be the slightly better pitcher of the two. However, Tyler is a great hitter, clobbering a lot of home runs."

"What's with the nursing home that MaryAna mentioned?"

"Oh," Coree responds. "Your sister goes to the big nursin' home across from the hospital almost every Sunday afternoon to talk to the patients."

"Is this some kind of church thing?" I ask, suspecting that a nursing home would not be a place that my materialistic sister would pick out to visit.

"As far as I know," Coree answers, "she just got the idea last spring and has gone on Sundays ever since. MaryAna says that she likes talkin' to the old people, and they're always happy to see her. She says that some of them think that she's their granddaughter."

"It's nice that she does that," I comment, extremely surprised. It's an aspect of my sister's personality that I would've never suspected.

"At first, your sister was secretive about where she was going on Sundays," Coree says. "Maybe she started 'cause she had no grandparents to visit. Your mother's parents have passed away, and she didn't know about the ones in New York."

"I'm not sure Tyler will enjoy the nursing home," I speculate. "It may not be his idea of a terrific date."

"Get real," Coree says with a laugh. "Tyler will be with MaryAna. If your sister suggested they visit the garbage dump, that boy would be all for it."

Obviously, I don't look convinced, so Coree adds in a hushed tone, "Remember, you just accepted a date with me to a mental institution."

As Coree giggles, I realize that she's just made an excellent point. If she invited me to join her at a nursing home or even the garbage dump, I'd just ask when we were leaving. My friends in New York would say that I'm "whipped," and they'd be right.

"Well," I say, as happy as my chirping little blue jay buddy is, "it's great to have you here today. I love being with someone who also believes that football is the most important thing in the world."

Wrinkling her nose and looking at me strangely, Coree corrects me. "While I believe that football is very important, the most important thing in the world? No way!"

"I'm sorry," I tell her. "I just thought that..." I don't finish as she places her finger gently to my lips.

Obviously trying to make me feel better, Coree says, "There's no need for an apology. Football is extremely important to both of us. But don't you think there are a few things in life that are a little more essential?"

"Like what?" I ask, actually surprised that she doesn't agree with me.

Suddenly sounding extremely wise, Coree says, "First of all, family and friends. My mother's illness and your father's death prove how important it is to spend time with your loved ones."

"I suppose you're right," I concede. Her argument is logical, but I'm still not convinced.

Coree continues, "My church teaches me that God is always most important. However, I believe they simply mean that God is part of all things, including family, friends, and, yes, football. To me, God isn't a separate entity to be placed above everything but an integral part of all we hold dear."

"Kinda like the Force in *Star Wars*," I suggest.

"Kinda but not exactly," Coree says, smiling. "You have to decide what *you* believe. Just don't believe anyone who claims they know what God thinks. They don't."

Awestruck by her words, I gaze directly into my dream girl's hypnotic brown eyes. "You're amazing."

"That's what you are supposed to think, sir," she says, wrapping her arms around my neck for a little kiss.

Once again, I like the sound of "sir." Along with "ma'am," it is a reflection of Southern culture. It isn't only a simple means of expressing respect, but also a nice way of making someone feel important. Their widespread usage indicates that "sir" and "ma'am" are taught to many Mississippians at an early age.

"Yes, ma'am," I say respectfully, conveying the same sentiment back.

Smiling at me, Coree says, "We're gonna make a Southern gentleman out of you yet."

Turning back to the NFL game, I notice excitedly that Coree has removed her ChapStick once again from her purse. I've always thought that televised games include too many commercial breaks. However, with Coree here, I look forward to each one. By the time the first game is over, I'm working on a master's degree in "kissology."

Stopping to catch my breath, I'm glad to have discovered an activity as exciting to me as football is. I'm no stranger to the saying, "All good things must come to an end." Holding Coree tightly as if someone is about to take her from me, I hope that day never comes.

This pleasant distracting, coupled with the noise of the television, prevents us from hearing Mom enter the house. She walks into the dining room to set a bag on the table. By now, Coree is sitting on my lap and we are entwined in a passionate embrace. It's really embarrassing when your mother catches you making out. Mom doesn't say a word. She simply spins on her heels and returns to the kitchen.

I pull away from my dream girl as if a fire alarm just went off. Coree looks at me and with wide-eyed innocence asks, "What's wrong?"

Slipping her off my lap, I whisper, "Mom's home. We better cool it."

Worriedly, she asks, "Do you think your mama saw us?"

"Yep, I'm sure, unless she suddenly went blind."

She whispers, "We weren't really doin' that much, but with my rep, she probably jumped to conclusions."

With a nervous little laugh, I whisper back, "We weren't exactly just sitting here innocently watching football either, were we?"

"No, not exactly." Coree bites her lower lip and twists her bracelets. "Do you think we're in trouble?"

"I don't know. Let me talk to Mom." I feel like a kid caught with his hand in the cookie jar. Nonchalantly ambling into the kitchen as if nothing is wrong, I ask my mother if she needs any help bringing in groceries.

She says coolly, "Thanks, I already have everything." Seeming nervous, Mom adds, "We need to have a talk later." Her tone doesn't indicate anger, but obviously, she's upset.

"About me getting a car?" I ask, since we were supposed to discuss that topic today.

"No, something much more important," my mother says sternly. I notice that she didn't call me honey, sweetie, dear, baby, or darlin', as has been her custom. I realize that I've quickly become accustomed to those little terms of endearment, which weren't thrown around so freely back in New York.

Retreating to the living room, I sit down on the couch next to Coree, who whispers, "Is your mama real mad at me?"

Hearing my mother's bedroom door close, I answer, "I don't think she's angry at either of us, just upset. I can't explain it. She wants to have a talk with me."

"What about?" Coree asks with alarm. "Us?"

"Probably. Obviously, it has something to do with what she saw us doing."

"I'm so sorry," Coree says. "I didn't want to get you in trouble."

"I don't think you did," I say. "Just let me talk to her, and everything will be fine. It's not like she caught us in bed together."

We watch the rest of the game doing no more than holding hands. I want to have the talk with Mom as soon as possible. When MaryAna arrives a couple hours later, I tell her that I need some time alone with our mother. My sister offers to take Coree home and stay at Calhoun Castle for a while. Apparently noticing our somber expressions, my twin avoids asking any questions.

As they prepare to leave, MaryAna says, "Text me when it's OK to come back."

"I'll do that," I promise. Turning to Coree, I say, "Everything will be OK. Why don't you fill MaryAna in on the way to your house?"

Giving me a little hug, Coree says meekly, "OK."

After the girls leave, I nervously approach Mom's bedroom. The door is still closed, so I knock softly. When she opens it, I enter hesitantly and then sit on the edge of her bed. She sits across from me in a chair at her small desk. The redness in her swollen eyes indicates that she's been crying. Remaining silent, I wait for her to speak.

For the last few days, I've thought that my mother has had something significant to tell me. I hope this is my chance to find out what it is.

Chapter 36

NEED TO KNOW

Clearing her throat, Mom takes a deep breath and begins by saying, "I'm sure that you're tired of hearing my secrets. Nobody else knows what I'm about to tell you—not MaryAna, not your grandparents, no one. I've simply been too ashamed and embarrassed to let anyone know what happened."

"I see," I say, thinking back upon my mother's previous secrets. I can't imagine how this one could possibly be any more embarrassing for her. Of course, I'm wrong, as usual.

Apparently finding it difficult to choose the right words, Mom takes another deep breath before finally stating, "I'm *not* goin' to make you promise to keep this secret, as much as I want to do so. You must use your own good judgment about telling others. However, there's no doubt that you *need* to know."

"OK," I respond, wondering what in the world she's about to tell me. Recalling our conversations over the last few days, I search for a clue. It certainly appears that seeing Coree and me earlier has triggered this reaction. However, she knew that I went out with Coree last evening and seemed all right with it.

With her upper lip trembling slightly, Mom looks as if she could burst into tears at any moment. Struggling to continue, she says, "The entire story that I've told you about your father and me is absolutely true, but…"

As Mom pauses, I wonder why there always has to be a "but" in these confessions. Why couldn't she just tell me the entire story last September?

With the saddest eyes that I've ever seen, my mother goes on. "There are some hard truths that you should know about what happened before you and your sister were born. When I came back from California to Mississippi the first time, I was here for over two months.

"One night, I ran into my former boyfriend from high school. He was havin' marital problems. I really needed a shoulder to cry on, and he listened to my problems. We began spendin' time together. He claimed that he still loved me and wanted us to get married after we both got divorced."

Wiping the tears that have finally burst forth, she continues, "Joseph was callin' and beggin' me to return to California. I told my former boyfriend that I'd decided to go back to my husband." As she fights back the tears, I realize she needs a few moments to compose herself.

"Mom, how about I get you some water."

"That would be nice," she responds, grabbing a tissue.

When I return, Mom seems better. After taking a few sips, she continues her story. "I went back to California about a month later, but soon I began feelin' poorly so I saw a doctor. He informed me that I was expectin'. I knew the baby's daddy was my former boyfriend, who was back with his wife by then."

Sitting as motionless as a rock, I'm once more frozen by another chronicle of events from the distant past. "Well, that explains why I don't look much like Dad," I interject, having no idea whatsoever how I should react to this shocking bit of knowledge.

Sadly nodding in agreement with my statement, my mother goes on. "Joseph and I wanted children. By not tellin' him right away, I was hopin' that he'd assume he was the father."

Having difficulty grasping that these events are true, I just sit in silence. It's as if her story is a reality show. Actually, it *is* a reality show in which I have a starring role.

Mom goes on. "I led Joseph to believe that because you were twins, you were born prematurely. That helped explain what appeared to be my less-than-eight-month pregnancy. My husband never gave me any indication that he knew you two were not his children."

"Do my grandparents know this?"

"Nobody knows but us," Mom tells me, shaking her head to emphasize the point.

Suddenly realizing that Papa and my grandmother aren't really my grandparents, I get a cold chill. I'm not the fourth Joseph Edward Collins in a line that goes back over a century. I have no real connection to Fulton's history other than the last sixteen years. My ancestry doesn't trace back to John Conley from Canada. For all I know, I'm not even Irish. My whole life has been one big lie!

"You see, JoeE," my mother continues as I half listen, "one of the reasons that I agreed to Joseph's proposal was that you babies weren't actually his children. When I first agreed, I thought there'd be only one child. If it was a girl, I'd take her to Mississippi, and no one would ever have to know how she was conceived. Of course, things didn't work out exactly that way."

Apparently, I screwed up the plans by being born. How rude of me. Now all I want to do is scream, and it takes every ounce of discipline in my body not to.

My mother admits, "I wanted to tell MaryAna the truth about her father so she wouldn't hate Joseph so much, but that would've led to a host of other questions."

The truth is just beginning to hit me like a load of bricks. Why did my mother *need* to tell me this story? Like a machine gun, I rattle off questions. "Well, who's our father? Where does he live? Do you think he might want to meet us?"

What my mother says next is unbelievable.

Driving the five words into my heart like daggers, she lets the silence that follows twist them at their hilts. Five little words, as sharp and deadly as knives, plunged straight into my heart. That's all it takes to tear my world apart.

Trying to speak, all I can do is sit there, stunned and mute. I struggle to form words, but the questions die in my throat. It's as though the ground has shifted out from under me. The world wobbles, the planets scatter out of alignment, and the stars fall from the heavens.

In the end, all I can manage to mumble is, "What did you say?"

But already the truth is settling in. The five little daggers are doing their work. The damage is done, the curse cast, the façade shattered forever. Like a house of cards teetering on the edge of collapse, my new life suddenly comes tumbling down.

Part 3

DEALING WITH TRUTH

Chapter 37

WHO'S YOUR DADDY?

The *truth* is a far more complex concept than I ever imagined. In court, we swear to "tell the truth, the whole truth, and nothing but the truth." That "whole truth" part now has new meaning to me.

Over the last few months, my mother has been feeding me the truth piecemeal about her and my dad, or at least the man I thought was my father. I figured that Mom's secret about me having a sister was the final twist of her fantastic story. Now I know it's a mistake to make any assumptions regarding my parents and their lives.

A new wrinkle has emerged. It turns out that the man who raised me wasn't my biological father. My mother apparently had an affair with a married man while she was separated from her husband. To make matters worse, she led Dad to believe that MaryAna and I were his children. Implementing their questionable child-rearing agreement, Mom and Dad remained in a long-distance, never-to-meet-again marriage. That's the truth, at least as far as I know right now.

"What did you say?" I ask again, wanting her to give me a different response.

Slowly repeating those five daggers, Mom says, "Your father is Rhyan Calhoun."

"You mean Coach Calhoun? Coree's father?" I ask, still clinging to the hope of a different response.

"Yes, JoeE," my mother says. She's on the verge of tears.

"You mean Coree is my..." All of a sudden, my throat constricts again.

Like a tornado, my mind spins with questions, but I'm afraid I already know the answers. Is this why MaryAna and her best friend look so much alike? Is this why Mom freaked out when she saw Coree and me kissing? Should I start calling Coree my "nightmare girl"?

Our mother has obviously been walking a tightrope for years with MaryAna and Mason. My twin said that Mom has encouraged friendship with the Calhoun family while discouraging any romantic involvement. This now makes perfect sense. My mother obviously thought that she could take the same approach with me.

At least this situation has an upside. I've always wanted a brother, and now I have two. Maybe Mom's secret isn't as confidential as she believes it is. Has Coach Calhoun already figured out that we are his children? Has he told anyone else? Could Mason know the truth? Is that why he's being so helpful to me and why he has ignored MaryAna's affections? From Coree's romantic advances, it's quite apparent that she's totally unaware of the facts.

Secrets, secrets, secrets, I think, shaking my head in utter defeat. I'm already finding it hard to keep Coree's secrets. How in the world will I deal with this avalanche of skeletons from the family closet? My grandfather would quote a line from his favorite poet, Sir Walter Scott, to describe this situation: "Oh, what a tangled web we weave, when first we practice to deceive."

Suddenly feeling overwhelmed, I wonder how I will explain to Coree that we can't have a romantic relationship without telling her the truth. If I explain that she's my sister, how in the world can I expect her to keep quiet about knowledge that involves her whole family? If this explosive information already feels like an unbearable burden for me, how can I unload it onto her?

I have no insightful answers to any of these questions. In fact, no ideas about where to start come to mind. I can't even think of any options. Mom has started sobbing uncontrollably, reminding me that she's been carrying around this secret for over sixteen years. I can't help but wonder if her tears are from shame or relief. Probably both.

As much as I feel like yelling at her for withholding the truth, I realize that throwing a temper tantrum will serve no purpose except to upset both of us further. My mother needs me to be a man, not a child. Instinctively knowing what I must do next, I reach out to my mother and give her a reassuring hug. What I need is time to think, to step back from the volcanic emotions of the moment, and use some clear, cool logic.

Brimming with false confidence, I boldly say, "We'll figure all this out, Mom. Don't worry. If it makes you feel any better, this doesn't change how I feel about you. You're my mother, and I love you."

She relaxes against my chest, apparently appreciating my gesture.

It's impossible for me to imagine how my mother has shouldered such a burden alone. It would've been difficult, if not impossible, to get back with Coach Calhoun, since he was still married. My mother tried to make her marriage with Dad work, but he wanted to raise me without interference. For a moment, I actually feel her pain and confusion. Apparently, Mom has had no one to help her cope with her personal problems. Possibly by default, I've fallen into that role.

"Is there anything else that you need to tell me, Mom?" I ask.

Thinking for a long moment, she finally answers. "Just some information about your trust fund, but that can wait, honey."

"For sure. There's enough on my plate already. I'll talk with Coree."

"Are you goin' to tell her everything?" my mother asks, choking back her tears.

"I don't know yet. Give me some time to figure things out. It's a lot to take in." Now I understand why Mom said "Thank God!" when MaryAna went out with Tyler.

After saying good night to my mother, I seek solace in my bedroom. Collapsing onto the bed, I actually consider moving back to Fulton—running away from this whole mess. I want my old, simple, black-and-white world back. I want the life with no mother, no sisters, no brothers, and no girlfriend. I don't want all these distractions from football. For the first time, I'm angry with Dad for dying.

A sinking feeling envelops me. I feel as if I'm in a maelstrom, being sucked down into the swirling abyss below. My whole identity is under attack, being ripped away piece by piece. If I'm no longer that self-assured quarterback, son of Joseph Collins, the latest in a proud line of football players going back nearly a century, who am I?

Suddenly, I see myself as a refugee in a strange land, living with a mother and a sister whom I hardly know. I'm a shy introvert who's terrified by girls, pretending that I'm able to handle a romance. I can't lie, even to myself, and I certainly can't be something that I'm not. JoeE Collins hates wearing the latest fashions, doesn't require Apple's latest gadgets, and can certainly do without wealth. He's a Spartan who leads a simple life. In less than a week, JoeE has disappeared.

I want him back.

Of course, I quickly realize that going back to my previous life is now a fantasy. No matter where I live or what I do, I'll always have this new family. Moving to Mississippi didn't make my grandparents or friends in Fulton vanish. I must face the fact that my life will never be simple again. I must also face the newly revealed truth about my family and deal with the situation. Like a phoenix, a new JoeE must arise from the ashes of my old life and soar into the complexity of this new world.

I notice that Coree has sent me a text, asking me to call her when I get a chance. I now wish that I felt the same brother-sister way about her as I did MaryAna when we first met. It certainly would make things easier.

One lesson I've learned is that you can't change the past no matter how much you wish you could. Debating what to do about Coree, I decide that first I need to calm down our relationship. That means no holding hands, no hugging, and certainly no more kissing.

It also means that I can't pay her any special attention, which will make these next few days—or even weeks—feel like walking a tight-rope. There's only one catch in this plan: it may be next to impossible to set in motion. But if there's another option, I'm not seeing it. Step one is this: don't call or text Coree back tonight.

Of course, even that minor step makes me feel like an inconsider-ate jerk. As promised, I text MaryAna to let her know that it's OK to return home. In a minute, my twin replies, asking if everything is all right. As I text back that everything is just fine, I wish that were the case. It's only a small lie, but I know that it's how I will begin to weave my own tangled web.

It isn't long before I hear MaryAna's voice echoing through the house. Hearing a second voice, I realize that Coree is with her. Great.

As the two girls enter my bedroom, MaryAna says cheerfully, "I brought you a present, Bro, and here she is." Upon telling me that her friend is spending the night, my twin has a devilish grin, as if she is keeping a secret.

Coming over to me, Coree leans in to give me a kiss and a hug. Trying to act cool, I return neither, remaining as rigid as an ice statue.

Immediately sensing the change in my behavior, Coree says, "I see that your mama cut me off, didn't she?"

The girls giggle as I try not to smile. If she only knew how *off* she has been cut, she might not be so happy.

With a giggle, MaryAna asks, "What did Mama want to talk to you about? The birds and the bees? I can't believe you two got caught making out."

"That's kinda what we talked about," I reply, hoping that answer will satisfy their curiosity.

MaryAna says teasingly, "I'm gonna give Coree my pink teddy to wear tonight. You'll probably like it better on her than me." She, of course, is referring to her own lack of modesty the first morning that I was in Brandon.

Sister or not, envisioning Coree so scantily clad proves too much for me to handle. I completely lose it. "I don't want to see Coree dressed like that! Why don't you airheads get serious for once? Grow up and at least act your age!"

My Spartan-like control has just disintegrated. It's as though I'm falling apart, and I regret the harsh words as soon as they leave my mouth.

At first, my sudden emotional outburst simply prompts surprised looks on the girls' faces. It's the first time that either of them has heard me raise my voice in exasperation, frustration, or yes, anger.

Realizing that I'm serious, MaryAna glares at me. "Whatever!" she hisses.

The expression that spreads across Coree's face is that of a puppy that has just been scolded for the first time. She rushes from my room, down the hall, and into MaryAna's bedroom, slamming the door behind her. I feel absolutely horrible. So much for my ridiculous plan of walking a tightrope.

I take a deep breath before apologizing to MaryAna. "I'm sorry, Sis. I didn't mean it."

Her eyes seem to penetrate me. "Did we do something wrong?"

"No, nothing. It's just been a weird night. I've got a lot to deal with right now."

"So things aren't really fine, are they? Do you wanna talk about it?" MaryAna asks.

"I've got some serious things to work out by myself. We'll talk about it soon. I promise," I say, accidently committing myself to telling her the truth about our father.

"I just wanna understand what's goin' on," MaryAna says, almost pathetically.

"I know, and I swear that you'll know everything soon," I reply, almost praying that she won't pursue the issue any further tonight.

"I'd better check on Coree. She seemed really upset," my sister notes. "You know, JoeE, she's extremely sensitive and definitely not an airhead."

"It was a stupid thing for me to say. Do you think it'd be OK if I go to your room with you?" I ask sheepishly.

"I guess so," MaryAna tells me. "I've never seen Coree get that upset so quickly. I think you really hurt her feelings, badly so mabe the sooner you apoligize to her, the better."

Walking to her bedroom, MaryAna softly knocks on the closed door. I hear a tearful "Come in." When my twin opens the door, I see Coree sitting on the edge of the bed, tears streaming down her cheeks. I've never felt so terrible or so guilty. Knowing that I'm responsible for such pain makes me feel absolutely horrible.

I walk over to Coree, saying, "I'm so sorry. I didn't mean what I said. I know you aren't silly. said It was really dumb and totally uncalled for. MaryAnacan dress you up any way she wants."

Looking up at me with eyes glistening with tears, Coree mutters, "Hey, I'm not a Barbie Doll, you know."

"My brother is really sorry," MaryAna says. "Actually, it was kinda nice seein' him get angry for a change. He's been actin' so perfect, I was afraid that Mama would start expectin' me to act that way too."

Sniffing back her tears, Coree gives me a little smile. With a sudden urge to hug her overwhelming me, I put out my arms. She slowly stands up and leans into me. As I wrap my arms around her, I try to keep it as brotherly as possible. Somehow, I just don't feel like her brother yet.

When we finally break apart, MaryAna whispers something in Coree's ear. As the girls giggle, I'm actually wishing that Mom hadn't told me her secret. In Fulton, my best friends were macho football players. Here, two cheerleaders are quickly becoming my best friends. How weird is that? I tell my sisters that it has been a long day and I'm heading off to bed.

MaryAna says, "Better lock your door, Bro. I heard that my best friend is givin' you kissin' lessons."

Shuddering, I cringe at the thought.

"Hush, MaryAna. That was supposed to be a secret," Coree says, brushing away the last of her tears. Smiling at me, she adds excitedly, "We've got plans for you tomorrow, JoeE."

"What plans?" I ask, alarmed.

My new sister says with a smile, "It's a secret. You'll just have to wait."

Just what I need: another secret. Trying to sound interested rather than fearful, I say, "Awesome. I can't wait."

Desperately needing to get my mind off everything, I return to my room and lock the door. I heave a sigh of relief when I see my savior waiting for me. No, I don't mean a vision of Jesus coming to save me, although I have to admit that at this moment, that would be comforting.

Basking in the glow of my bedside lamp is the Brandon playbook. I plug in my earphones and let classic rock wash away the day. Sitting down at my desk, I crack open the book. For the next several hours, my world is nothing but football and music. I'm on the clock, absorbing a system of x's and o's, the written language of my favorite sport.

After several hours, I've absorbed the entire playbook. Of course, I need more study to feel totally comfortable with the Brandon system. Although his notes in the margins helped immensely, I still have several questions for Mason. At least, I should be able to talk to him intelligently about various aspects of their approach to the game.

As good as it feels to get lost in football again, it's still just a temporary reprieve. As soon as I slip into bed, passes and plays fade away and are replaced by the five terrible daggers that my mother buried in my chest.

Chapter 38

LET'S ROLL

Lying in bed on Monday morning, I rethink my whole "Coree strategy." The totally cold approach backfired last night, so it's back to the drawing board. Recalling the sorrowful, almost devastated expression on her face when I yelled, I realize that I must eliminate any type of harsh treatment. Although that approach would definitely put a stopper on our relationship, I can't, and won't, hurt her. She's my sister, after all.

There's only one possible way to address this situation: with complete honesty and no more secrets. I don't know if the girls are ready for that just yet, and last night proved that I'm not ready, either. I need to talk about this problem with someone. But who? I really want to call Papa and ask for his advice. Obviously, that is out of the question for the moment. I can't see myself starting the conversation with, "By the way, Papa, you aren't my grandfather."

For the first time, I truly understand why my mother kept this information to herself. Her long-held secret is a time bomb, and Coree and I aren't the only ones in its radius. Last night, Mom was forced to light the fuse, and it's only a matter of time before everyone I care about is caught in the blast.

However, the only solution seems to be to tell the truth. I simply need to inform Coree of the facts, letting her and God deal with the consequences. Should I give her the same option that my mother gave me? Should she feel free to tell anyone about our family ties? Could this lead to even more collateral damage? It's possible. No, it's *probable.*

Then there's MaryAna. She has every right to know that Rhyan Calhoun is her father. I keep my promises. But I should probably talk to Coree before I deal with my twin. MaryAna has waited sixteen years, so a day or two more doesn't matter. On the other hand, my relationship with Coree depends upon being truthful with her as soon as possible. The big question now is when should I tell her the truth? We need to be by ourselves. Today, there appears to be plenty happening, so we may not have an opportunity to be alone.

Tomorrow, we're planning to go to the mental institution to visit Coree's mother. Mason won't be going with us, so that may be the most opportune time to talk privately. Stopping somewhere on the way back will allow for an uninterrupted conversation. This way, I'll also have a chance to break the news to Mom that I've decided to reveal her secret to both girls.

Although it's time for me to rise and shine, instead I turn over and try to go back to sleep. As I think about Coree, I realize that I'm facing the bitter end of my first romance. Despite its short duration, I suppose that the memories will linger.

Unable to go back to sleep, I eventually get out of bed, take a shower, and meander into the kitchen. No exercises, no run this morning. What's the point? I hear my mother rustling around in her room. I'm glad; this gives me an opportunity to inform her of my decision.

After hearing my plan, Mom says that she understands my predicament and will support me.

Soon MaryAna and Coree emerge, already dressed and apparently ready to leave the house. "Our surprise," my twin explains, "is that we're fixin' to take you on a grand tour of Brandon. We realized that you've been here for nearly a week and haven't seen much of our fair town."

Relieved that I won't be alone with Coree, I look forward to this little adventure. However, the expected trauma of tomorrow looms like a specter in my mind. Once more, I arrogantly believe that I know exactly what the future holds.

"I've got music for the ride," Coree says enthusiastically. She holds up some CD cases. "I hope you like Taylor Swift, Miley Cyrus, and Katy Perry."

216

"Don't they all sing about how guys treat them badly, lie to them, cheat on them, and generally mess up their lives?"

"Yeah, pretty much," MaryAna says. "And your point is?"

I just need to shut up and go along with the program. Apparently, my musical tastes are as irrelevant as my fashion opinions.

The sky is a blindingly bright blue as I climb into the backseat of MaryAna's car. This way, my dual tour guides can sit up front to coordinate the musical program with our travel itinerary. Noticing that there are two opened beer cans in the cup holders, I also spot a half-dozen empty ones on the floorboard of the backseat. The nursing home may not have been the only stop that Tyler and MaryAna made yesterday. I'm beginning to wonder whether my sister has a drinking problem or she is just trying to grow up too fast.

Putting in a Katy Perry disc, Coree says, "Let's roll, y'all!"

We pull out of the driveway with the speakers blaring. Settling back, I'm ready to be chauffeured around town as three female vocalists tell me how badly we males treat them. They're probably right.

After turning onto Highway 18, we drive less than a mile before seeing a red brick complex that Coree tells me is their high school. She says it was built just a few years ago. Another new building in Brandon—why am I not surprised? It doesn't look that much different from my school in Fulton. However, the area around it is much more open. There are no trees close to the buildings.

Getting out, we walk around. Ever since we left home, the girls have been receiving and sending text messages at a furious pace. They tell me that their friends are suggesting where we should go on our grand tour. It's a bit disconcerting to realize that I'm now a community project. I get the odd feeling that the female population of Brandon is running my life.

"Maybe Katy Perry will text you some suggestions on where we should go!" I say, but the girls ignore my stab at humor. Settling back in the car, I add, "Be sure to tell all the girls that I ate cereal for breakfast."

"We need to talk about your eatin' habits," Coree says. "You need to eat a more balanced breakfast. It's the most important meal of the day, you know." This from a girl who just skipped breakfast.

"What are you, my mother now?" I respond. She glares at me, says nothing, and goes back to texting. I wish that I hadn't challenged her thoughtful advice.

"I'm sorry. You're right," I say, quickly backtracking as she interrupts her texting to blow me a little kiss. I guess that I need to adjust to having two sisters running my life.

Turning north onto College Street, we pass Calhoun Castle. A short distance beyond, we come upon an older part of Brandon. The hills remind me of the east side of Fulton. Making a left at a large building, we drive down a small incline.

Near the bottom is a well-kept baseball field. Rising behind the field is a large football stadium. As it comes fully into view, I note that the expansive concrete stands are actually built into the side of the hill. Across from them are extensive metal bleachers for fans of the visiting team. This stadium is certainly too large in capacity for a high school.

In the background on College Street, I see several buildings. I say to the girls, "I didn't know that Brandon has a college."

They look at each other and giggle. Coree informs me, "That's Brandon High's football stadium. The school at the top of the hill used to be the high school. Now, it's the middle school."

"This stadium is awesome!" I exclaim. "What kind of attendance do you have for games?"

"It's always pretty full," Coree tells me. "I've heard numbers like eight or nine thousand fans. It could be more because it's always overflowing."

"Seriously? For every game?"

"For as long as I can remember," she answers matter-of-factly.

Impressed, I just shake my head, thinking about our home field in Fulton. I remember my dad being happy when we had almost two thousand people in attendance for big games. I might actually be on a team playing in this stadium next fall. That would be awesome.

Then I realize that my brother, Mason, has already experienced that thrill. Coach Calhoun has played in and coached many games here. My sisters have been cheerleaders in this stadium. Mom has marched in the band. This is the home stadium of *my* family. Why shouldn't I be a part of that tradition?

We now head north and make a right turn onto Highway 80. In a couple of blocks, we come to a tall statue in an area that divides the highway. The statue has a sculpture of a soldier at the top. There are also flagpoles, one flying the Stars and Stripes. I don't recognize the other two flags, both of which have single red, white, and blue stripes. One of them has the Confederate Stars and Bars in the upper left corner. That might be the Mississippi state flag, since the state continues to celebrate its rebellious past.

As we pull into a parking area, MaryAna points out a rather impressive old building. "Over yonder is the Rankin County Courthouse."

Motioning to the statue, I say, "So this is where the Union soldiers stacked their guns."

I receive a weird look from both girls. Coree asks, "What guns?"

I tell them about Sherman's army and the facts I learned on the Internet.

MaryAna says, "Yankees in Brandon? Yuck! How do you know that? Are you, like, some kind of genius?"

"I'm not any smarter than you," I say. "I just looked up the information on that awesome new laptop that you guys picked out for me."

MaryAna snorts. "JoeE, you need to stop with that *you guys* thing. It's *y'all* down here. You don't want that Rebel soldier to come down off that there statue thinkin' you're a Yankee, now do you?"

We all laugh at the thought of me being chased around downtown Brandon by a Confederate soldier. I promise the girls that I'll try to speak "Southern" from now on. The girls send some more text messages, keeping the entire female population of central Mississippi up to date on our progress. A good share of Brandon may have just learned why there's a statue in front of the local courthouse. Resuming the grand tour, we turn right at the next traffic light. A couple of blocks later, we turn onto Mary Ann Drive.

Coree points at a nearby house and says, "This is where Mary Ann Mobley grew up. She was Miss America about fifty years ago."

"Wow!" I say admiringly. "It seems like Brandon has produced beautiful and talented girls for a long time." Both of them giggle, knowing that I'm including them in this statement. "I read that Faith Hill is from Mississippi," I add, trying to enhance my genius status.

"Duh!" MaryAna says. "That's why she sang 'Mississippi Girl.' It was only a number-one country hit."

"I'm not that familiar with country singers," I admit.

Coree says, "JoeE probably only knows Faith Hill from the intros on Sunday Night Football. Are you a fan of *American Idol*?"

"Sure," I tell her. "If I miss anything, Papa and my grandmother bring me up to date. They watch it all the time."

Coree tells me, "Skylar Laine, who finished fifth this year, is from Brandon. She sang the national anthem at our football game against Petal High School last month when we won the south Mississippi championship."

"She has a great voice," I say, recalling seeing her on television.

"You know," MaryAna says, "Tyler claims he's gone out with Skylar."

"Seriously?" I ask, actually impressed.

Coree says, "Tyler probably claims that he has gone out with Faith Hill too." We all laugh as she changes our music.

Now listening to Miley Cyrus sing "Nobody's Perfect," I think about Coree—especially how she *is* almost the perfect girl. This tall, athletic young woman is strikingly beautiful, but it doesn't take a genius to know that real beauty can't be seen from the outside. She's also witty, caring, compassionate, intelligent, loves football, and, of course, has a great sense of humor. Her perfection is certainly not just skin-deep. She makes the perfect dream girl except for one fatal flaw—she's my sister.

Apparently, nobody is perfect.

Chapter 39

NEW VERSUS OLD

MaryAna announces that she's hungry and craving Chick-fil-A.

I ask, "What kind of restaurant us that?"

Coree explains, "They serve chicken."

MaryAna teases, "You really don't know much about eating places. I guess I need to scratch that genius comment."

"Don't pick on my JoeE," Coree says. "He's just restaurant-challenged!" She's probably right.

Continuing our grand tour, we pass Community Bank. I proudly announce that it's where I have my checking account.

"Good," MaryAna says, bursting my little bubble of pride. "Then you can pay for lunch."

"What about that 'girls want to pay their own way' thing?" I ask.

The two girls glance at each other, and my twin informs me, "I reckon girls in New York might fall for that propaganda. Down here, it's different. We need our money to make ourselves more beautiful!"

MaryAna's logic isn't always that clear. Either way, it's obvious that I'm paying for lunch.

Pointing out the police station, Coree informs me that the next building is the public library.

"When is the library supposed to be finished?" I ask, observing the structural steel above the white concrete columns at the front entrance.

The girls look at each other and giggle. "It's been finished for years. That thing over the front entrance is some kind of artwork," MaryAna says.

"It looks really weird," I say. "Fulton has a beautiful old public library."

"I'd love to see it someday," Coree says, giving me a little smile.

"It's on the National Registry of Historic Buildings," I proudly inform the girls. "I guess if Schubert can compose an unfinished symphony, then Brandon can build an unfinished library." From the looks on the girls' faces, I may have just reclaimed my genius status. I don't inform them that I only know about that piece of music from playing Trivial Pursuit.

A little farther along the highway, there's a small lake on the right. Coree points to the far side, saying, "That's Crossgates."

I remember that this is where my mother lived when she was young. MaryAna tells me that it is supposedly the largest subdivision in the world, with about three thousand homes. She also says that Mom still owns a bunch of houses in this area.

At the huge Ford dealership, with cars and trucks on display almost as far as the eye can see, we turn left. The dealership appears to have vehicles in every color imaginable, including Mustangs, my favorite car. I may desire to return to my Spartan life, but this time I want to have my own chariot.

Just before we get to Interstate 20, we pull into Chick-fil-A. Even though we've landed between breakfast and lunch, the place is still packed.

"Let's eat inside," MaryAna suggests as she parks the Malibu.

After entering the restaurant, I'm still perusing the menu when I realize the girls have already ordered for me. I forgot for a moment that I'm restaurant-challenged! When they hand us our food, we find a table. I pull out the hot chicken sandwich and take my first bite.

"Awesome," I tell the girls as the food collides with my taste buds.

Coree asks me, "Have you seen the commercial where the cows parachute into the football stadium and attack the hamburger vendors?"

"Yes, I remember that ad. It's hilarious." I recall seeing it during football games.

"That's a Chick-fil-A commercial," she informs me.

"I don't think we have any of these restaurants in New York, at least not near Fulton."

"Hey, Coree," MaryAna says, "maybe we should move to Fulton and open one. And maybe a Mexican restaurant, too."

"JoeE," Coree asks, "do you think that you'll ever wanna move back to New York?"

It's an interesting question, considering that last night I was ready to pack my suitcase. "I honestly don't know," I answer.

Coree then asks, "Do you like Brandon?"

"Yeah, but I still feel like a fish out of water."

"In what ways?" MaryAna wants to know, taking a short break from her sandwich.

"First of all," I say, "it's kinda like learning another language."

"What do you mean?" Coree says. "We all speak English!"

"Words like *y'all*, *fixin'*, and *yonder* aren't exactly common back in Fulton."

Coree giggles. "Well, they're English, aren't they?"

I think for a moment. "Let me give you some better examples. Yesterday, Coree, you asked me to 'catch the light,' but it wasn't falling."

She smiles, probably remembering the confused look on my face.

"I guessed that 'turn off the light' is what you actually meant. You use English words, but you're always putting them together in unique ways."

The girls grin as I continue. "This morning, MaryAna asked me to 'plug up' the toaster. Obviously, that would have damaged it, so I figured that she actually wanted me to plug it in, not up."

MaryAna asks, "JoeE, are you makin' fun of us?"

"No, not at all. I love to hear you guys, I mean *y'all*, talk. It's awesome."

They both smile, seeing that they're making minor progress with my Southern education.

I go on. "I know that movies and television shows often ridicule Southerners, so I understand why you might get a little defensive. But I think your accents are charming and your colorful sayings are unique and interesting. It's just that sometimes I have no idea what the heck you mean."

"Oh," MaryAna says. "You just need a Southern dictionary!"

Coree asks with real concern, "In what other ways do you feel uncomfortable here?"

"It may sound funny," I answer frankly, "but it's hard to get accustomed to how openly trusting and friendly people here seem. In Fulton, people tend to be more reserved and suspicious until they're familiar with you. Once they get to know you, they're very friendly if they like you or hostile if they don't."

The girls are quiet as they digest my answers along with their chicken sandwiches.

"Do you miss Fulton?" Coree asks.

"Yes, in some ways very much," I answer.

Like a detective conducting an investigation, she asks, "What do you miss the most?"

"My grandparents and my friends, mostly," I say. "You were right yesterday, Coree, when you pointed out that family and friends are really the most important part of life."

Remembering our conversation, Coree's eyes light up as she squeezes my arm.

Probing deeper, she asks, "Do you miss the girls in New York?"

"Well, Coree," I admit, "our first short conversation last Wednesday was longer than any that I've had with a girl my age. I guess a lot of the girls back home could've been wonderful friends if I'd only made an effort."

It's almost as if Coree is studying me, attempting to determine exactly what I'm thinking. I decide to explain further. "My father always said that girls and football don't mix. I never openly questioned anything he told me. No girl ever interested me enough to upset him or the routine that we'd established. Dad made the rules, and I followed them, period."

Both girls are looking at me with wide-eyed disbelief. When I talk about Fulton, I feel like I'm describing an alien planet. Of course, there are the superficial differences: weather, accents, ethnic makeup. The list goes on. If you want to find the real differences between the

North and the South, you have to read between the lines. The divide runs much deeper—right down to attitudes, priorities, and customs.

"There's something else that I miss about Fulton," I add longingly.

"What's that?" Coree asks, seeming intrigued by my answers to her inquiries.

I hesitate as I gather my thoughts. "On this tour of Brandon, about 90 percent of what we've seen is relatively new—not necessarily brand new, but definitely not old. It appears that many of the buildings aren't much older than we are."

"That's right," MaryAna agrees. "Except for the area around the old courthouse, most of Brandon is fairly new. We've watched much of the city being built as we grew up."

"In Fulton, it's just the other way around. The vast majority of the city is at least fifty years old, and most of the houses and other buildings are way older. Besides the library, Fulton has nearly a dozen historic sites on the National Registry, primarily buildings. I've seen very little construction in my lifetime."

"Doesn't havin' everything new make Brandon a better place to live?" MaryAna asks.

"Not necessarily," I say. "Do you like antiques?"

"Oh, of course," my twin says. "Most of them are very beautiful but kinda expensive."

Aware that I sound like a teacher, I explain, "Imagine if you lived in a beautiful old mansion, filled with exquisite antiques. However, the plumbing in this old house has serious problems, and the roof leaks. You decide to move to a brand-new house with good plumbing and no leaks. However, you have to leave behind many of your beautiful antiques because they were built into the old house or they would look completely out of place in your modern dwelling."

I pause for a moment to let the girls visualize my imaginary scenario before continuing, "There might be times when you miss your old place, despite its problems. There's a different kind of beauty in old things."

Coree says, "JoeE, you have such a nice way of explainin' everything."

"If you spent as much time listening to my grandfather as I have, you would think of all of this stuff yourself," I tell her. "Papa puts all kinds of ideas into my head whether I want them there or not."

"I can't wait to meet Papa," my twin declares.

"Mom says that my grandparents are coming down here to visit us in the next few months," I tell her.

"Don't you mean *our* grandparents, JoeE?" MaryAna corrects.

My mother's latest secret requires that I must lie. "Yes, I mean *our* grandparents. Mom says that she's planning a trip with us to Fulton next summer."

"I'd love to join you," Coree says excitedly.

Since I'm going to drop the sister bomb tomorrow, I might as well invite her along. "Sure," I say with a smile. "It would be great if you could join us. I know that they would love to meet you too."

"It's a date!" Coree responds gleefully, blowing me a kiss.

I shudder uncomfortably. "Date" may not be the best choice of words at this point.

Chapter 40

MONEY MATTERS

As we go back to MaryAna's car to continue our excursion, my twin asks if I'd like to drive. "No, but thanks for offering," I reply.

Leaving the parking lot, she asks, "You do have your license, don't you?"

"Well, not exactly," I explain. "In New York, you need to be sixteen to get a learner's permit, which I have. However, to obtain a driver's license, you must be sixteen and a half. I took driver education last fall. I understand that you only have to be sixteen in Mississippi, so hopefully I can get one later this week."

Coree says, "We got our permits when we were fifteen. That's one thing that's certainly better about Mississippi than New York!"

"I doubt that my grandfather would agree," I respond with a smile. "He thinks that teenage drivers are a menace to society."

MaryAna adds, "Based upon their rates, the insurance companies agree with Papa. Mama makes me pay my own car insurance out of my allowance. She says it'll make me appreciate how expensive havin' a car is, especially if I have an accident or get a ticket."

"Well, if I get a car, I suppose I'll have to pay the insurance too," I speculate.

"I asked Mama if she was gonna get you a car when I got mine. She told me that she plans to buy you one soon."

"Seriously! *That's* the kind of secret Mom should have," I blurt out.

"Mama still has more secrets?" MaryAna asks, looking worried.

"I just meant like you being my sister," I respond quickly, hoping that she doesn't pursue the subject.

"Oh," she replies as I sigh thankfully.

The remainder of the tour consists of driving around the nearby suburbs of Pearl and Flowood, which are between here and Jackson. By the time we start back home, it's around noon, and Coree is making a new musical selection. Taylor Swift's melodic voice booms from the car's speakers. The girls sing along, knowing every word.

Upon returning to the house, they hurry off to plan their wardrobes for the New Year's Eve party and catch up on text messages. Heaven help the world should they miss a text. However, I have to admit that I'm beginning to get hooked on the habit myself.

After what MaryAna told me about getting a car, I want to talk to Mom. I find her in her bedroom, typing away at her laptop. "Hi, are you busy?" I ask, entering the room.

"Not really, JoeE," she answers, looking up from her screen.

"Last night, you said that you wanted to talk about my trust fund. What do you want to tell me?" I'm hoping that it's about a car after what my twin revealed earlier.

"I told you that we needed to consult your grandfather before withdrawing money early from your trust fund. Well, I said that so it wouldn't influence your decision to move here. Although I would seek his advice in such a matter, I actually control it."

"That's fine, Mom," I interject, "but it really doesn't matter to me which of you controls the fund."

"As you know, baby, I bought MaryAna a car for Christmas."

My heart starts to pound, and behind my back, I cross my fingers.

"The money for her car came from one of my personal accounts. I plan to buy you a car as soon as you get your license. I won't use your trust-fund money for it."

"Awesome, Mom," I say. I wonder when the DMV opens. I want to be the first one in line.

"Now, dear," my mother warns, "you must keep your grades up, pay your own insurance, and *no* tickets. Those are the same rules that I gave MaryAna."

I tell my mother, "That sounds great. I appreciate it."

"One more thing, JoeE. A few days ago, you asked me if we were rich."

"Yes, ma'am," I say, showing off my new Southern etiquette.

Smiling at my respectful response, she says candidly, "Through various investments, I've substantially increased the value of your trust. The amount isn't a secret. If you ever want an estimated value, all you need to do is let me know."

"Does MaryAna know how much is in the trust fund?"

"Not exactly. I told her about it several years ago," my mother informs me. "MaryAna said she didn't want to worry about it until she turned twenty-one, so she hasn't asked since."

"I'd like to know a ballpark figure," I tell her.

On her computer, Mom brings up what appears to be a financial report. "This is a summary as of last quarter."

She scrolls the down to a line that reads, "Total Estimated Value."

My eyes bug out when I see the amount.

"Wow! It looks like MaryAna and I should never have to worry about money."

Mom surprises me again. "That's just *your* trust fund, sweetie. Your sister has one with about the same amount."

"So you're saying this money is all mine?" I say, almost skeptically. After recounting the zeroes, I get even more excited.

Mom reminds me, "It's not all in cash. I've got it invested in a wide variety of assets. Except for college, honey, you must be twenty-one before you have access to this money. It would be a good idea to take some financial management courses in college."

"That sounds like a great idea," I agree wholeheartedly.

My mother shuts the laptop. "I'll give you some advice that I was given when I was a teenager. Keep your financial business to yourself. That way, you never have to worry if a friend is only interested in your money. We'll talk more about this later. It never hurts to start a habit from the beginnin', and for you that time is now."

My mother told me that we're "well-off." Seeing the immense amount of wealth in my trust fund, I know that in a few years, I'll be rich by most standards. I feel as if I've just won the lottery. However, there's another feeling creeping into the back of my mind.

In the movie *Spiderman*, Uncle Ben tells Peter Parker, "With great power comes great responsibility." I suspect that the same is true about having a great deal of wealth. My mother already trusts me with a significant amount of money for someone my age. Maybe she's trying to teach me how to use it wisely before this small (actually not so small) fortune falls into my lap.

Continuing to explain our financial situation, she says, "Joseph had a very substantial amount of life insurance. I've deposited the proceeds into a special account, separate from your trust fund. Although you and I were joint beneficiaries on the policy, I feel that it's rightfully your money. You can access the funds anytime you wish. If you prefer that I invest any of it for you, we can discuss that at another time."

"You mean I've got *more* money?" I say, not sure how to react. "And I can use it any way I want right now?"

"Yes," my mother tells me, "you're free to use the insurance money as you see fit. And if you ever need advice, you know where to find me."

This information is coming at me so fast that I forget to ask her how much money we're even talking about in this other account.

"As for my financial situation, we have more than enough money for us to live comfortably." Seeming to be finished, she sighs as if she is somewhat exhausted.

"Now, is that *all* of your secrets, Mom?" I hope that no more "confessions" will be necessary in the future.

Taking more than a few moments to consider my question, she says guardedly, "That is everything that you need to know."

The way she phrases her answer, it confirms my belief that she has other closely held secrets that she won't—or possibly can't—share with me. I suppose that many people have personal secrets that they take all the way to the grave.

I give my mother a big hug. "You're the best mom in the whole world."

I know that she doesn't believe me, and it may not be true. However, despite all that has transpired in the past, to me she's the best mother in the world for one reason—because she's mine.

Chapter 41

THE AUDITION

After talking to Mom, I'm on the way to my bedroom when the front doorbell rings. Opening the door, I find Tyler and Mason there, dressed in sweats. The voracious Tyler is munching on what appears to be a corndog on a stick. Mason has footballs tucked under each arm.

"What's up?" I ask, pleased to see them.

"We're about to toss the ball around. You wanna join us?" Mason asks cheerfully. "We want to see firsthand what your arm is like."

"Sure, just a sec," I say, not trying to hide my enthusiasm.

I rush back to my bedroom and hurriedly throw on a blue New York Giants football jersey, some sweatpants, and my running shoes. Coming out of my room, I almost trample MaryAna and Coree, who have emerged from fashion central, curious about who rang the doorbell.

MaryAna asks, "Who was at the door?"

"Two Mormon missionaries here to offer my sinful twin sister a path to salvation," I respond, trying not to grin.

"Seriously?" MaryAna asks with a worried look on her face.

"No," I admit, smiling. "It's Mason and Tyler. We're going to throw a football around."

MaryAna delivers another stinging strike to my arm in retaliation for my little prank.

Coree says, "Let's go watch them. It'll be fun!" Apparently not convinced about the "fun," MaryAna reluctantly agrees, and they follow me outside.

Seeing the girls, Mason says teasingly, "Oh, great, we have the Airhead Twins for cheerleaders."

MaryAna quickly retorts, "We just came to see the Three Stooges. Aren't you Mo?"

It's nice to see that MaryAna no longer has a "deer in the headlights" expression just because Mason is here. Maybe our half-brother will soon start absorbing his share of those karate punches. It's a beautiful day with a temperature somewhere in the sixties. There's no wind, and only a few lazy clouds are scattered around the sky. Today reminds me of a nice fall day in Fulton. This ideal football weather makes it difficult to believe that it's December 31.

Walking around to the back of our house, Mason tells us that we're going over to Rachel's yard which is even larger than ours. I notice his Toyota is parked in her long driveway. His girlfriend is out in front of the house, waiting for us. With the Taylor's house set so far back from the highway, their expansive front yard will provide ample space for me to demonstrate my passing proficiency.

MaryAna, Coree, and I say hello to Rachel, who seems to be surprised to see the girls with us. Noticing that my twin is exceedingly friendly to her previous archrival, I hear them chattering about what they're going to wear to the party tonight.

Although she's with the other two girls, Coree's eyes are following me like a hawk. Her longing expression shows that she'd like to join us rather than remain an observer. Whose idea is this impromptu exhibition? Mason's? Maybe Coree's? The other guys begin throwing the ball to each other. As I'm about to suggest that we invite Coree to join us, Mason yells, "Heads up!" and whistles a pass in my direction, but a few feet away. With outstretched arms, I snatch the ball out of the air, diving to the ground to catch it.

"Well, he can catch," says Tyler, as I throw a much softer and more accurate pass in his direction.

Mason's a starting quarterback, and I know there's no way he'd intentionally throw a pass that bad. Odds are he wants to test more than just my arm.

"It'd be nice to have a receiver on our team who can actually hold on to the ball," Mason teases Tyler with a smile.

Maybe Mason believes that I could make the team as a receiver. More than capable of catching a football, I know pass routes and I'm fast. If catching passes is what it takes to play for Brandon High, I can adjust my ambitions. It's a team sport. I'll do whatever it takes to help win games.

"Having a quarterback who could throw the ball somewhere near us would be awesome," Tyler retorts. Although their jesting seems like friendly banter, I feel like a pawn on a chessboard as the more powerful pieces maneuver around me.

Still grinning, Mason replies, "Well, maybe JoeE will put it right in your little ole hands next fall. We wouldn't want y'all to have to make any extra effort."

I'm confused even further by that statement. What can Mason possibly be thinking? I know that the two guys are just kidding with each other, but Mason didn't make that last remark in a joking manner. Tyler's silence demonstrates that his friend's comment also caught him off guard. Does Mason really think that I might replace him as quarterback?

With each throw, we move farther apart. It feels good to loosen up my right arm; I've not thrown a football since an impromptu game at Thanksgiving back in Fulton. My left arm is still stinging from MaryAna's little love tap. That girl has a heck of a punch.

I tell Mason that I have a few questions for him about the playbook.

"How much of it have you had a chance to look at?" he asks.

"All of it."

"Really?" he responds, flashing his dynamite smile and sounding pleasantly surprised. "I guess you *are* after my job."

Why does he seem so happy about that possibility? I finally tell him, "I don't think that I'll replace you. I just hope I can make the team."

"We'll see," he responds, certainly right about that fact.

I glance over at Coree. She's still studying us intensely and appears to be listening to every word we say. I ask Mason a few questions about several terms, and he answers in detail, making sure that I understand.

MaryAna lets us know her opinion of our little game of catch. "Boring. Boring."

"What would you like us to do to entertain y'all, somersaults?" Mason asks.

"Something interestin'," my twin replies. "Tyler, show JoeE how fast you are."

Mason turns to Tyler. "I guess it's time to check out JoeE's arm, Ty. Y'all ready?"

I nod my head affirmatively as Tyler replies, "I was born ready." Mason tosses me a football, and Tyler lines up as if he's a wide receiver, about a dozen yards to my right.

"Run a post-corner. Break the post at about thirty yards. I'll let it fly when you break. Since it's supposed to be a corner route, I'll drop it over your right shoulder at about sixty yards," I tell him.

Tyler looks over his shoulder at Mason. "Who is this guy, Drew Brees?"

Before Mason can respond, I point to the number ten on my Giants' jersey and say proudly, "No, Eli Manning."

Tyler grins. Mason warns me, "Ty is really fast. He's outrun my arm before and, besides, he wants to impress your sister."

After last night's revelation, the last thing I want to be reminded about right now is sisters.

Using some of the Brandon cadence, I bark out some signals and Tyler takes off down the lawn. Standing sideways with my left shoulder forward, I take the classic quarterback stance. At about thirty yards down the lawn, he makes his break and cuts to the right at about a forty-five degree angle. As promised, I step forward, delivering the ball effortlessly. The football rockets out of my hand and into a perfect spiral as Tyler accelerates to full speed. When he looks back over his right shoulder, the ball drops perfectly into his outstretched hands, hitting him in stride. A perfect route. A perfect pass. Touchdown!

Tyler runs a few more yards, slowing down before doing a little touchdown dance in our imaginary end zone.

"Impressive!" Mason says as the girls clap and cheer behind us. "How consistently can you throw that pass?"

"Well, at least nine out of ten times," I answer and quickly add, "However, that's standing here in ideal conditions with no wind, no rain, and no nasty defensive players trying to tear my head off."

"That does make a difference," Mason agrees, having also experienced those conditions firsthand. "Are you busy this afternoon?"

"No plans at the moment," I respond, curious as to what he has in mind.

"Sweet." He motions for the girls to follow him to his Toyota. When he gets to his car, I see him take out his cell phone, text something, and show it to the girls.

Tyler has walked back from our imaginary end zone. "Nice pass, JoeE," he says.

"Thanks; nice catch," I reply, knowing that I could've thrown it much farther but I don't want to show off, at least not yet.

Observing Mason and the girls at the car, Tyler asks, "What are they up to?"

"I have no idea," I tell him, wondering myself.

While we wait, we discuss pass routes, and Tyler tells me his favorites. Then, unexpectedly, he asks, "JoeE, do you think MaryAna really likes me?"

I wonder if I have *Psychic Love Connection* tattooed on my forehead. "Yes, Tyler," I tell him. "I think she does, but I'm no expert on girls."

"Is anyone?" he responds. Then he hesitantly adds, "So, if I ask MaryAna to go out on a date, do you think that she'd say yes?"

When I don't answer immediately, he looks worried.

"I think she would be a fool if she didn't," I tell him. "Besides," I add, smiling, "she really wants those World Series tickets."

Chapter 42

HAVING FUN

While the girls frantically text, Mason comes back to where Tyler and I are talking.

"What's up, Mas?" Tyler asks.

"I've got the girls invitin' a few guys from the team to play a little football with us," Mason answers. "I figure that within a half hour, we should have ourselves a competitive little scrimmage."

While we wait, Mason and Tyler go over some more of the signals and other parts of Brandon's offense. In about ten minutes, the girls report to Mason that they have reached everyone. The girls' phones continue to ring, and MaryAna asks him if it's OK if some other players come too.

"Sure," Mason says cheerfully, "the more the merrier."

Pulling me aside, Coree whispers, "I sure hope that my brother doesn't get into trouble over what he asked us to send."

"What did it say?" I ask curiously, wondering how a simple invitation to play some football could possibly cause any trouble.

Coree touches her cell screen a couple of times and holds it up so that I can see the message. It reads, "Mason says 2 come see the new Brandon QB."

I can't believe my eyes. There's certainly no question now as to what he's thinking. The only question is why.

She tells me worriedly, "I'm not sure that Daddy will like this at all. Mason might just be stirrin' up a hornet's nest!"

Surely that little text can't cause too much of a problem. But then again, it's not the words that concern Coree; it's the implications.

A white pickup turns into Rachel's long driveway, pulling up behind Mason's car. As two young black guys get out, Tyler shouts, "Well, Thunder and Lightnin' are here."

"Thunder and Lightning?" I ask.

"Yeah, it's on their birth certificates," Mason says jokingly. The two guys amble over to where we are standing. "This here's Bud Townsend and his cousin, Jarvis. Bud's nickname is Thunder, and Jarvis is Lightnin'. Long story."

Bud is just under six feet tall and built like a basketball power forward. Jarvis is slightly shorter and built as sleek as a greyhound.

Bud asks, "What's all this noise about a new quarterback?"

Mason motions to me. "This is JoeE, MaryAna's long-lost twin. Just gonna toss the ball around, Bud. You feelin' up for it?"

Shaking my hand, Bud nods. "Sure." Looking at me warily, he adds, "So you're the Yankee dude your sister has been talkin' about. And you're a quarterback?"

"We're about to see." Mason tells him. Turning to me, he says with a smile, "JoeE, these jokers go around claiming to be pass receivers. You wanna see if they can catch anything today?"

Jarvis shakes his head. "Just bring it, man."

Tyler says, "Hey, Lightnin', I betcha can't outrun JoeE's arm."

Backing up to give us even more room, I nod to Jarvis. He sprints down the field, his nickname appearing to be well deserved. As he hits full speed, I step forward and launch the ball, putting plenty of air beneath it. The football rockets in a perfect spiral. Looking back over his shoulder, he watches the ball drift down into his outstretched arms about seventy yards away. I still could've thrown it farther, but that should be far enough for today.

Apparently not easily impressed, Bud says, "So you have a cannon for an arm; is it a rifle too? How about a twenty-five yard out, Yankee?" He tosses me a football.

"Where do you want it?" I ask, wanting to make the throw a little more challenging.

He puts his hands out in front of him at about shoulder height, palms up. "Put it in the old breadbasket."

Trotting down the field, he plants his foot at about twenty-five yards and sprints to the left sideline. Requiring exact timing, this pass must be delivered with little arc, getting to the receiver as quickly as possible. I drill a pass like a frozen rope in his direction. The spiraling football lands in Bud's hands right where he told me he wanted it.

That football didn't arrive at its exact destination by accident. Dad not only taught me how to throw the ball, but also all the little tricks and nuances that allow me to be like a high-powered rifle with a sophisticated scope. I'm able to judge the speed of the receiver, the angle of delivery, quickly release the football, and fire my "bullet" on target. Most importantly, thousands of repetitions allow me to make split-second decisions and adjustments. There is always room for improvement, but I like the challenge.

As he jogs back to us, Bud says to Mason, as if I weren't standing there, "Your new QB has some skills. Are you retirin'?"

"You never know," Mason answers. He turns to me. "Take Bud and Jarvis while Tyler and I play a little defense."

"OK," I tell him, "but I need a center." I turn around and yell to Coree, who's still watching us intently. "Hey Coree, you said that you wished girls could play football. Get over here and play center."

With a big grin lighting up her face, she makes a mad dash to us. Bud flips the football to her, and she places it on the ground. She puts both hands on the ball like a center in a shotgun formation. With her blue jeans drawn tightly across her posterior, Coree isn't in the most ladylike of positions. However, she's the most attractive center that I've ever seen. Maybe girls *should* be invited to play football more often.

Looking back, Coree yells, "When y'all are done checkin' out my butt, maybe we can play some ball!"

A chorus of "yes, ma'am's" quickly rings out as everyone takes his position.

I back up about five yards behind Coree to simulate Brandon's shotgun. Bud trots out to the right as Jarvis mirrors him on the left.

Taking a defensive position a few yards in front of Jarvis, Tyler jokingly yells to me, "JoeE, are you sure you don't wanna be up under center?"

Before I can respond, Coree stands up, glares at him, and says, "Why don't you get up under this, Tyler!" Gesturing in his direction, whatever she does seems to end the sexist joking for the moment.

"What route do you want us to run?" Bud yells to me.

"Both of you run seven-yard crosses," I tell him. "Let's see if Tyler the clown can keep from running into anybody."

I bark out some signals, and Coree snaps the ball back through her legs into my waiting hands. Her snap is surprisingly well executed. It's obviously not the first time she's hiked a football.

Both receivers run toward the middle of the field after taking a few strides forward. Jarvis, with his quickness, has gotten about a half step ahead of Tyler. As he darts to the middle of the field, he passes Bud shoulder to shoulder. Swerving to avoid a collision, Tyler must slow up slightly. Coming out of the traffic jam, Jarvis is now a couple of steps ahead of his pursuer, requiring only a routine pass that I deliver on time and on target. Snatching the ball out of the air, my speedy receiver completes the play.

A couple more vehicles pull into the Taylors' driveway, and four people get out. Greeting the new arrivals, Mason shouts, "Well, the defense is finally here." Yelling out some rapid introductions, we set to the line to run another play.

One of the fellows is about six foot tall with dark-brown hair. His name is Trevor; Mason says he plays one of the safety spots for the Bulldogs. Later, I learn that he is the boyfriend of Bonnie Lee Wilson, whom I met in Sunday school. She's one of the two girls who exit the car. The other girl is Shandra, whom I also met yesterday. They join our ever-growing band of spectators.

The other guy is taller, about my height, but with bright-red hair and bulging muscles. He looks like he could pick up the car that he just exited with no problem. I've got muscles, but he has *muscles*! The Incredible Hulk is Mitchell, whom I learn is a linebacker, the kind of defensive player that quarterbacks fear the most. He appears to be one of those guys who hangs out at the weight room because he thinks it is fun. I don't want Mitchell hitting me unless I'm totally padded. But even with pads, he's still someone to avoid.

After completing several passes in a row, I realize that it's been a long time since I've had this much fun playing football. The pressure to be perfect sometimes made it seem like a job rather than a sport. It's also nice to receive admiring looks from Coree.

One time when she says, "That was a nice pass, JoeE," I just nod and smile. It takes all my restraint to keep from boasting, "Girl, you haven't seen anything yet.

Chapter 43

EXTRAORDINARY SKILLS

"Is the center eligible now?" Coree asks.

"Sure," Mason yells. "Cover her, Ty."

Recognizing an opportunity to display another of my skills, I want to let Coree have some fun at the same time. She deserves a little joy today, considering what I'm about to unload on her tomorrow.

Gathering my team into a huddle, I say, "Let's clear it out for Coree. Jarvis, run a deep post. Bud, a ten-yard out. The Hulk should follow you." They all laugh, knowing exactly whom I'm talking about. I tell Coree, "Run a five-yard out to the left. Make it a stop-and-go. Let's see if we can burn Tyler."

As everyone takes his or her positions, I bark out some signals, and the action begins. To the right, Bud runs his pattern with Mitchell glued to him. On the other side, Jarvis sprints down the lawn with Mason on him step for step. Playing safety, Trevor begins to backpedal to help double cover the speedy Jarvis. Coree runs out to the left and turns toward me, stopping abruptly. Tyler is in the perfect defensive position just behind her.

After first turning to the right to create some misdirection, I rapidly pivot to my left, pumping the ball as if I'm throwing it to Coree but quickly pulling it back. Dad emphasized that to carry out any type of fake effectively, the motion must appear as real as possible. Falling prey to the pump fake, Tyler jumps in front of Coree to intercept a pass that isn't thrown.

When Tyler makes his ill-advised maneuver, Coree turns, sprinting at full speed down the left side of the lawn. Reloading the football instantly, I launch a pass in her direction. Even though I underestimate her speed, she slows up, adjusting perfectly to the underthrown football. To my genuine surprise, she reaches back, making an impressive catch.

With Tyler barreling after her, Coree continues to race down our imaginary sideline. When he's about to catch her, she stops, turns toward him, flips him the ball, and mimics his earlier touchdown dance. As all the girls behind me holler and cheer loudly, Tyler just shakes his head and walks back up the field, having suffered the ultimate humiliation—being beaten by a girl.

Scampering back to me, Coree is all smiles. "Nice catch," I compliment her.

After we high-five, Coree gives me a little kiss on the cheek. Breathless, she says, "That was freakin' awesome!"

I'm about to apologize for misjudging her speed when Tyler yells to us. "Come on, y'all. There's no kissin' in football!"

We laugh as Mitchell responds, "Get an interception, Tyler, and I'll kiss you!" I almost want to let Tyler intercept a pass just to see what happens.

Yet another car pulls into the driveway, and a small mountain emerges from it. A young black man with arms like tree trunks is introduced to me as Dedric. Coree proudly tells me that he finished second in the state power-lifting competition and plays defensive tackle for Brandon. In size and build, this Goliath reminds me of my best friend, Jonathan. If other high schools down here have defensive players like Mitchell and Dedric, I'll need Jonathan here to be my personal protector.

"Nice to meet you, Dedric," I tell him, glad to know that all those muscles will be on our team.

"Ditto," he answers. "Can we rush the quarterback?"

"Sure," I tell him reluctantly. Three-hundred-pound Dedric dwarfs Coree as she stands next to him. I say to her, "All you have to do is block *him*."

"No problem," Coree says with true gridiron spirit and determination.

On the next play, I can't help but laugh watching her attempt to slow Dedric down. Finally, she jumps on his back and goes for a ride. He carries her as if she's an oversized backpack.

After the play, I tell her, "I think that's a holding penalty."

"I don't see a flag. It's not a penalty if the ref doesn't call it," Coree says like a true football player.

We all laugh again, especially Dedric. He's obviously been blocked a thousand times, but I doubt anyone's tried to take him down with a piggyback ride.

I hear a great deal of laughter behind me. Turning around, I see that my mother and a couple about her age have joined the girls. As all the players kid Coree about her antics, I quickly run over to say hi to Mom. Rachel introduces me to her parents, Justin and Evangeline Taylor. I thank them for letting us tear up their lawn.

"It looks like you are drawin' quite a crowd," Mr. Taylor says, glancing around his front yard. I turn around to see several more cars have pulled into the driveway. Some people are walking over from the subdivision across the highway. For the next hour, we continue to draw spectators as well as add players to our little game.

Beginning to feel more comfortable with these guys, I decide to take my play to the next level. I call a play that sends the speedy Jarvis deep down the left side of the field as I roll out in the same direction. As he streaks down the lawn, I launch the football. He catches it in stride, over fifty yards away.

Dedric, the closest to me on the play, asks incredulously, "Did you just throw that with your left hand?"

Mitchell answers for me. "He sure did. Looks like the Yankee has some awesome skills."

Coree looks at me, shakes her head, and simply says, "Amazin'!"

As the rest of the players come back up the field, those who didn't see the throw are quickly informed that I'm able to pass with either hand. Even though I've always been proficient with my left, everyone moved the pencil to my right when I was learning to write. Playing baseball, I bat left-handed and in volleyball, I serve with my left. Even in tennis, I rarely hit a backhand; I simply switch my racket.

Dad came up with the idea of training me to be an ambidextrous passer when I was about eight years old. He recalled how hard it was to throw right-handed when moving to his left. From then on at football practice, I threw about half of my passes with each hand.

Mason yells to me, "That was freakin' awesome. What else can you do, JoeE? Play another position?"

"Actually, all of them," I tell him, not boasting but telling the truth.

"Hear that, y'all?" Mason warns his teammates. "JoeE just might take your position instead of mine."

Dad insisted that I play various positions as much as possible. He knew that it would help me understand what other players were facing. In junior high, I was already six feet tall and nearly two hundred pounds, bigger than many of our high school players. Since seventh grade, I've been given the "privilege" of practicing with the high school varsity. Dad demanded total effort from all his players, but especially from me.

Lining up for the next play, Dedric asks me rather sheepishly, "You mean you can play defensive tackle?"

"Don't worry, Dedric," I tell him, "I suck at it!" I have to admit that it's the one position I never came close to mastering.

We soon have at least thirty players and an ever-growing number of spectators. Mason puts extra players on defense, making it even more difficult for receivers to get open. Coree reluctantly gives up her position when Brandon's sophomore center, Clint Covington, arrives. His butt doesn't cause nearly the distraction that hers did.

For the rest of the afternoon, it's "game on." We run a simulation of Brandon's offense against most of the players that will make up the Bulldog's defense next season. I scramble around, completing passes as defenders unsuccessfully try to disrupt my rhythm. They fail as one pinpoint pass after another reaches its target. Brandon's array of sure-handed receivers makes my job easier.

After completing about twenty passes in a row, I make a horrible throw that bounces harmlessly at Bud's feet.

He turns to Mason, saying, "I'm glad to see that the Yankee is human. I was beginnin' to think that y'all brought us a robot."

On one play, a frustrated Mitchell comes blitzing into the backfield. Although he tries to avoid a collision, I inadvertently step directly into his path. He knocks me into the next zip code.

As he helps me up, the muscle-bound linebacker says apologetically, "Sorry, Yankee, I get a little carried away sometimes." My earlier thought about needing to wear pads when Mitchell is around has proven to be accurate.

After a few more plays, Mason takes himself out of the game and goes over to talk to some men on the edge of the lawn. They're standing next to Tyler's sister, Lainey, and her friend, Noe, the two cute girls who were at the Calhouns' little get-together on Friday. I don't recognize any of the men, but they seem to be intently listening to what Mason is telling them.

Realizing that the "Yankee" nickname is probably going to stick, I think it could have been worse. In *Remember the Titans*, they start calling the quarterback from California "Sunshine." Even though I was born in California, Sunshine Collins doesn't appeal to me. Yankee Collins, Super Bowl MVP, has an interesting ring to it.

Since I'm losing my dream girl, I need a new fantasy.

Chapter 44

NEW FACES

By the time we decide to call it quits more than two hours later, almost every Brandon football player has joined us. As the game went on, a host of people encircled the field. It's hard to believe that a touch football game has drawn so much attention. Afterward, Mason introduces me to several of the spectators.

The first is a young man who is as tall as I am and has bulging muscles and a broad smile. He's wearing a unique white-and-gold pointed ring. Obviously an athlete, he's wearing a Southern Miss football jersey, like the ones that MaryAna and Tyler wore Friday.

"JoeE, this is Kane Robinson," Mason informs me as I shake his hand, feeling his powerful grip. "His younger brother, Matthew, was one of your receivers out there today. Kane graduated from Brandon last year and is on a football scholarship at Southern."

"We had a terrible season at Southern Miss this year," Kane admits in a deep, almost gravelly voice, "but next season I plan to help change that, no matter who they get for our coach."

I smile as if I agree. I don't want to burst his bubble. I fear it'll take more than him and a new coach to turn a winless team back to winning ways.

When his brother Matthew—a fast, tall wide receiver—joins us, I'm shocked that the two are related. They look absolutely nothing alike except for having dark-brown eyes and rather unique eyebrows: straight slashes without any arch.

After acknowledging Matthew with a quick wave, I turn to his older brother. "Nice to meet you, Kane. What position do you play?"

"I'm a linebacker. I like to hit people."

Motioning to Matthew, I say, "Your brother has a great pair of hands. He caught everything I sent his way." The younger brother appears to be on the shy side, and he quietly accepts the well-deserved praise.

Kane says, "My brother tells me that you're MaryAna's twin."

"That's right," I reply, wondering how well he knows my sister, since he's several years older than she is.

"I see MaryAna over there looking as good as ever," Kane says with a devilish grin. That statement may answer my question. "Say hey to her for me. See y'all later."

Kane turns to leave. Matthew doesn't say anything but gives us a wave of his hand before following his older brother.

"Later, guys," I tell them.

Next, Mason introduces me to a man who's a math teacher at the high school as well as the baseball coach and the defensive coach of the football team. As I gulp, wondering what this guy is thinking, Mason says, "Coach Butler, I'd like you to meet JoeE Collins."

Ruggedly handsome, the man looks to be about forty, but his slightly receding hairline suggests he may be older. The coach isn't super tall—he's less than six feet—and he has wide shoulders and a thick neck. He appears to be in excellent physical shape.

Coree joins us and grabs my left hand as I'm being introduced. Obviously, she knows Coach Butler, since he's on her father's coaching staff. The coach has a strange look in his dark-brown eyes, as if he's surprised that she has taken my hand. For a few moments, he stares at me like a father sizing up his daughter's new boyfriend.

"Nice to meet you, JoeE," he finally says, thrusting out a meaty paw to shake hands. "You really tore my defense apart today."

Smiling, I respond humbly, "Thank you, Coach. They were going easy on me."

He turns to Coree. "Nice to see you, too."

She acts as though Coach Butler is invisible. Failing to respond to him in any way, she adopts an icy-cold stare that I catch out of the corner of my eye. I have to admit, I'm perplexed by her sudden change in demeanor.

Ignoring Coree's stony attitude, Coach Butler says to Mason, "The first practice, we're gonna have to put some real heat on your friend and see how well he passes while runnin' for his life!"

"I'd appreciate it, Coach, if you don't let Mitchell beat me up too badly," I say, half joking and half pleading.

"Yeah, that boy's a load," Coach Butler says. I just nod in agreement. "Nice to have met you," he says as he begins to walk away.

"Nice to meet you too, sir," I say, practicing my Southern etiquette.

As Coach Butler leaves, I have a feeling that he may be on his way to make a phone call to Coach Calhoun. I'd certainly love to listen in on that conversation. Coree explains to me that besides coaching football and baseball, JJ Butler also teaches karate. She says that he was Mason's, MaryAna's, and her instructor or "sensei" (the Japanese term for teacher).

"Do the three of you still take karate?" I ask.

"Mason and MaryAna still do, but I quit a couple of years ago," my dream girl answers, not explaining why she quit or gave Coach Butler that icy stare. I figure that if and when she wants me to know, she'll tell me.

Bonnie Lee Wilson and her boyfriend, Trevor, who just impressed me with his play at safety, come over next. He says, "You're a heck of a passer, JoeE. I'm glad you're goin' to be on our side."

"Thanks," I reply, "but I was lucky that you didn't intercept any. You're an excellent safety, and I need to sharpen up a bit."

"JoeE," Bonnie Lee says, "I hope that I didn't embarrass you in Sunday school. MaryAna told me afterward that you're kinda shy."

"It's OK," I say, laughing. "MaryAna's embarrassing me plenty all by herself." They smile and nod, obviously familiar with my twin.

Coree continues to hold my hand as I meet more people. I doubt that she's going to feel quite so possessive when she learns that I'm her half-brother. Now feeling even more guilty for not telling her already, I realize how awkward it'll become for both of us if Mom's little secret becomes public knowledge.

For the next hour or so, I meet players, some of their families, and others who are simply fans of the Bulldogs. Lainey and Noe come over to say hi. With them is a man who Mason introduces as Mr. David, a US history teacher at the high school. He and JJ were two of the men to whom Mason was talking so intently earlier.

Everyone seems friendly and complimentary. I begin to have the uneasy feeling that Coach Calhoun may be receiving more than one phone call. I begin to suspect that Coree's fears about Mason's text may be a problem after all.

As darkness begins to fall, MaryAna and I head back to our house while Coree rides home with Mason.

As we cut through the trees, I mention to my twin, "Mason introduced me to Kane Robinson. He told me to tell you hey." I leave out the part about him saying how good she looks.

An almost visible chill seems to sweep through MaryAna. Shaking her head slightly, she makes no reply. I've no idea how to interpret her reaction. Maybe another secret?

When we get home, Mom is waiting for us. She says, "I really enjoyed seeing you play football, honey."

"It was only a little game of touch."

"I know," she says, wiping a little tear at the corner of her eye. "Are you hungry?"

"Always, Mom," I say, realizing that she still doesn't know me any better than I know her.

"I'll fix you a really big sandwich," she informs me as she goes to the refrigerator. It's great to have a mother.

After we all have a bite to eat, Mom and MaryAna go to their rooms to make themselves beautiful for the New Year's Eve celebration, and I take a much-needed shower. Seeing my eyes in the bathroom mirror, red-rimmed with fatigue, I consider taking a nap.

Instead, I grab my iPad, lean back in the recliner, and go automobile shopping. Now that I know I'll be getting a car soon, I check out the latest selection of makes and models. Although a Mustang would be awesome, I should take my selection a bit more seriously.

When it's time to leave, MaryAna finds me in my bathrobe, sound asleep in the recliner. Staying up most of the night finally caught up with me. My clothes for the party are neatly laid out on the bed. I'm beginning to appreciate the efforts of my stealthy fashion coordinator. My twin informs me that Mom has already left for what she called "a little get-together" at the governor's mansion.

On the way to the party, I ask my twin, "Who does Mom know that's close to the governor?"

"She knows alotta of politicians," MaryAna answers. "She's on the board of directors for a bank, and she gives money to political campaigns. Mama rubs elbows with powerful people here and in Washington. She doesn't talk about it much."

I wonder why my mother hasn't mentioned anything about this. Still more secrets, perhaps?

By the time we arrive at Calhoun Castle, it's well past ten o'clock. In the clear sky, the stars are like pinpoints of light against the blackness. It will be the perfect backdrop for the fireworks later.

Chapter 45

CONFRONTATION

When we reach the Calhouns' home, Coree meets me at the door. Leading me to the kitchen, she proudly shows me the great spread of culinary delights that she and Julie have spent hours preparing. Already into the food, Tyler leads the attack.

Starving, I match him bite for bite. I get the opportunity to try turnip greens. They look like a cooked version of what I clean off the bottom side of the lawnmower when I mow for my grandparents. After my first bite, I'm very polite and say that I don't really care for them. I believe turnip greens, like okra, are an acquired taste that I may never acquire.

As Julie and the girls prepare dessert, Coach Calhoun motions for me to join him in the far corner of the living room. Mason is already waiting for us, and I can tell from his nervous fidgeting that he probably would prefer to be elsewhere.

Coach says in a gruff tone, "I heard about your little football game this afternoon." I feel my stomach turning into tight knots. I don't recognize the look on Coach's face, but it's not one of pleasure.

Mason doesn't make matters any better when he says rather aggressively, "Well, sir, you now have that awesome passer that you've always wanted." With those words, it looks like Coree was right—Mason is stirring up a hornet's nest.

With his piercing blue eyes narrowed, Coach Calhoun looks at Mason and, obviously irritated, responds sternly, "So you're the big expert now, huh? You think that you can pick who we should play at quarterback after one game of touch football?"

"No, sir," Mason responds emphatically. "But you'll see for yourself come first practice!"

Coach seems speechless at Mason's loud outburst. I'm also stunned at both Mason's words and his frankness. He's actually telling Coach that I should replace him at quarterback. Now, standing almost toe to toe with his father, Mason adds in a surly tone, "For the record, it didn't take all afternoon. I knew after the first pass!"

When Coach responds, his voice is agitated and his words a little bit slurred. "Boy, it takes more than a good passer to make a quarterback!"

"Yes, sir, I know that all too well," Mason tells him, lowering his voice slightly. "I knew JoeE had everything else covered before I ever saw him with a football in his hands. If you don't believe me, ask Coree!"

I wonder what in the world Mason is getting at. Ask Coree? What does that mean? I'm happy that he believes I can play quarterback for Brandon, but this confrontation scares the heck out of me.

In a slightly softer tone, Mason informs his father, "Daddy, don't worry about gettin' JoeE a playbook. I gave him mine yesterday, and he already knows it better than me. I probably won't need one anyway."

Walking off to the kitchen, Mason leaves us standing there in astonishment.

Turning to me, Coach Calhoun says, "What's gotten into his head? It's just not like him. That boy has never talked to me like that. Something must be really wrong. Has he said anything to you?" There's real fear creeping into Coach Calhoun's voice.

"No, Coach," I tell him. "All Mason did was invite a few guys. Things just got out of hand."

"What happened this afternoon isn't really a big problem," Coach Calhoun assures me. "It's stirred up quite a buzz about you, and I'm gettin' a lot of questions about Mason. My phone has been ringin' all night."

"I'm not sure that I should replace Mason, Coach," I say, now really wondering what I've stepped into. "What are people saying about me?"

"Well." He stops for a moment to collect his thoughts. "Mason isn't the only one who thinks you would be a great quarterback. Coach Butler gave you the highest compliment. JJ said that he would hate to try to design a defense to stop you. We'll work all this out at practice. By the way, do you really throw just as well with either hand?"

"I'm actually a little bit better with my left hand. It feels more natural," I whisper to him as if I were a spy exposing a state secret.

A part of me would like to mention that my ability with my left hand runs in our "new" family. However, this is neither the time nor place for that discussion. It is slowly starting to sink in that I'm actually talking to my flesh-and-blood father rather than just another coach.

"Even an awesome passer needs dessert," Coach Calhoun tells me, crushing his empty beer can. "Let's get our butts into that kitchen before Tyler devours everything." He's beaming his usual great-big grin, but I can tell that he's forcing it.

The knots that have been building in my stomach for the last few minutes loosen up somewhat. However, I'm starting to see why Dad tried to keep my life simply black and white.

For dessert, I cut myself a large slice of what I believe to be pumpkin pie. I heap an excessive amount of whipped cream on top of it. It tastes wonderful but seems sweeter than the ones my grandmother always makes for dessert at Thanksgiving.

"How do you like the sweet potato pie, JoeE?" Julie asks, sensing that I probably have no idea what I'm eating.

"It's delicious," I tell her, "but I thought it was pumpkin."

After we eat, Coree and I stroll outside to where Mason and Rachel are talking. The girls begin complaining about how cold it's getting. By Fulton standards, we wouldn't call this temperature cold, just chilly. Coree invites Rachel to come upstairs with her to get something warmer to wear. After they leave, Mason motions for me to follow him, and we begin walking toward the rear of the large backyard.

He says, "JoeE, I'm so sorry that I put you through all that with Coach."

"Oh, that's OK," I tell Mason. "I certainly don't want to come between you and your father. I can play another position. Quarterback is your spot. I really don't want to screw everything up."

"No, JoeE, you don't understand," Mason says, sounding a little desperate. He goes on in a very deliberate, somber tone: "I want you to replace me as Brandon's quarterback."

Is he serious?

As I stare at him in stunned silence, Mason continues, "You'll make a great quarterback for our high school. First of all, you deserve it. You're better than me, fair and square. And if we're being honest, I'm done. Not just with quarterback." He must read the bewilderment on my face. "You see, I would have quit football a long time ago if it wasn't for Dad. He pushed for it, and I liked makin' him proud." I nod, sensing exactly where he's coming from.

As I try to grasp what's happening, Mason goes on. "However, as the years went by, I began feelin' more and more responsibility for my team, my coaches, and now for all of Brandon. Look at how many people showed up because of one simple text message. Believe it or not, football is the real religion of Mississippi. I feel like everyone is dependin' on me to lead us to the Promised Land. Whether it's intended or not, that pressure falls directly upon the team's quarterback. I really believe that you can handle that pressure. I can't anymore."

When Mason pauses, I ask, "What makes you think I can handle that pressure any better than you?"

Mason smiles. "Partly because of what you said to me yesterday. You asked someone who you practically just met why he likes his girlfriend! Just like that. That took some real balls. I know you were doin' it for MaryAna. I also know that I couldn't have done anything like that for Coree. Anyone with that kind of courage isn't goin' to be intimidated by a blitzin' linebacker."

I return his smile, but picturing Mitchell bearing down on me makes those balls shrivel a bit. Mason continues, "Your confidence is exactly what you need to play quarterback for our high school!"

"Thanks," I tell him, "but you said that was only part of the reason. What else convinces you that I can handle it?"

"That's simple," Mason answers. "Because Coree said you could handle the job. My sister knows her football—better than you and me. Maybe better than some of the coaches."

There is no longer any doubt in my mind that Coree is an expert on the sport. No way would Mason make that statement unless it was true. It appears that I actually have the opportunity to be the next quarterback for the Bulldogs after all. Mason has just handed me the keys to the kingdom. My heart is flying like an eagle, soaring to the heavens

Chapter 46

FIREWORKS

Thinking back to Mason's confrontation with Coach Calhoun, I say, "Your father's worried about you. He says he's never seen you act like this before."

Mason puts the back of his hand over his mouth, drops his head, and looks at the ground. As fireworks explode somewhere in the distance, he finally lifts his head and wipes tears from his eyes. Trying to speak, he chokes up.

I want to say something but decide that it's better just to give him a chance to regain control of himself. Recalling how Jonathan's arm felt when my father lay on the sidelines after the heart attack, I want to put my arm around Mason's shoulder but refrain. I just stand there motionless in an awkward silence.

Finally making eye contact, Mason says, "I promised Rachel not to say anything about this, but if I don't talk to someone, I'm just gonna fall apart. Coree says that you're a great listener, but I hate to burden anyone else with my problems."

Seeing anyone in such pain would bother me. Knowing that Mason is my brother just adds to my concern. "I'll be glad to listen," I say, trying to sound sympathetic.

Taking a deep breath, Mason says, "It's Rachel. Her cancer..." There is panic in his voice.

He can't finish, but the awful truth is all too clear. Like a clay pigeon, my heart is suddenly shattered into a thousand pieces. I suck in a breath, totally stunned. No wonder my brother is so upset. Against every tenet of my Spartan programming, I feel a cold lump rising in my throat.

"She goes back on chemotherapy this week. I want to spend as much time with her as possible. JoeE, I think I may lose her."

This time, I do put my arm around his shoulders. We stand there in silence for a couple of minutes until I notice Coree and Rachel are at the back door. They yell to us that it's fireworks time. I remove my arm, and we begin a slow walk back toward the house while Mason regains his composure. My next thought is what, if anything, can I do to help them?

"Are you going to tell Rachel that you told me?"

"Yes," he says, wiping his eyes. "We don't like havin' secrets between us."

"You should tell Coree," I suggest, trying to make myself useful. "You've told me that Coree's been through a lot. She could be a big help. Of course, I promise I'll never mention anything about the relapse to anyone."

Hearing about Rachel's condition sure puts my little problems into the proper perspective. As we reach the house, Coree asks me what Mason and I were discussing so intently out in the yard.

In order to keep my promise to him, I tell her the truth but not the whole truth. "Mostly football."

Remembering my mother's piecemeal story, I feel badly that by not telling Coree the whole truth, in a way I'm still lying to her. I hastily add, "And some other stuff," hoping that she won't ask anything more. Luckily, she doesn't. Instead, she leads me through Calhoun Castle to the front yard.

Mason and I are informed that the boys are "fixin' to set off the fireworks." I'm assuming the "girls" aren't invited to participate in such a dangerous activity. More likely, they're smarter than we are and are staying out of harm's way. Despite several attempts to blow ourselves up, including one really close call for Mason, who seems preoccupied, we manage to survive with all of our fingers intact. We have a great time, and the girls applaud our amazing pyrotechnic display from a safe distance.

Reentering the house about ten minutes before midnight, we prepare to celebrate the New Year. Earlier, MaryAna called our grandparents. She explained to them that I couldn't come to the phone as I was playing demolition man. They had already watched the ball drop in Times Square, which doesn't have much meaning here, since it drops at eleven o'clock our time.

There's a televised celebration from Memphis, where a giant guitar will drop down at midnight in our time zone. As the New Year approaches, I suddenly recall the time-honored tradition of kissing your wife, girlfriend, or date at the stroke of midnight. I hope that in the South, they don't follow the same tradition, since my date tonight is my half-sister. Maybe they just shake hands.

As Coree takes my hand and leads me to the back patio, I realize with horror that the New Year's kiss must be a tradition throughout America. Staring into her big brown eyes, I resign myself to the fact that she isn't expecting a brotherly peck on the forehead.

I feel like a condemned man who is being offered his last meal prior to his execution. I decide that for the next few moments, I'm not going to think of Coree as my sister. Instead, I only see my dream girl. As the Calhouns' grandfather clock strikes midnight, I feel Coree's arms wrap around my neck along with the chill of her metallic bracelets in the crisp night air. Then her soft, warm lips are against mine. I close my eyes in surrender and enjoy my last romantic moments with her.

If God is going to strike me dead for this kiss, I only hope that he will wait a minute or so. If I'm dead, at least I won't have to face Coree tomorrow.

I live through the kiss. God, apparently, has decided to punish me by forcing me tell her the truth in the morning. It's a fair punishment, and I accept my fate.

Julie announces that she has some eggnog and hot peach cobbler for us in the kitchen. For the first time, Tyler isn't at the front of the chow line. In fact, he's nowhere to be seen, and neither is MaryAna. Coree and Rachel help Julie serve the cobbler. It's fabulous, as I've come to expect in the Calhoun home.

About ten minutes later, MaryAna and Tyler wander in to join us. My twin's always-perfect lipstick is smeared, and there's some extra redness to Tyler's lips. It appears that both of my sisters know how to ring in the New Year.

When it's time to leave, MaryAna hands Coree her car keys and asks her to drive me home. My about-to-be ex-girlfriend says that she's spending the night at our house again. My twin informs me that Tyler will drive her home.

"Don't forget," Coree reminds me as we climb into MaryAna's Malibu, "we're leaving about ten o'clock in the mornin' to visit Mama. Is that OK with you?"

"That's fine," I respond, still feeling like a prisoner on death row. I start the countdown to the hour of my execution.

Chapter 47

MAKE BELIEVE

Soft, melodic sounds greet us at the door as Coree and I step over the threshold. At the piano, my mother is playing and singing along. Unaware that we've joined her, she continues a song that I don't recognize. The melody is striking and her voice is strong and vibrant.

As Mom's passionate voice fills the room, I realize that she's playing the song from memory—there's no sheet music to be seen. The words describe a dark, longing fantasy about lost loves. Did Mom long for Dad to come back to her before he died? Is she thinking about Coach Calhoun despite their tragic relationship? Or is there someone else?

Considering all her ill fortune with past lovers, it's no wonder Mom's gone and made one up. My dad spurned her decisions at every turn and didn't even let her escape the marriage. But the question remains—why did my mom agree to go along with his idea of splitting up MaryAna and me? There must be a piece missing, and that throws the entire puzzle into doubt. Now I've learned that Coach Calhoun broke up with my mother not just once, but twice. The first time, he ended up marrying Coree's mother; later, he married Julie. I try not to judge the actions of others; however, in these cases, it's difficult not to.

When Mom finishes the song, we applaud loudly. She jolts and smiles shyly, realizing she had an audience.

"Encore, encore!" Coree calls out.

My mother laughs, her cheeks reddening. "Maybe some other time."

"That was great, Mom," I say. "I had no idea you were that good."

"Well, I'm still trying to shake off some of the rust. But thanks."

"What's the song about?" Coree asks.

"Pipe dreams and fairy tales," she answers jokingly. "My mother made me learn it for a recital when I was young. I didn't appreciate it back then, but now I like it. How was the party?"

We tell her about the fireworks and the gargantuan feast. Apparently having stayed up to wish us a Happy New Year, she asks why MaryAna isn't with us.

"Tyler is bringing her home. They should be here soon," I tell her, surprised that they aren't already here. Mom seems pleased at the news, obviously preferring her daughter to be with any boy but Mason at this late hour.

"How was the governor's party?" Coree asks.

"Nothing special. Just another political occasion," my mother says, shrugging. "Business as usual."

Before heading off to bed, she gives us both hugs, which seems to make Coree feel better. Sitting down on the couch, Coree asks me if I was pleased with the tour of Brandon.

"Yes, very much," I say, and mean it. "I had a great time."

She says regretfully, "It's too bad that we didn't have time to show you our new domed football stadium."

"You mean Brandon has a domed stadium?" I ask before noticing the mischievous grin on her face.

"Gotcha," she says, giggling, obviously quite proud of herself. I just shake my head for being so gullible. "It's just too easy to fool y'all Yankees," Coree continues, adding insult to injury. "You know, Robert E. Lee did it all the time."

I feel as if I'm at Fort Sumter and have just been shelled by Confederate cannons. It appears the War Between the States is back on.

Unable to let my fellow Northerners be insulted like this, I fight back. "I seem to recall that your brilliant General Lee got fooled a bit himself at a little place called Gettysburg."

Like a Rebel who won't retreat, Coree renews her full-out attack. "Well, if Stonewall Jackson hadn't gotten himself shot and Jeb Stuart hadn't turned tail and run to heaven knows where, things would've been different. We would've pushed the Yankees right outta Gettysburg, all the way to Fulton, and straight on into Canada. Besides, y'all cheated!"

"Cheated?" I raise my eyebrows quizzically, noticing how she's personalizing her argument as if she actually fought and bled in the Civil War.

"Yeah, y'all had more men and more factories and more money and more cannons and lots of stuff! It just wasn't fair to us," she says belligerently. Her brown eyes sharpen like knives.

Suddenly, I recognize that this anger isn't an act. Coree is actually becoming upset. I've never realized that a war fought a century and a half ago could still evoke such fervor. Apparently, reminders like battle sites and the statue in downtown Brandon have kept the war very much alive in the South.

I decide a strategic withdrawal is my best option. "You're right," I tell her truthfully. "That war wasn't fair."

She calms down, her eyes soften, and she seems to accept my surrender. After our short Civil War reenactment, I tell her that I'm really tired and need to go to bed.

"Alone, I suppose?" she teases, that mischievous little smile lighting up her face again.

"Most definitely alone," I riposte but with a smile, not wanting to upset her again.

Pretending to pout, Coree slinks off to MaryAna's bedroom. I get ready for bed, glad that the long day is finally over. I'm about to turn off the light when I hear a soft knock. Quickly throwing my jeans back on, I open the door. As Coree steps inside my room, I'm thankful that she's wearing some pink-and-white striped pajamas rather than MaryAna's pole-dancing outfit.

"I'm sorry about losing it over that Civil War stuff, JoeE."

"It's fine," I tell her. "I like your passion."

"I don't want to get you into any trouble," she says, mischievous eyes gleaming, "but would it be too much to ask for a good-night kiss?"

I should go ahead right now and tell her that she's my sister, but I'm just not ready yet. Plus, I'm way too tired for the lengthy discussion that is bound to follow. So I kiss her, keeping it as brotherly as possible.

Batting her big brown eyes at me, she obviously expects a little more enthusiasm on my part. Finally accepting my G-rated version of a good-night kiss, she leaves again, pouting. This time I don't think she's pretending.

After sliding into bed, I have trouble finding sleep with so much weighing on my mind. As I'm just about to drift off, there's another knock at the door. What could Coree want this time? Is this some biblical test of will?

Putting my jeans on once more, I open the door saying, "Come on in, Coree."

This time, however, MaryAna is my late-night visitor. She's still wearing her party dress, which is slightly crumpled. Her hair and lipstick are a mess. When she gives me a little hug, I smell beer on her breath.

She asks, "You got a minute?"

"Sure," I say reluctantly, yawning and rubbing my eyes. "Make yourself comfortable."

Closing the door behind her, MaryAna slurs, "If you're expectin' Coree, I'll leave."

Shaking my head, I say, "No, I wasn't expecting anyone."

As usual, my twin plops down sideways into the recliner, throwing her bare legs over the arm of the chair and kicking off her shoes. As her dress rides up her thighs, she reclines in a position that she somehow finds comfortable. Sighing, I take a seat at the desk, yawning once more.

She glances over at me. "I've got a question about makin' out."

Oh, God. MaryAna has just jolted me out of my drowsiness. Now I'm sure that I have *Psychic Love Connection* tattooed on my forehead. Not having the slightest idea what she's about to ask, I sit in stunned silence.

After pressing her finger to her upper lip as if she's checking to see if it's numb, my sister finally asks, "Do guys just expect us to act like the girls in R-rated movies?"

"So you watch R-rated movies?" I blurt out in a lame attempt to change the subject.

"Of course," my sister says with an expression that borders on disgust at how naive I am. "So, do most guys just expect us to go all the way like those girls in the movies?"

Taken aback by such directness, I have no idea how to respond. "I-I d-don't know, Sis," I stutter, not understanding why MaryAna would even want to ask me such an intimate question. Hoping to end this uncomfortable discussion quickly, I say, "I guess it just depends on the girl. I'm not a love guru."

Not letting me escape that easily, she responds, "I know it's not the same for everyone, but..." Her words trail off. Taking a deep breath, she continues, "Let me put it this way: Do you expect Coree to go all the way?"

Obviously, the last thing I want to talk about or even think about is being intimate with Coree. But it looks like MaryAna is demanding a serious answer, and I fear she won't give up until she gets one.

"I don't want to talk about Coree. Please, just leave her out of it," I request.

"OK, but I really want to know what's goin' on inside guys' heads," MaryAna insists, almost begging for an answer.

Wiping the beads of sweat off my forehead, I take a shot at it. "I can only make an educated guess. From what I've heard, most guys around our age aren't really sure how far they expect to go with any given girl. We're not exactly known for our complicated thought processes. In the heat of the moment, our hormones kinda rule, not our brains."

After giving me a little smirk from her recliner throne, my sister purses her lips, obviously trying to focus. I'm sure I haven't told her anything that she doesn't already know.

Trying to apply pure logic, I continue, "It really shouldn't matter what the guy wants. Why should it? It's your choice in the end. You have the most to lose, so you should decide."

"You're right," my sister replies, nodding in agreement. "I hadn't really looked at it that way. All these years, I've been savin' myself for Mason. Now that I know he'll never feel that way about me, I've got to reevaluate and move on."

"These kinds of situations are never easy," I say, giving her time to gather her thoughts again.

Looking up at the ceiling as if seeking divine guidance, she goes on, "I kinda like Tyler, and God knows he likes me. If I hadn't put on the brakes tonight, no tellin' how far we might've gone." Taking another momentary break, she adds, "Girls are more mature than boys, but we have hormones too, you know?"

"If it were left up to your hormones," I say, "you'd probably already have a kid or two. That might be acceptable in some cultures, but our modern world frowns on such behavior."

"You know that Tyler and I were drinkin' a bunch tonight, don't you, JoeE?" my twin bluntly admits, although it's obvious that she's feeling no pain.

"I kinda figured it out," I tell her, trying not to sound judgmental.

"Coree's got a bunch more experience on this stuff, so I guess I should talk to her." Before I'm able to respond, my sister says, "Thanks, Bro. You're so easy to talk to, and you give really good advice."

"You're welcome, Sis," I reply. I'm not sure that I even gave her any advice.

Unbelievably, MaryAna instantly seems to forget what we were discussing and asks, "Do my legs look fat?"

"They're perfectly fine," I tell her. "It's just the way you're sitting."

"Oh, yeah," MaryAna says, scooting to a slightly more upright position. "By the way, where are y'all takin' my car tomorrow? Coree said that you need some private time. What exactly are you two up to?"

"Can't say. It's our little secret," I reply. As she pretends to be upset, I tell her gratefully, "We really appreciate you letting us use it."

"No problemo," she spits out, grunting as she struggles to extricate herself from the recliner. "You know that I'm gonna check the mileage, right? That way, maybe I'll figure out where y'all went."

Laughing and helping her out of the chair, I say, "You watch too much *CSI*." Staggering off, MaryAna closes the door as she leaves my bedroom. I get back in bed, hoping to get somemuch needed sleep.

Chapter 48

A GOOD LISTENER

Despite getting to sleep so late, I rise at my usual time on Tuesday morning. As much as I would like to stay in bed, the Spartan in me won't allow it. Somehow, I just can't skip exercising and running again today. I can imagine Dad pressuring me to maintain my routine and stay in perfect shape. If he were here, I'd point out that I played football yesterday, so I actually did get some exercise. However, he'd still tell me to get up and get going.

Yawning, I roll out of my comfortable bed, intent on returning to my normal routine. As I prepare to go for my morning run, I hope that the fresh air will clear my muddled head. Maybe running will help me think of a way to reveal Mom's secret to Coree.

Quietly leaving the house while it's still dark out, I'm greeted by a chilly mist somewhere between rain and fog. Although it's the coldest morning since I arrived, it's still a good thirty degrees warmer than when I left Fulton. In my old hometown, these conditions are often a prelude to snow. In Mississippi, they seem only to threaten showers.

Enjoying the cool, refreshing breeze hitting my face, I go around the hedge at the front of our house. An unfamiliar maroon Nissan Sentra is parked in our driveway. I'm surprised to see Rachel's short red hair peeking over the steering wheel. As I walk over to the passenger side of the vehicle, she rolls down the window.

Leaning toward me, Rachel says, "Hey, JoeE, get in if you have a minute. I need to talk to you, please."

Opening the door, I slide into the front seat. "What brings you out on a morning like this? We can go inside if you want."

"No thanks," she says. "I don't want anyone to hear what I'm going to say."

"OK," I say anxiously.

"Mason said y'all talked about my relapse. I was upset at first, since I don't want to bother people with my problems. Then I realized that he needed to talk to someone besides me." She pauses, as if afraid to continue. "Mason said that you're a great listener."

Living up to my new image, I just nod. It's ironic that I'm getting this "listener rep," since I earned it with my shyness rather than any unique ability.

Rachel speaks softly, as if she's still afraid that someone might over-hear. "I've seen you out runnin' early in the mornin', so I took a chance that you would be here today. I need someone to confide in too."

"Well, I don't know much about cancer," I admit, concerned that she's looking for advice on her treatment.

Rachel surprises me when she says, "It's not about cancer. You see, last night, Mason asked me to marry him."

My mind freezes for a moment, and all I can do is repeat her words. "Marry him?"

"Yes. Mason is willin' to quit school so we can get married right away. He says that there's some money saved up in a college fund, enough for us to live on till he gets a job. He wants to spend more time together while I go through chemo."

"What did you tell him?" I ask, trying to get my thoughts back in order.

"I almost said yes," Rachel says, her voice cracking a bit. "I want to be with him, but I need time to consider whether or not we should get married right away. I don't want Mason to drop out of high school or use up his college money."

"Do you really think he means it?"

"He was absolutely serious," Rachel says. "Mason has already looked into blood tests, a marriage license, a weddin' ceremony, and even an apartment."

"Sounds like he's given it a lot of thought," I agree. "Do you mind me asking what—" I trip over my own words, not sure how to ask. "I mean, how long do you…"

"We don't know," Rachel says, having guessed what I was getting at. "Relapses can be unpredictable. But since they found it quickly, my chances are good. My oncologist recommends that I get a bone marrow transplant, but it's hard to find a compatible donor. They've started the search already. What do you think I should do about Mason?"

For a few moments, I consider the situation. "The thing is," I say slowly, "I couldn't possibly come close to what you two are feeling right now. But if it were my decision, I would take a step back. Take the emotions out of it. Don't get married right away. Wait and see how the treatments go, and take things as they come."

I see the slight hint of a smile on Rachel's face. "Fair enough, JoeE. It's kinda what I've been thinkin', too. Do you mind if I tell Mason that we talked?"

"Of course not, Rachel," I reply, trying to sound comforting.

"Mason was right," she says, seeming as though a burden has been lifted off her shoulders. "You are easy to talk to. Sorry I interrupted your run."

"Did Mason mention anything about telling Coree?" I ask. "I know he respects her opinion, and she can definitely keep secrets."

"If you think it's a good idea," Rachel says, "go ahead and tell her. Can I ask you about one more thing?"

"Sure."

"Yesterday, MaryAna was acting really strange toward me. By strange, I mean she was actually being friendly again. Did you have something to do with that?"

"We've had a couple little talks," I admit.

"What did you tell her?"

"Just the truth. I told her that Mason is in love with you and that she needs to get on with her life."

"Well, I'm grateful," Rachel responds. "I really missed havin' MaryAna as a friend. Who knows? Maybe we can even be close again."

Climbing out of the car, I say, "I appreciate your confidence in me, Rachel. If you need anything, just let me know. Good luck with your treatments."

She waves good-bye as I jog across the highway, starting my run. My problems really do seem pale and petty next to hers. God needs to focus on Rachel while I deal with my little problems on my own. Deep in thought, I notice my friendly blue jay perched on his favorite tree. We have a short conversation; I talk and he sings. Somehow, my mind is clearer after our little chat.

The run this morning is practically an exorcism. Reevaluating the loss of my romantic relationship with Coree, I look at the bright side, thinking, "I'm losing a girlfriend, but I'm gaining one heck of a sister!"

After running several miles, I return home in sunlight. The chilly mist has disappeared. It's warming up quickly, and I anticipate another beautiful day. The sudden change in weather matches my change in attitude. Resigning myself to my fate, I am happy that, as my sister, Coree will always be part of my life.

After I'm done showering, I get dressed and head to the kitchen. I find Coree is cooking breakfast.

"Do you like omelets, JoeE?" she asks invitingly.

"Sure, that would be awesome," I tell her, drawn toward the tantalizing smells coming from our kitchen.

"One ham and cheese omelet comin' up."

What can't this girl do? I wonder. "Where did you learn to cook?"

"Well, mostly from my stepmom, but Mason taught me how to make omelets. Julie works the night shift a lot, so she's usually asleep during the day. Daddy isn't exactly a morning person, so Logan and I help Mason fix breakfast, then my brother carries us to school."

In a few minutes, I'm feasting on a perfect omelet, toast, orange juice, yogurt, and hot cocoa. There's also something white on the plate. It looks like cream of wheat but isn't.

"What's the white stuff?"

She tells me they're grits, made from cornmeal. After I take a bite, I realize that unlike okra and greens, these are actually pretty good.

"This is the type of breakfast that you should be eatin' every mornin'," Coree advises, sitting down to join me.

As the great smells from the kitchen circulate throughout the house, Mom and MaryAna appear. Coree gives my mother her omelet and heads back to the kitchen to fix two more.

"Do you cook, MaryAna?" I ask.

My twin gives me a half-awake, blank stare and groans in my general direction.

"The only time I remember MaryAna cookin'," Coree calls from the kitchen, "she was burnin' marshmallows over a campfire."

We all laugh. Except for MaryAna.

Chapter 49

MARTY

After breakfast, Coree follows MaryAna to her room, where they catch up on text messages. Meanwhile, I help Mom load the dishwasher and ask her if we can talk privately.

After closing the door to her bedroom so we won't be overheard, I ask, "Is there enough money in my insurance account to buy a house in the subdivision across the highway?"

My mother looks at me curiously. "You could buy a few if you wanted. Why? Are you thinking about investing in rental properties? Or buyin' a house down here for your grandparents?"

"Something like that," I say. A house might make a great wedding present if Mason and Rachel decide to get married. Maybe then, my brother might not have to leave school or tap into his college fund.

By the time I leave Mom's room, it's almost time for Coree and me to head out. Before we go, I pop open my laptop for some quick research about marriage laws in Mississippi. I wonder if Mason has bothered to check them out, especially the age requirements.

Then Coree and I take the Malibu and head southwest on Highway 468. As we're driving, I ask about her mother's family.

"Mama was brought up in Brandon," Coree tells me. "Her father died when she was just a baby. When she was only twelve, her own mama abandoned her and left the area."

"That must have been rough on her. Where did she live after that?"

"Mama was brought up by Sarah's mother, Kimberly," Coree informs me.

"My maternal grandmother?" I ask incredulously, realizing that our families are more entangled than I ever imagined.

"Yes, your grandmother, JoeE," Coree confirms. "As far as I know, Mama has never heard from Corinna since she was abandoned. Mama has an older sister named Penny who ran off to Texas with some guy when she was a teenager."

"It sounds like your mother had a pretty tough childhood," I say.

"It makes me feel bad for Mama. Her family situation wasn't exactly ideal," she responds.

"What about your father's parents?" I ask.

"There's just Grandma Rosalee, but she doesn't like being called that. She says that she's way too young to be called Grandma. Her husband, George, died several years ago. Ever since he died, she's been mostly bouncing around Europe—Paris, Venice, you name it."

Pausing a moment, she gives me a moment to get all these names straight.

"Our whole Calhoun clan celebrated Christmas together this year," Coree adds proudly. "We got together before we left for Disney World and Grandma Rosalee flew back to Europe. My Uncle Rick drove down from Starkville. He used to play ball for Brandon and then at State, just like Daddy. He has two young sons, a little younger than Logan. They're always going on about how they're gonna play football like their daddy."

"It's good that you could celebrate the holiday together," I tell her. I want to say that since MaryAna and I weren't there, it wasn't really the *whole* clan.

The weather is clearing and warming up now that the sun has finally peeked out from behind the clouds. About four miles down the road, Coree points out a brick building to the right.

"That's the Mississippi Highway Patrol. Sometime this week, you'll need to go there for your driver's test."

Across the road is an expansive complex of buildings and yards surrounded by a high fence topped with razor wire. Large, intimidating guard towers are nestled at every corner.

"Is that a prison?" I ask, having never seen such a facility up close.

273

With a giggle, Coree replies, "I believe that, officially, it's called a correctional facility. But I bet that the inmates would say that they're in prison."

"On the way back, let's drive somewhere private," I say nervously. "I want to talk to you about something important."

"OK, but can't you tell me now?" she whines like a child wanting a Christmas present early.

"No," I say firmly. "It can wait. Let's visit your mother first."

Driving over some railroad tracks, Coree says that up ahead is the entrance to Whitfield. She turns right toward a sign that reads "Mississippi State Hospital."

We show the guard at the first building our identification: Coree, her driver's license; and me, my learner's permit. After looking at them, the officer issues us a parking permit. We're then ushered on to the administration building.

There are buildings and vast grounds for as far as the eye can see. We step inside a brick building. Coree tells the woman at the desk why we're here, and we're each issued a written visitor's pass.

Before we leave, I ask the woman at the desk, "How large is this place anyway?"

The woman informs me that it's about three and a half thousand acres. She says that there are over five hundred employees and over three thousand patients, who are called "residents."

"I understand," the woman says proudly, "that this is the largest mental hospital in the country."

I guess there are plenty of insane people in Mississippi, not to mention the "crazy" ones like MaryAna.

As we drive to a large building at the far end of the complex, I'm amazed at the beauty of the grounds. If I didn't know better, I'd think that we were touring a nature park. We pass at least twenty buildings. Coree finally pulls up in front of a large, redbrick building.

Entering, I notice Christmas decorations still adorning the walls. A friendly nurse greets us. Probably remembering Coree from previous visits, she escorts us to what she calls the south dayroom.

Glancing around the spacious room, I estimate that there are a couple dozen people scattered about. The curtains are parted, inviting warm sunlight inside. Some of the residents are playing cards, while the rest are at tables reading, talking, or just sitting. Spotting a pool table in one corner, I wish I were here for that kind of fun.

"What should I call your mother?" I ask, starting to feel uncomfortable as my shyness rears its ugly head.

"Martha, I guess," Coree tells me, seeming a bit nervous herself. Apparently, modern psychiatric drugs are quite effective, as everyone in the room appears calm and relaxed except us.

Taking my hand, Coree leads me to the far side of the room. Sitting at a table by herself is a pretty woman with a worn, yellow-paged novel clasped between her hands. She's not wearing any makeup, but she doesn't need it. Even at first glance, it's easy to tell they are mother and daughter. The only telltale difference is the dull, tired, blue eyes that lack the sparkle of Coree's bright-brown ones.

I immediately note something even more amazing. Although Coree favors her mother, Martha bears an uncanny resemblance to my own mother. It's no wonder that MaryAna and her best friend look so much alike because their mothers could very well be twins.

"Mama," Coree addresses the woman softly.

Martha looks up and smiles. "Corinna! Happy New Year."

They embrace, and Coree introduces me. "Mama, I'd like you to meet my friend, JoeE Collins."

"It's nice to meet you, Martha," I say cordially. When I look into her blue eyes, I get the feeling that something isn't right. However, I can't put my finger on what it is.

"Oh, just call me Marty," she says in a friendly tone. "Everybody here does."

Coree tells her mother, "Let's walk outside, Mama. It's gettin' warmer, and you probably need the fresh air."

Marty grabs a white sweater from the back of her chair. We stroll to a sunny patio at the rear of the building. Here, the view of the grounds is even more spectacular. There are trees, hedges, and, despite the time of year, even a few wild flowers. In the distance, I observe a lake.

Geese paddle leisurely along the shore. We sit down at a small table overlooking the grounds. Marty asks Coree if she had a nice New Year's Eve. Her daughter tells her about the fireworks and Mason almost blowing himself up.

Trying to break the ice, I say, "I didn't know your daughter's real name was Corinna."

"Oh, yes, JoeE," Marty says rather proudly. "Her middle name is Rosalee. She's named after her two grandmothers." She goes on, a tone of annoyance playing at the edge of her voice. "Calling her Coree was Rhyan's idea. He didn't like her being named after my mama. He took the "Cor" from Corinna and the "ee" from Rosalee and made up my daughter's name." She shakes her head disapprovingly.

Marty seems to be getting herself agitated, but she calms down when Coree changes the subject. "JoeE is from New York."

"That's nice," her mother says. "I've never been there. How do you like Mississippi?"

"I like it very much," I tell her, "especially the weather. It's a lot warmer here, and it is great not having to deal with all the snow."

Smiling, Marty turns to her daughter. "How did you meet JoeE, dear?"

"He's the brother of my friend, MaryAna Lindley," Coree tells her.

"You mean he's Sarah Lindley's son?" her mother asks, her tone no longer friendly.

"Yes, ma'am," Coree answers hesitantly, "JoeE is MaryAna's twin brother."

Curling her index finger, Marty motions for me to move closer. Then, in almost a whisper, she says, "I know a secret about your mama, JoeE."

Oh great, I think, *another secret!*

I've no idea how to respond to Marty. Coree says, "JoeE doesn't want to hear any secrets about his mama."

Seeming slightly upset with her daughter, Marty says emphatically, "He's practically a grown-up, Corinna. He needs to know this." She pauses and then states rather loudly, "Sarah Lindley had an affair with my husband!"

"Mama!" Coree pleads, burying her face in her hands.

Tears well up in Marty's eyes. "Rhyan and I had hit a rough patch and were sleepin' in separate rooms. Then I heard that Sarah had slipped back into town and that she was having an affair with my husband. I was afraid that he was about to leave me for *her*."

"Mama, stop!" her daughter pleads. "JoeE doesn't want to hear any of this!"

"It is OK, Coree," I say reassuringly. "Please, let her finish." I believe it's much better for her to hear about the affair now from her mother rather than later from me.

Standing up and beginning to pace, Marty continues her story. "I couldn't bear the thought of bein' rejected and divorced. I didn't want to be a single mom and go back into poverty. So I came up with a plan to save my marriage."

Coree and I look at each other. I can see that neither of us has any idea of what Marty might say next.

"Maybe I'd better get a nurse," Coree suggests. "You're gettin' yourself all riled up, Mama. All this happened a long time ago. It doesn't have anything to do with today."

"No, I'm fine, Corinna!" Marty snaps, intent on finishing. Her memories seem to be crystal clear. While Coree might only hear the ramblings of a mad woman, I know that the heart of her story must be true, since it's agreeing with what Mom told me.

Still pacing, her mother continues, "I knew that if I got pregnant, Rhyan wouldn't dare divorce me. His coaching career meant the world to him. The public humiliation of leaving his pregnant wife and one-year-old son to fend for themselves would have been too much. His family would have disowned him. I knew that he would have no choice but to come back to me."

Coree asks, "So, Mama, if Daddy and you weren't sleepin' together, how did he get you pregnant?"

It's obvious that Coree is trying to talk some sense into her mother, to tear apart her mad rant brick by brick.

"Well, darlin', I *did* get pregnant, and it wasn't long before Sarah hightailed it back to California." Marty then looks at her daughter and says candidly, "Oh, Corinna, my dear, I never told you…but how could I? How would you take it?"

"What, Mama?" Coree's on the edge of tears, apparently anticipating her mother's answer.

Marty ends the suspense. "Well, the truth is, dear, Rhyan Calhoun isn't your daddy."

Chapter 50

WHAT?

Thank you, God! Coree's *not* my sister! I want to shout it out as loud as my lungs will allow. Instead, I put my hand to my face to hide my growing smile.

In my jubilation, I almost fail to notice that Coree is about to faint. With her bright-brown eyes glazing over and her face turning ashen, she clutches the table for support. Quickly grabbing her arm, I steady her until some color returns. The news has hit us in very different ways.

Almost incoherently, Coree gasps, "Oh my God! What? No!"

Putting my arm around her for support, I whisper, "It's OK; everything's fine. I'm here with you."

Her eyes glistening with tears, my dream girl just shakes her head, making it clear that she doesn't agree that everything is fine. Finally, she says, "I'm so sorry. I had no idea."

Again trying to make her feel better, I say softly, "You'll be OK." My words don't seem to register with her; Coree gazes off into the distance.

Apparently oblivious to the impact of her words, Marty goes on. "I loved Rhyan with all my heart, even sacrificing my dream of a career for him. I didn't bug him about his little flings, but that wasn't enough. Not for him. He had a wife, a son, everything. Still, he wanted more. More, more, more."

Coree continued to look away, apparently lost in her own thoughts.

Marty chokes back a bitter laugh. "Then he got serious with someone again. Someone else who couldn't see through his little charade."

Her eyes widen and her teeth clench, and just like that, something in Marty seems to change. "Look at me when I'm talking to you, Corinna."

Slowly, Coree turns back as her mother continues the tirade. "Julie was my friend. She was always so nice. Do you believe her betrayal? Can you even understand what that felt like? Like being stabbed in the back. I bet he told Julie all the same things he told me, rattled off all the same lies..."

Marty's voice trails off as she loses herself in her memories. Then, with a shake of her head, she continues, "Anyway, he and I had a fight in which he told me that it was none of my business who he was with. One thing led to another, and I told my husband that he didn't have exclusive rights to me. I let him know that there were plenty of men who enjoyed what he rejected!"

In a trembling voice, Coree asks, "So Daddy knows that I'm not his daughter?"

"Yes, dear. Durin' that argument, he found out. He slapped me so hard it knocked me to the floor. Then he just went to his old recliner to drink more beer like always. The next day he moved out, and about a month later, we had the fire. And you know what? I bet that bully started it."

Marty bites her lip and cranes her head forward, instantly adopting a softer voice. "Corinna my dear, I just think it's time you knew the truth about Rhyan Calhoun. He hates me, and he doesn't love you. He doesn't love anyone except himself. I wish you were in here with me, not out there in the world with him. Wouldn't that be nice? I could protect you from him here." Tears glisten at the corners of her eyes.

The dejected expression on Coree's face indicates that whether or not her mother's telling the truth about Rhyan, her daughter seems to agree with her. There's now a barely noticeable quiver in my dream girl's hands as if her nervous system has reached overload. I've witnessed the friction between her and Coach Calhoun firsthand. Maybe it runs far deeper than I imagined?

Silent tears flow down Coree's cheeks. Seeing the deep sadness in her daughter's eyes, Marty reaches out and takes her hands. As their eyes meet, their hearts seem to touch, and Marty pulls her child into her arms as only a mother can do. Stroking Coree's long blond hair, her mother plants butterfly kisses on her forehead as they continue the embrace.

Coree makes a brave attempt to smile, but it's clear that she feels buried beneath this previously well-kept family secret. I feel terrible that before the day is out, I'll be heaping more onto her. However, as her focus returns, her expression indicates that she's starting to grasp the implications of Marty's all-too-shocking admission.

Saying it to herself as well as to us, she speaks slowly, "I think I'm gonna be sick."

I've been so happy about the fact that she isn't my sister that I'm not being very sensitive to what she's going through. Turning to me, Coree says, "Well, they probably have some pretty good drugs here. How about gettin' me a bottle?"

I smile, thinking how great it is to know that she at least hasn't lost her sense of humor. Suddenly, I realize that she isn't smiling. Her reference to taking a bottle of pills suddenly takes on a much more sinister meaning.

As Coree seems to regain her composure, she asks the obvious question: "Well, Mama, who *is* my daddy?"

I know exactly how she feels, as I asked that question two days ago. I'm sure that the answer can't be as shocking as the five daggers that Mom threw at me. I'm wrong once again.

At first, Marty doesn't respond. Her mother sits down in her chair and seems to be considering her answer. At least she's starting to relax a little bit.

"I hate to admit it, Corinna," Marty says finally, "but I'm not entirely sure. There're more than a couple of candidates."

I can't imagine what I would've thought if Mom had given me an answer like that.

Amazingly, Coree just shakes her head and looks at me when she says, "And *I'm* the one who has the bad rep!"

Leave it to Coree Calhoun to joke around when she's just been told that she may never know who her real father is. This girl is something else. If I weren't already head-over-heels in love with her, I would be now. Recalling the musical *Mama Mia,* I suppose when Coree gets married, no telling how many potential fathers she'll need to invite to her wedding.

My dream girl then says dejectedly, "I guess that I can add 'illegitimate' to my resume."

Marty twirls her hair absentmindedly and drops her voice to just above a whisper. "This is a mess, isn't it? I was just supposed to sit here and talk. And I mucked it up, didn't I?" She pauses, glancing in the direction of the open field. "Oh, Corinna, I guess that I shouldn't have told you and JoeE about all this. I should have just kept my big mouth shut. These drugs mess me up sometimes."

Coree glances at me and with a sigh, turns to her mother. "It is OK, Mama. For some reason, it doesn't seem to be botherin' Mr. JoeE."

We spend another thirty minutes talking to Marty, who's now quite calm and very pleasant. For the rest of the conversation, we avoid anything to do with fathers, affairs, pregnancy, and secrets.

Finally, we return to the dayroom and say good-bye to Marty, promising that we'll visit again soon. When I tell Marty that I enjoyed meeting her, she apologizes again for bringing up old wounds. Of course, I'm glad that she took us on the enlightening excursion down memory lane.

Driving away from the mental institution, Coree says, "If I were old enough, I'd just get drunk right now. I think I need it!" Sounding emotionally drained, she adds, "Let's drive to Brandon Park. We can talk there." She pauses, her gaze shifting to the road. When she finally speaks again, her voice is calm and cool. "Do you think that Mama was tellin' the truth about Daddy not bein' my father?"

Thinking about Marty and looking at Coree, a bell goes off in my brain. I suddenly realize why I experienced the strange feeling when I first met her mother. It's one of those eureka moments when an answer to a difficult question suddenly pops into your head.

"Your mother has blue eyes," I announce confidently.

"And so?" Coree asks.

"Coach Calhoun also has blue eyes, so he can't be your father!"

"Oh my God, you're right!" Coree exclaims. "How could I be so dumb? It was right there in front of me, and I never even caught it. Two blue-eyed people can't have a brown-eyed child."

"You have brown eyes, no doubt about that," I tell her. "Blue is a recessive gene, so your mother was telling the truth."

"Well, don't sound so happy about it," Coree says.

"I don't know if your mother was telling the truth when she said she didn't know who your father was. But you can definitely count out Coach Calhoun."

"That now narrows it down to a couple billion brown-eyed men," Coree says sarcastically.

Sensing that she may be too emotional to learn any more secrets, I tell her, "We don't have to go to the park and talk right now. You're probably too upset."

"Darn right I'm upset!" she snaps. "I can't believe that Mama told you about your mother having an affair. I'm so sorry, JoeE."

"It's all right. I already knew all about it," I tell her, a little afraid of her reaction.

"*What?*" she screams as she slams on the brakes and pulls the car over to the shoulder of the road. "You knew and you didn't tell me? It just slipped your mind? Forget the park—I want to hear about this right now!"

Peeling myself from the seat belt that has become embedded in my chest, I search for a place to begin. Her expression is a mixture of anger and curiosity, but mostly anger.

Gulping hard, I finally begin what now feels like a confession of my own. "I know what you're going through."

"You have no idea!" she says, gritting her teeth.

"I kinda do," I confirm. "Sunday night, Mom told me about how she got pregnant. All my life, I thought the man who raised me was my father. But I was wrong."

Coree's eyes seem to widen in disbelief.

"My mother told me that my real father is Coach Calhoun."

"*What?*" she exclaims. "So since Sunday night you thought that I was your sister?"

I nod and say apologetically, "I've wanted to tell you but just didn't know how."

"No wonder your mother was so upset when she saw me sittin' on your lap. Oh, God. What she must've been thinkin'. So that's why you were actin' so uptight that night." Coree giggles. "You know, JoeE, that New Year's kiss wasn't very brotherly, was it?"

"Give me a break. I just had a weak moment." Then I add, "I'm glad that you're having a good time with this. It's been killing me trying to figure out how to tell you."

"Oh, I'm sorry," my dream girl says, "you poor thing. Luckily, it doesn't matter, since we're not blood related."

Putting out her hands, she takes mine. Coree just looks at me for a few seconds and then says, "Now I see why you weren't upset when we found out that Daddy isn't my real father. I'm really glad that I'm not your sister."

"I'm sorry you learned about your father that way. It must have been brutal."

"It's OK," Coree says. "Wow! What a mess. Are we gonna tell our families the truth?"

I consider her critical question. "MaryAna needs to know. Beyond that, I'm not sure. We need to think this through. We need to tell Mom right away that we aren't brother and sister."

"Definitely!" she agrees. "We don't want to be accused of incest!"

"Are you going to be OK?" I ask her, concerned that my dream girl has so much on her mind.

"I just need a minute to clear my head. I'm just kinda mad."

"At me?" I ask.

"No," she says to my relief. "Daddy mostly, for sleepin' around in the first place and startin' this whole mess."

"Well, if he didn't sleep around, then there would be no MaryAna, no JoeE, and probably no Coree," I tell her, probably being too logical.

"I suppose that's one way of lookin' at it," Coree responds. Not sounding convinced, she asks, "Do you think that Daddy had Mama committed to get revenge?"

"Possibly. But maybe he just thought he was protecting you and Mason," I offer in Coach Calhoun's defense.

"I'm not so sure," Coree says. "Well, he should've told Mason and me about Mama instead of lyin' to us!"

Agreeing with Coree on that point, I remind her, "Sometimes people keep secrets because they can't face the truth."

From her guilty expression, I know that she realizes that I'm referring to her deceptions with MaryAna.

Sounding like an injured puppy, Coree says, "You may be right. After I stew over it awhile, I might be able to see things clearly. Right now, I just feel overwhelmed and betrayed."

"I know the feeling," I tell her.

As Coree pulls back onto the highway, she says, "I'm driving to the park. We have a lot to talk about."

Sitting back in my seat, I try to relax. At every turn this week, I've encountered more and more secrets. I begin to believe that I finally know everything about my family. Then I catch myself, realizing that as each secret has been exposed, it has revealed another hiding in the shadows.

Could there possibly be more to my family's story? As my grandmother said just a week ago, "Only time will tell."

Chapter 51

COREE THE WISE

There's no doubt that our family tree is a tangled web of unfaithfulness and deceit, spun by those who came before us. My brothers, my sister, and Coree deserve lives unburdened by the mistakes of the past. For some reason, it has fallen upon me to untangle this mess. I hope that I can use the truth to rip this web apart strand by strand.

However, the situation with Mason and Rachel overshadows our other family problems. Regardless of what decision they make, they have my support. The last thing I want to do is burden Coree with another secret after her mother's confession and my revelations. But if Rachel and Mason have to deal with their nightmare, they need all the help they can get.

Driving to the park, Coree asks, "You sure are quiet. What are you thinkin' about? About our messed-up families?"

"Yes, that and something else," I admit.

"Can you tell me about it?"

"I'll tell you all about it when we get to the park," I say, trying to put her off for the moment.

"JoeE, do you really think you can top what Mama told me?"

"Maybe," I say grimly.

"Come on," Coree practically pleads. "At this point, I can take anything."

"Well, OK," I say, pausing for a moment. "Rachel's cancer is back."

"Oh, no!" she exclaims, obviously as shocked as I was upon hearing the news last night. "When did she tell you?"

"I talked to her this morning before I went running," I explain. "But Mason told me last night."

"When you were out back at our house?" Coree guesses correctly.

"Yes," I confirm. "Obviously, he's taking it pretty hard."

"So that's why y'all looked so depressed," she says. "Mason must be devastated. He tries to act all macho, but he's really sensitive."

"He was pretty emotional. He even asked Rachel to marry him."

"What?" Coree exclaims, shaking her head. "They can't get married. They're still in high school. That's crazy!"

"Mason plans to quit school and use his college money for them to live on."

"They're too young, aren't they?" Coree asks with alarm. "Rachel's our age, for heaven's sake."

"I looked it up on the Internet," I tell her. "All they need is parental consent."

Coree thinks for a few seconds. "I don't know about Rachel's parents, but good luck gettin' permission from Daddy!"

"That may be true," I tell her, "but I don't think that will stop Mason from dropping out of school. He says he loves Rachel and wants to be with her."

"Does she want to marry him?"

Recalling my conversation with Rachel this morning, I tell her, "Yes, some day in the future she wants to marry him, but not now."

Completely silent for about a minute, Coree is apparently digesting what I've told her. Finally, she says, "Mason needs to stop sayin' he loves Rachel and start actin' like he loves her."

"I don't understand."

"My brother needs to stop thinkin' about his own feelings and pain. Instead, he needs to consider what's best for Rachel. I'm sure he's puttin' more stress on her when she already has enough. He doesn't understand what marriage means to girls. He needs to chill out. After I talk with him, he will."

I'm simply amazed at the insight and clarity that Coree has instantly brought to the situation. What she's saying makes perfect sense. It seems that she's confident of convincing our brother not to take any drastic actions.

The park is behind Brandon's library, which still looks unfinished to me, but what do I know about art?

When we arrive, I step out of the car while Coree stays inside and calls Rachel. After a short conversation, Coree follows me onto the blacktop. "Rachel agrees with me."

"Are you sure that Mason will agree also?" I ask her, still concerned.

"If MaryAna and I teamed up on you, do you really think you'd stand a chance?" Coree asks with a little grin.

"I see your point," I reply, ending the discussion on that topic. Once more, I learn a lesson about the power that females wield over us poor, unsuspecting cavemen.

We walk down an asphalt-paved path beyond a playground. Coree takes my hand as we stroll. It is wonderful to have my dream girl back.

In her little singsong voice, Coree says, "Let's sit down at one of these picnic tables."

Looking around, I spot a small table not far from the path. There's almost no one around, so we shouldn't be disturbed. I tell her my idea about using the truth to untangle the web of secrets and lies.

"Who do you think we need to tell about all of this?" Coree asks apprehensively.

It's a simple question, but it's difficult in so many ways. Even when I was a youngster, Dad taught me to use clear, crisp logic, taking emotions and feelings out of the equation. He might point out the why, how, and if of a situation, but he always came back to the facts.

Although I'm aware that the emotions of individuals should always be taken into consideration, in this case I have to look at the big picture. Dad encouraged me to digest the available information and quickly make a decision. It's essential in football, and I'm about to apply it to life.

Dismissing irrelevant information that might cloud my judgment, I find that one crystal-clear fact remains: this farce must end. It's about time for the truth to prevail in our families, regardless of the collateral damage.

Looking into Coree's anxious eyes, I give her the simplest of answers: "Everyone."

Chapter 52

LATER, SIS

By the time we leave the park, Coree and I have agreed upon a plan to enlighten the Calhoun-Lindley-Collins family about the truth, the whole truth, and nothing but the truth. I've convinced her that the only way our plan will succeed is if she is willing to share the information about her mother with everyone in our families. This decision to tell the entire truth will lead to an interesting day, indeed.

Suddenly, an earsplitting siren blares. It's a penetrating sound that I imagine can be heard all over Brandon. Lasting about a minute, it finally subsides.

Coree says, "It must be noon."

Checking the time, I see that it's one minute past twelve. Noticing my confused expression, she explains, "They test the tornado warning system on the first day of each month at exactly noon."

"Well, except for deaf people, I'm sure everyone heard it," I tell her. "I hope that I never hear it again, except on the first of the month."

"We do have real tornado warnings," Coree informs me. "Living here, you get used to them but never comfortable. Twisters usually occur in the spring, but bad weather can spawn them anytime. When you hear a warning siren, you need to take it seriously. It means a tornado has been spotted in the area."

"What should I do if there's a warning? Find a basement?" I ask, having never even thought about the possibility of tornadoes before this moment.

"I doubt that there's a single basement in this entire county," she informs me.

"Why no basements?"

"Most everything here is built on concrete slabs. Our soil is a kind of clay that would crush basement walls pretty quickly."

"So what do you do?" I ask. "Hide under your desk?"

"Unless you have a storm shelter, your best bet is a room with no windows. And the closer to the center of the house, the better."

"Have you ever seen a real tornado?"

"No, and I hope that I never do," she replies. "I've seen some of the damage and heard stories about those who've died."

We spend the rest of the ride back lost in our own thoughts. It seems like today, Coree and I are the tornadoes that are about to shatter lives.

My dream girl has the additional burden of convincing Mason to refrain from jeopardizing his future. Via a text from Rachel, Coree learns that Mason is at Rachel's house. The first step in our elaborate strategy is now only minutes away.

As Coree parks the car, I tell her, "Good luck with Mason." My dream girl smiles and without saying a word heads off to Rachel's house.

Entering our home, I see MaryAna on her laptop at the dining room table. Looking up, she asks, "How's my car?"

"Perfect, Sis," I tell her, "and thanks again. Can I give you some gas money?"

"Not necessary," she says with a smile. "I'm lookin' up stuff on the Internet. I've decided that I'm gonna be as smart as you. Some of this stuff is actually interestin.' Do you know what state is the widest from east to west?"

"Texas," I guess. "Or maybe Alaska."

"Nope," my sister informs me. "Hawaii. It's about fifteen hundred miles from the farthest eastern island to the farthest western one. That's really amazin', since they always make it look so little on a map."

"Wow," I say, actually impressed. "You're gonna be tough in trivia games." I pause. "I've got another favor to ask."

"Sure. Anything for you, Bro," MaryAna says, smiling.

"Could you give Coree and me a little time alone with Mom?" I ask. "Maybe an hour or so."

"Coree isn't pregnant, is she?" my sister asks as her imagination kicks into high gear. "Is that the secret? Isn't she on the pill?"

"Coree isn't pregnant," I tell her, calming her down. "It's nothing like that. We'll tell you all about it when you return."

MaryAna seems satisfied with my promise. "Should I leave now?"

"No, there's no hurry," I say, relieved that she's being so agreeable. "Coree is at Rachel's house. She should be back in a few minutes. You can wait until then if you want."

I'm pleased to see that the mention of Rachel's name no longer draws any negative reaction. Apparently, my twin's interest in Tyler has made her forget about Mason. What we plan to tell MaryAna will provide a permanent end to any remaining romantic feelings.

"Is Mom in her bedroom?" I ask.

"I guess so," MaryAna answers, going back to her Internet research.

Entering my mother's room, I see that she's working on her computer. Closing the door behind me, I ask, "Are you busy?"

"No, dear, I'm just finishing up."

"Coree will be here shortly. We want to talk with you together, if that's OK?"

"All right," she replies. In a quiet voice, she asks, "Did you tell her about Rhyan and me?"

"Coree knows everything," I say. "There are just some things we need to talk about."

"What things?" Mom asks, seeming curious. It feels strange to be the one who knows the truth while my mother's mind whirls with possibilities.

"We need to wait until Coree gets here." At least I'm not asking her to wait sixteen years.

"All right, honey," Mom says, resigning herself to the wait.

I return to the dining room, where my sister is continuing to increase her knowledge base. She asks, "Which state has the most ocean coastline?"

"Hawaii," I guess, figuring that she's on a website with facts about that state.

"Nope, Alaska," MaryAna says, seeming pleased that she's finding trivia that I don't know.

"I've got one for you, Sis," I tell her. "What's the difference between intelligence and wisdom?"

"I don't know," she admits, after thinking a moment. "I thought they were the same."

"No," I inform her. "Intelligence is knowing that a tomato is a fruit and not a vegetable. Wisdom is knowing not to put a tomato in a fruit salad!"

As Coree comes in the front door, MaryAna looks at me, grinning. "Are you implying that I'm intelligent but not very wise?"

I smile. "I wouldn't be surprised, Sis, to see you put a tomato in a fruit salad just to see how it would taste. That's what makes you so incredible: you have a vivid imagination."

For once, my twin lets me have the last word.

I'd love to continue swapping trivia questions with my sister. Unfortunately, we have slightly more serious matters on the agenda.

"How did it go?" I ask Coree, anticipating a problem but hoping otherwise.

"Fine," she answers, seeming pleased. "It took a little gentle persuasion, but he finally agreed with us."

Looking perplexed, MaryAna asks, "How did what go? Who agreed to what?"

"Later, Sis. We'll tell you everything you need to know," I promise, not willing to deviate from our plan.

"Text and let me know when I should come home, OK?" MaryAna asks, grabbing a jacket as I nod in agreement. Heading for the door, she adds, "I'll be at Tyler's house. Maybe *he* won't keep secrets from me."

Soon my twin's curiosity will be appeased, and she'll learn that we're not the only ones keeping secrets from her.

Chapter 53

GUT-WRENCHING CONVERSATIONS

With MaryAna out the door, I ask Coree, "Are you ready?"

"Sure, but I need a hug first," she says, seeming nervous.

I wrap my arms around my dream girl. At this moment, she seems as vulnerable as a newborn kitten. After embracing for about a minute, I use my Spartan-like, unemotional tone and say, "It'll be over soon. We can end this drama and give our families a fresh start."

Looking up into my eyes, Coree says, "Only five more gut-wrenching conversations to go." She wipes some dampness from her eyes, takes a deep breath, and says firmly, "I'm ready. Let's roll!"

While Coree sits down at the dining room table, I ask Mom to join us. On the way back, I snatch a couple bottles of water from the fridge and place them strategically on the table. A box of tissues is nearby. For a change, I'm determined to be prepared for what I expect to be an emotional conversation.

Mom sits at the table, saying to Coree, "JoeE says that he told you about Rhyan and me."

My dream girl nods. "Yes, ma'am. I have some secrets of my own to tell you."

With my mother now extremely nervous also, Coree goes on cautiously. "I don't know how much MaryAna has told you, but some of the things she believes about me just aren't true. First of all, I haven't been sleepin' around with boys, but I've led MaryAna to believe that I have."

I'm a bit shocked at how blunt Coree is being. However, I realize that the time for subtlety is long past. We agreed to present the unvarnished truth and let the chips fall where they may.

My mother responds kindly, "I know the kind of pressure and feelings that you girls face. I went through the same thing when I was about your age."

Continuing her confession, Coree says as she fidgets with her bracelets, "I led MaryAna to believe that my real mama in Atlanta got me on birth control. Neither of those things is true. I'm not on the pill, and Mama doesn't live in Atlanta. Since I've been little, she's been at the state mental institution. Daddy lied to Mason and me, but Julie told us the truth a couple of years ago. We were sworn to secrecy."

Mom gasps audibly and then sits in stunned silence. Coree lets this admission sink in before going on, "After our house burned, Daddy had her committed."

My mother has a strange look of disbelief on her face. "You mean Marty has been there this whole time?"

"Yes, ma'am," Coree responds, nodding.

Taking Coree's hand for a moment, Mom whispers, "I knew your mama would never desert you kids. She and I have had our differences, but that's water over the dam. She's had to overcome a lot in her life."

As they both reach for tissues to wipe their eyes, Coree says, "Thank you, ma'am. Mama needs people who believe in her. Today, JoeE and I went to the mental hospital. When she found out that he was your son, it must have triggered her memories. She told us about your affair with Daddy. Mama told us that she broke up your affair by gettin' pregnant with me."

"Oh," my mother says, seeming surprised. I know that she can't possibly guess what's coming next.

"Mama also told me that she got pregnant by some other man, so Daddy isn't really my father."

"What? Rhyan isn't your daddy? Let me get this straight," Mom says, as if she's not sure that she's heard correctly. "Marty said that she was tryin' to wreck an affair between Rhyan and me?"

Nodding, Coree says, "That's right and Mama doesn't even know who my real daddy is." With that, Coree finally starts to sob.

Mom reaches over to embrace her, trying to hold back her own tears. However, she fails, and soon they're both crying like babies. I now understand what Coree meant by gut-wrenching conversations.

As the crying subsides, I tell my mother that we've decided that it's time for everyone in our families to know the truth. I notice that her eyes widen in alarm and there is a little tremor in her bottom lip.

It's obvious that Mom is hesitant. She points out that telling everyone might cause some problems. We convince her that it isn't fair for our generation to suffer for our parents' mistakes.

"I don't know how Rhyan will react," my mother warns. "He may get really upset, especially with me. Do I have to be there when you talk to him?"

"No," I reassure her, "that won't be necessary."

I hear her sigh of relief and realize that my mother is shaking as if the very thought of being near Coach Calhoun scares her.

"We'll try to handle him with kid gloves." I'm not exactly sure what that might involve, but I really hope Coree does.

After texting MaryAna to let her know that she can come home, I ask Mom if she's willing to stay while we talk to my sister. She agrees and asks if she can be the one to tell my twin about her father. I'm pleased that she's offering, and I accept her assistance readily.

"After you finish talkin' to MaryAna, I need to have a few words with her," Coree says, twisting her bracelets. "She needs to know all about me and that Mama has been at the mental hospital."

Having no idea how my volatile twin may react, I volunteer to catch her if she faints or restrain her if she starts throwing things.

Returning home surprisingly fast, MaryAna bursts through the door, obviously anxious to know what's going on. We make a seat for her at the table between my mother and Coree. I have another bottle of water and the tissue box at the ready. I'm becoming an expert at these emotional situations, a skill I hope will be unnecessary in the future.

MaryAna breaks the silence. "What's up, y'all?" she asks in her usual carefree tone. Glancing from one anxious face to another, our expressions immediately dampen her excitement.

My mother begins by telling MaryAna the story I heard Sunday night. My sister seems to react as I did until Mom reaches the point where she reveals that our father is actually Rhyan Calhoun. I was shocked and upset by that fact. My twin's reaction is different. She's not happy, but she seems relieved that this time she's being told that her father is actually alive.

Sounding very upbeat, MaryAna says, "Well, they have been kinda like my family anyway. I guess now it's just official. Why isn't everyone here? Do they know that Coach Calhoun is our daddy?"

After I explain that we'll be bring them up-to-date later, all MaryAna has to say is, "Well, Mason has always treated me like his sister. Now I can treat him like a brother." Having been treated as MaryAna's brother for the last week, I feel a certain amount of sympathy toward Mason. I should warn him, especially about his clothes.

Next, my sister turns to Coree, reaching out her arms to give her a hug, "Sister," MaryAna says as she hugs her best friend. Then she glances over at me with a sudden realization. "Oh, JoeE!" she says with real concern in her voice, "Coree is your sister too!"

Quickly jumping back into the conversation, my dream girl says, "Before you feel too bad for Mr. JoeE, there are several other facts that you need to know."

As MaryAna listens intently, her best friend explains about the years of deception. At times, my sister's face reflects some anger, but she also seems to sense how difficult it is for her friend to admit so many untruths. My sister even laughs when she finally hears the real reason that Coree was so mad at Tyler a few years ago.

When MaryAna learns that Coree isn't on birth control, my sister says, perplexed, "I know I've seen you take pills from a prescription bottle a lot of times."

After a quick glance at me, Coree explains, "Those were my prescription antidepressants."

"Why do you need those?" MaryAna asks, concern written all over her face.

"You know I get really down sometimes. And they are supposed to help."

Antidepressants? I recall when Coree told me her secrets; she'd made it quite clear that she had been very depressed. Now aware of her mother's struggle with mental illness, I understand why my dream girl might be prescribed such a drug. It makes perfect sense.

As Coree explains about her mother at the state mental hospital, my sister's expression turns to disbelief. MaryAna asks, "Why didn't you tell me? I'm your best friend. Don't you trust me?"

"It isn't that I don't trust you, MaryAna. There were so many times that I wanted to tell you," Coree explains hesitantly. "But I was really messed up and afraid that I was losin' my mind. I was ashamed of havin' a mama in a mental hospital and afraid that you might start treatin' me like you treated Rachel when she got sick."

Coree's last statement really stuns MaryAna. At first, her expression seems to reflect bitterness. Then I can see a rosy hue creeping up her face. It seems that my sister may recognize that shunning Rachel was both excessive and unnecessary behavior. After a few long moments of deafening silence, she appears to relax, apparently accepting the explanation.

MaryAna admits contritely, "You're right, Coree. The way I treated Rachel wasn't right. We used to be such good friends. I see why you were afraid that I wouldn't understand about your mama or your other problems. I guess I wasn't much of a friend, was I?"

"Neither was I," Coree says. "I'm so sorry. I should've told you everything."

The girls tearfully hug for a moment, seeming to forgive each other instantly for past mistakes. Now I know for sure that they will be best friends forever.

MaryAna says hopefully, "Let's start now and promise always to tell each other the truth. Also, I'll make sure that I treat Rachel like a good friend."

Nodding in agreement, Coree says, "JoeE and I went to see Mama at Whitfield today." She proceeds to tell my sister all about our conversation with Marty.

When Coree finishes her story, MaryAna says, "So you *aren't* our sister! That's sure enough lucky for JoeE." Turning to me, she says, "You really dodged a bullet, Brother." Looking at our mother, she adds in the same breath, "Mama, did you know that he actually got mad and yelled at us?"

MaryAna glances back at me with a huge smile. "At least now I know where my car has been today. You better treat Coree right from now on. No more yellin' at her, or I'll kick your butt!"

Surprisingly, there have been practically no tears for the last fifteen minutes. Maybe Coree and my mother have cried themselves out.

Then Coree says, "MaryAna, thank you so much for forgiving me," and tears start streaming down my dream girl's cheeks. I guess I know absolutely nothing about the female gender.

My sister starts crying as all kinds of emotions spill out. She embraces Coree again and then she gets up from her chair and comes over to me. I barely have time to stand up before she throws her arms around me.

"At least we have a daddy again, JoeE."

My "strong, silent type" image is beginning to crumble under this intense emotional pressure. Still embracing each other, MaryAna and I move toward Coree and Mom. We each reach out an arm, and soon we have a group hug going. My shirt becomes damp from tears. As much as I hate to admit it, a couple of them might be mine.

The thought crosses my mind that a man isn't a father just because the genes say so. Will Coach Calhoun even acknowledge us as his children? Will he love us? Will we lose him before we ever have him? Once more, only time will tell.

Turning to Coree, I ask, "Are you about ready to move on to the next stage in the Consequences of Truth game?"

She smiles, saying, "Next contestant, please."

Chapter 54

TRUTH BETWEEN FRIENDS

MaryAna asks us if the other members of the Calhoun family know about all this. I tell her that some people know some secrets, but no one is aware of everything. I tell Mom and MaryAna how we intend to enlighten all of the Calhouns by the end of the day. Coree texts Mason, asking him to come over because we have something important to tell him. He texts back that he will be over shortly and he's bringing Rachel, since they have no secrets between them.

Although Rachel wasn't part of our original plan, I know she's definitely good at keeping secrets. Coree points out that she's likely to be part of the family someday.

When I tell Mom that Rachel will be joining us when we talk to Mason, my mother is uncomfortable with the idea. I ask her to trust me, and she reluctantly agrees. MaryAna accepts the idea with no problem. Apparently, my sister is serious about treating Rachel as a valued friend.

In a few minutes, the doorbell rings. Once Rachel and Mason are inside, everyone takes a seat on the couch while I strategically position myself in the chair on the opposite side of the coffee table. This way, I'm facing everyone and all eyes are on me.

Noting the wary expression on Mason's face, I suspect that he believes that I've betrayed his confidence and told others about Rachel's illness. Possibly fearing that this is some kind of intervention, he may not be ready to hear our secrets. Before revealing the reason we're all here, I must put him at ease.

"Mason," I say in as relaxed a tone as possible, "the reason we brought you here is so we can talk about something that happened a long time ago. You should know the truth about our families."

The expression on his face instantly changes, and his body language indicates that he's relaxing. Now both he and Rachel have looks of curiosity as they lean forward, anxious to hear what we're about to say.

After Mom relates her story about Rhyan fathering MaryAna and me, Mason seems pleased that we are his siblings but not especially surprised that Coach Calhoun fathered us.

"Wow, another brother and sister," he says. Then turning to Coree, who's sitting quietly by his side, he says, "Oh, I'm sorry, Coree. I know how much you like JoeE."

"Thanks, Macy. However, I've got something to tell the two of you also. Have you told Rachel about Mama?"

"Yeah," Mason answers. "I thought that she should know everything. I don't want any secrets between us."

"Good, that makes things easier. I've told the others. In fact, JoeE went with me to visit Mama today." Coree ends the tale with, "Mama told me that Daddy isn't actually my father and that she has no idea who my real daddy is."

After Mason has a few seconds to sort things out, he asks, "Do Daddy and Julie know all of this?"

Coree replies, "Well, Mama said that he's known since I was little that I wasn't his daughter. I'm not sure how much Julie knows. We're gonna tell both of them that we all know everything in a little while."

So far, Rachel has been sitting silently. She glances at her boyfriend, who nods. In her normal soft, unassuming voice, she says, "I have something that I need to tell MaryAna and your mama." With the room eerily silent, she reveals, "My cancer is back."

I hear my mother gasp while my sister stands up and walks over to Rachel.

MaryAna, with her voice cracking slightly, says, "Rachel, I'm so sorry." They embrace, and my sister manages to squeak out, "I've been so mean to you because I was jealous. Can you ever forgive me?"

Mason puts his arms around both of them. My mother starts tearing up again, and Coree moves over toward her. Being practical, I scramble to make sure that there are plenty of tissues. I hope Mom has a good supply, since they're vanishing rapidly.

As the emotional reactions of the girls continue, I motion for my brother to come to the dining room. "Mason, could you get a hold of Julie and ask her to join us?"

"Sure," he replies. "She should be at home now."

"Please ask her to come alone," I tell Mason. "It would be easier to tackle Coach Calhoun later."

After calling Julie, Mason announces, "She's on her way, and she'll be by herself." Out of the corner of my eye, I notice that Mom seems relieved by the news that Ryan will not be coming along.

"That's great. Thanks, Brother," I tell Mason.

He flashes me his dynamic smile as I, too, sigh in relief. We need to have everyone up to speed before we tackle Coach Calhoun.

"By the way," Mason says to me, "your idea about gettin' Coree involved was smart. She and Rachel straightened me out. I guess I was too busy having a pity party to see the stress that I was puttin' on Rachel."

"Coree is awesome," I tell him, "but I'm sure glad that she's your sister and not mine."

Chapter 55

ANOTHER CONFESSION

Although the crying has stopped, Mom and the girls all have red and swollen eyes when Julie arrives. I explain to everyone that it would be better if Mason and I let our stepmother know what is going on while the others freshen up.

We bring Julie up to date on family history. Our stepmother seems elated to learn that she has two more stepchildren, although MaryAna has played that role unofficially for years. As we continue to talk, I notice that she becomes very quiet, as if she is considering the ramifications of the situation. We leave it up to her to decide whether to inform Logan that he has two more siblings. Our stepmother is devastated when she learns the news about Rachel's relapse.

When Mason tells her that everyone here knows that Marty is at the mental institution, I watch for her reaction. As a worried expression spreads across her face, I say, "Today, Coree took me to the mental hospital. Marty told us that Coach Calhoun isn't Coree's matural father."

Not seeming surprised, Julie admits, "Marty once told me that Marty got pregnant with Coree by some other guy, but she never mentioned who. I guess I owe you kids some explanations, since I've had a hand in this mess."

"You did?" I ask, having no idea what she means.

"You see, beginning in high school, Sarah, Marty, and I all had serious crushes on Rhyan or, as we called him, Rhino. He asked Sarah out first, and the two of them started going together when we were juniors. Marty and I were extremely jealous of our friend."

Having believed that the revelations were over for the day, I'm curious where this confession is leading.

Hesitantly, Julie continues, "When Rhyan went off to Mississippi State, Marty was secretly goin' up to Starkville to visit him. That led to Rhyan breakin' up with Sarah. When he graduated, Rhino married Marty, but they soon had serious marital problems."

"Oh," I blurt out almost unconsciously.

"Not long after you were born, Mason, your mama told me that her marriage was falling apart. She aeemed desperate," Julie says candidly.

Mason remains silent, and I have no idea from his stoic expression how he is taking this information.

"I was livin' in Jackson when Sarah returned from California the first time. One night, Rhyan and his brother, Rick, met us at a club in Jackson for drinks and dancing. Rhyan took Sarah home, and you know what happened after that."

Looking at my brother, Julie admits, "Mason, I'm the one who broke the news to Marty about Rhyan's affair with Sarah. The look on your mama's face was…" Julie shakes her head. "Well, maybe after today, all this drama will finally be over."

Then Julie asks the question that is on everyone's mind: "How are we gonna tell Rhyan about all this?"

We explain our plan to tell him at Calhoun Castle, and Julie agrees that it's the best way to go. I hope that in a more familiar environment, he will feel a little less threatened. Making it clear that my mother won't be there, I suggest that she take Logan to our house while the rest of us talk to Coach Calhoun.

As Coree joins our discussion, she asks, "Julie, do you think Daddy will be really mad that you told us about Mama being hospitalized?"

"He won't take it very well, that's for sure. But eventually, he'll get over it," Julie answers. "I need to do some prep work on him. I'll send Coree a text when it's time for y'all to come to our house."

Envisioning their conversation, I don't envy her job of talking to Coach. At the park, Coree warned me that dealing with her daddy would be by far the most difficult part of our game plan. I'm afraid she'll be right, but I hope he will bereasonable.

With the final pieces of our plan now decided, Julie and Coree join the others in the living room. While the females console each other, Mason and I sit at the table. We're both looking forward to ending this long day.

"I really like the fact that you're my brother," Mason says, flashing me a smile.

"Likewise," I reply.

"I talked to Coach Butler today about how I wanted you to replace me at quarterback next season," my brother informs me. "He said that he would love to have me play some defense for him."

"Seriously?" I respond. "Would you like to play on the other side of the ball?"

"I think so," Mason replies. "But we'll just have to see what happens."

Before Julie leaves, one unanswered question rears its ugly head: Who will talk to Coach Calhoun? Everyone exchanges nervous glances.

"I will if I have to," Mason says, standing up. "He's my Daddy, after all."

"He's my father, too," I say, leaving my seat and putting a hand on his shoulder. "You've got enough on your plate right now. And I owe you one. I'll talk to Coach."

Everyone agrees, probably because no one else wants the job. However, since I normally keep my emotions in check, I'm the logical choice. That will be a challenge. Dad always told me he that he was getting me ready for football *and* life. His training should come in handy today.

An hour after Julie leaves, we still haven't heard anything from her. Everyone is on pins and needles, ready to leave but dreading what might happen. I tell Rachel that if things are going badly, I won't mention her illness.

Mason advises me, "Daddy's bark is worse than his bite." I suppose that the young Spartans were told something similar about the hungry wolf.

As we continue to sit around nervously, Mom asks Coree, "When does Julie go back to work?"

"She'll be back at the hospital bright and early tomorrow morning," Coree says.

"What does she do at the hospital?" I ask, grasping for something to take my mind off confronting Coach Calhoun.

"She's an emergency room doctor at River Oaks Hospital in Flowood. I thought that MaryAna would've told you," Coree explains. "She took a couple weeks of vacation so we could take Logan to Disney World for Christmas."

"I guess it's handy to have a doctor around the house," I say, realizing that Julie's profession might explain the Calhouns' expensive home.

"We definitely needed her that one time," Coree says, without explaining why or when, as if I already know to what she's referring.

I'm about to ask her about that "one time" when she receives a text from Julie. We're quickly off to the Calhoun Castle. We park in the circular driveway in front of the house. Julie is waiting in the doorway accompanied by Logan. As we arrive, the seven-year-old comes running to greet us.

Wrapping his arms around my legs, Logan gives me a hug. "Did you come to play with me? I've got lots of toys in my room to show you!"

"Maybe later, buddy," I tell him. "Right now, I've got to talk to your dad. My mother's going to take you to our house for a little while, OK?"

"Oh, that's cool," he says. "Coree never lets me go to MaryAna's house. She says that's her getaway, whatever that means."

I tell my little brother, "My mother loves kids, so you two will have a great time."

Logan waves to all of us as Julie walks him to Mom's Escalade, making sure that he fastens his seat belt. Before they drive off, Julie says something to Mom that I can't hear.

Entering the house, everyone is silent. It feels as if we are attending a funeral, and you could cut the tension with a knife. Recalling Dad's training, I act as if it's the start of a football game, and I'm leading my team onto the field.

I calmly think: My name is Joseph Edward Collins the Fourth, but I'm known as JoeE to my friends and family. I am a sixteen-year-old high school student. Today is Tuesday, January 1, and I'm about to face Coach Rhyan Calhoun. My purpose is to inform him that my twin sister and I are his children. I will stay calm and cool no matter what happens. Reminding myself that we've all thought through this plan, I'm ready to face the consequences of revealing the truth. Reassured, I take a deep breath and already feel my nerves settling down.

Now all too aware that Mississippi is often plagued by violent weather, I wonder if this is the calm before the storm. I'm afraid that before it's over, this particular storm may earn the title Hurricane Rhyan.

Chapter 56

NOBODY'S PERFECT

While Coach Calhoun sits back in the security of his recliner, his stone like silence notches up my anxiety. Julie takes a place on the couch next to her husband, possibly to act as a shield. Coree and MaryAna occupy the other two spots next to our stepmother, while I sit in a chair directly facing them. Rachel and Mason park themselves on the loveseat. I know that the stage is now set and the real drama is about to begin.

The stern look on Coach Calhoun's face is hard to read. However, his body language is obvious. Papa told me that a person crossing his arms in that manner is projecting a very defensive attitude, as if he's preparing for an attack. I'd like to say something to relax him as I did earlier with Mason. However, absolutely nothing comes to mind.

Julie is the first to speak. "Rhyan, these young people have something to tell you, and they've decided that JoeE will speak for all of them."

Before I can say anything, Coach Calhoun says stiffly, "I understand that my family has ripped the scabs off some old wounds. I sure hope that you brought plenty of bandages, boy." I assume that he's referring to all of us knowing about Marty being in a mental institution.

Feeling like an awkward schoolboy, which maybe I am, I say, "Well, Coach—"

He cuts me off immediately, stating coldly, "Call me Mr. Calhoun. I'm not your coach."

"Daddy!" Coree says pleadingly.

"Hush your mouth, girl. Nobody asked for your opinion," Rhyan demands sharply. "Julie said that your friend, here, would do all the talkin' for y'all, so keep quiet!"

Coree struggles to keep both her anger and tears in check. She's biting her lower lip and almost frantically twisting one of her bracelets. Like a "tell" in a poker game, I've come to recognize these little habits as signs that she's extremely nervous.

Out of the corner of my eye, I see Mason's angry expression and clenched fists; he's obviously upset that his father yelled so viciously at his sister. Rachel quickly pulls him close and strokes his arm as if trying to calm an agitated animal. It works, and he settles back onto the loveseat.

MaryAna looks tremendously hostile. She's pursing her lips, and there is disgust in her eyes. I feel like the room is a powder keg, and I'm holding a match.

As the room settles into yet another deadly calm, I say bluntly, "Mr. Calhoun, we all know what happened between you and my mother seventeen years ago."

"Now, wait just a minute!" Rhyan exclaims in a thunderous voice. Rising from his recliner with fists clenched, he yells, "I don't care what Sarah told you. I'm not gonna be judged by a bunch of teenagers in *my own home!*"

As Rhyan begins to stride away, Julie grabs his arm tightly. Despite her small stature, he stops abruptly as if he's reached the end of an iron chain.

In a firm, yet calm voice, his wife tells him, "Rhyan Calhoun, sit right back down in that chair! JoeE is a guest in *our home!* You will show him respect and courtesy!" I hold my breath, not knowing what will happen next.

Something flashes in Rhyan's eyes—whether it's anger or resentment or even fear, I have no idea. To my surprise, he reluctantly settles back down in his chair, scowling even more than before. He crosses his arms again, apparently resigning himself to the fact that he's going to hear what I have to say. The beating of my heart is now like a bass drum pounding in my chest.

"I'm not interested in judging you, Mr. Calhoun. All I'm interested in is the truth." As I speak, Rhyan says nothing. He sits motionless. "Your romantic relationships are none of my business. All that matters to me is that when my mother returned to California, she was pregnant."

Rhyan's demeanor changes abruptly. The scowl on his face remains, but he leans toward me. "You mean Sarah told you we had an affair and she was expectin' when she left Brandon?"

"She said that during your relationship, she got pregnant," I say, feeling too awkward to use the word "affair." "MaryAna and I are *your* children!"

I finally have Rhyan's undivided attention.

"So that's what this is all about?" Rhyan asks. "Sarah told you that we had an affair?"

"Well, sir, she didn't use that word exactly; she mostly told me the outcome of your relationship before she went back to my dad. She probably would have carried that secret to her grave, but she was forced to tell me the truth because of my growing affection for Coree."

I pause as he slowly reaches for another beer, pops the top, and takes a swig. "When she found out that Coree and I were dating, she had no choice but to tell me her secret."

Surprisingly, Rhyan suddenly seems relieved rather than upset. He even has a little smirk on his face like a criminal who's gotten away.

Wanting to get everything out quickly, I continue, "You should also know that Coree and I went to see Martha today at the mental institution."

"Yeah, my wife told me about that," he interjects, shooting Julie an angry glance.

I go on quickly, "When your ex-wife discovered that I was Sarah's son, she told us that Coree isn't your biological daughter."

Coach Calhoun's expression turns angry again. "That crazy woman has a big mouth and no morals." Glancing toward Coree, he attempts to mask his anger. He tentatively utters, "Oh, Coree. I'm sorry that you found out that way." He reaches his hand to her, but she doesn't take it.

"It's OK," Coree says icily, staying on the couch.

Next, Rhyan reaches out toward MaryAna. "Come here, dear."

My twin seems hesitant but goes over to him. "I guess I need to start calling you Daddy."

Pulling MaryAna into his lap, Coach Calhoun gives her a big bear hug. Looking at me and turning on the charm, he says, "Forgive me, son. You can call me Coach or any other darn thing you want. After the way I just acted, 'darned old fool' is probably appropriate."

He seems extremely happy, but I can't put my finger on why. I hope that it's because he's excited to have us as his children, but his smile doesn't reach his eyes. They remain hard and wary.

I'm certainly willing to give him a chance as my new father. Smiling, I tell him, "Coach works just fine for me."

"It really took some balls to be so upfront about all this. I can be kinda rough sometimes," he says, glancing over toward Julie, as if that was more of an apology to her than to me. His reaction reminds me of a child who's only sorry about being caught.

Coree looks over at Coach. "I told you that JoeE was something special."

Coach Calhoun says sarcastically, "Maybe you should be the football coach, Coree, since you can evaluate people so well."

Without hesitation, she replies, "That's a great idea! When can I start?"

I don't believe that she really expects an answer, and she certainly doesn't get one.

I look over at Mason and Rachel to see how they're hanging in. I'm about to add the news about Rachel when Mason motions for me to join them.

He tells me in a hushed voice, "We'll tell Daddy about Rachel later. You've been through enough. I knew that you would be cool under fire, and you just proved me right."

As Rachel smiles at me, I say to Mason, "Thanks, Brother."

I walk back toward Julie, who says, "You did great. Can you come help me in the kitchen for a minute?"

Before I can follow Julie, Coach Calhoun commands, "Hey, Jules, get me some more beer. I need to celebrate."

As far as I can tell, Coach Calhoun is always celebrating.

Smiling at Coree, I say, "I'll be back in a minute."

As we enter the kitchen, I tell my new stepmother gratefully, "Thanks for the help, Dr. Calhoun. I don't think that I could've done it without you."

She grins. "You know that I'm just Julie here."

"Yes, ma'am," I respond, still working on my Southern etiquette.

After I help my stepmother bring in some ice from the storage room, we get something to drink for everyone. We join the others just as the doorbell rings. Answering the door, I think that it might be my mother bringing Logan home. Instead, it's Tyler.

Entering the house, he asks curiously, "Hey, y'all. What's up?"

Everyone is silent for a moment before Julie looks at Coach Calhoun. "Tyler's practically family," she says, as if testing the waters. "One more teenager knowin' the family secrets won't hurt."

Coach's expression seems to indicate that he doesn't exactly approve; however, he says nothing.

"Knowin' what secrets?" Tyler asks, sounding confused, as would be expected.

Mason tells him, "Come here, Ty. I've got a story to tell you, if you can keep a secret."

"I can keep a secret, but can you tell me in the kitchen? I'm hungry!" We all laugh, and everyone heads to the kitchen except for Coree and me.

My dream girl puts up her hand up for a high five as she congratulates me, "Nice game plan there, JoeE Collins."

Recalling the all-too-predictable interviews after football games, I say mockingly, "It was a tough game. We hung together and executed well. I want to thank God, my teammates, my coach, and the love of my life."

"And who would the love of your life be, Mr. JoeE?" she asks expectantly.

"Why, Eli Manning, of course!" I say.

"JoeE!" she exclaims, punching my arm in true MaryAna fashion.

Once again, I figure I deserve the punishment for my smart remark. Noticing Coree holding her wrist, I realize that when she hit me, she must have injured herself.

"Are you all right?"

"It's OK," Coree assures me. The edge in her voice implies otherwise.

"Let me see your wrist," I demand, reaching toward her.

"It's OK, really," she says, recoiling a bit.

"I know a thing or two about sprains," I tell her.

She finally lets me take her hand and I gently begin to remove her bracelet to examine her wrist. They're the same wide, silver bracelets that she was wearing when I first noticed her in the Atlanta airport.

As I remove the bracelet and touch the top of her wrist, she winces in pain. Unlike the rest of her arm, her wrist isn't tanned. Thinking back over the last few days, I realize that I've never seen her without something covering her wrists, either bracelets or wristbands.

As I begin to roll her wrist over to examine the underside, she tries to resist. But apparently, the pain is too great, and she allows me to turn it over.

Then I see it.

Coree's face betrays much more than pain—it's a sorrowful expression somewhere between agony and embarrassment. With my fingertips, I softly caress the straight, thin scar on her wrist. Obviously, it's the result of a cut from a very sharp object, most likely a razor blade. I suspect that there's a matching one beneath her other bracelet.

All of the pieces fall into place, and I feel stupid for not seeing it earlier. How she cried for two day when she was thirteen, how her world was falling apart, and how she had been so depressed that she just wanted to die. She asked me if I "understood" and if I was "OK with it." Even with all my logic, I was still too dumb to see what was right in front of me all along.

Even earlier today, Coree mentioned that once they needed Julie, an emergency-room doctor, at their home. She acted as if I already knew the event to which she was referring.

Now I do.

Apparently, Coree thought she had told me what happened without uttering the dreaded words: suicide attempt. I was so hung up on preserving my *dream* girl image of her that I paid no attention to the *real* girl telling me she'd tried to kill herself.

Ignoring her scar for the moment, I look into her sad brown eyes and say, "We better get some ice on this wrist and have Julie take a look at it."

"JoeE, I thought—" She stops abruptly as I gently place my finger to her lips.

"It's OK," I say softly. "Nobody's perfect."

EPILOGUE

While Julie examines Coree's wrist, a storm of thoughts races through JoeE's mind. He tries to step back from the emotional trauma of the day to reflect upon his new life. With the dawning of a new year, he gazes toward his future as if peering into a crystal ball. Although uncertainty clouds his view, he optimistically envisions the path ahead of him.

Next week, he'll become a student at Brandon High, where baseball season is just around the corner. Soon his grandparents will be visiting, and there's a trip planned to visit them in Fulton in the summer. In the fall, there'll be the excitement of the next football season with parties to attend, people to meet, and games to prepare for. With his social director, MaryAna, in charge, there shouldn't be a dull moment.

However, JoeE now knows more than ever that he doesn't have a crystal ball. If the events of the last few months have proven anything, it's that life may take an unexpected turn at any moment.

Teenage romances are an endangered species, but JoeE can't imagine doing anything to harm his relationship with Coree. In an extremely short time, they've forged a strong and hopefully enduring bond. His dream girl has been to the depths of hell and wears the scars to prove it. He doubts that drugs alone can subdue her demons, but now she doesn't have to face them alone.

And still, there are unanswered questions. How will Rachel's illness progress? Is Sarah hiding more secrets? What's going on between MaryAna and Kane Robinson, and does it have anything to do with her drinking habit? Is JJ Butler to blame for Coree's attempted suicide?

315

What else is Coach Calhoun hiding besides Marty's mental illness? The list of questions only gets longer.

When his cell phone rings, JoeE answers, only to hear his mother's frantic voice on the other end. Excusing himself, he walks into the empty living room. The short phone call puts him into a state of shock.

Returning to the kitchen a few minutes later, he asks MaryAna, "Can you give me a ride home, Sis? We need to pack. We're flying to Syracuse first thing in the morning."

As the heads of everyone in the room snap around, his twin asks frantically, "What's wrong, JoeE? You're as white as a ghost!"

Although he's soon on the receiving end of another dozen questions, he simply tries to think clearly. His only lucid thought is that this was supposed to be the conclusion of the drama but, apparently, it's only the beginning.

Ignoring the questions for a moment, he simply says to his sister, "I hope you'll like New York in the wintertime, *MaryAna*."

Secrets, Secrets, Secrets

Book One: *JoeE*
Book Two: *MaryAna*
Book Three: *Coree*
Additional Books: To Be Announced
For information & publication dates: *www.secrets3.com*
For questions, email us: b*ooks@secrets3.com*
Find us on Social Media:
On Facebook: facebook.com/secrets3books
On Twitter: @secret3books

Made in the USA
Columbia, SC
15 December 2017